Jonni Jordyn

Books by Jonni Jordyn

The Lost Art of Magic Series
The Lost Art of Magic
The Untold Prophecy
The Old Child
The Orb of Destiny

The Mother of All Viruses Series
The Mother of All Viruses
The Queen of All Viruses

The Valley of Hope Series
The Calling of the Grull
The Hammer and the Chain

The Beat of a Different Drummer

The Diva of Mud Flats

Something About Nobility

Dedicated to Leann Hardy, who barely even knows me,
yet knows a deeper, more personal part of myself than
most, and was there when I needed her.

Age is just a number...

... especially when a person's apparent age is a different number.

Jonni Jordyn

 The Old Child

Tome III

Jonni Jordyn

CHAPTER 1

Day seven

> *It was a battle like none the modern world had ever seen before; a conflict as old as mankind's memory itself; a clash between an old world that had vanished centuries ago, and the new world with its mechanized technological war machines. It was a war that was measured in hours, not years. It ended, not when one of the warriors had proven victorious, but when neither opponent was able to answer the bell for another round.*

A deathly quiet had replaced the cacophony of shells and missiles raining down and exploding over the two combatants, but it was more of a shocked silence than a reverent respect. The putrid scent of death and decay wafted up from the rubble and twisted steel that surrounded the crater at the center of the destruction, but even the horrible smell of burning flesh was easily overpowered by the strong and unnatural odor of rotten eggs from the sulphur that laced the smoke.

A trail of dead bodies and broken war machines led from the earlier standoff in downtown Salt Lake, where a tall building was brought down onto the street by the sheer will of a single disturbed teenager, to the highway leading to Cheyenne where the National Guard took their stand against the same ambitious young girl. Their charred remains littered the battlefield, but were barely noticeable next to the crushed and twisted hulks of their tanks and armored vehicles. The death toll in Utah was staggering, but it was the army's defeat in Cheyenne that garnered most of the military's attention and well deserved concern. One little girl faced off against the United States of America, armed only with her hands and a power beyond their comprehension. It was a disaster unlike any other in recorded history and would have been much worse if it hadn't been for the other girl.

It is said that in war, there are no victors. The same holds true in a private battle between two girls wielding fire and magic as their weapons. Athletes like to boast to the media that they give one hundred and ten percent, but in reality, giving it all would leave them lying in a heap on the ground, dying, or limping away, unable to claim the victory for which they compete. So it was with these two girls. No winners, only losers, and only one of them was able to limp away.

The mood surrounding the Planchette plantation had sunken far below a somber melancholy. They were short of facts, but those among them with the gift of sight were sure of what they had seen, and the visions they were granted could not have been any worse. Even the swamp that surrounded them seemed to show some modicum of respect for the dead this morning. Gators drifted silently along the shore of the bayou and the birds of the swamp kept their normally boisterous opinions to themselves. Only Mrs. Planchette, who didn't have the gifts, went about her normal duties and busied herself in the kitchen preparing breakfast. Out in the yard, four stunned women wept, searching to console each other but still unable to comprehend what had transpired.

"She can't be dead," Ashlin cried. "She just can't be! Where was Blake? I thought he was going to protect her!"

Michelle pulled the distraught child to her bosom and cried with her. "I don't rightly know what happened to that boy."

"You never did trust him," Ashlin said. "Maybe you was right all along."

Michelle nuzzled the young girl's face into her neck and said, "No, Cherie. That tain't it. I know how I was suspicious at first, but I come to believe in him. If he warn't with her, then he musta had some good reason. Could be dat sumpin' happened to him, too."

Ashlin pressed her face into the older woman's neck, blotting out the light, then pulled back and wiped her tears on the back of her sleeve. "We have to go. We can cry later. Right now, we have to find a way to get there and see for ourselves what happened to her."

"Yeah, you right," Michelle replied. She released her embrace and stared at the young redhead. She shook her head slowly and said, "You really is my mama all over agin. Not jest da red hair, but dat be just what she woulda said."

Ashlin straightened out her dress and headed for the car, but stopped when she realized that she was walking alone and looked back only to see the panic on Michelle's face. "What're you waitin' for?"

"You knows I cain't drive, and besides, dat ain't even mah car."

Mrs. Planchette came up behind Michelle with a plate full of pancakes and said, "I sought zat all of you were looking too serious before, but now ze looks on your faces just got worse. Who died?"

"Nobody died!" Ashlin spat back at her.

"Oh, my," Mrs. Planchette replied. "Je m'excuse. I make you ze crepes. Zere is some syrup and jam in ze kitchen."

"I'm sorry," Ashlin said. "It was nice of you to make us some flap jacks and I shouldn'a yelled at you like that. It's just that something happened to Destiny and we need to go see that she's okay."

"That's about the size of it," Michelle said, "but I cain't drive and we don't have no car, anyways."

"Tut, tut," Mrs. Planchette said. "If zis be as serious as ze looks on your faces, zen I'll drive you where you need to go."

"Cheyenne," Ashlin said.

"Cheyenne?" Mrs. Planchette asked as she took half a step back. "As in Wyoming?"

Ashlin and Michelle both nodded.

"Zat would be a very long drive. How about I drives you to ze airport instead?"

Michelle started to cry softly and Ashlin said, "We cain't afford no airplane tickets."

"Well, it be a good sing for you zat I can."

"No," Michelle said. "You can't... "

Mrs. Planchette interrupted her, "If you sink for one moment, zat you can tell me what I can and can't do with mon aime husband's money, zen you can just save your breath. I'm doin' it."

Michelle wiped a tear from her eye and mouthed the words, "Thank you."

Mrs. Planchette put the breakfast on the table and said, "You may as well eat what you can while I get my sings together."

<hr>

A thick smoke hung over the battlefield. The army had thrown everything they had at the one called Honey, but nothing in their arsenal could even touch her. Their missiles and tank shells showered her with fire, but fire was her first gift. Nobody taught it to her. She just discovered it and now she could summon fire with hardly a thought. The battle was over, but was still as fresh in her memory as the sour odor was that clung to her clothes. The army was against her and tried their best, but they didn't stop her. They couldn't stop her. It was her stupid cousin that had ended her assault and sent her cowering from the battle. Honey was winning the fight. She had already beaten the army and she could feel her cousin weakening, but that bitch did some last ditch witchy thing and drained Honey of her strength. Such desperation was a sure sign of the witches coming defeat at Honey's hands, but her bitch cousin refused to go down alone. That stupid cow would have brought them both down if Honey hadn't escaped before it was too late. She refused to die at that bitch's hands.

She scanned the field around her for cover, but while there were plenty of large objects for her to hide behind, the vast ground that needed to be crossed between them was naked and void of cover. Earlier attempts to summon a thick smoke to cover the ground like a fog so she could escape had failed, but Destiny countered that by calling in a heavy storm that rained down upon them, cleansing much of the obnoxious fumes that had carpeted the ground. She could have used the rain for cover, but that witch had made sure that the shower was too short for Honey to make her escape. The ground had already dried, and the rain hadn't even left the teeniest mist to aid her. Honey didn't have far to go to; she only had to reach her friends in the car that had brought them here, but soldiers still stood between her and the car, and they weren't going to allow her to pass if they saw her.

The burned-out hulk of a tank that had been tossed aside in an explosion hid her as she watched the soldiers crouching down behind their vehicles. If she kept her distance and skirted around the battle zone, she should be able to reach the car since all eyes were still on the center of the conflict and not on the fallen casualties that surrounded the field.

The battle with her cousin left her feeling weak and unable to finish what she had started, but she resolved that there would be another day. She hated to admit that she might need anyone's help, but Richard had guided her this far, and he was the one who had advised her to build an army rather than take on the world by herself. She hung her head and stared at the ground. Admitting that any man might have been right was even worse than admitting that she might need help.

The limo was still where she had left it and Richard was still inside with her other friends. She saw only a single guard left to watch the vehicle, but it was still a long distance away from her. The guard didn't appear too keen on watching the occupants of the car, so maybe they weren't in custody. Maybe Richard had convinced them that Honey had forced them to come with her. He was a smart man when he wanted to be.

Honey tried producing some more smoke to cover the ground. Smoke wasn't all that different from fire, and she was real good with fire, but Destiny had left her too weak to create even a little spark. She squeezed the amulet that hung from a chain and bounced between her breasts, but for the first time since she had taken it from Destiny, it was cold to the touch. It used to pulsate with a warm heat against her chest, but she had drained it of every last bit of its power while fighting that filthy witch and now she was completely powerless.

An awkward quiet hung over the battlefield. Some fires still burned and occasionally a metal shard would bend from the heat sending an eerie screech across the silent field. She crept around the perimeter of the battle, hiding behind whatever was available, but the smoke was too thin and there was precious little between her and the limo. She kept her eyes pinned to the guard as she snuck up to the car. He spent most of his time looking away from her, but he turned around in a full circle now and then to check the surroundings. He probably wanted to make sure the car was still there and hadn't flown away. Normal people can be so stupid sometimes.

Her foot scraped across the sandy ground, close enough now for the guard to hear, so she fell to her belly just as he turned around to spot the noise. A small crop of weeds hid her from him, but she had a clear view of his face. He was young and awkward looking. That could work in her favor. She may not be able to fry him right now, but that didn't mean she couldn't warm him up a bit. She waited for him to return his attention to the battlefield, then brushed back her hair with her hands and popped open another button on her blouse. Stepping carefully onto the road, she crept as silently as she could up to the back of the car. She hid from his view behind the car until she was alongside the bumper, then stood up and opened another button for good measure. "Hey sugar," she purred as she approached him with an exaggerated sway of her hips. "What'cha doin' here when all the excitement is way over there?" She pointed to the center of the battlefield where people had begun to congregate around her cousin's limp body. She cooed and batted her eyes while running her finger down the buttons of his fatigues. "I guess you seen one dead witch, you seen 'em all. Besides, we got us something way more interesting going on over here. You see that girl inside the car you is guarding?" Honey stepped in close and rubbed her lips on the poor man's ear while she whispered, "Ain't she pretty? She's my lover, but we likes boys too. You ever done it with two hot chicks like us before? Maybe this is the chance that you been waitin' for all your life. Think about the stories you gonna tell when those boys over there tell you about the dead girl they saw. You kin tell them all how you didn't see no dead girl, but you shore did see two real live girls and you did more than just see us. They is all gonna wish that they was left guardin' this here car instead of you."

Perspiration moistened the private's temples as he gasped in shallow drafts of air.

Honey tucked her finger into one of his pants pockets and pulled him away from the car door towards the rear of the vehicle. She glanced briefly over at Richard and winked while she deftly reached down and gripped the tab to his zipper. The private's mouth fell open as she started to pull his zipper down. He never heard Richard sneak out of the car and just as Honey was about to slip her fingers into his fly, Richard bashed the poor man on the back of the head with a crystal decanter from the back of the limo.

The private slumped to the ground and Honey cooed, "Well, if you cain't keep it at attention, then the hell with ya."

Richard bowed his head as he held the door and invited her in. Honey placed her hand on his chest and said, "Thanks Dick. For a moment there, I thought you was gonna let me actually do him."

"For a moment there," Richard stuttered, "I thought you might have wanted to."

Blake yawned broadly as he opened his eyes and rubbed the sleep from them. Something was different about the plane they were in. He heard a metallic clink from the front of the cabin and saw the pilot working on the same broken seat that he had been fixing when they first found him and hired him to fly them to Cheyenne. The shades were drawn in all of the small jet's windows, but something didn't feel right. He climbed to his feet, but felt a bit woozy as he took his first steps down the aisle. A brilliant light shone through the open door in the front of the cabin. They were on the ground. Thirty seconds ago, they were circling in the air, waiting for clearance to land, and now they are on the ground. That can't be. He spun around to find Destiny, but she wasn't in her seat. Panic struck him as he rushed down the short aisle to the exit.

"She's gone," the pilot said without looking up from his work. "She said you were all very tired and just wanted to sleep. I wasn't in any hurry to go back, so it made no difference to me."

Blake didn't remember falling asleep, and he didn't remember her leaving. In fact, they were sitting together at the back of the plane waiting to land. He closed his eyes and groaned as the truth sunk in. She tricked him into one of those dream worlds like her teacher Mala used to make. She let all of them believe that they were circling over the airport waiting to land while she ran off alone to face her cousin. When did she learn how to do that? He shook his head slowly. Of course she knew how to do that. Magic came too easily to her. He took a deep slow breath to calm his heart, and called out into the ether, "Destiny?" She didn't respond. She should have responded.

Even knowing that she had tricked them all, she still should have responded. In that silent moment, afraid of what she may have done, his heart began racing again.

Tommy and Maggie made a space for Honey between them in the back of the limo. The thought of taking the seat that they offered flashed briefly through her mind, but she was too exhausted to play with them; in fact, she felt a twinge of disappointment that they wanted to play after everything that she had been through, so she sat across from them next to her mother instead.

Honey hadn't realized just how much she smelled like smoke and sulphur until Maggie crinkled her nose soon after she had taken her seat. She grabbed the lapel of her blouse and sniffed it. She couldn't remember ever feeling so vulnerable and was afraid that she might cry, but she couldn't allow herself to appear so weak in front of her subjects. Especially now that she was their self-appointed queen, and she had gained her title by being the toughest and strongest bitch of all of them, or anyone else on the planet. A melancholy beat gripped her heart. How could she remain their queen if they ever learned the truth? She closed her eyes tightly to hold the tears in. If any tears did escape, she would have to blame it on all the smoke.

Abilene had watched Honey taking her seat through nervous eyes, but now looked away from her daughter and tried acting as if nothing was wrong. She pretended to look out the window, but her trembling lips betrayed her true feelings. There was no escape for her.

She couldn't bear to look straight across at her daughter's sexual playmates, and she couldn't really look at the destruction outside. If she closed her eyes, her mind would replay the terrifying scene of bombs and missiles exploding around her only daughter. She didn't know which scared her the most: the fact that the army fired rockets at her little girl; or that her Honey had just stood there, impervious to the army's might. There really wasn't anyone in the car that she felt comfortable looking at, so her eyes just darted around the cabin with no place for her to safely rest her focus.

Honey was born on the farm, surrounded by witches, but her mama never told her who her daddy was. Whoever he was, she doubted that he was one of the men on the farm. Her first inkling of her powers came to her shortly before her thirteenth birthday when she lost her virginity to one of the men on the farm and accidentally singed the bedsheets, but she had only become powerful enough to be truly dangerous in the past few days. Those few days had been a whirlwind that had taken her from a simple country girl who could light kindling with her hands to a power crazed megalomaniac bent on ruling the world. Even though it had only been such a short time, she couldn't remember ever feeling as helpless as she did now. She looked at her mother, hoping she might find some comfort there, but her mother wasn't looking at her. Honey had never wanted anything touchy feely from her mother before. They had never had that kind of a relationship, but now she felt like she really needed it. She certainly didn't want the same kind of comfort she could get from Tommy or Maggie, although she was pretty certain that they would freely offer up plenty of that, but now she needed something different. An emptiness inside of her made it difficult to smile right now, leaving her confused by her desire for her mother's comfort. She shouldn't even need to be comforted. Destiny was the one whose lifeless corpse was sprawled out in a crater at the base of the state capitol steps. Honey was the one who should feel victorious, but this didn't feel like a win. Honey felt weak and powerless and immensely sad. She had to sneak away from the battlefield and felt like she was the one who had been defeated.

She leaned away from her mother and rested her head against the window, letting her eyelids fall shut. Her mission wasn't done yet, but maybe she was done for today. She promised herself that this wouldn't be the end of her. She'll be back one day. These strange feelings will eventually go away. Maybe that witch did something to her, but she was gone now and Honey would eventually return to her old self. She just needed to rest and heal so she could do this all over again. At least, she hoped that she would heal and recover her powers, but she won't make this mistake again. Next time, when she comes to attack the capitol, she'll mean business, and they won't have her cousin to protect them anymore.

Captain Saunders was one of the first people to reach Destiny at the bottom of the crater. The depression where her body lay was oddly clear of smoke, but the harsh odor still clung to her hair and her clothing. Witnesses came and gathered in a large circle around her, then slowly converged towards the center, pushing each other as they inched along for a better view. Other spectators hesitated at the rim of the crater where they waited for more of the smoke to clear or maybe they were simply afraid to get too close, but there were those who had no fear and wanted to see the body at the center of the commotion, and Saunders was at the head of the pack. "Give her some room," Saunders ordered, more as a means to establish that he was in charge than to give her any air. "Corporal, see to it that we have some space here, and by God, will someone get a corpsman in here to look at her?"

The corporal's knees shook as he positioned his men around Destiny to keep the curious that had followed Saunders at a safe distance. He thought it was odd that this many people would want to get this close after witnessing the supernatural battle between the two girls. They didn't know what she was or how she did what she did, and even with the battle over and one girl apparently dead, he worried that there might be some kind of residual radiation surrounding her body.

The crowd was strangely quiet. Coughing was unavoidable as wisps of smoke blew across the rim of the crater, but the onlookers were oddly muted, with little chatter amongst them, either from respect for the dead, or simply a stunned silence from what they had seen.

Saunders had never been this close to either of the girls before. She looked like an ordinary girl. He didn't know why he would have expected anything different, but he was pretty sure that his commander, Major Flinch, would have expected gills or horns, or anything that said she was an alien from another world. She had no outstanding features that any normal girl couldn't have had. Even her hands, the source of her fire, appeared as normal as any other girl's.

He knelt down to check Destiny's pulse. Saunders was no medic, but he thought that he should at least be able to tell if she was dead, but he couldn't find a heartbeat. He glanced around to make sure that Honey wasn't hanging around among the onlookers. They say that arsonists like to linger so they can witness the fruit of their destruction, and that girl sure could make fire, but then so could this one. Saunders felt again for a pulse, but he felt nothing. She was gone. He straightened out her legs and placed her arms at her sides. He wished that he could have gotten to know her instead of the one that called herself 'Honey'. It probably wasn't her real name. How could it be? It sounded more like a stripper's name. No, that's not fair. It could have been a hippy name. She could have been a perfectly nice hippy, except that she tried to take over the world and used her mind to toss tanks around like empty milk cartons.

Major Flinch didn't want to ally with either of the girls. As far as he was concerned, they were both aliens and that made both of them enemies, but it was clear to Saunders that no matter what these girls really were, this girl was on their side, or at least she was against Honey, and that whole enemy of my enemy saying meant something special to him, and that made her his friend.

The corpsman finally arrived; huffing and puffing from the climb down the crater, and immediately went to work, checking for a pulse.

"It's about time," Saunders said. "If you'd have been sooner, you might have been able to save this girl. If that other one ever comes back, we might need her."

Saunders' radio squawked and Flinch asked, "Do you have her in custody yet?"

"Major Flinch, sir, she is dead, at least, I think she is dead. I couldn't feel a pulse, but the medics are looking at her now."

"If she's not dead, then you make sure you slap some irons on her and post guards around her twenty-four hours."

"I'll handle things," Saunders replied. He didn't care what Flinch had said, he had no intention of putting her in handcuffs. She had helped them and if she was still alive, he intended to do everything he could to return the favor. What was it that Honey had called his superior? Major Butt Flinch or something like that? She was a monster, but he did like the way she talked to his commander.

Saunders watched the corpsman check her wrists for a pulse. He repositioned her wrist in his hands, but found no trace of a pulse and tried the vein on her neck. He re-gripped his fingers under her chin, but could only shake his head slowly for Saunders.

"NO!" Saunders shouted. He leapt to Destiny's side opposite of the medic and pressed his ear to her bosom. "We need her! She saved us all. She deserves better!"

"I'm sorry, sir."

Blake shaded his eyes as he looked out from the airplane's hatch, but Destiny was nowhere to be seen. Johnson and Logan were sleeping peacefully in the midsection of the small plane with their seat belts still strapped around their waists. Destiny probably sucked them into her dream world, too. Blake had no doubt that they believed that they were still in the air circling the field, waiting to land. She must have gone on ahead of them to face Honey alone. Blake wasn't going to make the same mistake. He needed to find Destiny fast, and they might be able to help. Fortunately, he didn't have Michelle around telling him what he could or couldn't do. He could do this his way, which always seemed more expedient than anything that Michelle would allow. He woke up Logan and Johnson. "Come on. We don't have much time."

"What happened?" Logan asked.

"It was Destiny. She did something to make us sleep."

"Are you crazy?" Logan asked, still rubbing the sleep from his eyes. "We weren't asleep. We're still circling the airport, waiting for traffic to clear so we can land."

"Look outside," Blake suggested, "and tell me if you remember landing."

Logon slid up one of the window blinds and blinked from the blinding light, but saw enough to tell that they were already on the ground. "Son of a bitch. I could have sworn we were still in the air."

"Me too," Johnson said. "Just like you described it."

Blake pulled Johnson out of his seat and pushed him towards the exit. "I'm pretty sure that she did that. She created a dream world, and we were too stupid to tell the difference."

"She can do that?" Johnson asked.

"Why not?" Logan asked. "You thought fire was her only spell? Fire's not really even a witch spell, and she appears to be a very talented witch."

Johnson shrugged his shoulders and Logan gently pushed him out of the jet into the brilliant day, but he paused at the top of the ramp, shielding his eyes as he squinted to see the surrounding buildings. "I wonder if we are even in Cheyenne."

"Yep," the pilot said as he tightened a nut on the front seat. "This is Cheyenne alright. This is the private side of the airport. If you follow the road in front of the hangar, you'll find the car rentals right before you get to the commercial airlines' ticketing counters."

Blake squeezed between his companions at the top of the ramp and ran down the ramp and into a parking area. He checked off a couple cars that looked too big or too slow, then found a sedan that looked like it would be fast enough. He entered the lock tumblers with his mind and opened the door. "Come on, guys. Let's go find her."

Johnson paused for a moment to ask, "How'd he..."

Logan chuckled and replied, "Don't ask."

Saunders repositioned himself to hold Destiny's head in his lap. He sighed forlornly as he stroked her hair. He didn't even know her, but he had witnessed heroism of the highest order and had to choke back the tears when he recalled how bravely she had fought against Honey. The corpsman waited with him until the civilian ambulance arrived at the top of the crater. Two emergency technicians carried a stretcher down the steep embankment to their position. The crowd parted to let them through, and one of them immediately fell to the ground and started checking for vitals. Saunders locked eyes with the lead technician and briefly shook his head, but they still attended to her as they would any emergency.

Saunders' corpsman pulled him away as the lead EMF listened with a stethoscope and moved it around on her chest, looking for any sound of life from her heart while his partner setup the portable defibrillator and lubricated the paddles. He opened her blouse and held the paddles to her chest and her side. "Clear…" Her body twitched as the power coursed through her. The primary EMF still heard no pulse. Nearby, the secondary dialed up the power a bit. The defibrillator squealed as it charged up for the next burst. "Clear…" Destiny's body jerked and again, they heard no pulse. The primary frowned and shook his head.

"No!" Saunders said. He didn't know why he cared so much, but he felt as if she were his own daughter. "Keep trying. Rush her to the hospital, but keep trying!"

They carefully lifted Destiny's body onto the stretcher and Saunders hand signaled some soldiers to help them carry it up and out of the crater. Saunders followed them and cringed each time the stretcher leaned to one side or the other, but she was securely strapped and the soldiers quickly righted her each time.

Atop the edge of the crater, they slid her into the back of the ambulance and started to close the door, but Saunders held the door open and climbed into the back with them, and before they could object, he cited, "National Security."

The lead EMF glanced between Destiny and Saunders and wondered what kind of security risk she could possibly represent, but it wasn't their job to ask about a patient's politics.

Saunders pointed to her and said, "Keep working."

The two EMF's looked at each other hopelessly. They knew that she was gone, but Saunders was so distraught, it would be easier to care for her and let the hospital explain it to him. They saw little point in plying their skills on a corpse, but Saunders needed to see something, so, since she looked severely dehydrated, they administered I.V. Fluids and attached an EKG monitor.

The driver closed the doors and took his place at the wheel. The squeal of the sirens wound up until they blared outside and the vehicle roared to life, rocketing away from the crater and down the road towards the hospital.

***

The governor of Utah still sat behind the wheel of the limo, where Honey had appointed him as her driver. He was helpless to defy her and fearful to even object. As long as she lived and held such ungodly power, he was her pawn to command. The limo's engine roared to life with the touch of his finger on the starter. He ran the wipers to clear the ash off the windows, but the black residue just smeared against the glass until he squirted enough washer fluid to rinse some of it off. The oily black ash still smeared across the glass, but it was clear enough that he wouldn't have to get out and scrape it by hand. Unlike the army, he had already seen Honey at her worst, so what she had done here came as no great shock to him. The blond girl, on the other hand, was quite a surprise. She matched Honey flame for flame and if it hadn't been for the final blow that fell the girl, he might have given her the match on points, but Honey was the only one who had walked away, and his fate, through no choice of his own, was somehow aligned with hers. He turned his head to the back seat and forced a thin smile as he asked, "Where to?"

She thought about it a moment, and without even opening her eyes, said, "Your place. Take us to your home."

The governor stiffened a bit, grateful that her eyes were closed, but still tried maintaining the already weak smile on his face. Terror filled his heart as he said, "Home… yes ma'am. My home." His knees shook as he faced front and gingerly pressed the accelerator. The car weaved slowly around the myriad of broken tanks to get back to the main road and the highway that led them back to Utah.

"Don't worry," Honey said. "I ain't gonna do nothin' there. You can go back to your Ophelia and tell her everything that happened. Or, you can tell her nothing. She sounded plenty worried to me. I'm sure she'll be glad to have you back. You done good, as my driver, but I won't be needing you no more. In fact, you can go back to being the governor, for now at least, but I'm gonna keep the car. Richard will take the rest of us back to my base."

The governor kept his face forward, but worried that she might have opened her eyes and wondered if his face showed how happy he was to let her have the car and drive as far away from him as possible. He didn't know what other unnatural powers she might have and worried that she might be able to read his thoughts, but he couldn't stop thinking about any of it.

CHAPTER 2

Tempest's jaw fell slack as she watched her mother and Ashlin walk toward Mrs. Planchette's car without her. Both of them had been an anchor for her when she had felt the voices of the world drowning out her own thoughts, and now they were abandoning her. Even with Zeline staying behind to help her, she didn't know if she could avoid becoming the person that she used to be when she ended up in the hospital, but they didn't want to take her and she didn't want to stop them from going to help her daughter. Destiny was in some kind of trouble. They all felt it. A hollow life-sucking fear twisted in the pit of her stomach, but she just gritted her teeth and waved weakly goodbye.

Ashlin felt the concern well up in Tempest. She came back to the older woman and wrapped her arms warmly around her waist. "You'll be fine. You've been doing so much better, but if you start to feel crowded again, Zeline can help you and you know how to reach me, no matter how far away I am." Ashlin released her grip on Tempest's waist and ran to the car, then climbed into the back seat, closing the door behind her. Tempest felt the world shrink away as

Ashlin latched her seat belt and waved goodbye to her and Zeline through the window.

Michelle was already settled into the front seat next to Mrs. Planchette. She pressed the button to roll down the window and said, "Don't you worry. We'll call you as soon as we know anything."

Tempest knew in her head that Ashlin was correct. She had been doing better, but she sure wasn't feeling any better right now at this moment. She heard her baby calling out in agony. It echoed in her head. Something was wrong, and she needed to be there with her daughter, but they were leaving her behind. She would have to find her own way to wherever Destiny had gone, but for now, she didn't need them to worry about her. She smiled meekly and waved back at them, but she didn't feel right about it.

A lone sentry stood guard by the portable fences that blocked the roads coming in or out of the battle zone. The governor pulled the limo smoothly up to the guards and said, "I'm Governor Vale. Let us through."

Honey cracked open an eye and snickered, "Vale? Percival Vale?" Percy Vale?"

"Shhh," Richard said. "Let him deal with this."

Honey playfully pretended to look shocked that he would shush her.

The guard looked incredulously at the man behind the wheel of the limo and asked, "Can you show me some identification?"

The governor rifled through his coat on the seat next to him and pulled out his wallet. He smiled professionally as he handed it to the guard and said, "I think you'll find that everything is in order."

The guard glanced back and forth between the governor and his id. "It looks real enough," the soldier said, "but why would the governor of Utah be driving his own limo in Wyoming? Where's your driver?"

The governor smiled sheepishly and said, "He's in the back, with the girls."

The guard leaned in close so he could see through the tinted windows.

"I lost a wager," the governor said, "so I'm driving him around."

"This is all very peculiar," the sentry said. "I'm not supposed to let anyone through. I think I should call this in."

"Oh hell," Honey said as she opened the car to face the sentry.

"What are you going to do?" Richard asked with a hint of fear showing in his voice.

"Shhh," she replied. "Let me handle this."

The guard whistled and said, "I guess you're one of the girls he mentioned."

"That's right," she cooed as she started to undo the remaining buttons on her blouse. "In fact, I'm the wager he lost, but I don't mind. I like to party and I'll party with just about anybody. Do you like to party?"

Honey opened her blouse all the way, but coyly covered her breasts with her hands. "Would you like to come inside for a better look?"

The guard shook his head and said, "I don't think that would be such a good idea."

"Oh, come on," Honey prodded him. "It will be fun and I have lots more to show you."

The guard hesitated.

Honey turned her head towards the car and said, "Maggie? Say hello to the nice guard."

Maggie giggled and said, "Hello nice guard."

The guard leaned over and saw Margaret through the open door.

"Be honest," Honey said. "Haven't you always wanted to have a threesome with two girls like us? You may never have another opportunity like this again. Come on in and we'll show you the best time of your entire life."

The guard nodded his head deliriously and started to enter the limo, but Honey said, "Whoa there soldier. What'cha gonna do with that?" She pointed to his rifle, but his eyes were glued to her single exposed breast.

Honey cupped both hands below her breasts and lifted them to give him a better view. "These are going to take both of your hands to operate. You better give Richard your rifle and prepare for the ride of your life."

The guard blindly handed his rifle to Richard. Honey quickly pulled her blouse closed and said, "Kill him."

Arlene Planchette rolled down the driver's window and wondered when she would see her home again. The honeysuckle's aromatic scent that filled the yard wafted into the car. She closed her eyes and breathed deeply to savor the perfume. "Michelle, Cherie. I loves you and your petit cherie, but I jest don't think zat I can stand to leave ze bayou for even a minute. I'm gonna drive you to ze airport like I promised, but I wants you to go on from zere wisout me."

Tempest walked around to the front of the car and thought to Michelle, "I don't like this. Take me with you. She's my little girl, and she needs me. You're going to need me there."

"We cain't," Michelle thought back. "I ain't gots da money for your ticket."

"Look at her," Arlene said. "Since I ain't goin, she can have my ticket. We just has to cash mine in and get another one for your sweet Destiny's mere."

Michelle stared at Arlene and asked, "Is you psychic? Has you been holding out on me all dese years?"

"I don't have to be psychic to know how a Mama should be with her daughter at a time like zis."

Tempest climbed into the back seat. "Thank you so much Mrs. Planchette."

"Call me Arlene hon. You be takin' my seat on ze plane, so's you might as well call me Arlene."

* * *

"What do you mean 'you lost her?'" Major Flinch growled.

"There was a lot of smoke," the quivering lieutenant explained, "and fire everywhere."

"You're the United States Army and you just got your butts handed to you by an unarmed girl?"

"I wouldn't say that she was unarmed....not exactly."

"Don't you talk back to me!" Flinch barked. "That little girl just handed it to you up your backside and you let her go! What did you do? Did you go run and hide?"

"What were we supposed to do?" the lieutenant argued. "None of our weapons worked against her, and we used missiles! We'd all be dead if it weren't for that other girl."

Flinch turned his back and pretended to cover his ears with his hands. "I don't want to hear about that other girl. You go find the first one."

"You mean the bad one?"

"Bad one?" Flinch asked. "Are you suggesting that there is also a good one? As far as I'm concerned, and as far as your government is concerned, they're both bad ones until proven otherwise."

"But…"

"Don't but me! You go find that first girl."

"And what if we f-find her?" the poor lieutenant stammered. "Wh-What do we d-do then?"

"You bring her in. We're the God damned army! That's what we do."

"B-but we're on American soil. We're n-not even supposed to be here, and you just saw what she did to us, and that was with tanks and missiles…"

"Why are you still here?" Flinch barked. "We're here now, and both the FBI and the national guard asked for our superior firepower. End of story."

The lieutenant stormed out of the room, mumbling under his breath, "Then they should have asked for the other girl, not the army."

***

"You cain't be goin' without me," Zeline sang out as she ran around to the front of the car.

"Oh Lordy," Michelle said. "What now?"

Zeline scrunched up her face and focused her thoughts to the witches in the car. "Mebbe I ain't been part of your coven for so long, but I be one of y'all now."

"You right about that," Michelle thought back, "but…"

"But what?" Zeline asked. "Is I too black to travel wit' you?"

"No," Michelle replied, "it tain't dat. It's just…"

"Just what?" Zeline interrupted her. "You tink dat my grand daddy's voodoo tain't good enough magic for your kind?"

"No," Michelle shouted into her mind. "No. No. And no! If you just let me gets a word in edge wise. It's just dat I ain't askin' Mrs. Planchette to pay for another ticket just so you kin go with us."

"Don't you worry 'bout dat. Zeline has money. What you tink? Just cause I's a old black woman dat lives out in da swamps, I ain't gots no money? You tink I was born in the swamp? I be payin' my own way. Asides, I been gettin' plenty good acquainted with Miss Tempest. Ain't dat da truth?"

"True dat," Tempest thought.

"And da old child dare in da bag o' da car may not always be available for Miss Tempest all da time."

"I do my best," Ashlin replied.

"Zeline knows you do," she continued, "but it still could be dat you be needing me more dan you knows."

"I have enjoyed our talks," Tempest said.

"You see dat?" Zeline said. "We be gettin' close and all."

"That's true," Tempest admitted, "but still, I don't think you should come. I don't mean to hurt you, but I got this bad feeling about this. It's going to be real dangerous and it may not go so well for you."

"Zeline knows. I seen it too, but I seen it bad for you too and I believes dat I needs to be there, no matter what happens."

Mrs. Planchette watched the women glancing back and forth between each other without even a syllable passing between them. "What is ze strange looks between y'all? I understands if zis be some secret between y'all zat I cain't know about, but I also knows zat we gots to move it along."

"Get in," Michelle said aloud, "but I be afeared of what's gonna happen to all of us."

The highway was eerily deserted as Blake rocketed the sedan down the road. "At this rate, we'll be there in no time."

"This don't feel right," Johnson said as he craned his neck to look up and down the road. "Where is everyone?"

Logan frowned and turned on the radio. Country music blared from the speakers. He changed the radio to the AM band.

"Hey," Blake said. "I like that song."

"Sorry," Logan said, "but I'm looking for the news." He hit the search button, and the radio found another country station. Another press of the seek button led to a non-English speaking station coming from the speakers. Several more presses finally found a talk station.

"... are closed. The KMCP traffic copter has been grounded by order of the state police, but sources close to our own Tracy Bluss tell us that the order actually comes down from much higher. Numerous tweets from our listeners described some kind of military action at the state capitol, but these reports remain unconfirmed and we, here at KMCP, have lost access to the internet. Mark Burr is en route, but...just a second...this just in...internet access is down across the state...just a second...it seems that one of the cellular networks is also down, scratch that...I'm told that all cellular networks are down." The reporter covered his microphone with his hand, but could still be heard to ask, "What is this? Are we under attack? Is this a terrorist action?"

"Is this a joke?" Johnson asked. "Did you tune into the news or some old-fashioned radio drama?"

"I don't think they're joking," Blake said. "Look ahead of us down the road."

Logan looked up from the radio and saw the dark smoke swelling on the horizon. "That's not terrorists," Logan said. "That's Honey. I saw her pull a building down in Salt Lake. That's pretty much what it looked like from a distance."

"Don't write Destiny off just yet," Johnson said. "I seen what she can do."

"Well," Blake said, "I guess we're heading in the right direction, at least."

"Hey look!" Johnson shouted while pointing down the road in the opposing lanes. "A car! I'm a little surprised we don't see more of them trying to get away from that."

"If they only knew what we know," Logan said, "then the people might try to evacuate, but the radio told them to stay put."

"And," Blake added, "I'll bet money that the police are keeping them off the streets."

"More like the national guard," Johnson added. "It's probably Martial Law within the city limits."

Blake pressed the accelerator and pushed the car from ninety to one hundred miles per hour.

Logan glanced over at him and asked, "You okay driving this fast?"

"Don't know," Blake replied. "Never drove this fast before."

The bland surroundings blitzed past them, but the oncoming limo was going equally fast in the other direction and zipped by them in a blink.

Blake let off the accelerator and said, "That was her."

"Destiny?" Logan asked.

"No, Honey."

"Should we go after her?" Johnson asked.

Blake pressed the accelerator again and said, "No. Destiny needs us."

⸻

The EMFs still couldn't detect a pulse from Destiny, but they sure felt the pulse of Saunders' intense stare, so they continued to administer first aid to her lifeless body. The flat lines of the EKG spiked and Saunders was quick to point to the recording. "Look!" He shouted. "She's not dead yet!"

"That was me," the technician said. "I bumped the electrode."

"What about her brain?" Saunders asked. "She must have active brainwaves!"

The lead tech shared a forlorn look with his partner and said, "Relax, Captain. The doctors will check all that at the hospital. In the meantime, we are doing everything we can to get her there."

Saunders' radio squelched. That would be Flinch, but he ignored it. Flinch would be furious if he knew that Saunders was trying to save the girl. He'd rather let her die and see if the autopsy told them how she did what she did. The Pentagon would probably support Flinch, especially if they ever thought there was any way to take what she did and implant it into their soldiers. He pictured the idiots in the Pentagon reading comic books and believing in such outlandish fairy tales.

The country side continued to zip past them. Saunders peeked outside through the tiny window in the back door. "How much farther to the hospital?"

"Not much farther," the driver said.

"I thought we would be there by now."

"We would have, but we've been rerouted to the V.A. Hospital."

"No!" Saunders shouted. "You take her to the nearest trauma unit."

"But we have our orders…"

"And I have a gun. I'm giving you new orders." Saunders didn't know why he would risk his career for a girl that he didn't know, but he was sincere and unbuckled the clasp over his sidearm. "I will shoot you and drive her there myself if I have to."

"That won't be necessary," the driver said as he turned the ambulance around, adding the squeal of the tires to the blaring sound of the siren.

Saunders held Destiny's hand and said, "Don't worry. I'll take good care of you. You'll see."

Blake reached the off-ramp where Flinch had closed off the highway with tanks to force Honey off the road. He slowed the car and exited the highway, but found sentries standing at the end of the road.

Johnson pointed at the soldiers and said, "Those aren't national guard. They're regular army. No way regular army should be out here like this."

"Halt!" the nearest soldier ordered. "This road is closed. What are you doing on the road, anyway? Haven't you heard the warnings?"

"I only just turned the radio on," Blake said, "and what we heard made no sense."

"Nothing makes much sense," the sentry admitted. "Terrorists bombed the state capitol. Why would terrorists bomb Wyoming?"

Blake shrugged and said, "My girlfriend works at the capitol. How do I see if she's okay?"

The sentry sighed and said, "You don't. You'll have to turn around and call the hospitals from somewhere else."

"I can't do that," Blake said as he entered the man's mind. "You don't want to stand in the way of true love, do you?"

"No," the man mumbled, "I don't want to do that, but I still can't let you in."

"But wasn't that your commander on the radio just now?"

"Huh?" the man asked. "I didn't hear anything."

Blake pushed the man's mind as he said, "You didn't just hear your commander tell you to let us in?"

"Oh that?" the man asked. "Yeah. I guess I heard that."

"Well?" Blake asked.

The sentry's eyes twirled in their sockets as he waved them in. "Go on then. You're cleared."

Blake put the car back in gear and pulled through the checkpoint.

"What was that?" Johnson asked. "I didn't hear nothing."

Blake chuckled and asked, "Aren't you the one taking orders from a voice in your head?"

Johnson sat back and crossed his arms defensively. "Sure, but it ain't like I'm crazy. They're real voices."

"But you're the only one that hears them."

Johnson scowled, but remained quiet.

Ashlin held Tempest's hand as they entered the airport. To all the world, Tempest might have been a mother leading her young daughter safely through the crowds, but in reality, it was Ashlin that provided security to Tempest who squeezed her hand a little tighter as they passed through the doorway and saw how many people were going this way and that. Ashlin looked around the terminal, eager for her first flight. "I never been on a plane before."

"Me neither," Tempest replied. "There sure are a lot of people here. I never thought it would be so crowded. It reminds me of the bus station, only bigger."

"Kinda," Ashlin agreed, "only it don't smell like truck exhaust."

"You girls wait right here," Mrs. Planchette said to them, "while I go get ze tickets."

"I'm right behind you," Zeline said. "We wants to make sure our seats be together."

"Well," Michelle said, "that Zeline sure does have a surprise or two."

Tempest hooked her arm into Michelle's and said, "That's just cause you never gave her a chance to know you before."

"She just never seemed quite right," Michelle said. "I always thought she was a little bit crazy, especially when she got to jawin' about being a witch."

"Why?" Tempest asked. "Don't you believe in witches?"

Ashlin laughed and said, "You guys are funny."

Michelle frowned and sighed. "She still seemed a bit on the crazy side."

Tempest snickered. "Like you don't know how to deal with crazy."

"Mebbe it be more like I gots me enough crazy in my life to deal with."

"Yeah, Mama, that's probably it."

Mrs. Planchette returned and said, "I got us some good news and some bad news."

Ashlin bit her lip, waiting for Mrs. Planchette to continue, but when no explanation immediately followed, she blurted out, "We're still going, aren't we?"

Mrs. Planchette tussled the child's red hair and said, "Yes, Cherie. You're still going, but jest not so soon. We couldn't get you all on ze same flight until zis afternoon."

"That be fine," Michelle said. "It be like they say, beggars cain't be choosers."

"You don't need to put on ze brave face for me," Mrs. Planchette said. "I know how anxious you be to get to Destiny, but it's ze best we could do at ze last minute."

Michelle hugged Arlene and said, "I know you tried, and I appreciates it. We'll just have to see her later tonight."

"We might not see her till the morning," Zeline said. "We gets in pretty late, but don't you be worrying about where we is gonna stay the night. I gots dat all handled."

Michelle looked at Zeline and didn't know what to say. Mrs. Planchette had been a longtime friend, and Michelle already felt uncomfortable taking her charity, but Zeline was a stranger.

"I heard dat," Zeline said. "I ain't no stranger to you just acause you didn't know dat you liked me so much. Tings be different now. You taught me somethin' dat I cain't never repay you enough for."

"Maybe I hasn't told you yet about not listenin' to people's private thoughts."

Ashlin tugged on Michelle's sleeve and whispered, "You kinda shouted your thoughts."

Michelle's cheeks warmed. "I apologize to you, Zeline, but I don't understand why you think you owes me nothin'. I was pure mean to you."

"You was dat," Zeline said flatly, "but I don't tink you'll be so mean to me no more."

"No," Michelle admitted. "I reckon not."

"And," Zeline thought to her, "not because I got us a hotel, but because you knows I is one of you now. We be kindred spirits now."

Michelle impulsively wrapped her arms around Zeline and thought, "That we be. That we be."

CHAPTER 3

Winding their way through the security line was relatively easy, even for such inexperienced flyers. Michelle held Ashlin's hand because it just seemed appropriate to hold on to the younger girl, although Ashlin was a pinch too old for hand holding and Michelle was the more nervous of the two. Zeline stayed close to Tempest, ready to help her if the voices overwhelmed her, but most of the people in the line had a singular focus which made the voices seem fewer in Tempest's head, kind of like a choir all singing the same song.

Ashlin knew that their flight was still hours away, but the anticipation within her grew with each step that they took as they shuffled through the slow-moving line. She had always assumed that only rich people or businessmen took airplanes to go places, but the line was full of more kinds of people than she could have possibly imagined. She was wrong when she thought that their little troupe would stand out against all the seasoned travelers, but she wasn't wrong about how exciting this trip would be. The further they delved into the busy airport, the more she realized that this was shaping up to be one of the most momentous events of her young life.

Michelle, on the other hand, grew more nervous with each passing second. The tension within her began to derail her as the voices had always done with Tempest. When she reached the first checkpoint and was asked to show her I.D., she blindly pulled it out of her wallet and moved to the next line when the TSA officer had motioned her to move along. Ashlin cocked her head when Michelle had walked away with the TSA guard holding his hand out for her identification. "I'm with her," Ashlin said with the voice. "My sister is real sick and my nana is getting real worried for her."

Michelle heard Ashlin and turned back to say, "I'm sorry, darling. Your nana is feeling a bit distracted, but I promise to do better."

The TSA officer nodded his head and waved her on.

Tempest didn't have an official government id. It wasn't something they issued in the sanitarium where she had lived for so many years, but she showed him her name tag from the hospital and used the voice to convince him that it was a driver's license, which he gladly accepted.

Once they were past security, Ashlin squirmed around in Michelle's hand trying to peer into all the shops that lined the mall. "Have you ever seen so many shops in one place before?"

Michelle said, "I know. It sure be something."

Zeline chuckled. "You needs to get out more. You don't has to go to da airport to see a mall with lots of shops. All of da cities have malls, only dem regular malls don't rob you blind for daer goods, well mebbe not so much."

"I seen a mall before," Ashlin said, "but it didn't have so many restaurants all together where you could see all the people eating."

"Yeah, you right," Zeline admitted, "but I suspect most of dem people dat you see is just waitin' and drinkin', speaking of which, we gots us a pretty long wait, so I is gonna buy everbody lunch. Why don't y'all have a good look around and tell Zeline which of dese restaurants looks da best to ya."

Michelle sucked in her breath to protest, but before she could get a word out, Zeline blasted in her head, "Don't you dare tell me dat I cain't buy you lunch jest because you is too poor. I ain't hearin' a damn word of it. I is buying you lunch and dat be dat."

Johnson's attention was locked on the military presence that lined the roads outside. He never liked his time spent in the army and he barely followed their rules, but to his surprise, those rules and procedures jumped to the forefront of his memory as he watched and recognized the activity outside. He could tell the difference between those soldiers that were on duty and the others that were awaiting orders. The familiar looks on their faces told him who did not want to be there.

"That's far enough," a voice boomed in Johnson's head. "Tell him not to go any further. Tell him to stop the car and turn around."

"I can't do that," Johnson mumbled.

"What was that?" Logan asked.

"Nothing," Johnson said. "Just thinking out loud."

Logan shook his head as he looked at Johnson, but returned most of his attention to the activities outside, leaving just a glancing eye to monitor the ex-soldier.

"You shouldn't get any closer," the voice said.

"He wants to save his girlfriend," Johnson said. "I can't tell the dude to abandon her. He's committed. When I said that we should follow that 'Honey' chick, he refused because..."

"You said WHAT?"

Logan turned back and said, "Seriously, what is going on?"

"Nothing!" Johnson snapped back.

The three librarians put their heads together and conferred before telling Johnson, "Watch over him. Do NOT let him go after Honey, but watch out for the military. They may want to experiment on him if they ever get the chance. They'll probably want to experiment on you, too."

"Why?" Johnson asked. "I'm not like him."

"They don't know that. They'll want to dissect you to see if you are like him."

The restaurant was crowded, and the service was understandably slow, but that was fine, since the four women needed something to pass the hours until their flight. Michelle tapped her fingers on the table as her eyes darted around the room. Her nerves made small talk difficult for her. "I'm afraid dat we may be too late."

"Too late?" Zeline asked. "We is hours too early."

"Not about the plane," Ashlin explained. "She's talking about Destiny."

"Let's not talk about that right now," Tempest said. "It's too upsetting for all of us, since we can't do anything but sit around and wait right now."

"Especially you," Zeline said. "I kin feel da tension in you somethin' fierce. Maybe we just talks about nothin'."

"I don't think I can," Michelle said. "I just cain't stop worrying about her."

"You needs to clear your mind," Zeline said. She reached over and held Michelle's hand. "And mebbe I kin help you."

Ashlin and Tempest left Michelle in Zeline's hands. They were able to accept that they couldn't do anything for Destiny from here, but they were too full of curiosity to think calm thoughts. They watched the myriad of people walking by and made up stories about who they were and what they were doing.

"Look at that guy," Ashlin said. "He's obviously a cat burglar. See how stiff his left leg is? I bet he has a painting rolled up around his leg under his pants."

"How can the two of you play a game like that?" Zeline asked. "It be just too easy to peek into daer minds and know exactly what they is up to."

"That would be cheating," Ashlin explained.

"Plus," Tempest added, "their real lives are probably a lot less exotic than the ones we are making up for them."

Zeline chuckled as she watched the 'cat burglar' walk by and nodded her head. "True dat."

Once the food was delivered, all the games and conversation ended. Nobody at the table had realized just how ravenous they were until the aroma of freshly heated food was just under their noses. Breakfast had been hours ago, and they had barely nibbled at the pancakes that Mrs. Planchette had offered them. The food placed before them, regardless of its true quality, stood no chance against the four hungry women. The drinks were refilled repeatedly during and after the meal.

Michelle's mood hadn't improved, so Zeline suggested that she might want something a little stronger to drink, but tempted as she was, Michelle wanted to keep her wits about her and settled on iced tea which had been refilled several times. Tempest also considered something stronger, which would have helped dull the voices, but a little Ashlin voice in her head reminded her that she didn't need that anymore, so she also drank iced tea.

Zeline kept track of the clock and brought the meal to a close as they neared their departure time. Once they were out of the restaurant, Ashlin again twisted her head all around to see everything that they walked past while Michelle and Tempest remained more narrowly focused on the path in front of them.

"Dis way," Zeline said as she started them towards their gate.

Michelle walked hesitantly down the airport terminal, bumping elbows with other travelers as her eyes stared off into space. Part of her wished that she had accepted Zeline's offer for a stronger drink.

Tempest tugged at her hand and said, "Come on mother, we don't want to miss our flight."

"I'm coming," Michelle said, but the tone of her voice was laced with horror and her face had grown pale.

"I know," Tempest said. "I saw it too, but I've also seen what the army plans to do to her. They want to open her up to see what makes her tick. They want to know what makes us all tick."

"I know," Michelle replied. "Dat tain't what I's afraid of."

"You don't think they'll try to experiment on us, do you?"

Michelle didn't answer. Her already slow pace slowed a bit further.

"Oh, my God!" Ashlin exclaimed. "You're afraid of flying!"

Zeline broke out laughing. "You gots to be kidding me! After all da shit you done seen and all da magic dat you done yoself, you be afraid of flying?"

"It don't look safe," Michelle said. "Does you see how big dat daer airplane be? What holds it up in da sky? Tain't magic. It's a machine dat's held aloft by motors. Men made dat thing, and not none o' our kind neithers. In fact, it be more likely dat some damned sorcerer helped design dat contraption, and he didn't put no magic into it neither."

"Uhuh," Zeline muttered. "You is one crazy white woman."

Tempest couldn't help laughing a little, too. "Come on Mama. I'll hold your hand and if we need it, I'll even add a little magic to keep the plane in the air."

Michelle hit Tempest lightly on the shoulder and said, "You ain't no sorcerer. You be a witch and you cain't keep no plane in da air."

"If my baby kin do it," Tempest said, "then so can I."

Michelle scowled and said, "Your daughter may have got some sorcerer blood in her, but I promises you dat your daddy didn't have none of dat blood in him."

"Wow," Tempest said. "That's probably the most you ever told me about my daddy."

"And it be more dat you ever needs to know," Michelle said. "Besides, you warn't da most receptive child, now was you?"

"That just ain't true Mama. I was a perfectly good child before I come to my womanhood and got all sick in my head."

"Well," Michelle said, "be dat as it may, you didn't need to know nothin' about your daddy then, an' you still don't."

"We're here mama."

Michelle was so engaged discussing her fears and trying not to think about Destiny dying, that she hadn't even noticed that they had led her onto the plane already.

Tempest pointed and asked, "Do you want the window seat Mama?"

Ashlin jumped up and down repeating, "I do! I do!"

Michelle smiled and said, "Let Ashlin have da window."

Ashlin squeezed past them and climbed into her seat.

"You next," Michelle said. "Ashlin can help if you hears da voices, and after all dat iced tea I drunk, it might be dat I needs to go see da cahbin before we be done."

"You right about dat," Tempest said. "We probably shoulda all gone before we left the restaurant."

***

Smoke had already blotted out most of the sky, casting a dark shadow upon the landscape well before Blake had brought the car close to the battle area. Johnson crinkled his nose from the unpleasant, but familiar odor of fire laced with sulphur that had seeped into the car. He would never forget how the sulphur tainted the already rotten smell of the swamps, but this time, the swamp odor was replaced with gunpowder. While he and Logan could only see what was visible through the windows, Blake could see the battle as easily as he could smell the fumes. He saw how intent the army was, with their weapons all trained on Honey and Destiny. He also saw how divided some of them were when they realized that she was helping them. Now, with the battle done, they circled the main field of destruction with nothing to do but keep onlookers away. Once the soldiers that were present had desisted their futile attempts to win this battle, there were only two combatants left and only one of them had been hostile, yet, she was the one who got away and none of them were too interested in actively pursuing her.

Blake's skin prickled from the magical energy that led him to the large depression in front of the state offices. She was here. They had both been here. He shook his head slowly when he thought of Destiny and Honey going against each other. It's a wonder they didn't leave an even larger crater.

A very annoyed sentry held up his hand and ordered Blake to stop the car.

Blake rolled down the window and said, "It's okay. We're supposed to be here."

The sentry eyed them cautiously and asked, "You are? Who are you?"

Blake had to think up a good excuse. He should have thought of one beforehand, but had to improvise. "We're…"

Before he could finish, Johnson jumped out of the car and barked, "We're homeland. What did you think? Now, do you intend to keep jawing at us until the evidence grows cold or what?"

Blake turned around and looked at Johnson with a half-smile. Johnson climbed back into his seat, and Blake gave him a quick nod.

"You're homeland?" the sentry asked sarcastically. "If you're homeland, then I'm the king of England."

Blake smiled and bowed his head dramatically. "Your majesty. May we pass?" As he spoke, Blake entered the poor man's head and asked, "Don't you recognize a four-star general when you see one?"

The sentry bent low to peer at Johnson through the window. He squinted his eyes and cocked his head to the side while his mind worked to cope with the new image that was forming before him. His eyes suddenly opened wide, and he snapped to attention with his right hand held sharply to his temple. "I'm sorry Sir. I didn't see you. Of course you may pass."

Blake still wore the half-smile as he put the car back into gear and drove forward to the capitol steps. The whole area was alive with residual power. "They fought here. This whole area still tingles with energy from their battle."

"I don't know about that," Johnson says, "but it sure stinks. That's a lot like the smell from hell that I remember from the bayou." As soon as he had said it, Johnson wished he could take it back. He and Blake were part of a group that had gone into that island with the intention of killing Destiny, but things had changed since then and he did not want to stir up that memory. The smile left Blake's face and Johnson knew that he had heard what he said. He bowed his head and said, "Sorry."

Logan didn't know what had just passed between Blake and Johnson, and he didn't care. "If they fought here, and from the smell of it, they did, then we are too late."

"Don't say that," Blake said.

"You can't duck it," Logan said. "From the looks of things around here, they had one hell of an epic battle with more firepower than the army could muster. They fought, and we saw Honey heading the other direction. I think we know what that means, and I think maybe it's time that I should be leaving."

"You want to leave?" Blake asked. "Why? This changes nothing!"

"Doesn't it?" Logan asked. "They fought. That means our people fought. We won, and you lost. I don't think there's much more reason for us to be together."

"Really? You know Honey. Do you really want to live in a world with that bitch as your queen?"

"I don't," Johnson said.

"You have no choice," Logan said. "She won the battle and there's nobody left to stop her from crowning herself queen."

"Destiny can," Johnson said.

"Don't you get it?" Logan asked. "If they fought, then only one was left standing, and we saw Honey leave."

"I don't believe it!" Johnson yelled.

Blake struggled to hold back his tears as he heard Logan take the conversion where he did not want it to go.

"Believe it!" Logan barked. "Destiny is dead, and there's nobody left in the world to stop Honey."

"That's not true!" Johnson growled. "She's not dead. She can't be! I would know if she were dead!"

Blake started to like Johnson a little bit more.

"Do you see her around here?" Logan asked. "She's gone and without her, there's nobody left who can stand up against Honey."

"Blake can," Johnson said.

Logan laughed and said, "Don't you know that Blake is one of our people?"

"No, he ain't," Johnson replied. "He's with Destiny."

Logan was still laughing as he mockingly asked Blake, "What would you do against Honey?"

Blake held his hand out with his palm up and formed a perfect globe of fire that pulsed and danced.

Logan's eyes widened as he sucked in his breath and said, "Oh. Well, you know that she made a lot more than just that little fire."

"They both did," Blake said, "and I intend to find her."

"Yeah," Johnson said. "'Cause she ain't dead."

Blake really was starting to like Johnson more and wished they hadn't gotten off to such a bad start in the beginning. "When I do find Destiny, we're going to go hunt Honey down."

"Yeah!" Johnson exclaimed. "That's a good idea."

The librarians screamed into Johnson's head, "No! That's a terrible idea!"

"So," Blake continued. "Which side do you want to be on when Destiny and I go destroy Honey together?"

The librarians urged Johnson, "Tell him that's a bad idea."

"I see your point," Logan said, but all he really meant was that he'd better wait until he confirmed that Destiny was dead.

Tempest tried sitting still in her seat, but she couldn't help fidgeting. Before boarding the plane, everybody in the airport shared a common thought; getting on board and finding a seat, and that made them seem like fewer voices, but now that they were settling in, people's thoughts diverged into a cacophony of noise bouncing around her head. She tried focusing on a single voice, as Ashlin had shown her, but the excitement level of the passengers raised the volume of their thoughts to a level of shouting in her head. It already felt to her that the voices that surrounded her were pressing in on her, but the seats were too closely spaced for her to escape them and when the seat in front of her had pushed back, she could add claustrophobia to her overwhelming misery. She pushed back on her seat, hoping to get more airspace, but it didn't budge. She leaned forward slightly and tried slamming her back into the seat, but it still wouldn't recline.

Ashlin leaned over and asked, "Are you okay?"

"I'm fine," she replied, "but I'm feeling a bit crowded and was trying to lean back."

Zeline leaned forward and whispered, "You has to push da silver button, but I wouldn't bother jest now. Dey won't let you lean bag until we's in da air."

Tempest turned around to face Zeline and pointed her thumb at the seat in front of her. "Someone should tell that to the guy in front of me."

Tempest's words had barely escaped her lips when they heard the stewardess say, "Excuse me, sir. Please return your seat to its upright position until the captain turns off the seatbelt sign."

Ashlin couldn't contain her giggles.

Tempest settled back into her seat and closed her eyes. She reached over and squeezed Ashlin's hand and quietly thought to Zeline, "Thank you."

Zeline felt good to help and smiled as she thought back, "You ain't got nothin' to worry about. Flying is a piece of cake."

"It's not the flying," Tempest thought back, "It's the girl across the aisle that had too much water to drink. She has to go to the bathroom, and it's all she can think about."

"Now that you mention it," Ashlin thought, "I wish I had stopped at the toilet on the way here."

"If dat be all daer is to bother you," Zeline thought, "then you gonna be jest fine."

"Nah," Tempest thought back, "Three rows up, there's a guy that's demanding drinks from them. I think he's already had a few before boarding."

Zeline snickered and thought, "Sounds like he be more scared dan you. To tell da truth, I wouldn't mind a sip o' someting myself, not dat I is afraid or nothin'."

"Not me," Tempest thought. "I done that when I was young and it took me down a dark path. Only good what come from it was my baby girl."

"Don't you worry none," Zeline thought. "If you starts a-feelin' crowded in your head, you jest has to talk to Zeline. You squeezes da old child's hand and let Zeline talk you through it."

Destiny's EKG showed a steady flat line where her heartbeat should have registered. The emergency technician looked forlornly at Captain Saunders, wishing desperately that he could ease the captain's pain and draw him away from the false belief to which Saunders so desperately clung.

"No!" Saunders yelled. "Keep trying! I know there is more that you can do until we get to the hospital. You just keep her blood flowing!"

The tech greased the defibrillator paddles and applied them to her chest and side. "Clear!"

Destiny's body arched into the air as the electricity flowed through her and contracted various muscle groups, but her heart remained flat.

"Again!" Saunders ordered.

"But…"

Saunders let his hand fall to the grip of his sidearm and growled, "I said do it again!"

The tech didn't want to challenge Saunders. "Clear!"

Her body convulsed again, but this time a tiny blip appeared on the scope, then another. But it wasn't a normal rhythm. The tech put his hands together and applied CPR to her chest while the second tech administered adrenaline.

The ambulance pulled up to the hospital's emergency entrance, and the driver ran around to swing the door open. Saunders stepped out and bellowed, "Where is everybody? We should have had doctors waiting here to meet us!" He ran in through the automatic doors and barked, "I need your best people out there five minutes ago! Move it!"

A nurse took a step towards Saunders to explain who was in charge, but then thought better of it when she saw the crazed look on his face and the holster around his waist.

"I got this," a doctor said as he ran out the door with Saunders. "What do we have here?"

"She's the most precious resource this country has. This is a case of national security. You have to save her!"

The tech said, "She was flatline for over five minutes, but then we got an irregular heartbeat from her. There are no visible signs of trauma, but she shows signs of massive dehydration. Look doc, I don't know what went on over there, but it looked like a war zone, and she was in the center of it."

The doctor checked her for signs of bruising as they wheeled her into the ER. "A war zone? What kind of war zone? I served two tours in Afghanistan and I see no lacerations or burn marks, nor any other injuries typical with war trauma."

"You should see the crater we found her in."

"A crater? There was an explosion?"

"There must have been!" the tech exclaimed. "But it wasn't just the hole in the ground. There was smoke everywhere, and it smelled like gunpowder...and...and...and something else like rotten eggs. And there were tanks all over the place!"

The second tech added, "And some of the tanks looked like they were destroyed."

"Yeah!" the first tech agreed. "They were bounced around and some of them were even crushed!"

Destiny was transferred to an emergency room gurney and attached to a battery of monitors. Her heart still blipped erratically. The doctor gave her a more detailed examination, but still found no indication of trauma. He pulled her eyelids up and checked her pupils. "Pupils are fully dilated. Give me a tox screen. Let's see what she's on."

"What she's on?" Saunders asked.

"What's he doing in here?"

Saunders flashed his military id and said, "Homeland security. I stay."

The doctor groaned and returned to checking her vitals. Alarms went off when Destiny stopped breathing.

"Intubate her!" the doctor shouted as another alarm indicated that her heart went flat-line again.

Destiny's mind was numb. She was stuck in that hazy state between sleeping and being awake. She wasn't dreaming, or at least, she couldn't remember any dreams, just a vague dreamless existence where she was aware of nothing, except that in that nothingness, she felt at peace. And now, she was acutely aware of a tingling in her fingers. Her arms and legs were asleep. Something tugged at her core, pulling her out of her slumber, but she wasn't sure that she wanted to wake up. The air was icy cold and stung her throat and her lungs as she sucked in a deep breath and felt the world forming around her. The pounding in her ears accelerated as her heart raced at the prospect of returning to the world of the living, but when she opened her eyes and saw the deeply concerned bright blue eyes of

Marvalaine staring back at her, she knew that she was somewhere else.

His mustache wiggled as he scrunched his face and played with the long white beard that hung below his face. "You're not looking too good," he said to her.

She tried sitting up in her bed, but fell back against her pillow. "She was a lot tougher than I thought she would be."

"Of course she was," he replied, "and she had you to thank for that."

"If you're going to lecture me about what a terrible idea it was for me to go after her alone, then you can save it. I know what I did, and I just don't want to hear about it."

Marvalaine had always been a decent friend to her. Sometimes he was like a father to her, and other times he was more like a cousin, or the brother she never had. Their souls had known each other many times throughout history, and were lovers through most of those lives. Even now, he was married to Nimisen, who shared her soul. He meant the world to her, but right then, at that moment, she wished she weren't lying in that bed with him staring at her and before he could scratch his whiskers; she was gone from his place and time.

She recognized the sensations that accompanied the changing of a vision and was prepared for a new view of the world to form around her. It was like that when she traveled through time, but, instead, she found herself in a dark room lit only by a glowing orb which spun around on the fingers of a much younger Marvalaine.

"Oh," she said. "It's you again."

"I'm hurt," he said, feigning a pain in his heart.

"I still don't want to be lectured. I thought I was getting away from you."

"That's the thing about wishes. They are like dreams. Everything is so imprecise. You must concentrate on your magic if you want to control it and have more predictable results. Your mistake was that you wished to get away from that bed, not from me."

"I'll try better next time."

Marvalaine continued to play with the glowing orb, letting it roll across his knuckles, from finger to finger until it rolled around to the underside and continued across his fingers without falling until it eventually rolled back up around to the top side.

"That's a neat trick. In my time, you would have done well as an illusionist."

"Except," he replied, "that this is no illusion."

"Is that it?" she asked.

"Is what what?" he asked with a mischievous twinkle to his eye.

"Can I see it?"

"I believe you already do," he replied, "but you may not touch it, if that is what you are asking. It is not for you."

"Not for me? I thought you said the orb of destiny was named after me."

"It is true that you share a name with the orb of destiny. Perhaps you were named after it."

"I really need it. It's not for me. It's for my mother. She needs it. I need it to heal her."

He tucked the orb away in his robes and poked the coals in his hearth. "You need it for much more than just that, but, still, you may not have it."

"Really," she said. "I need it to save my mother."

He saw that the tears collecting in her eyes were authentic, but he would not let them sway him. "Fear not," he said. "If your need is true, then it will come to you when you need it most."

"Riddles?" she pouted.

"No."

"Then what? Why can't you just give it to me?"

He pulled his pipe from his cloak and touched the contents with his finger to light it. "Everything has a time and place, even for you, the mistress of time."

"But it can heal my mother!"

"It can do much more than just that."

"Then why can't I have it?"

He drew a deep breath through the pipe and blew a perfect smoke ring in the air. The ring hung there and expanded beyond the size of a dinner plate, at which point he blew three perfectly round orbs of smoke through the center of the ring. "I cannot give the orb to you, because it is not for you to collect. You have played your role, and now it is for another to find the orb."

"But I thought you said it would come to me?"

"When the time is right, but first it must be found, and before it can be found, it must be sought."

"Oh," she said with a frown. "Not riddles, but games."

Ashlin kept her face glued to the window and was rewarded with an extraordinary view as the plane rocketed down the runway and tilted up into the heavens. She pressed harder against the glass as the buildings shrunk below her until they looked like models on a table. The tiny cars and trucks rolling down the miniature highway disappeared into the roadway and were ultimately replaced with the colored squares of farmland that also shrunk away during their ascent. Then it was all gone as they pushed up through the clouds, wrapping the plane in a thick fog until it emerged over the weather and all Ashlin could see was the brilliant white tops of the clouds below them.

With little left to see below her, she cast her eyes forward slightly, but remained pressed against the window, where she could feel the drone of the jet engines through the fuselage and the rush of the wind against the window. Her eyelids drooped and for a while, she thought she could still see the fluffy clouds in her mind, but they turned dark and began to swirl around her. The swirling dark mass transformed into a tumbler of chocolate milk that she vigorously stirred in circles, creating a whirlpool with a depression in the center of the glass. She stared into that depression, and then fell into it, landing in a large crater.

Smoke hung on the ground and blanketed the air around her. She coughed as she waved the obnoxious odor out of her face. She wanted to close her eyes to keep the smoke out, but her eyes were drawn to a point of light in the center of the crater. A light in the darkness like that should have been more inviting to her, but there was something ominous about it that she did not want to see. A deep fear gripped her soul as her feet stepped slowly towards the light. She did not want to go. Her knees shook from fear of what she might discover there, but her feet continued to take her, anyway.

She fell to her knees when she arrived at the bottom of the crater and saw Destiny's lifeless body with its legs twisted beneath her. She reached out to stroke Destiny's hair and saw old wrinkled hands with liver spots at the end of her arms. Frail fingers hung from her wrinkled hands. Lines and spots crisscrossed the back of her hands like a map, almost as if the pattern that the lines made had some cosmic significance. Her fascination with her wrinkled skin was interrupted by thunder that clapped all around her. It was an unnatural thunder with no lightning. It shouted to her, "Ashlin! Wake up!" The smoke thickened around her. The wind slapped her in the face and the thunder shouted again, "Ashlin! Wake up!"

She opened her eyes and saw Tempest stroking her cheeks and saying, "It was just a dream; just a very bad dream."

***

"So, where is she?" Logan asked. "Do you want to check the hospitals before we check with the morgues?"

"She's not dead," Blake said. "I would know it if she were dead."

"Uhuh," Logan replied, but under his breath, he mumbled, "You're just in denial."

"She's not here," Johnson said. "I say we go with your instincts."

Blake closed his eyes and cocked his head around. "Destiny?" he thought. "Can you hear me?"

Johnson watched Blake intently and knew he was trying to pick up her trail. "You got anything?"

"She's not responding."

"You can talk to her?" Logan asked.

"Yeah, we can do that."

Logan was jealous. He had heard stories that in ages past, the witches could communicate telepathically. His people could never do that. "So, what do you do when you can't reach her?"

Blake reached out with his senses, but she had vanished.

"You did it before," Johnson said. "I was there. I remember. You took us right to her."

Blake shrugged and said, "I didn't really do anything then. It just came to me."

"It just came to you?" Logan asked.

"Yeah," Blake sighed. "It came to me in my sleep."

"So why are you still up here in the driver's seat talking to us?" Logan asked. "Get in the back seat and take a nap. I'll drive."

Blake didn't hear him. A searing pain sliced through his brain and overwhelmed his senses. The pain devolved into a throb that left him with an image of an emergency room. Destiny was lying on a gurney, and he was looking down at her from above. The image shrunk before him as if he were being pulled away from it. His vision flew across the ground, away from the hospital until he was back in the car staring off into the distance."

"Are you listening to me?" Logan asked. "I'll drive while you sleep."

"That won't be necessary," Blake said. "I know where she is now."

Chapter 4

Normally, the doctor would have had more time to compose his statement as he walked from the treatment room to the waiting room, but Saunders wouldn't leave her side, so the attending physician just turned to him and shrugged his shoulders. "That's all we can do for her. She's in a coma. The best we can do is keep her body alive and hope that she returns."

"Are you sure?" Saunders asked. "She's the most important person in the world right now. Is there no treatment you can recommend for her? Something that would bring her out of the coma?"

"I don't know what makes her so precious to you or why you think she is so vital to the world," the doctor said, "but every patient is important to me and I'm telling you that there is no treatment for her condition. I've found a bed for her in ICU. We'll watch and wait, but I don't know how long we can devote that bed to her."

"You don't know how long?" Saunders growled. "I can tell you how long. You will continue to take care of her for as long as it takes."

"She may never come back," the doctor said. "Strike that. There is very little chance that she will return to consciousness. In my expert opinion, she is gone already."

Saunders glanced over at the monitors that reflected her heart and breathing rates. They were all active and strong.

"The machines are keeping her body alive," the doctor said. "Those monitors would be flat without our hardware."

"What about her brain?" Saunders asked. "Are you even measuring her brain?"

The doctor sighed and said, "I've dealt with this kind of trauma for over ten years. Trust me when I tell you she is gone."

"You didn't answer the question. Have you measured her brain activity? You can trust me now when I say that you have no idea what you are dealing with here. You have never in your life treated a girl like her before."

The doctor had seen this before. The patient's family was unwilling or unable to accept the fact that they were gone, only this time, her family had a uniform and a gun. He looked at Saunders and saw a man who was out of his mind with grief. He had absolutely no idea what Saunders was talking about, but there was nothing the doctor could do to shake his faith in what he believed.

When the doctor didn't reply quickly enough, Saunders simply ordered him. "Do it. Check her brain. Now!"

Ashlin's heart raced as her nightmarish vision of Destiny's lifeless body lying at the bottom of a crater still lingered in her mind. A shiver ran down her spine as she sucked in her breath and leaned her head on Tempest's shoulder. Her voice quavered as she admitted, "I'm glad you're here."

Tempest stroked her hair and said, "Usually it's you comforting me through my bad moments. It is nice that I can return the favor for a change."

Ashlin turned back to look out the jet's window, but she found herself looking down a long white hallway instead. The steady noise from the wind rushing past the window was replaced with a church-like silence. She turned back to ask Tempest what was going on, but Destiny was sitting where Tempest had just been. Ashlin looked beyond Destiny and saw a room filled with sad looking people.

"Where are we?" Ashlin asked.

Destiny silently shrugged her shoulders, like a mime that was unable to speak.

Ashlin jumped when the quiet was broken by a shrill alarm bell that rang in a room down the hall. It frightened her, yet she was drawn to it. "I have to go," she said to the now empty seat next to her. Her knees quaked as she walked slowly down the hall. Part of her wanted to run down the deserted corridor, but most of her wanted to take off in the other direction instead. Her feet moved haltingly in front of her and carried her slowly towards the alarm. A door at the end of the hall swung open, admitting her inside, where she saw Destiny lying on a gurney with a dark-haired woman that she didn't know standing beside her.

Ashlin's stomach twisted as she neared Destiny's bed. It was the knotted feeling in her gut that witches get in the presence of a sorcerer. It had to be the woman standing over Destiny. She didn't look particularly scary, and she wasn't even very old, but she was from the sorcerer clan, and that alone made her dangerous.

Ashlin wanted to ask the woman what she was doing there. She wanted to scream for her to get away, but she couldn't. She stood in the doorway, frozen and mute, staring at the bizarre scene until doctors and nurses rushed into the room, shoving Ashlin aside.

Honey leaned her head against the car window and watched the road roll past. The white lane divider flashed in her eyes, matching the droning rhythm of the tires on the road. Her hair fell against her cheek and she smelled the smoke from their battle again. Why was she running away like a whipped dog? She kicked ass. She beat the chosen one. Why did she feel like she had lost?

Part of her wanted to turn right around, but she knew the answers to her questions. Even with Destiny out of the way, she still had to deal with the military, and she was drained. She reached between her breasts and squeezed the amulet that she had stolen from her cousin. It was cold and lifeless. Gone was the potent thrum of power that she had become so accustomed to feeling against her chest.

Destiny faced her without the help of a talisman, and Destiny had stopped her. Even though Destiny lay dead at the end of their battle, she had stopped Honey from becoming queen of the world. Honey squeezed the amulet again, hoping it would come to life for her. She needed it to rule the world, but she didn't know if the amulet would ever recharge itself.

Saunders waited in the ICU for the guards, which he had ordered, to arrive. He couldn't request guards through the regular channels or Flinch would simply have them escort her to the base hospital for study. Flinch didn't know what Saunders knew. Maybe because he wasn't actually there like Saunders was. Flinch couldn't feel the heat that radiated from their hands. He didn't feel the concussion as the missiles that impacted into the protective field that surrounded the girls. He couldn't smell the God awful smoke from their bombs and the girls' fire. Most of all, he hadn't seen how much this girl fought against Honey. Flinch had no way to fully understand how impotent they were against Honey and how much they needed the other girl. So instead of asking Flinch for a guard detail, Saunders called a retired friend who now worked for a security firm and asked for some men to stand watch.

A commotion down the hall alerted him that they may have arrived. He heard the doctors and nurses complaining about having soldiers in their hospital, and he knew for sure that it must be them. He knew they wouldn't be regular army, but when he left the room to greet them, he was disappointed to see that they were too young to even be veterans. This was not how he thought that he had explained the situation to his friend. He hoped there might be a chance for some retired rangers or seals that would want to get in on this action, but what he found was a couple of kids that looked more like college football players.

He must not have made himself clear, but then, how could he explain it to someone else when he didn't fully understand his own compulsion to protect her? He didn't even know who he was protecting her against. If the threat came from more people like Honey, then these boys would be outmatched. Even the best soldiers in the world couldn't stand up to her kind, whatever that was. Nobody could, except for the girl in the ICU.

Honey had told him that they weren't aliens from another planet. She even laughed at the thought, but he had no better explanation. She told him that she was from Mississippi, as if she were a regular human, but even though she looked human enough; there was nothing regular about her. He went back into the room and looked at Destiny. She looked like a normal human girl too, but that can't be either. She was like Honey and they were something else entirely.

"Sir?" one of the guards asked. "We were told to report to you."

"You see this girl?"

They both nodded.

"She is the most precious resource we have in this country. I don't know what you've been told..."

"We were briefed about Salt Lake before we were sent here, sir."

"Good. Then you have some idea what we are facing."

One of the boys pointed at Destiny and asked, "Is that her, sir?"

"She's not the girl from Salt Lake, if that's what you are asking. She's the girl that did what you and I could never do. I'm talking about stopping the girl that destroyed downtown Salt Lake."

"She killed the other girl?" the guard asked.

Saunders shook his head and exhaled sadly. "No. I wish that were true, but Honey escaped. That's why this one is so precious to us. Apparently, this girl is on our side and we need her."

"Did you say her name was Honey?"

"I spoke with her on the phone. She told me that her name was Honey, but she also said she was just a girl from Mississippi, so I don't know how much of her story we can believe."

"Our orders, sir?"

"Don't let anyone in or out, except for her doctors and nurses, of course. I want one of you in here watching her at all times and one of you out in the hall."

"You think the Honey girl will be coming back?"

"God, I hope not. One more thing; nobody can know that she is here. That's why I called for you. Even my brass doesn't know that she is here."

"Yes, sir."

"Of course he's looking for her," one of the librarians said. The dim light from the glowing coals barely illuminated his sweaty face within the large hood. "He thinks he loves her."

"He does love her," another librarian sad. "Don't minimize his feelings just because they are so young."

"Well," the first librarian continued, "he's obsessed with the notion of saving her. It's our job to prevent him from harming himself."

"That would be a lot easier," a third librarian said, "if he weren't so hell bent on rushing into harm's way."

"He's in love," the second librarian repeated, "and he's not going to listen to us."

The first librarian pulled his hood back and let if fall onto his shoulders. He leaned back, letting the soft grey material fall further down his back. The heat from the coals mixed with the cool air against his now exposed face, evaporating the sweat off of his skin as he took a deep slow breath and released it in a long exaggerated sigh.

"What are you doing?" the second librarian asked. "He told us to get through to the boy."

"I know what he told us," the first replied. "He's been telling us the same thing for years. Protect the boy. Get through to the boy. Convince the boy to leave it alone."

"So?" the second asked. "Are you going up against him? I'm not, and I don't think you would last two minutes against him."

"There's no point," the first said. "The boy won't listen."

"Then let's figure out why he won't listen," the third said, "and don't tell me it's because he is in love."

"What do you want us to tell you?" the second asked. "You don't think he knows what kind of danger he is heading into? If he won't listen to his own fears, what makes you think he'll ever listen to us?"

"First of all," the third said, "I don't think he knows where the true danger lies. He still thinks that the other girl is the only danger. He doesn't realize just how much danger this girl will put him in."

"She's not the problem," the first said.

"No, but she's the chosen one and everything you see outside stems from her."

"That's not a very realistic view," the first replied. "Haven't we all learned by now that fate always seems to get its way no matter what we do? Have you ever considered that the world was already in decline before she came along? For all we know, the others may have found the power without her, and then she may not have been there to save the world."

"Have you looked outside?" the second asked. "There is nothing but rubble and fire across the globe. How can you even call that saved?"

"She holds time in her pocket," the first said, "much more so than we ever will, and she simply hasn't saved the world yet."

"And," the second added, "she won't be able to save the world if we let her die."

"Or," the first said as he climbed to his feet, "if we stop him from getting to her."

"He's not going to like this," the third said.

The first librarian crouched down so he could look into the second's eyes. "He probably already expects us to fail. This won't even faze him, and I seriously doubt that it will surprise him in the least. Let's go research what happens next."

Blake, led only by his innate connection to Destiny, pulled the car into the hospital's parking lot and swung around to the emergency entrance.

Logan examined the hospital from one end to the other, but saw nothing to suggest that Destiny was more likely to be in this hospital than any other. "So, were you planning on going from one hospital to another looking for her?"

"No need," Blake said. "She's here."

"Oh," Logan said frowning. "Those witch senses you got from your mother's side?"

"Yeah," Blake said as he pulled the car into a slot and shut down the engine.

Logan looked around and whistled. "You'd think they'd be busier after all the destruction and smoke we just drove through."

Blake wasn't listening. He jumped out of the car and ran across the lot and into the emergency room.

The nurse at the admitting desk could tell that he wasn't injured and tried looking around him to see who was.

Blake didn't bother waiting to catch his breath. "I'm looking for Destiny Boutin."

The nurse checked her registry, but Destiny's name wasn't on it. "I'm sorry, but we have no Destiny admitted here. This is the emergency room. Perhaps you should ask at the main desk."

"She would have been brought here. She's sixteen years old, medium height, with blond hair, and she probably smelled like smoke."

His description matched the Jane Doe that came in with the army officer, but she was directed to not disclose any information about her. "I'm sorry," she lied, "but we don't have anyone matching that description."

It was too late. Blake had already heard her thoughts. "What's her condition? Can I see her?"

"I told you," the nurse said, "whoever you are looking for is not here." But as she said the words, her mind thought, "Coma."

"Coma?" Blake asked. "Can you help her?"

The nurse tried hiding the shock she felt when he said, "coma," but her mind involuntarily thought, "...being kept alive on machines."

Honey couldn't hide the sorrow or the shame from her face. She shouldn't have to run away like a kicked dog, but that is exactly what she felt like she was doing; riding away from the conflict with her tail between her legs. She looked around the limo's cab and caught Maggie's eyes for a moment, but Maggie was quick to turn her attention back to Tommy. Honey knew why Maggie didn't want to look at her. Why would she? Honey must be the biggest loser on the face of the planet, except for her cousin Destiny, of course, but even that thought brought her no joy.

She leaned her head against the window, unable to suppress the tears that now leaked from her eyes. Abilene brushed back a few hairs on Honey's face and said, "Don't cry, baby. Everything's going to be just fine. You'll see."

Honey flopped her head over to her mother's shoulder; something neither of them were accustomed to doing. "Oh Mama. I made such a mess of things."

"Oh hush," Abilene said. "You done what you set out to do. You defeated my sister's bitch whelp, and you done it in front of the whole damned world."

"Then why is it that I has to leave like this?"

"I don't know, sweetie. Why is we leavin' before you makes your-self queen of the world?" Abilene had an idea what was wrong. She saw how dark the amulet that Honey wore was now. It no longer glowed and throbbed with power. Honey would never admit it to her, but Abilene knew that it was the source of her new power. Abilene had even tried stealing it from her daughter while she slept, but Honey had always stirred before she could. With Honey leaning against her now, in her distraught condition, it would be easy for Abilene to remove it from her neck, but it looked dead now. It was useless to her.

"I never suspected that she would be so tough. It took everything I had to kill her. Now I don't even have the strength to overcome one measly man."

"You got us past the guard just fine," Abilene said.

"Sure, Mama, but that warn't by using no powers. Men is silly around pretty girls. You knows that, I mean, you used to know that. Didn't you?"

Abilene frowned. If she had taken the amulet while it was still charged up, she might have renewed her youth instead of wasting it on some damned fool crusade to conquer the world. "You jest needs to rest up some. You'll be getting your strength back in no time."

Honey reached her arms around her mother's neck, another ges-ture that was very unusual for them. "I hope so, Mama. I hope so."

She closed her eyes again and fell asleep against her mother's shoulder.

Chapter 5

Blake didn't get an exact location for Destiny from the nurse's mind, but it wasn't because she was somehow hiding her thoughts from him. He saw everything that she knew and it was simply because Destiny had been brought in before her shift had started, and she didn't know the actual room number. He could have forced her to look up the room while he was in her mind, but she had already grown suspicious of how much he had learned while talking to her, so he backed out of her mind, satisfied that she did at least offer what ward Destiny was in and how to get there.

Logan remained in the waiting room while Blake and Johnson followed the corridors to find Destiny. An open elevator was waiting for them and swiftly took them up to the proper floor, but when the doors opened to the ICU ward and they stepped out into the hallway, even Johnson knew what room she was in when they saw the guard posted out in front of the door. The guard that stood inside the room couldn't see them, but the other eyed them both suspiciously as they left the elevator. Blake walked nonchalantly down the hall and the guard remained at his post until Blake actually angled towards the door to her room.

"This room is private," the guard said, "no admittance."

"Private?" Blake asked. "How can that be? Don't you know who I am? I'm her boyfriend, I mean her husband. We're newlyweds. I'm barely getting used to saying that."

The guard stood his ground. "I'm under orders to admit nobody, and there's no exception for any boyfriend or husband."

The young soldier clearly didn't believe him, so Blake entered the man's mind and planted a story. "You know me. You've always known me. We go way back. In fact, you were the best man at our wedding. Don't you remember? You've been wondering where good old Blake was while she was lying alone in there, suffering from a coma, and boy, are you relieved to see me now?"

"Where the hell have you been?" the guard asked. "She's all alone in there. The brass won't let anyone in except them and the hospital staff. I think they would keep the doctors and nurses out if they thought they could get away with it." The guard nodded towards Johnson and asked, "Who's he? And don't try telling me he's her brother."

"You don't remember Johnson?" Blake planted more ideas into the guard's mind while he was asking the question.

The guard squinted at Johnson and said, "Oh yeah. Weren't you one of the groomsmen at their wedding?"

"Yeah," Johnson said as he recognized what Blake was doing and just played along. "That was me."

The guard opened the door and said, "Hey Jimmy, this is her husband and a friend. Don't worry, I know them."

The inner guard held his palm against the door and said, "I don't know."

Blake entered his mind and suggested, "You were at our wedding too."

"Wait a minute," the guard said. "I remember you. It's Blain, right?"

"Blake, actually"

"Oh yeah. Hurry up, and get in here, and be quiet."

Johnson snickered and whispered to Blake, "You know I love it when you Jedi mind trick them, don't you?"

Blake winked back at him.

"You don't ever do that to me, do you?"

"You better come on in here," Blake said, "so they can close the door."

"You didn't answer my question."

Blake ignored him and went straight to Destiny's side.

———

While Blake had been tracking down Destiny's room, Logan had gone to the nurses' station. He waited patiently for her to acknowledge him, but he had arrived too closely after Blake and she was already rattled by how much Blake knew about the Jane Doe, so she was automatically suspicious about Logan and tried to ignore him, shuffling papers around on her desk. She read patient charts that she didn't need to read, but still felt him staring down at her and when he wouldn't go away, she looked up and asked, "Can I help you?"

"I wanted to offer my support for the girl they brought in a while ago."

The nurse eyed him nervously and asked, "What girl?"

"Her name is Destiny."

"Are you family?"

Logan considered lying, but decided it wasn't necessary. "No. The poor girl barely has any family, and what family she does have is dirt poor, so I'd like to help."

The nurse scrolled through some pages on her computer and said, "We have no Destiny admitted here, but you couldn't have seen her, anyway. Only family is admitted in the ER."

"I don't wish to see her, but knowing her family's circumstances, I doubt that she has insurance, and I wanted to be sure that she got the best medical care available."

"I'm sorry, sir, but we have no Destiny here. I would remember a name like that."

"It's possible that you didn't know her name, but I saw your reaction when my associate described her. You recognized her description and sent my friend off in that direction. Would that be the way to the ICU?"

The nurse's heart raced. Nobody was supposed to know about their Jane Doe, and she wasn't supposed to reveal anything, yet two men had come to her already knowing too much. She tried finding something on her desk to occupy her time again, but Logan remained. She looked back up at him, clearly annoyed, and said, "I'm sorry, but I can't help you. Was there anything else?"

Saunders wished that he could have stayed with Destiny, but he had been ordered to report to Major Flinch. He couldn't explain, even to himself, why he cared so much about her, but he had this undeniable feeling that she was important and it was up to him to oversee her care. Flinch was never going to care for her, so it all fell upon his shoulders, but he had to do it in secrecy. He should be with her now, but the best he could do was post guards at her door and hope for the best until he could return.

Flinch's secretary was away from her desk as Saunders approached his office. He stood there a moment, staring at the closed door, ready to knock, but hesitating because he didn't have a rehearsed statement to give to his superior. He couldn't stand there forever, so he rapped his knuckles on the door.

"Saunders, if that's you, you had better get your butt in here and start explaining."

"Sir?" Saunders feigned innocence as he opened the door.

"Don't play dumb with me, mister. You know exactly what I want."

"Sir. I had to save her. She's our best defense, maybe our only defense against that other one."

Flinch chewed the butt of his cigar, wishing that they were still allowed to light them up like in the old days, so he could blow a thick billow of smoke into Saunders' face. "She was dead! Our best defense against that other one was to take her apart and learn what makes them tick."

"Not if I could save her."

"Save her? You think they can also rise from the dead?"

Saunders shrugged. "Who knows what else they can do? Besides, she wasn't actually dead! She was weak, but she wasn't dead, at least not yet."

That put a crimp in Flinch's rampage, but he wasn't quite done yet. "I want her looked at by our own surgeons. If she's still alive, then we'll transfer her to one of our V.A. hospitals, where we can care for her."

A part of Saunders wanted to laugh at Flinch's misguided confidence in the V.A. system, but he knew that it wasn't confidence on Flinch's part. He wasn't the least bit concerned with her well-being, and the moment he learned that she was on life support, he would pull the plug and turn her into a biology experiment.

"Yes, sir," Saunders said.

"Where'd you take her?"

"I'll find out for you."

"What do you mean, 'you'll find out'? Don't you know where you took her?"

"Sir," Saunders lied, "they were ready to transport her from the ER to someplace with a specialist, but they hadn't found a bed yet. I'm sure she's been moved by now. I'll find out where she is for you."

Flinch scowled. "You do that, and report back to me as soon as you do!"

The flight attendant's voice flowed smoothly from the sound system as she recited a well-practiced announcement, "Ladies and gentlemen; the captain has turned off the seatbelt sign. At this time, you may proceed to use your personal electronic devices. We will be starting our beverage service momentarily."

Michelle leaned her seat back, but clutched the arms of the chair and stared up at the air nozzles and lights below the overhead bins. Tempest saw how she had pressed the silver button and mimicked her mother to lean her own chair back.

Michelle glanced over at her daughter and said, "Oh, I'm sorry. I forgot how this be your first time and I was going to show you how it's done, but I sees dat you figured it out okay."

"I didn't know that you knew how to do it," Tempest replied, "seeing how you don't fly."

"I said I don't like flying, not dat I never done it." Michelle looked across Tempest at Ashlin who had her face pressed against the glass. "What be out there?"

"Not much to see right now," Ashlin said wistfully, "but I keep hoping something will happen."

"Nothing excitin' I hopes. I think I'm ready to catch me some shuteye."

"You go ahead," Tempest said. "I'm fine."

Michelle didn't need any more encouragement than that. Her eyes easily fell shut, and she drifted off, but even in her dream, she was still on the plane. She looked across Tempest and saw her mother in the window seat. "Mama?"

"You done real good," her mother said, "with the young ones, I means."

"How can you say that? My baby girl lived her life in a hospital for crazy people."

"You can't blame yourself for that," her mother replied. "You didn't put her there. I remember. I was there too."

"Well, I shore didn't do nothin' to keep her out."

"Sure you did. In da end at least. Look at her now!"

Michelle looked at Tempest and shook her head. "I'm still afraid for her, and for her daughter. You should see Destiny. She be somethin' to behold."

"I know. I seen her."

Michelle looked at her mother and wondered how she even recognized her. She didn't remember her mother having so many wrinkles etched across her face and her hair was shocking white when it used to be a brilliant red. "What happened to you, Mama?"

"Pardon?"

"It's just that I don't remember you havin' dem age spots on your hands and your..."

"Oh Lordy," her mother said, "is you calling me old? Ain't that the kettle callin' the pot black?"

"Who me?" Michelle asked, "But I'm still...that is, I just figured you'd be the same, that's all."

"Ain't I? My hair turned white long before I passed."

"But you wasn't a prune as I recall."

"Mayhaps not. Could be you just don't want me to look too young to be your mother."

Michelle nodded her head. "Das probably it."

Her mother's eyes twinkled as she smiled warmly at her daughter.

"You know mama, these be dark times. There be times dat I could sure use your guidance these days."

Michelle's mother just smiled and slowly shook her head. "You already gots all the guidance I could ever give you sitting all around you. Asides, you gots the best of me inside o' you."

Michelle sighed. "Destiny be the best of all o' us and I fears for her."

"She needs you. She needs you all."

"The boy too?" Michelle asked.

Michelle's mother smiled warmly and nodded her head. Michelle thought she saw some of the wrinkles smooth on her mother's face. "The boy, most of all."

Blake stalled when he reached Destiny's bed and got his first good look at her. Her cheeks were flaccid and pale. Tubes were taped to her chin, pumping air in and out of her lungs. He dragged a chair to the side of the bed and held her hand. The room was so frigid that he had almost expected her hand to be cold like a corpse, but she was thankfully warm to his touch.

She was the only one in the room. Monitors surrounding the bed traced her heart beat and her breathing, which seemed odd to him since the minds that he had read said that the machines were doing all the work. The room was almost as quiet as it was dim, with only the rhythmic whir of the breathing machine and the equally rhythmic blips from the heart monitors. There was something mesmerizing about the sound. It should be easy for him to reach into her mind and let her know he was there.

He closed his eyes and slid into the grey void. The soft rhythms of the room swirled around his head. He called to her, "Destiny?" Before she could answer, a grating, screeching noise jarred him from his trance. Blake glanced up at the guard that still stood his post at the door. He grimaced and nodded his head towards Johnson.

"Sorry," Johnson said as he dragged a chair to the far corner of the room near the window. "I thought I'd give you guys some alone time." Johnson grabbed a magazine from a wall rack and tiptoed to the chair and sat where a sliver of light pierced through the space between the closed blinds and the wall, projecting a thin stripe onto his page. He flipped through a few pages, looking for something interesting, but he was too tired to read and quickly fell asleep, with his head falling backwards against the wall.

Blake returned to his trance and entered the void again. "Destiny? It's me. I'm back. Can you hear me?"

He waited for a response, but none came to him. She should have heard him even if she was in an ancestral memory. Maybe she just couldn't respond. He refused to consider anything worse than that.

He returned from the void and entered her mind like he would if he had wanted to influence her. "Destiny? Yoo-hoo . Anybody home?" He still refused to entertain any ideas that she was gone from this world and convinced himself that she must be too busy to talk. She's probably doing healing spells and he should just leave her alone.

The bed was a bit stiff for a pillow, and gave little to the weight of his head as he lay it on the bed, still holding her hand. He fell asleep to the sound of the machines.

Michelle couldn't take her eyes off of her mother. She didn't care if it was just a dream; she hadn't seen her mother since Destiny was just a baby and she didn't want to lose a single moment of this opportunity. She even breathed softly for fear that she might break the spell.

When Tempest was a little girl, her mother was the first to see the great potential in her. Even though witches no longer wielded the same powers that their ancestors could, some of them still had the sight, and Michelle's mother had seen a great, but terrifying future for Tempest. As a young girl, Tempest was already very sensitive to the spiritual energy that surrounded all life, something that was rare in a girl that hadn't yet reached her womanhood, but it was puberty that had manifested her problems with her gifts. The voices in her head became overwhelming to her. She had refused her training and only wanted to find some quiet in her head, which had ultimately driven her to booze and all manner of distraction until she finally ended up hospitalized. She was quite a handful in those days, and Michelle could not have made it through them without her mother's help.

When Tempest ran away, Michelle and her mother had used the sight to search for Tempest together, and after several months, when they had finally found her, they learned that she had given birth to a little girl. Michelle was glad that her mother had lived long enough to see her great granddaughter. It was her mother that had seen the baby's future and had suggested that they name her Destiny, but she didn't live long after that and Michelle missed her often.

She stared into her mother's face. The sun blazed in through the jet's window and lit her hair like a halo that framed her features. Her white hair took on a red glow from the sun and started to look like the fiery red hair of her youth. The plane banked to turn and Michelle saw that it wasn't just the sun, but her mother's hair had returned to its bright red color, and her face had lost years as the wrinkles had smoothed across her cheeks. Her eyes remained bright and alive while the rest of her aged backwards, younger and younger, until Michelle was left looking at the red headed Ashlin, who smiled at her and turned back to look out the window again.

"Would you like a beverage?"

Michelle was startled out of her dream. She glanced up at the flight attendant and nodded. "Water please."

Destiny felt like Marvalaine had abandoned her. He knew where the orb was and refused to give it to her. She was the chosen one, yet he had told her that it wasn't for her to retrieve. If not her, then who? It couldn't be her mother, because her mother wasn't well enough yet, and they needed the orb to save her mother. She could always rely on her nana to get things done, but maybe not if she would require help from Marvalaine. Ashlin showed a lot of promise for a young witch, but she was too young for Destiny to burden with such a task. Besides, Ashlin was pretty busy helping her mother with the voices.

That only left one person that she could ask. Destiny closed her eyes and entered the void. "Blake? Can you hear me? I need your help."

The void had always been full of chatter, but now it sounded different to her, as if it were fading away. She couldn't focus on it enough to tell past from present, or maybe she just wasn't listening for the right clues, so she narrowed her focus only on finding Blake, but as she floated through the void, she did not hear him. She could usually tune in on him pretty easily, but that was when she was alive and the void didn't feel so distant. Maybe he was still stuck in the dream world she created of them flying in circles, waiting to land.

She refocused on the world that she had created to hold him captive and the void was promptly replaced with the cabin of the small jet, but it was empty. Blake and the others were all gone.

The captain's voice came from the loudspeakers, "The tower has informed me that they are still trying to clear the obstruction on the runway, but for us to hang in there. We should be getting you on the ground shortly."

Destiny frowned and returned to the void. "Blake? Can you hear me?"

Again, there was no answer. Something must be wrong. She had left them in the dream world, but they managed to escape. She should have known that she couldn't have kept him locked in the dream forever. What would they have done after escaping? They would have come looking for her. There were a lot of ways they could get themselves in trouble. The army could have taken them into custody for questioning or something, but why? He was more liable to be arrested by the police for trying to hitch a ride from the airport. No. He wouldn't hitchhike. He would push someone to give him a ride, but they wouldn't arrest him for that. Nobody would ever know that he had done it, and if anyone claimed that he had, the police wouldn't believe it. If he didn't push someone, he might have pushed the car. She remembered how easily he could open locks. He might have stolen a car, and that would land him in big trouble, but would that prevent her from contacting him?

Whatever was wrong with him went deeper than some trouble with the police. In order for him not to respond to her, he must somehow be unable to respond. Her heart raced as the panic coursed through her body, culminating in quakes that shook her from the core out. He must really be in trouble. She would have to try the hospitals to find him.

She reached out with her senses. Hospitals were fairly easy to locate. The healer within her could feel the concentration of sick people. A darker witch within her could sense the souls that had died there. She suppressed the darker side for fear that he might be among them and refocused her mind on the ill and tried to isolate him among the many suffering people that she found.

If he was hurt and in the hospital, it would be reasonable to imagine him dreaming, and his dreams should be a bit louder than the other patients in the hospital. She listened keenly to the dreams of the suffering and heard him call for her. His voice was faint and far away, but she closed her eyes and cocked her head while she followed it to its source.

It led her to a dimly lit room. She didn't find him lying in a hospital bed. Instead, she found him sitting aside the bed, holding onto the patient's hand. She tried seeing who was lying in the bed, but all she could see was vague blocks of color where the face should have been.

"Blake? I'm here."

He didn't respond, but after a few moments, she heard his thoughts. "Destiny? Where are you Destiny?"

"I'm right here," she replied, but again, he didn't hear her.

She floated above him, still unable to see who was in the bed. She hoped fervently that it wasn't him. Her eyes dampened as she realized how hard it would be for his spirit to hold his own lifeless hand and wonder where she was and why he had to die alone.

Blake dreamt of the first time he had met Destiny. He'd been raised to believe that her kind was the enemy, but it turned out that her kind was his kind, only he didn't know it until he met her. Unlike Destiny, he was one of the results of highly secret breeding experiments held by the sorcerer clan to produce a crossbreed that could fulfill an ancient witch prophecy. He was raised by them and went to school with them, but he was never really accepted by the other students or the clan. He had thought that he would finally gain some respect when he was tasked with tracking her down, and he did it well, but she wasn't what he expected. When he found her, believing that she was the enemy, but in truth, he was the true enemy. She came to him in a dream and could have killed him, and nearly had, but she let him live. It was just a dream, but his life had still been in her hands.

When he woke from that dream and saw her in person for the first time, something started to change within him. He couldn't hate her kind anymore, because he finally realized that they were the same. They both shared blood from both clans. His dream now took him to that morning on the island where Destiny lived with her nana. He was supposed to leave. Michelle had told him to leave at sunrise. Even in his dream, Blake found the humor in his thoughts. Michelle didn't just tell him to leave. She ordered him to go and threatened his life if he didn't, but Destiny didn't want him to go. She saw in him what he saw in her. She was the most wonderful person he had ever known, and now she was gone.

He lingered in the dream and watched her walk away from the smokehouse, where they let him spend the night, to the main house where she lived. She was really something.

"She certainly was," Marvalaine said behind him.

Blake spun around and saw an old man with a long white beard and an odd curly pipe. He searched his memory, but couldn't quite place where he knew this man in the billowy robes. "How is it that I know you?"

Marvalaine smiled and said, "You've known me all your life."

"Uhuh," Blake said disbelievingly. "Why are you here? You aren't supposed to be here, that is, you weren't here that day."

"No?" Marvalaine asked. "You might say I've always been with you."

"What does that mean?" Blake asked. "Are you telling me that you are God or something?"

"No," Marvalaine said with a slow shake of his head. He took a long, luxurious puff from his pipe and blew smoke rings into the air, then returned his attention back to Blake and said, "I am not Him."

"So, why are you here?"

"I've come to you because you cannot come to me."

"Really?" Blake asked. "This is a dream. This is my dream. I can go anywhere I want in a dream, but I can't dream forever and I have no time for odd figments of my imagination. I want to concentrate on her, so, if you don't mind..."

"If you are so interested in concentrating on her," Marvalaine said, "then why are you wasting your time in a dream? Scratch that. I don't want you to wake up yet. I came to you in your dream because you cannot come to me. She could, you know. She's the only one that I know of who could do that."

"You're not making any sense."

Marvalaine took a long draw on his strange coiled pipe and blew another perfect smoke circle into the air. "Destiny would visit me often, in my time."

"Oh, yeah?"

"We had a special relationship."

"You?" Blake laughed. "A shriveled up old man like you?"

"Nothing like that, and I wasn't always as you see me now. I am a distant ancestor of hers."

"I know who you are," Blake said, but I don't know why you are in my dream."

"Didn't I already say? You cannot come to me, so I came to you."

"Yeah, I heard you the first zillion times, but why do you need to see me?"

"Because," Marvalaine said, "you are the only one who can save her."

Blake's mind swirled for a moment. Marvalaine finally said something that was relevant to him. "I can save her?"

"It is for you to find the orb."

"Sure," Blake replied. "Just tell me where."

"I cannot. It is for you to find. It is a hand-me-down of sorts. I had it during my time, and I passed it down. I cannot tell you the lineage that has carried it over the ages. But I can tell you that it seeks you out as much as you must seek it."

Blake thought about it for a moment and asked, "If it seeks me out, then why must I look for it? Why don't I just wait for it to find me?"

Marvalaine smiled as he nodded his head and said, "That is a good question, but even if it comes to you, you won't see it, or at least, you won't recognize it, unless you are looking for it."

"This is all very strange," Blake said.

"It is," Marvalaine admitted, "but then, isn't that the way with all magic?"

Logan squirmed in the waiting room chair, passing the time by watching the people come and go, but he wasn't really waiting there to learn how Destiny fared. He was waiting to spot anyone else that might be coming to see Destiny. He had thought that the ER would have been a busier ward late at night and on the weekends, especially after the incident between the two girls, but, although it was much quieter than he had anticipated, there was at least enough traffic to keep things from being too boring. He stirred his cup of coffee but frowned at the stale taste of the machine dispensed java. He held the cup close to his lips, debating whether to try another sip when Saunders returned from his briefing with Flinch. "Excuse me," Logan shouted as he sprang out of his chair, almost spilling the coffee, "are you here to see Destiny?"

"Who?"

Logan took a half step back and cocked his head. "Are you telling me that you don't even know her name?"

Saunders looked at Logan suspiciously and replied, "I don't know your name either."

Logan offered his hand and said, "My name is Dr. Francis Logan, but you can call me Frank. I realize that you are trying to keep her presence here a secret, but I already know she is here, and I only wanted to help with her care."

"Are you her doctor?"

"Yes," Logan replied, "but I'm not a physician, I'm a psychiatrist."

"You're her psychiatrist? Hmmm." Saunders was intrigued that the girl with the supernatural powers had a psychiatrist. "I don't suppose you can tell me why she needed a psychiatrist?"

"No," Logan said. "I couldn't, because I wasn't treating her. My interest is as a friend of the family. I only wanted to offer financial help to be sure she gets the best care possible."

"I've already seen to that," Saunders said. "You can sleep easy knowing that she'll get the best medical attention available."

Logan pursed his lips as Saunders turned abruptly and marched down the hall towards the elevator, leaving him with his bitter coffee and no answers.

Blake swam around in the void, unsure if he was drifting through the memories of his long-lost ancestors, or just dreaming that he was. Marvalaine's words echoed in his head, but it was hard to take a man seriously when he looked like such a crackpot. Blake needed a little more substance right now and Marvalaine delivered mostly character, and not necessarily the good kind. How could anyone trust an old coot blowing smoke rings from a pipe that looked like a pig's tail? Destiny did. She trusted him implicitly.

The already dark void that surrounded Blake turned darker. He felt the ground form below his feet and sensed that it was more than just a dream. Thick smoke blotted out the sun and burned his eyes. His throat gagged from the wretched odor of burning sulphur and rotting flesh.

A flickering light in the distance produced a soft, round glow in the fog-like smoke that grew larger as it neared him. This didn't feel like it would be a particularly pleasant memory, so he turned and tried running in the other direction, but his feet were bogged down in the muddy ash.

"Where would you go?" a deep raspy voice asked from the vicinity of the light. As the stranger neared him, Blake saw the shadowy outline of a hooded figure in a long robe. "You cannot escape your fate," the man continued. "You have a quest before you. It is a rare honor to have such a pivotal role in what is to come. It is your destiny to find the orb."

"Seriously?" Blake yelled. "If I didn't believe the other nut-job, do you really think that a mysterious world and spooky robe would work any better?"

The librarian didn't know what Blake meant by the other nut-job, but remained on point to fulfill his own mission. "It is necessary for you to find the orb."

"Yeah, yeah, I know. Find the orb. Save Destiny. Believe me when I tell you that I want to save Destiny more than anything else."

"We understand your personal motives to save the girl," the librarian said, "but we also know that if the others find the orb first, and learn to control it, your life will be in grave danger."

"What does my life matter to you?"

"One day, you will know the answer to that question. For now, you only need to worry about finding the orb."

"But," Blake said, "I don't know what this orb is or where to find it."

"It's hidden, of course; hidden so they don't find it before you, but they are already perilously close to it."

"I don't suppose you can tell me what it looks like? Or are you going to be as vague as that other guy?"

Again, the librarian didn't understand Blake's reference. "It sounds to us like you already know that we cannot reveal the orb's appearance to you, but we are confident that you can fulfill your quest and you will know it when you see it."

"What makes you so sure that I can find it?"

"Because," the librarian said as he tented his fingers and bowed his hooded head, "it is your destiny to do so."

Blake scowled as the hooded figure faded away. The strange visitor left a worse taste in his mouth than the awful smoke that surrounded him.

Saunders had been away from the blond girl for far too long. A thousand things could have happened while he was busy reporting to Major Flinch, and meeting Logan in the waiting room had only made him more uneasy. It was bad enough that his commander would rather put her on a table and dissect her, but he couldn't afford to have the media find her and expose her before he could save her. He guessed that Flinch would already have contacted the NSA to put some kind of spin on the events that would hide the truth, but he also had no doubt that any attempts to bury the events would be unsuccessful. Truth had little to do with perception when the public was concerned. There were those that would always mistrust anything the government said. It would be like Area 51, except this time, someone probably captured video on their phone.

The battle between the two girls was epic, and even though he witnessed it firsthand, he still didn't know the real truth behind what he had seen. He didn't know that the battle was between a witch and a sorcerer. He didn't know the history of violence between the two clans. Nor did he know that magic was a real force in ancient times, or that the power that they displayed had been merely dormant for centuries. In his mind, the possibility of them being aliens from another world was more plausible than having a Dark Age magical power reborn, but he didn't really care how they did what they did. He only cared that the other one was violent and aggressive, and this one seemed to be on his side.

Saunders left the elevator on the third floor and turned towards Destiny's room. An antiseptic odor in the hall tickled his nose as he followed the sky blue line on the floor to ICU. Just outside the ward, he saw Destiny's doctor and asked, "How is she?"

"She's no better than before, but the machines are keeping her organs fresh. Have you located a next of kin to see about organ donation?"

Saunders wanted to lash out and rip the man apart. "No! Maybe I wasn't clear to you before, but we aren't giving up on her. Bring her back. Do you hear me now? You have to bring her back!"

"Do something extraordinary to return her to us! Do something to reboot her brain! I don't care what you have to do or how experimental it might be, but you must revive her, and if you aren't the man to do it, then find someone else who can!"

Johnson's head had flopped back against the wall. It rocked gently with his breathing while the magazine that he had tried reading had long since slipped to the floor. His mind had taken him back to the bayou when he was tromping through the swamp, trying to escape the carnage, but his body snored uneasily as he slept.

"Johnson!" the voice boomed in his head, jolting him from his dream. It was them again. He was glad to be free of the swamp nightmare, but he doubted that having them in his head would be any better.

"Johnson, we want you to encourage him to find the orb."

"The what?" Johnson asked sleepily.

"The orb. It's a…oh never mind, he'll know what you mean. We'd send you, but he's the only one who can find it. Don't worry though; we want you to go with him."

"Sure," Johnson said, still half asleep. "I'll go with him."

"It's important. He needs to find the orb before they do, and you must protect him along the way. Don't take any unnecessary risks."

"Got it," Johnson said drowsily as he settled back to sleep. "Get the orb. Protect Blake."

Michelle wanted desperately to see her mother again, even if it was only a dream. She sipped the water that the stewardess had given her and closed her eyes, but when she closed her eyes to resume her dream, she didn't find her mother. She found herself in a cold hospital room. The skies outside were dark and gloomy, but they weren't really clouds. She could smell the smoke through the closed window and occasionally spotted glowing red embers drifting past the window and landing far below at ground level.

Blake was at Destiny's side, holding her hand and crying, when Tempest burst into the room. "What are you doing here?"

"I had to see her," Blake cried.

"You should be out there finding it!"

"I know what I should be doing," Blake cried, "but I can't find it. He said it would come to me. He said that I was destined to find it, but I don't even know what it looks like!"

"I don't care," Tempest screamed. "You go back out there and start looking again! We need her or all is lost!"

The vision burst abruptly as the flight attendant shook her shoulder and told her to raise her seat back for landing.

The doctor's eagerness to harvest Destiny's organs left Saunders wondering if this really was the best place to bring her. He needed physicians that would be willing to do anything to bring her back, and this doctor spoke as if it was too late already. His concern didn't improve any when he reached her room and saw an uncomfortable expression on the guard that he left posted in the hallway.

The guard swallowed hard as Saunders approached.

Saunders eyed the guard suspiciously as he asked, "Is there a problem?"

"Ummm..."

Saunders wasn't waiting for bad news from the guard and burst into the room. He immediately saw Blake with his head on her bed and pulled his sidearm. He pointed it directly at Blake and barked, "Who are you?"

Johnson instinctively reached for a weapon, but he was unarmed. Saunders saw his move from the corner of his eyes and turned to aim his weapon at Johnson instead.

Blake raised his hands and said, "I'm her boyfriend."

"Her boyfriend?" Saunders asked. "They let you in because you are her boyfriend?"

Blake smiled sheepishly and admitted, "I told the nurse that we were newlyweds."

"I don't care about how you got past the nurse. I want to know how you got pasts my guards!"

"Oh," Blake said. "That might be a little harder to explain."

Saunders turned to the guard and barked, "Tell me why you let him in."

The guard gulped hard and said, "He's okay. I know him, sort of. I was even at their wedding. Ask Milton. He was their best man. He knows him way better than I do."

"Milton?" Saunders barked. "Is that true? Do you know this man?"

"Yes sir, absolutely."

"And you were the best man at their wedding?"

"Yes, sir."

"Then why did he tell me he was her boyfriend?"

Milton laughed and said, "They're newlyweds. He keeps forgetting to say he's her husband."

"Of course," Saunders said with a fake smile. "How long have they been married?"

Blake hadn't planted that information in the poor man's mind. Saunders saw him searching his memory, but no answer came forth.

The hackles on the back of Saunders' neck prickled. "Come on Milton. You said you were there. When was the wedding?"

Again, Milton was unable to respond.

Saunders trained his weapon on Blake again. "Who are you? What are you? Are you like her?"

Blake smiled sheepishly again and said, "You got me. I'm like her. Can you lower your gun now before you start to shake? By now, your mind must be telling you that your weapon isn't going to help you against me, but you might accidentally hit Destiny while she sleeps."

Saunders wasn't willing to lower his weapon just yet. "How many of you are there? Are there more than just the three of you?"

"Three of us?" Blake asked, confused at first, but then he smiled, hoping a friendly face would ease the tension a bit. "Oh, that's Johnson. He's not one of us, but he knows about us. He's actually one of you. He's ex-military."

"I meant the other girl. The one that called herself Honey."

"Oh her," Blake said with a scowl. "She's definitely not one of us."

"Not one of you?" Saunders asked. "I saw what she could do."

"She's one of them," Blake explained, "and she could only do what she did because she stole some of Destiny's powers."

Logan stepped into the doorway and said, "Maybe you can relax a little, captain, so we can explain. We're all on the same side here."

Saunders pointed a thumb to Logan and asked, "Is he one of you?"

Blake leaned to the side so he could see around Saunders and said, "Not exactly. He's one of them, but he doesn't like what Honey is doing either, and he's sort of with us."

Saunders' head spun. He barely was able to cope with the two girls. Now he has to deal with both 'them' and the other 'them'. "I don't know what kind of history has gone on between you and the others, and I'm not sure that I want to know. My only interest is in the security of this nation and our way of life, something that Honey had plans to upset, but this girl was willing to help us preserve our way of life. She proved herself. I don't really know where the rest of you stand. I can tell you this, though, the United States Government has a much narrower view than I personally do and you would do well to cooperate with me as much as you can."

CHAPTER 6

Day eight.

Was it the quiet after the storm or just a lull before the next storm rolled in? The battle between the two girls was certainly unlike any fight before it, at least in contemporary history, and it wasn't over yet. It was the greatest conflict ever witnessed in modern times, but while Honey may have won the battle, the war had not been settled and no peace had been brokered. As much as possible, the world was kept in the dark while a race was on, by only a select few, for humanity to prepare before the next skirmish began.

Honey nestled her head against her mother's shoulder, but her mind remained locked in battle with Destiny. She didn't have the witches' gift to relive memories as if she was there, but she could dream. In her dream, she sneered at her cousin and flaunted the

amulet that dangled between her breasts. She undid another button and smiled at her cousin while toying with the glowing stone.
"Hey cousin. You lose something? You must be awfully brave to
come face me without it."

"That bauble?" Destiny asked. "Did you think that just because
all your power came from some old rock, that mine did too?"

Honey feigned another smile. It was just tough talk from a
desperate woman. "You ain't foolin' me. You cain't bluff your way
past me, cousin."

Destiny stood her ground in front of the steps to the state
offices and said, "If you think you can get past me, then come on."

Honey wrapped her fingers around the amulet and felt the
warmth pulsate through her hand. Her cousin sure talked tough,
and for what? Why would she risk her life for these people?

"Well?" Destiny taunted her. "Are we gonna dance? Or do you
plan to stand there playing with that toy?"

"Now I know you is lying," Honey replied. "Cause this shore
ain't no toy."

Honey squeezed the amulet with her left hand while summon-
ing a huge fireball in the other, but before she could throw it, the
dream exploded in a brilliant orange fire storm.

Abilene stroked Honey's hair and cooed, "It was just a dream.
You be fine. We all is fine."

Honey was unsure how to respond to this kind of affection from
her mother and sat up straight in her seat. She looked at Schaefer
and waited patiently for him to notice her. He felt her staring at
him, but failed to look away in time. She waited until she knew
she had his attention and said, "I think maybe you was right."

At first, he wasn't sure she was talking to him, but she never
looked away. "About what?" he asked.

"About me makin' a army instead of going up against her
myself."

"Oh," he said. He wished she had listened to him before. "It won't be so easy now."

"Why?" she asked. "You think I cain't do it? You think that just 'cause I got a little tired, that I lost my powers?"

"No," he replied, carefully crafting his words so he wouldn't upset her. "I think it won't be easy because they know you are here now and eventually, they'll get their nerve back and hunt you down. When they find you, they're going to find the rest of us, too."

"I ain't afraid of no witches."

Schaefer took a deep breath and sighed. "I'm not talking about the witches. I'm talking about the government."

"Oh," she said demurely, afraid she may have sounded dumb. "Then we better hurry so we is ready for them too."

"They are probably going to try developing some new kind of surveillance to locate any major fires like you made."

"Oh," she said meekly. "I guess we'll have to do something about that."

Michelle tried finding her mother in every shadow of the airport. Even on the car ride from the airport to the hotel, she constantly glanced around hoping to find a vision of her mother sitting in place of one of her companions, but no more visions came to her and by morning, after a full night's rest, the compulsion had faded away.

She eased herself out of bed, anxious to see Destiny, but also dreading what she might find when she got there. Zeline was already up and smiled at her over the breakfast table. Michelle smiled back, but inside, she was wracked with guilt over the way she had treated Zeline for as many years as she had known her. "You be too kind, putting us up in this hotel. Especially after how I been to you for so long."

Zeline made a face and said, "I don't wants to hear no more about dat. It be water under da bridge. Is you gonna eat nothing? You may as well while I goes to turn in our room keys and den we has to find dat girl of yorn. Where does we go from here?"

Michelle shrugged her shoulders and said, "I don't know."

"Hmmm," Zeline looked around, but she had absolutely no clue what they should do next. "You ain't got no idea where she be?"

Michelle didn't know, but she could feel her and pointed towards the front of the motel and said, "I think she be dat way."

"Dat-a-way?" Zeline asked. "You cain't get no name for where she is?"

"I dunno," Michelle said with a shrug, "I just has a feeling. It be the best I kin do."

Zeline frowned as she rose from the table. "Well, it may be dat it comes to you while you eats."

Michelle was too worried to eat, but she thought a nice muffin and some coffee might be nice. Ashlin and Tempest were already loading eggs and bacon on their plates as Michelle browsed the breakfast trays. Tempest saw the solitary muffin in Michelle's hands and said, "Come on Mama. You're gonna need more than just that in your stomach. Here, you take this while I load another plate for myself."

"You take that and go sit down," Ashlin added, "while I get you a coffee."

"You see dat?" Zeline said when she returned to find the three of them eating. "Bacon cures all ills. Dat's what my Pappy used to say."

Michelle shrugged as she scooped up some scrambled eggs. "I dunno if it cures all ills, but I must admit dat I feels better dan I did afore."

"So…" Zeline said, satisfied that she had contributed something meaningful to the quest, "what about dat beau that was so sweet on Destiny?"

"Who? Blake? You know about him?" Michelle asked.

"Of course I knows about him," Zeline said. "I seen 'em in da court and it don't take no magic to see what dey gots together. You tink dat he might know where she be?"

"Could be," Michelle said, "but I ain't heard from him in a spell."

"Well then," Zeline said as she stood from the table a second time, "we still got da car for a few more hours, so I spose we should get on then."

Michelle nodded her head and mumbled, "Mhm."

As they left the motel, Zeline pointed off in the general direction that Michelle had suggested and announced, "I guess we is going dat-a-way. Everone get in da car."

Thomas leaned in close and whispered into Margaret's ear, "Look at her. Don't you think she needs a little cheering up? How long is she supposed to feel sorry for herself?"

"As long as she wants," Margaret whispered back. "She knows we're here, but she doesn't look like she's in any mood to party."

Thomas frowned. "She didn't used to have any other mood. Something's wrong."

Maggie slapped him in the chest with the back of her hand and chided, "You want to tell her to snap out of it? That's on you, but I advise against it."

Thomas considered it. If Honey would only have looked at him, he might have said something, but he didn't want to interrupt her.

"What's wrong?" she asked with a devilish smile. She poked him in the ribs and asked, "Did little Tommy chicken out? Does little Tommy need some encouragement from Maggie?"

Thomas nuzzled her neck and said, "You know I don't like it when you call me little Tommy."

"Oooh," she purred. "Maybe if Maggie looked around, Maggie can find BIG Tommy again."

Thomas reached under her blouse and whispered, "That's entirely possible."

Honey tried getting back to sleep, but she heard them whispering and kept her eyes shut, preferring to stay out of it. She couldn't make out what they were saying, but she peeked at them through her eyelashes and saw them fooling around. How could they play games like this after what she had just gone through? She may have to find new play friends that were more sensitive to her moods, but not just yet. Her mama had always told her not to burn her bridges while she was in a mood, but to wait on it until she was thinking clear, then burn those bridges clear to the ground.

Her mother's heart beat pleasantly in her ears. She remembered resting her head against her mother's shoulder and hadn't noticed when it had slipped off and rested on her breast. She froze for a moment, but told herself that it wasn't dirty or nothin', then closed her eyes again. There was a moment, on their trip from Salt Lake to Cheyenne, when she thought she was capable of killing her mother; frying her until she was just a pile of ash, but lately, her mother had become quite a comfort to her and was helping her deal with her defeat. She was glad now that she hadn't killed her and would have to find a position of respect for her mother, assuming she ever returns to having her own administration again.

Her chest heaved as she took a deep breath and sighed. She was supposed to be the queen of the world, but now she just felt like a big failure. She should be on one of those talk shows where everyone ridicules her, only she doesn't know that they're against her. They're always looking for trailer trash to make fun of, and she sure looked the part.

Abilene's heart continued to beat comfortably in her ear. Her own heart fell into a sympathetic rhythm and the sounds of her friends fooling around eventually faded away as she fell asleep.

The governor pulled the limo off the freeway, down the exit ramp and onto the shoulder of the road. He looked into the back seat through the rear-view mirror and said, "Well, this is it. From here, you can easily hop back onto the highway and you'll be home in no time."

Honey opened her eyes and yawned. She looked out the window and cocked her head to the side in bewilderment. Looking out the other side of the car was just as perplexing. "You live on a off ramp? I thought you was the damned governor, not a hobo."

"No," he admitted, "I don't live on the off ramp, but you don't know this area and from here, it will be much easier for you to get back onto the interstate without getting lost."

Honey pretended to be sad as she said, "Percy, are you afraid to let me see where you live?"

"No," he said as panic gripped his heart.

"Then what is it?"

"It's Ophelia. She's never seen your faces, and I thought it might be best that way."

"Why? What's wrong with my face?"

"Nothing...it's just that...I mean..."

Honey giggled. "I'm just messing with you, Percy, but I would like to meet your wife."

The governor's mouth parted slightly, but nothing came out.

Honey sighed and said, "Some other time. I'll call you if I ever be needing your services again."

The governor's mind spun as he considered her calling on him again. He sat frozen in his seat, afraid of what she might request next.

"Don't you think that you should get out now," Honey asked, "so Dicky here can drive?"

"Yes ma'am," he said as he opened the door, "I mean, your highness. Please call on me anytime." He stood outside her door, hoping that she would never call upon him again. He bent at the waist, hoping she couldn't see how much his knees quaked, fearful of what she might do if she recognized how much he really hated her.

———

Destiny wasn't sure where she should go to find help or who she should seek out. Blake was no use, and she wasn't in the mood to wander aimlessly through the ancestral memories, looking for answers where they probably didn't exist. She floated through the void, seeking out Marvalaine again. He had already refused to give her the orb once, but maybe if she went further back in time, she could trick him into giving it to her.

She found him standing on the balcony, looking out over the castle courtyard. The weather was pleasant, and judging from the leaves on the trees, she guessed that she may have landed there in late spring or early summer. He looked good, with a full head of dark hair. She snuck up behind him and covered his eyes. "Hey there. Guess who?"

"Phoebe?" he asked. "Haven't I asked you not to get so intimate in public?"

"Phoebe?" Destiny asked. "Are you still toying with her? Don't you know that nothing good will ever come of it?"

"Cousin Destiny," he said, "it is so good to see you." He hugged her and cleared his throat before continuing, "Something good has already come of it, but Phoebe had the extraordinarily good sense to refuse my hand in marriage."

Destiny sucked in her breath and asked, "You mean...you and Phoebe had a..."

Marvalaine's cheeks reddened behind his neatly trimmed beard. "Indeed. Father was none too pleased, but I am not the first prince to have sired a bastard whelp."

"Bastard whelp?" she asked. "Is that how you refer to him? Her?"

"Her, and those were father's words."

"You are taking care of them?"

"Of course."

"Well," Destiny said, "it seems that Phoebe hit the jackpot. She got all the money and I imagine most of the privileges without having to deal with you day in and day out."

"Ow," Marvalaine said. "That hurts."

"Sorry, "she said. "Listen, I'm here on a mission."

"What kind of mission would that be?"

"A mission for you, actually. You sent me back in time to collect something from you, or for you in this case, but you wouldn't give me too many details. You said that you'd know what it was."

Marvalaine chuckled as he said, "How very mysterious of me."

"Yeah," Destiny smiled back. "Like you've never been obtuse about things before."

"I am never obtuse. Tell me what clues I gave you regarding these things that I have."

"Just one thing," she said. "It's an orb. You said I should come back and get this particular orb from you."

"You can't give me any clues better more than just an orb?" he asked. "I have many orbs."

"No. You wouldn't even tell me how far back to go, just to find you when you were younger. You said that it is a very special orb. You said that it was very powerful, and it's named...well, you called it..." She suddenly felt very self-conscious as she tried to say the name.

"Go on," he urged her. "What did I call it?"

"You called it the Orb of Destiny."

"Really?" he asked. "I named it after you? How peculiar. And you say that I sent you here to get it?"

"Yeah. Pretty funny, huh?"

"Sad, actually. I never heard of it."

Destiny frowned. Either he was lying about it and hiding it from her, and she had never known him to do that, or he really did not know what it was. If that were true, then she might have come back too far. She wasted no more time with idle conversation and shimmered out of his time.

Johnson's eyes never left Saunders' gun hand, which rested on the butt of the sidearm that had already been loosened slightly out of its holster. Even though he was pretty sure that Blake would not have let Saunders use it, he breathed a sigh of relief when Saunders returned it back to its resting place. He was even more relieved when the captain's attention turned back to Logan. While Logan was busy listening to Saunders, Johnson hissed, "Pssst. Blake."

Blake glanced over at Johnson, then back to Saunders, who sounded like he might never stop talking to Logan. "What?"

Johnson beckoned Blake with his fingers. "Come here."

Blake patted Destiny on the hand and said, "I'll be right back." He joined Johnson in the corner of the room and asked, "What?"

Johnson turned his head to be sure that Logan couldn't see his lips and whispered, "They contacted me again. They want you to do something for them. They said you have to find some kind of orb."

That rang a bell. It was something in Blake's dream, but he wasn't inclined to do anything to help them. "Why should I care what they want?"

"They said that you needed to find it before the others do."

"You mean Honey?"

"I guess so," Johnson said, but he added a nod of his head towards Logan and said, "and maybe him too."

Logan couldn't hear everything that Johnson was saying over Saunders' strong voice, but he did pick out a couple of words. He heard, "find" and "orb". He also saw Johnson's head jerk towards him and knew something was up that probably involved him.

Destiny's mind was muddled with strange and conflicting thoughts, but at least they were all her own thoughts. She no longer sensed stray concerns from other people in the world. It was a very strange and lonely feeling for her, but not necessarily a bad one. Maybe this was how it was away from the living. If only the world could have been this calm when she was alive, then her life would certainly have gone differently.

The void around her morphed into a pleasant-looking world. She was no longer wandering aimlessly through the nothingness, but this was definitely not Marvalaine's home. She didn't recognize anything about where she was, yet something about this new place felt like home to her. It didn't feel like a memory or a vision. Those usually focused on traumatic events in other people's lives, and this place felt completely free of anxiety. Nobody greeted her upon her arrival and there was no calamity awaiting her. She simply found herself lying on her back in an open meadow of a strange and empty world. It was a beautiful place with lush green grass and crisp blue skies. She had never felt so at peace before, nor had she ever felt so alone. There were no birds or animals to break the silence. A gentle breeze carried the scent of flowers across the meadow, but there was no sound as the wind whipped past her ears, and there was something very sterile, even about the floral fragrance. There was absolutely no trace of animal musk on the wind. The world seemed somewhat bland to her.

This wasn't the world of the living, with its myriad of conflicting scents and sounds. She worried that she had left her Nana in a bind, facing all the problems that she was supposed to tackle, but she couldn't shake the notion that this place was where she belonged. It didn't feel like it was part of her destiny, but it was her new home, none the less, and that feeling came with a sense of finality to it. This certainly wasn't what she had expected to find after death. Maybe it was only a mid-point; a test even. She probably had to wait here until she fully accepted that she was dead now, but she wasn't the one who was in denial. It was her family that still clung onto the hope that she was still alive. Maybe she would be stuck here until they finally accepted the fact that she was gone. She sighed sadly as she thought about how long that might take.

A stream gurgled off in the direction of a stand of trees. It was a pleasant sound and practically the only sound she heard. It was definitely something worth following. The splash of the water was the closest thing to life that she could detect. Even the trees didn't rustle in the breeze. She giggled as she wondered if that made this place too perfect or slightly imperfect.

Before she reached the edge of the forest, she came across a dirt path that ran from her left to her right. It wasn't an animal path. As far as she knew, there were no animals to wear down a path here, but even if there were, she could tell that this was definitely a manufactured road with pea gravel layered on top of a wide dirt base.

She looked left and right, but saw no end to the road in either direction and randomly turned to the right, away from the sound of the stream, and followed the path, which led her up a small rise. From the top of the hill, she saw homes along both sides of the road below her, but she sensed no people in any of those homes. As she walked down the hill, she felt a hunger pang and wondered if she might find any food down there. She wouldn't have expected hunger in the afterlife, but she was ready to accept whatever test they put before her. Since the village appeared to be abandoned, she hoped nobody would mind if she looked for something to eat. She stepped up her pace and bounded down the path.

CHAPTER 7

Honey was sound asleep, with her head resting against Abilene's shoulder, when Richard pulled the limo into the compound's parking lot and announced, "We're here." She looked out the window and rubbed the sleep from her eyes. She hadn't even noticed when they had left the highway, but here they were. The last thing she remembered was getting back on the interstate after dropping off the governor. She should have fried the little chicken shit. He was afraid to let her meet his wife. She felt the old meanness enter her heart, but remembered that she couldn't conjure up enough fire to fry an insect and shrunk back into the melancholy little girl she had been for most of the trip.

Richard parked the car and rushed to open her door for her.

"Listen," she said, "I don't want y'all letting everybody know how I got my ass kicked. I'm gonna rest up and train an army so we can try this again."

"But you didn't get your ass whupped," Abilene said. "You killt her and you is still standin'. You kicked the army's butt, and you is still walkin' free."

"About that," Richard said. "They no doubt tracked us with their satellites, so they know where we are now. We may have to relocate if you want to have someplace safe to train your minions."

Honey accepted Richard's hand and climbed out of the limo. He saw in her eyes how she would have preferred to slink in without being seen.

"Don't worry," he said. "I'll spin this so everyone knows you won a major victory."

Honey climbed the steps to the main entrance and already felt the stares from her people. "Are you sure they don't already know? It was probably on the news already."

"No," Richard said, "even if there were reports on the news, I'm pretty sure that they wouldn't know what really happened there."

"You mean that I lost? Is that what you mean what really happened?"

"No," he replied. "The government won't let the public know that two girls used magic to fight a war that the army couldn't stop, and they would never let the people know how you kicked the army's ass."

"Twice," Abilene added.

Honey still felt as if everyone knew and looked at her like the loser returning home to brood. She left her mother's side and ran through the halls to her room, slamming the door shut with both Maggie and Tommy still outside. The room was big and empty; just like she felt on the inside. It had only a few places for her to hide. She kicked off her shoes and threw herself into the bed, pulling the covers all the way over her head.

A shiver ran down Tempest's spine as Zeline pulled the car into the hospital parking area. The hospital was newer looking and a lot bigger than the one she had been confined to, but it still triggered the old feelings inside of her that fought against going in. Her first impulse was to stand at the curb, but her baby was in there and she wasn't going to let her fear stop her now.

Michelle was quick to leave the car, even before Zeline had turned it off.

"Where you goin' in such a hurry?" Zeline asked. "You best be waitin' for your family to come with you."

"Well, come on then," Michelle pleaded. "Climb on down from da car and catch me."

Ashlin climbed out of the car and took Zeline's hand. "You're coming with us, aren't you?"

"I spect they'll only be lettin' family in to see her," Zeline said, "and I be a few shades too dark for dem to tink I'm family, but I'll go as far as da waitin' room, I s'pose."

Ashlin kept hold of Zeline while she took Tempest's hand in her other and walked them up to Michelle, who took Tempest's other arm in hers.

"I sure is glad dat da weather be nice," Michelle said. "I been havin' da most depressin' dreams."

"No, you haven't," Ashlin said. "You dreamed about your mama on the plane."

"How in da world does you know about dat?" Michelle asked. "Has you been sneakin' around in my private dreams?"

"No," Ashlin replied. "I was there. Don't you remember?"

"I guess I does remember somethin' like dat, but I thought it was just one of dem semaphores."

"You mean a metaphor," Ashlin said.

The double doors swooshed open and the four women entered the main lobby of All Saints Hospital. A friendly receptionist smiled and asked, "Are you visiting? It's a bit early still."

"We just flew in," Michelle said. "My granddaughter..."

"My daughter," Tempest interrupted.

"Our baby was brought here yesterday," Michelle said. "Something be terrible wrong wit her."

"What's her name?" the girl asked.

"Destiny Boutin," Michelle replied.

The girl looked up and down the computer screen. "I'm sorry ma'am, but we don't have a Destiny Boutin registered here."

"You might not be knowin' her name," Michelle said frantically. "She be sixteen with long blond hair."

The girl did spot a Jane Doe on the list who was taken to ICU, but it was tagged top secret and no visitors. Top secret usually meant VIP, but...

"What's a Jane Doe?" Michelle asked. "Is dat what you calls my little girl when you don't know her name?"

The girl's mouth parted in surprise. There was no way that Michelle could have seen her screen.

"Well?" Michelle asked. "Is you gonna tell me where she be?"

The receptionist turned off her screen and said, "No. I don't see your little girl here. I think you should be leaving." She stepped away from the desk before Michelle could sneak any more information from her.

"Never mind," Michelle said. "I'll be findin' my own way to da ICU."

Destiny kicked the pebbles as she skipped along the path down to the deserted village. The sound of her footfall and the rocks skittering down the hill was a welcome relief to the overwhelming silence that surrounded her. She still sensed no other people in the vicinity and assumed that if the village was truly abandoned, then she could pick any house that she wanted and started with the first one that she came to. A narrow flagstone footpath led from the road to the porch with a trim lawn and flower bed on each side of the walkway. The door was unlocked, which she took as another sign that she was welcome here. She stepped inside and sucked in her breath when she saw the perfect interior. It was already furnished and even though the furniture was not covered with protective sheets, there was no dust.

She found the kitchen and opened the pantry. It was far better stocked than she would have expected, with crackers and soups and even a loaf of bread. She squeezed the bread and found it to be fresh and spongy. It made no sense that the village would be abandoned like this, when the food was still fresh. Either people would be returning, or it was left here for her. Why would anyone arrange an entire village just for her? If it was a test, was she supposed to accept these gifts or refuse them?

Her stomach growled, and there was no refusing her hunger. She grabbed the bread and a jar of jam and took it to the small round table in the nook. She found some cutlery in a drawer and butter in the fridge and made herself a jam sandwich.

She decided to not only accept the food, but to take up residence there. It was as nice a place as she could have ever expected, much nicer than where she had grown up, but it was still a lonely place, and if she ever grew tired of it, she could just move on to the next home.

Ashlin was anxious to see Destiny and had led Zeline into the hospital by the hand, but once they were in the reception area, her focus had become unhinged. Zeline sensed the confusion in the young girl and led her behind Michelle, but Ashlin's eyes were blinded by the myriad of bright and blinking lights. She no longer saw Michelle or Tempest. Instead of seeing the reception desk, she saw a young girl shuffling her feet as she slowly entered a hospital room to visit her dying aunt.

Ashlin left Zeline behind as she followed the little girl into the room where the youngster turned and said, "Shhh. Aunt Sophie is sleeping." Ashlin's confusion left her when she realized that she had wandered into a memory.

"It's okay," Sophie said from the bed. "I'm awake. I was hoping you would come visit me."

The little girl ran to the bedside. She couldn't reach up high enough to hug Aunt Sophie and laid her head on the woman's arm instead.

Sophie smiled broadly at the young girl. "I am so glad to see you."

The girl couldn't respond. She knew that her aunt was dying and didn't know what to say or not to say.

"It's okay," Sophie said. "It's not a secret. I know that I don't have much time left."

The girl looked up and tried wiping the tears off her face with her sleeve.

"You know something?" Sophie said. "I'm not even scared anymore. Pretty soon, I'm going to be with your papa. You want me to give him a message?"

The little girl shrugged.

Ashlin's host wrapped her hands on the girl's shoulders and said, "Tell her what you told me before."

The girl shivered as she looked over her shoulder and gave Ashlin a frightened look.

"It's okay," Ashlin said, "go ahead."

She leaned as close as she could and whispered, "I know that you're not allowed to come back to us from heaven, but I wish that you and Daddy could sneak back as horsies to live with Mama and me."

"Oh," Sophie said, "That's a fine idea. Don't you worry. I'll keep it a secret between you, your mama, your papa and me."

"That's good," the little girl said as she pointed up to the sky, "because I don't want any of them to know about it."

The memory popped and Zeline said, "I don't know where you was just now, but I don't never think dat I ever felt so much love from nobody afore."

Abilene saw Honey leave her playmates out in the hall. On any other morning, she would have steered clear of her daughter's apartment just to avoid the awkwardness, but this morning she felt the need to be with her. She had also overheard the conversation with Richard and knew that the government would be looking for them, so she didn't want to let her little girl dawdle all morning until they were discovered. She knocked gently on the door. When Honey didn't answer, Abilene let herself in and found her daughter still in bed, hiding under the covers.

Honey heard someone enter and was prepared to explode in anger until she heard her mother whisper, "Honey?" Their relationship was changing. Honey had never admitted that she had wished for a sweet, supportive mother, and had always hidden her desires beneath a tough girl facade, but lately, Abilene had become the mother Honey had always wished for and she found herself welcoming her to her bedside.

"Honey. It tain't good for you to keep yourself locked up like this. Look at you. You're hiding under the covers like you is afraid of your own shadow."

Honey pulled the covers down and said, "I know."

"Then come on," Abilene said. "Pull yourself together and come on out of there."

"I'll get up, Mama, but I ain't goin' out there. I'll just stick to my room."

Honey sat up on the edge of her bed and let Abilene hug her. "You knows that you cain't do that. You heard what Richard said. We cain't stay here or they'll find us. You said it yourself, in da car, dat you wants to create an army before you goes up against them again. So we has to get up and move on, and dat means outside of dis room."

"I just cain't. I told them all that I was gonna be their queen, but it was all just a bunch o' empty talk. I ain't nothin'."

"No? You're still their queen. That's how they sees you."

"Then they just ain't heard the truth yet. When word gets to them how I got whupped, they won't see me as nothin' but a failure and they sure as sure won't want to learn nothin' that I gots to teach."

"If any of them dares look down on you, then they'll have me to deal with."

Honey stood up from the bed and pulled her mother to her feet, wrapping her arms around the slender woman. She held the embrace until Abilene said, "That's enough now. We gots to get you out there so they can see their queen."

Honey felt emboldened from her mother's tone. She took a deep breath and started walking towards the exit.

"Not like that," Abilene said. "You might want to change into some clean clothes."

Honey looked at herself in the mirror and laughed. She was a mess.

Tempest pushed past Zeline and flexed her knuckles as she focused on the receptionist. "I'll get her to talk."

"Daer be no need for dat," Michelle said. "She told me all dat I needs to know."

"You plucked it outa her head," Zeline said with an impish grin, "didn't you? Tain't dat da same damned ting you been ridin' dat boy about? Da one she's so sweet on?"

"It tain't da same at all," Michelle growled. "Dat boy been puttin' ideas into people's heads. I only listened in on what she was thinkin'."

"Oh yeah," Zeline said sarcastically. "Dat ain't nuttin like da other."

Michelle scowled as she hustled off to the elevator.

Tempest and Ashlin just shrugged their shoulders and ran off after Michelle. Zeline decided to see how far she could follow them rather than automatically resigning herself to the waiting room.

Abilene waited by the door while Honey changed into some clean clothes. She should have made her shower too, but she didn't want to wait that long before getting her out into the public. It was enough that Honey had at least washed the soot from her face and brushed her hair. "Now," she said, "don't you feel so much better?"

Honey just shrugged and shuffled her feet until she was at her mother's side.

"Well, you look much better at least," Abilene said as she opened the door and gently guided honey out towards the hall, "and you even smells better." Abilene crinkled her nose as Honey passed her. Her hair still smelled like smoke, but at least her clothes smelled fresh.

Honey paused in the open doorway and counted how many people filled the hall. Fresh clothes didn't change the feelings inside of her. She felt like she was exposed as a failure. She couldn't have felt more exposed than if she had been naked and stepping into the hall. "Where are you taking me?"

"Nowhere special," Abilene said as she pushed her daughter out of the apartment and closed the door. "I just need to get you up and going."

Honey stared at the ground as she shuffled her feet slowly alongside her mother. She avoided eye contact with those that they passed in the hall. "They're all looking at me."

"They must have heard how you defeated the army."

"Look at them," Honey said. "They must have heard how I turned and ran with my tail between my legs."

"Nonsense," Abilene said. "You're imagining that. You're hardly even looking at them yourself. You're their queen. Hold your head up like a queen should."

"They aren't looking at me like I'm their queen."

"Well, what do you expect? You're hanging your head down and dragging your feet like a servant girl. You're making yourself look guilty."

Honey started to cry and turned her face to hide it in her mother's hair.

Abilene pointed to a passerby and yelled, "Wipe that smirk off your face! Don't you know you're in the presence of your queen? She just went out there and kicked the United States Army's ass! Not once, but twice!" Abilene pointed to another and continued, "You, too! You show her some god damned respect when you passes her in the hall."

The girls in the hall looked more confused than admonished as Abilene stared them down and continued walking her daughter down the hall.

"Thank you, mama."

Abilene broke away from Honey for a moment and pointed to another girl further up the hallway. "Is you laughin? Don't you look at my baby that way." Abilene summoned a ball of electricity in her hand and yelled, "Do you want some of dis? Da's right. You show me some god damned respect too. Y'all start acting a little different around us. You hear?"

"Mama," Honey exclaimed. "I ain't seen you do that since the farm."

Abilene bounced the electric ball in her hand and shrugged, saying, "Well, what do you know? I think that you and me is gonna own this place."

Blake was back at Destiny's side with his head resting on the bed when Michelle entered the room. The picture flooded her mind with the memory of her vision where Tempest burst into the room, demanding that he goes out and finds something. When the image of that vision faded, she saw that he was asleep and whispered, "Blake?"

Saunders' mind was still reeling from learning that there were two clans of whatever they were and he couldn't tell one from the other. He didn't know what to make of the sweet looking matronly woman who had just entered the room, but she did get past his guard, so he didn't need to imagine too hard that she was either one or the other, as were the parade of women that followed her into the room.

Blake barely stirred, so Michelle cleared her throat and said a little louder, "Blake?"

He opened his eyes and immediately felt the presence of more witches in the room. "Oh," he said softly, "Hi."

Michelle went to the bed opposite from Blake and held Destiny's other hand. "Has you been with her long? How is she?"

Tears welled up in Blake's eyes. "The doctor's talk like she's already gone, like she's dead, but I know it's not true!"

"You made them take care of her?" Michelle asked.

He shook his head and pointed towards Saunders. "I didn't have to. Captain Saunders took care of that. I didn't trust him at first, but," Blake lowered his voice to a whisper and said, "I peeked into his mind and saw that he threatened to shoot them if they didn't keep her alive. He meant it, but I couldn't see why he felt that way."

Logan quietly slipped into the shadows, away from the bed until his back was flat against the wall. He felt the unfamiliar pangs in his gut when the witches entered the room. He may not have been accustomed to the twisting sensation in his stomach, but he had read enough about them to suspect what they were.

Tempest ran to the bed and cried out, "Destiny? Destiny sweetie! It's mama!"

Blake wiped the tears from his cheek and said, "They say she's in a coma, but they don't think it's one that she can come back from."

"They're wrong then," Tempest cried.

Michelle's mind drifted back to the vision. "Blake? Is you supposed to be lookin' for something?"

"No," he said, but then he shook his head and said, "I don't know. How did you know about that?"

Michelle sniffled and shook her head. "How does any of us know any of the things dat we know?"

"I had a vision," Blake said. "An old man said that it was for me to find."

"That's right," Johnson chimed in. "They even told me to encourage you to look for it, too."

"And," Blake continued, "some dude in a robe with a hood told me that I had to find the orb to save Destiny."

"So?" Tempest asked. "Why are you still here?"

"The old man said that it would seek me out as much as I had to find it. Besides, I didn't want to leave Destiny alone."

"Well, she ain't alone no more," Zeline said. "We kin watch over her."

Honey continued to stare at her feet, letting her hair hang down to hide her face while Abilene guided her down the hall to the cafeteria. The sounds of forks on plates and glasses on tables echoed down the hall and reminded Honey that she was a little hungry. She couldn't tell how many people were there, but she heard them talking and laughing until she entered the room and the room fell silent.

"Do you hear that?" Honey whispered to her mother. "They're all talking about me and only stopped so I wouldn't hear them."

"Nonsense," Abilene replied. "They can sense the power you wield and grew quiet out of respect."

Honey looked up and scanned the faces through her bangs. They weren't really all watching her, but she felt like they were. She squeezed her mother's arm as waves of paranoia swept over her. Abilene led her to the breakfast grill where the line parted to allow Honey to the front.

"You see that?" Abilene asked. "That's respect."

Honey saw what they had done, but she didn't feel like it was out of respect. She walked to the counter and perused the trays of scrambled eggs and hash browns under the warming lamps. The chef poured another batch of bacon into the tray next to the sausage tray. The scent of fresh bacon perked up her spirits some, and she grabbed a plate and tray and began scooping some eggs.

"Let me do that for you," the chef said. "In fact, you tell me what you want, and Pepe will make it fresh for you."

A shiver ran down Honey's spine as she felt some of her old self return. "Bacon," she said, "and sausage with hash browns and eggs over easy."

"As you wish," the chef replied with a respectful nod of his head.

"No," Honey said. "I want an omelet with all those things and cheese. And I want toast, but not the square kind; I want some of those round things."

Pepe held up an English muffin and asked, "These?"

"Yeah, those," she said, "with jelly."

"And you, madam?" he asked, indicating Abilene.

"I'll have the same with coffee."

"Me too," Honey said. "Coffee. Lots of coffee."

"As you wish," the chef said. "Go ahead and find your seats. Pepe will bring it to you when it is ready."

Honey liked Pepe's attention and stood a little more erect, stepping out in front of Abilene, leading her onto the main floor, where she found Richard sitting alone at a table. Honey pointed to the table and raised her eyebrows.

"Of course," Richard said. "Please join me."

"I'm glad you're here," Honey said. "I wanted to talk to you about a dream I had."

"I'd be glad to listen," Richard said, "but dreams are not one of my areas of expertise. In fact, reading dreams is a witch thing."

"Remember when we talked about training an army?"

Richard nodded and sipped his coffee.

"And you wondered why I wanted to go after her on my own?"

Again, Richard simply nodded, but slower and with raised eyebrows as he wondered what she was about to share with him.

"Well, you probably thought it was just because I wanted to keep all the power for myself, but that wasn't it at all. I had a dream where I was gonna teach our people to be like me and use fire. In the dream, I even said that I wanted to teach our very best people to be part of my army, but what I got instead was a bunch of old farts. I was kind of pissed in my dream. Not only was they all old, but there weren't any women at all. Even though it was just a dream, I could tell that they thought they was so special, but they was just a bunch of old men who wanted my power and had enough money to arrange their ways into the class."

Richard stifled a laugh. "Are you sure you don't have some witch blood in you? That would be pretty typical behavior for our kind."

"Not no more," she said. "I want my army to be young people strong enough to win a war."

Richard smiled broadly. "I'm glad you feel so passionately about this. I'll see to it."

"And there better be some tits in my army. You hear me?"

Richard bowed his head and said, "I hear and obey."

Michelle eyed Logan suspiciously and asked, "Why is you still here?"

Logan swallowed hard. His hands trembled slightly as he counted how many potential witches had just entered the room. He had no clue how many of them could do what Destiny did. His voice cracked slightly as he said, "I just wanted to help. I told them to give her the very best care available and I would pay for it."

"Oh," Michelle said timidly. "I be grateful for dat."

"Why?" Tempest asked suspiciously. "She already went up against your girl. Where is she? Where is that bitch Honey? What happened? Why do you still need my baby? Do you still think she is gonna try and fight her again?"

Logan heard the anguish in her voice. It was natural for a mother to protect her cub. He wondered if she had the power to kill him for saying the wrong thing and drew a deep calming breath before explaining, "The fight between them was a draw. Honey has returned home to lick her wounds and unless someone else comes forward who can fight her, I see no other candidate to be our champion."

Tempest's voice ratcheted up two notches. "Our champion? Are you actually including yourself with us? What on God's green Earth makes you think that I'm ever gonna let my baby girl try that again?"

"Someone has to," Logan said. "Honey is clearly crazy, and she gets really mean when she feels the power. If she comes back to full strength again, who's going to stop her? You?" Logan immediately regretted the last part of his statement. He had no intention of challenging an angry witch to come forth.

"I just might," Tempest said. "Maybe if I'd accepted my gifts as a young girl, none of this would have ever happened."

"Don't say that," Michelle said softly. "You cain't be blamin' your-self for what's happened here."

"Honey is not going to win," Blake said. "Destiny won't make the same mistake again. We'll combine our powers to fight her together."

"You might just have to," Logan said, "because Honey wasn't the only one to have recovered her powers. If Honey finds more of my people with their powers back, you might need to start looking for more of your kind, too, but you might still need Destiny. She is The Chosen One."

Michelle gasped. She never expected them to know about that.

Saunders had played like a fly on the wall long enough. "Explain this to me. Pretend like I don't know anything about you people..."

"You don't," Tempest said sharply.

"So, help me understand." Saunders walked to the center of the room, near the end of Destiny's bed, where the light was better. "You're telling me that there are more of you with powers like her?"

"No," Tempest growled. "We ain't telling you nothing. You're just eavesdropping on our conversation."

"Tempest!" Michelle scolded. "Let the man talk."

"Thank you," Saunders said to Michelle with a polite nod of his head. "How many of you are there?"

"Nobody knows that," Michelle said. "We been scattered to the winds for centuries. You know the churches warn't too kind to us in the past."

"No?" Saunders asked. "You've had run-ins with the churches before?"

"Dey burn witches," Michelle replied.

"And a lot of our people, too," Logan added.

"Not to mention those regular humans that were either unlucky or unpopular with the church," Ashlin added.

Saunders nodded his head. "I see. Can you tell me what was up with that other girl, the one that calls herself Honey? Why do you talk like she is different from you?"

Michelle's voice dripped with disdain as she replied, "Because she ain't a witch like us."

"She's a damned sorcerer," Tempest spat while pointing to Logan, "like him."

Logan tried to shrink back away from the room, but there was nowhere for him to go.

Saunders glanced around the room, checking the looks on their faces. "You don't like sorcerers then?"

"You must be a damned college boy to figure that out," Tempest said sarcastically.

"Tempest!" Michelle scolded her again.

Tempest threw her hands in the air and cried, "What Mama? We don't got time to bring this soldier boy up to speed." She pointed to Blake and continued, "and he is supposed to go find some damned orb instead of sittin' around here with his thumb up his butt!"

"Quiet!" Michelle yelled.

"Yeah," Blake said. "That wasn't really general knowledge."

Logan stepped forward out of the shadow and asked, "What was that about an orb?"

"Nothing," Blake said.

"Are you sure?" Logan asked. "Maybe I can help you find it, if it will help."

"Thanks," Blake said, "but I got this."

Logan smiled broadly and said, "Well, at least let me arrange rooms for everyone to stay at."

Michelle thought to Blake, "You know he just wants to stay close enough to learn what we know."

"Yeah," Blake thought back. "I know."

Tempest stared angrily at Saunders.

Saunders didn't know whether she could or could not fry him with a look, but he wasn't going to be intimidated. He needed Destiny, and if there were more like her, he needed to be on good terms with them. "Look," he said to Tempest privately, "I know you don't like me, but I'm not the enemy here."

"Aren't you?" Tempest asked. "You may be a bit more sympathetic, but if push comes to shove, you're still a government puppet who will turn on us to save your career."

"I violated orders to save that girl..."

"Her name is Destiny," Tempest growled, "and she's my baby girl."

"Well, she was nobody to me and I still tried to save her. My superiors wanted me to take your baby into custody. If it were up to them..."

"I know," Tempest interrupted. "They would take her to some secret installation and do tests on her like a lab rat."

"That's right," Saunders continued, "In fact, she was already declared dead, and my superiors would have left her dead so they could dissect her, but I think that we need her more as an ally than a test subject, so I saved her at great personal risk to my career. A little gratitude would be appreciated."

"Oh, I appreciate what you done," Tempest admitted, "but I'm afraid of what you might do next. I'm afraid they'll order you to give her up."

"I won't tell," Saunders said firmly.

"And those two soldier boys you posted outside her door?"

Saunders frowned and admitted, "They're not army. I hired them privately, at my own expense, I might add, but still, you need to disappear. All of you need to disappear."

Tempest shook her head and said, "It don't look like my little girl can do much disappearing at the moment, but we do have a problem. Three of you know where we are. Does anybody else know?"

Saunders swallowed hard and asked, "What are you saying? Are you suggesting that you need to kill us? Could you really do that after everything I did to help you? The army would investigate, and they would find you."

"No," Tempest said with an evil snicker. "I ain't gonna kill you. What we really need to do is disappear from your memories."

Saunders' face registered real fear as he asked, "Can you do that?"

"Hey Blake!" Tempest called out. "Come over here."

Blake joined them and asked, "What's up?"

"You're real good with planting ideas in people's heads, aren't you?"

"Yeah," Blake said, "but your mother really hates it when I do that."

Tempest nodded her head. "I can see that, but do you think you can change people's memory? Can you erase us and this hospital from their minds?"

Blake shrugged and said, "I don't know. I suppose it could work, but I never tried that before and I don't know if it would be permanent."

"Is it safe?" Saunders asked nervously.

Blake nodded and said, "My suggestions are more like your own mind having an idea of its own. I suppose it would be like hypnosis."

"How am I going to be able to help her if I can't even remember her?"

"What more did you plan to do?" Tempest asked. "What exactly would you do if Honey came back?"

Saunders swallowed hard. "Maybe I can't deal with Honey, but I've been doing pretty good with the doctors."

"Don't worry about them," Blake said. "I can always get them to do what we need."

Saunders didn't like the idea of messing with his memory, but they were right. It would be easy to slip up or even be followed here. "Okay," he said. "Do it to Milton first. Show me that it works."

"Here?" Blake asked. "If I do it here in the hospital, you're still going to remember being here."

"Right," Saunders said. "Come with us. We'll take a drive to another hospital, and you can do it there."

Chapter 8

Richard slid away from the table and stood up. He bowed his head politely to Honey and said, "If you'll excuse me, I have some preparations to make for your first class."

Abilene beamed with pride as she waited for him to leave, then brushed Honey's hair to the side and gushed, "I'm so proud of you."

"I'm scared Mama."

"What have you got to be scared of? It's the rest of the world that's gotta be scared. Not only is you gonna have students meeting you face to face to learn something, but they is gonna be awfully anxious to prove themselves."

Pepe brought their breakfast to the table and said, "I hope everything is to your satisfaction."

The food was piping hot and carried with it a bouquet that promised them a wonderful meal.

"It smells real good," Honey said. "Thank you. What's your name again?"

"Pablo, but everybody calls me Pepe."

"Pepe?" Honey asked. "How do you go from Pablo to Pepe?"

Pablo bent low at the waist in a formal bow usually reserved for the royal court in ancient times and said, "My name is Pablo Ruiz Ortega Pasqual, or just Pablo Pasqual. Pepe sounds much better than P.P. No?"

Honey giggled and said, "Yes. Much better."

Pablo backed up a step and spun around to return to his kitchen.

Honey meowed as she watched him walk away. "A man who can cook and has manners."

"Kinda cute too," Abilene added as she noted Honey's interest in Pepe's butt.

"Kinda? He's yummy."

Milton pulled the car into the parking lot at Devlyn Children's Hospital and announced, "Okay. We're here. I don't know why we drove all the way across town to be here, but we are. What do you want us to do now? Shouldn't we report in that we're away from our post?"

"Under your orders," Jimmy added with a nod to Saunders.

Blake leaned over and whispered to Saunders, "You didn't tell them?"

Saunders shook his head and whispered back, "You said it was safe."

"It is," Blake said. Secretly, he thought to himself, "I think."

Saunders took a deep breath and said, "Okay then. Let's do this."

Blake reached into Milton's mind and suggested, "The past day has been really exhausting for you. You were ordered to pick up Captain Saunders at Devlyn Children's Hospital. Your orders were to wait outside for him while he finished up some paperwork. You waited in the car, but he was taking a really long time, and you were so tired that you fell asleep. The last thing you saw when your eyes fell shut was the hospital, so you dreamed that you were in one of the rooms where a girl lay in a hospital bed surrounded by her family. She was a pretty girl, and you dreamed that you had known her and her husband for a long time. You even dreamed that you were the best man at their wedding. It was a good dream, but a weird dream. It felt very real to you, but deep down inside, you knew that it was just a dream. You're still very tired. It's okay if you sleep now. You'll wake up when Captain Saunders comes for you."

Milton leaned his head against the window and snored softly as he slept.

Blake reached into the other guard's mind and planted, "Your orders were to stay in the car with Milton and wait for Captain Saunders. He wasn't supposed to be very long, and you figured it would give you guys a chance to talk about stuff, but Milton was too tired and fell asleep. You didn't realize how tired you were until you heard Milton snoring and talking in his sleep. You thought it was pretty funny when he talked about a girl in the hospital and her family. Eventually, you fell asleep too and dreamed about the girl you heard Milton describe. It's okay if you sleep now and enjoy the dream a bit more."

With both guards sleeping, he turned to Saunders and asked, "Are you ready?"

Saunders was a bit alarmed when he saw both of his men fall asleep. It frightened him to think that it was so easy for Blake to render them unconscious. "Maybe this is not such a good idea."

"Why?" Blake asked. "You thought it was a good enough idea an hour ago."

"That was before I saw my men pass out cold."

"They're fine," Blake assured him. "They're way better off than if I fried them."

Saunders eyes widened as he sucked in his breath and reached for the door handle.

"Don't worry," Blake said. "I didn't hurt them and I'm not going to hurt you."

"But how do I know what you did? How do I know what any of you do? Maybe the major was right. Maybe you should be studied." Saunders jumped out of the car and headed for a solitary taxi waiting in front of the hospital.

Blake quickly left the car and followed Saunders. "You agreed to this. You know it's the right thing to do...to protect Destiny."

"To protect all of you, you mean," Saunders growled as he double timed to the cab.

"You need her as much as we do," Blake replied. "You know that."

Saunders slipped into the cab and said, "I know, but maybe not like this." He reached to close the door, but Blake held it open a moment longer. Saunders looked menacingly into Blake's eyes as he gave the cabbie his destination.

Blake couldn't let this continue and entered Saunders' mind whether he was ready or not. "Calm down. You're over thinking everything. The girl you tried to help was on your side. Your instincts told you to save her, and they were right. You were right. You helped carry her into the ambulance, but you were too late. Her injuries were too severe. She expired in the back of the ambulance just as you arrived at the hospital. You ordered them to take her body to your army base for study, but you couldn't go with the body because you had too many reports to fill out, so you remained behind and called for a car to come pick you up. Deaths like this are always complicated by the forms you need to fill out. You waited by the emergency room entrance for your ride, but it never came. You eventually decided to search the parking lot on the other side of the hospital, but you never found them and decided to take a taxi instead." Blake gently closed the door and continued, "You were angry at first, but you were too exhausted to deal with it just yet and fell asleep in the taxi."

Saunders leaned his head against the window and snored gently as he slept.

Blake paid the cab driver with fake money as he had been doing so much lately, and watched it drive away, hoping for the best for their only true ally in all of this. He needed to get back to Destiny, but there were no other cabs around. He searched the lot for someone to give him a ride back to Destiny. Michelle would probably not approve of what he was likely to do next.

Logan tried keeping his true feelings buried deep down, hoping the witches wouldn't learn that he didn't really care about Destiny as much as he didn't want to live under Honey's regime. He smiled politely and was sincere in his offer to give her the best care possible, but not for any altruistic reasons. Normally, he would have had a secretary arrange hotel rooms for them, but he didn't want to explain who would be using the rooms, and more importantly, he didn't want Honey to learn that he was involved with the witches. The hospital was kind enough to let him use a phone in admitting, but the hotel had put him on hold and he felt the eyes of the nurses upon him, wondering how long he would keep the phone tied up.

The music on the phone stopped playing and the hotel clerk said, "Please forgive us for the delay, Mr. Logan. Your rooms are confirmed for two weeks. Will there be anything else that we can do for you?"

"No," he replied. "That's all. Thank you."

He hung up the phone and started back for Destiny's room when he heard a man's voice calling him, "Mr. Logan?"

A thin man in a well-worn suit held his hand out as he approached him. "Mr. Logan?"

"Dr. Logan," he said as he shook the man's hand.

"Dr. Logan. I am Dr. Gaines, the hospital administrator. I was hoping to discuss the young woman in ICU with you."

"Is there a problem?" Logan asked. "I thought I already explained that I would take care of all the costs."

"Yes, yes," Dr. Gaines said, "that's most generous of you, but I'd like to discuss her care with you."

"You'll have to walk with me then. I told your doctors to spare no expense," Logan said.

"I understand your desire, but I need to discuss the quality of her care."

"What's to discuss?" Logan asked as he entered the first floor elevator. "The best means the best. Not the second best."

"We just can't devote a private ICU room to a patient with virtually no hope of recovering."

"I'm not accepting any excuses," Logan said as he left the elevator with Dr. Gaines trailing behind, "and I thought I made it clear that I expect you to take whatever extraordinary steps were necessary to revive her."

"We have other wards that are better suited to the long-term care of patients like her."

"No," Logan said. "She stays right here. We aren't looking for long-term care. You need to keep searching the nation for the very best young minds until someone has an idea of how to bring her around. And if that is not good enough, expand your search to include the whole world. Find a way to save her."

"I need this bed," Dr. Gaines insisted as they entered the room, "and what are all these people doing in here, anyway?"

"It's a private room," Logan explained, "and they're her family."

"They can't stay here," Dr. Gaines said with an agitated edge to his voice. "She can't stay here. The long-term care facility is better suited to handle guests as much as it is for her care, and I assure you that you can get a room that is every bit as private as this one."

Logan buried his index finger into the man's chest and snarled, "Listen to me, bub. I'm paying for this party and I say she stay's right here."

Dr. Gaines brushed Logan's finger aside and asked, "Do I need to call security?"

Logan snapped his fingers and, without taking his eyes off of Dr. Gains, said, "Blake! Explain to this man, in that special way that you have, that he doesn't really want to move Destiny."

"I got this," Michelle said, using the voice. She peeked into his mind to learn who he was and continued with the voice, "Barry. May I call you Barry? The thing that you need to understand is that you don't need this room for anything other than my Destiny. You will do everything you ever thought of, and more, to help her and you will be nice to everyone you see in here because you think it be so wonderful that Destiny's family is here with her."

Barry's head throbbed with the commanding sound of her voice. "It breaks my heart to suggest this," he said, "because you're all such wonderful people and I truly like that she has family to be with her, but we just aren't setup to handle this many guests."

"We understand," Logan said. "We'll visit in shifts. I think Michelle could probably use some sleep, anyway."

"No," she said, "I'm not tired."

Ashlin hugged Michelle and said, "It's okay. I'll stay with her while you sleep."

"But I don't want to go," Michelle whined.

"Shelly!" Ashlin snapped. "You know that it's way past your bedtime. You go now and get some sleep while I sit with Destiny."

Michelle was shocked by the tone of her voice, but only pouted and hung her head instead of arguing.

Dr. Gaines mouth had fallen open during the short discussion. He pointed at Ashlin and asked, "How old is she?"

"I'm twenty-one," Ashlin said with the voice.

Michelle giggled and said, "Yeah, she's twenty-one alright. I'm going to go take a nap now. A little rest wouldn't hurt me none and I kin see now that everything here is in good hands."

"I'll take you to the hotel," Logan said. "And I think that maybe Blake and Johnson could use some rest, too."

"I'm staying," Tempest announced.

"I'll stay with them," Zeline said. "You go gets yo rest. Mebbe after dey gets dere rest, dem boys kin start lookin' for dat ting you was talkin' about."

"Where is Blake?" Michelle asked, while looking around the room for him.

"He went with Saunders," Ashlin explained. "He took Saunders and his men to that other hospital for that thing that they were going to do. He should be back soon."

"That's right," Logan said uneasily, as he remembered that Blake was going to help them forget about this place. "He can join us when he returns."

"I'll go down with you," Johnson said, "and wait for him in the lobby."

Dr. Gaines stood numbly in the middle of the room as the others had started to leave.

"Don't you have things to do?" Ashlin asked him as she returned to Destiny's side.

"I wish they'd stop starin' at me," Honey said as she speared a slice of sausage from her omelet.

"Dey know who's in charge," Abilene said. "You be like a movie star now."

"They don't look like they's staring at a movie star. They's lookin' at me like I'm just a crazy person."

"Nonsense," Abilene said. "Besides, you is kinda like a movie star. Better even. Ignore them if you feels that way. Das what a movie star would do. Eat your breakfast and den we'll go see what Mr. Richard has for you."

"I ain't really hungry, Mama."

"That's okay," Abilene said as she drained her coffee. "You don't have to eat all your food if you don't want to. You ain't a little girl no more. You is da queen."

Honey tried to smile, but it didn't fool Abilene. Her baby girl was hurting, and she didn't know how to help her.

Abilene stood and said, "Let's just go, then."

"Yes'm"

Honey rose and took her mother's arm. Abilene led her from the cafeteria. On the way out, Honey smiled at the chef and said, "Thank you. It was real good."

"Come on," Abilene said. "We'll go find Mr. Richard and see if he can come up with something for you to do."

Honey held on tightly to her mother and nestled her head in the crook of Abilene's neck.

Now it was Abilene that felt like people really were staring at them. Something was wrong with Honey. She was too nice. She was never polite like this before. Maybe that witch had done something to her.

Abilene patted Honey on the head and said, "Don't you worry 'bout nothin'. Mama is gonna take care of everythin' for you."

Blake hadn't given any fore thought as to how he was going to get back to Destiny. He looked around the lot and saw plenty of cars that he could take, but that would place a second stolen vehicle in the same hospital's parking lot and might draw too much suspicion. He figured that his best way to avoid undue attention would be to hitch a ride with someone who was going that direction.

He made his way back to the emergency exit and found a couple guys loading their equipment into the back of an ambulance. "Hey," he said, trying to sound friendly and not like someone that was about to take them for a ride.

The techs looked up at him, but said nothing.

"I was wondering if you could do me a favor," Blake explained. "I need to be over at All Saints and I was hoping that maybe you could give me a ride."

"Sorry man," one of the techs said. "We can't give out rides to strangers like that."

"But I'm not a stranger," Blake thought into his mind. "I'm your ride-a-long. You're showing me what it's like to do your job."

"We could get a call at any moment," the tech said. "We need to be ready. We can't just go to any hospital we want, especially one that's all the way across town."

"Not even," Blake thought to him, "to visit that new nurse? Wasn't she just on the verge of giving you her number?"

The tech thought about it a moment. He felt like she was just about ready to give him her phone number. "Hey Brad," he said to his partner, "you mind if we swing by All Saints for a minute?"

The other tech shrugged and said, "Sure. As long as we don't get a call on the way."

Abilene led Honey down the corridor to the hall where Richard had said he would be. It looked like a school gymnasium that also served as an auditorium for speeches. Half a dozen younger people were helping him setup mats in the center of the gym. Collapsible bleacher seating had already been pulled out from the wall.

"Lookit there," Abilene said. "Richard is already setting things up for you."

"This ain't nothin' like my dream, Mama."

"It's gonna be fine," Abilene said. "We ain't witches. We don't dream the future. I think you said that your dream wasn't so good, anyway. Now, lift your head up and stand tall."

Two of the girls helping Richard pointed at Honey and giggled.

Abilene flew into a rage and yelled at them, "You see something funny?" She held her hands in front of her and showed the girls short tendrils of lightning that extended from her fingertips. "You want me to show you something really funny?"

The girls froze when they saw Abilene.

"Mama, stop it."

"They gots to learn respect," Abilene said.

"Not like this," Honey said.

Abilene arced her lightning over the girls' heads, then had it split into four splinters that came down around the girls, trapping them into an electric cage.

"Mama!" Honey shouted. "I axed you to stop!"

"I will," Abilene said, "after they've learned some proper respect."

Honey screamed and fire surrounded her like it was her clothing. "THEY NEED TO RESPECT ME! NOT MY MAMA!"

Abilene retracted her lightning and said, "Sorry, baby. You is right."

"It's okay Mama. I know that you meant well."

Honey tried to hug her mother, but Abilene backed away, asking, "You think you could turn off the flames before we hug?"

"Ooops," Honey said with a giggle. She dropped the fire and hugged her mother warmly.

"Wow," Richard said as he joined them, "you certainly know how to make an entrance."

Honey blushed as she released her mother from their hug and tried to hide her overwhelming joy that she apparently had her powers back.

"Now," Abilene said. "You look at dem girls. Dey sho respect you now."

The girls held each other, shaking uncontrollably.

"That's not respect," Richard said. "That's fear, but we can work with fear."

Honey walked over to the girls and said, "I'm sorry that my mama did that, but you don't have to be scared no more. I took care of it. I'm Honey, by the way."

"You see that?" Richard said. "In time, I think she can learn to change that fear to respect."

"All I sees," Abilene said, "is my little girl gone soft."

"Or," Richard suggested, "maybe she's just finding some balance. We don't want another incident like we had at Salt Lake or Cheyenne."

"Or at that restaurant," Abilene reminded him. "She was almost killt there. Now that I think on it, you may be right. She could do with a little more control on her temper."

<hr>

Logan led Michelle through the hospital's lobby towards the exit, but froze just inside the large sliding doors at the entrance.

Blake nearly crashed into Logan as he ran into the hospital and asked, "What's wrong? Where are you going?"

Logan pointed to the car they had stolen previously and the police cruisers that were parked behind it. "I was just taking Michelle and Johnson to the motel for some rest. I think you could probably use some sleep too."

"Don't worry," Blake said, "I can get us another car."

"You'll do no such thing," Michelle scowled. "I kin already see what you been up to without me to guide you."

"Don't worry about it," Logan said. "Follow me." He led them to a couple of cabs taking a break at the coffee shop across the street.

Before Michelle could object, Blake placed a suggestion into the drivers' heads that they were done with their break.

Logan walked up to their vehicles and called out, "Taxi?"

Both drivers raced to be first, but slowed down when they saw that the number of passengers he had would take two cabs, anyway.

As soon as Blake had settled into his seat, he closed his eyes and returned to the void. "Destiny?"

"Blake?" she asked, but her voice sounded far away. "Is that you?"

"It's me. I need to talk to you."

The void swirled around Blake and pulled him into a spiral. He was no longer suspended in the empty ethereal space, but found himself falling, tumbling out of control. He fell into a bright green memory and landed in a soft meadow.

Destiny giggled and said, "Nice landing."

Blake frowned at first, but he was too glad to see her for the frown to remain on his face. "What are you doing here?"

Destiny laughed lightly and said, "I'm greeting you. You called for me, remember?"

Blake climbed up from the ground and brushed himself off. "I remember, but why here? Why didn't you come to me?"

"I don't know why," she replied, "but I can't seem to leave this place."

Blake took a better look around. The meadow was bright green and the sky overhead was a pure blue, but dark thunder clouds loomed off in the distance, like a barrier that surrounded the whole idyllic little paradise. "I see," Blake said. "The storm clouds must be holding you in. Is it a prison? Did Honey trap you here?"

Destiny looked around, but she didn't see any storm clouds. "I doubt that Honey can do anything like that."

She seemed unusually vague to Blake. Her voice was light and airy, but behind her eyes, he thought he detected something dark and foreboding. "If not Honey, then who?"

Destiny shrugged. "It's hard to explain, but it feels kinda like home to me."

"I been to your home," Blake said, "and this is nothing like it."

"I know," she replied. "It's not that home. It's a new home. It just feels like I belong here."

"You live in a meadow now?"

She hit him on the arm and said, "No, silly, but I didn't want you crashing through my roof."

"You already have a home," Blake said, "with your family, and this isn't it."

"I don't have a home back there anymore," she said sadly. "Don't you remember? It was burnt down."

"Well, you still have a family, and they love you and miss you."

"I know," she said, "and I miss them too, but I can't leave here."

His voice cracked as he said, "I love you, too."

"That sounded like it was painful to say."

"Not really," he said. "I'm just nervous that you might not feel the same."

She brushed his hair and said, "You know that I do."

"Then come back with me. Come back to all of us. Haven't you ever heard the saying that home is where the heart is? Your heart belongs with us."

"I can't."

"You have to," he pleaded. "I miss you. I'm all messed up without you. You have no idea how much I need you right now!"

"I know," she said, "and I miss you too."

"Can't you see what is going on? Don't you know where you really are?"

"Don't you?" she asked. "You've visited enough dream worlds to recognize one when you see it."

"That's my point," he said. "This isn't real. This is a trick. There's something wrong with this place. It's not safe for you to be here. You're not even really here. You're actually in a hospital; in a bed. We're all with you waiting for you to wake up."

"Come with me," she said, ignoring his pleas. "I'll show you my house. You can come visit me whenever you want."

"Didn't you hear me?" he cried. "You're in the hospital in a coma and we need you to wake up!"

"I'm not really there," she said. "That's just my body. This is where I am now."

Blake choked as he stifled a sob. He couldn't stop the tears from tracing little trails down his cheeks. "This is just a trick that your mind is playing on you."

She looked softly into his eyes and said, "You need to face the truth. I'm not there anymore. I tried to fight Honey alone, and I died."

"You're trapped in here just like your mother was! Remember that?"

Destiny looked concerned for the first time since he had arrived. "My mother? How is she?"

"She needs your help," he said. "Remember? You were going to save her."

A tear gathered in her eye. "I can't do that anymore."

"Maybe I can help with that. I'm supposed to find some kind of an orb..."

"I remember," she said. "The orb is supposed to help me save my mother. Who will save her now?"

"That's why I'm here. I need to find the orb."

She hung her head and said, "I can't help you. I saw it once, twice maybe, but I can't tell you where it is. Marvalaine wouldn't tell me."

"That crazy old coot wouldn't tell me either, but he said something about it finding me."

She cracked a small smile, but her eyes were still sad. "He's mysterious like that sometimes. I can't help you, but you need to find the orb and save my mother."

"Sure," he said. "I'll try."

He left her on the edge of the meadow, but he knew that he was really looking for the orb to save her, not her mother, and they all needed her to save the world.

"Here we are," Logan said as he helped Michelle out of the taxi. "I know it's not the Ritz, but it's close to the hospital."

"Close?" Michelle asked. "I think I kin still see the hospital from here. It makes a body wonder why we bothered wit dem taxis at all when we coulda just walked."

"Anything for you," Logan said. "besides, I didn't know just how close it would be until we got here. This way, we can go see your granddaughter anytime we want."

"I be grateful," Michelle said, "but I still don't fully understand your interest in her well bein'."

Logan held the door for Michelle and led her to the registration desk. "I've been privy to my people's oldest and most sacred documents. Our history is contained in those documents and the ancient scrolls tell us..."

"Your people has a written history of your kind?"

Logan handed his credit card to the clerk and said, "I'm Doctor Logan. I called earlier, and all these people are with me." The clerk took his card, and he turned back to Michelle to explain, "We have to write down our history. We don't have your ability to see the memories of our ancestors."

"You knows about that?"

"We know quite a bit, actually. Sadly, my kind hasn't been the fairest throughout the ages, but the best times between our people were those times when we had some kind of balance between the clans. In the beginning, the wars were fought to maintain that balance, but after a while, people got greedy."

"Your people," Michelle said.

"Mostly," Logan admitted, "but your clan had its maniacal leaders who tried eliminating us too, and let us not forget that it was your people that brought the curse upon us all that ended magic for the last thousand years or so."

"I don't know noghin' about that and I shore don't remember none of those leaders coming from our clan."

"Here you go," the clerk said as he handed over several room keys.

"Thank you," Logan replied. "Please be sure to take care of anything they need and bill it to me."

"As you wish."

Logan accepted their room keys and led Michelle to the elevator. "If our clans are going to exist together in the modern era, then we are going to have to cope with not only each other, but the rest of mankind too. Their technology makes them a greater threat to us than they ever have been before. I don't think we can survive if we start feuding with each other again."

The elevator stopped on the second floor and Logan waited for Michelle to exit first.

"Maybe you wants balance," she said, "but I don't think dat little girl of yourn wants no balance, and I don't think she's afraid of the world's technology neither."

"And that," he said with a serious and final note to his voice, "is why I am helping you. She doesn't know about our history, so she's not afraid of anything or anyone, and that scares me. We've seen enough really bad presidents running this country. I don't want someone like her ruling the world."

Michelle felt something else hidden beneath his words. "You don't want her leading your clan neither, do you?"

"No. I don't. We'll never have peace between the clans as long as we have a megalomaniac at the helm."

"A magalowhat?" Michelle asked. "Never mind. I can guess what dat means."

"So, I'll do whatever it takes to keep her out of power, even if it means helping you find the orb."

"You know about the orb?" she asked.

"I told you," he lied. "Our ancient scrolls have a lot of history recorded about both our peoples."

"You think maybe your scrolls can tell us where the orb be?"

Logan felt stupid. The scrolls and the archives were real, and they just might have something about the orb. "They might. I should have thought of that. It may take some time, but I can go back to them and do some research."

"Take da boy with you," she said.

"I don't think they'll let your kind in our sacred libraries."

"I know," she said, "but he used to be one of your kind, remember? On second thought, I think Honey might recognize him."

Blake floated through the void, wondering what Destiny did to contact Marvalaine, but even if he knew how she did it, he didn't have her flair for reaching out to people in ancient times. It was far easier for a talented witch to leave a message for someone in the future than it was to contact someone in the past. It was kind of like voice mail that waited for the right time to contact someone, but contacting someone in the past was a rare gift. Marvalaine said that he had come to Blake because Blake couldn't go to him, but Destiny could. She had gone to visit him at various times during his life, even when he was just a little boy. At first, they were just memories like any other, but she said that later on she had started to visit him for real. She could do that. She could cross the time barrier and somehow visit people in the past. She had even seen the orb once, but she said that he wouldn't give it to her or tell her where it was.

Blake floated through the void, eavesdropping on memories as they floated by. He called out randomly, "Marvalaine?" But no answer came back.

How was he supposed to seek out the orb if he didn't know what it looked like? And what was all that stuff about the orb finding him? This was pointless. He'd be better off seeking out Honey and taking back the amulet she stole from Destiny. It had power. Maybe it could save Destiny, or maybe it could help him find the orb. He'd probably have to kill Honey to get it.

"Don't do that," Marvalaine said. "You can't go up against her."

"Why not?" Blake asked. "I have all the same powers that Destiny has."

"You are gifted," Marvalaine said, "I'll grant you that, but you don't have, as you said, all the same powers that Destiny has, and you don't possess all of the qualities that are required to defeat Honey."

"And Destiny does?"

"She does," Marvalaine said flatly.

"Well, she's gone, and I don't know if we can ever get her back, especially without the orb."

Marvalaine pulled Blake into a memory, with them standing atop a large cliff overlooking the ocean. Blake's mind wobbled, and he spread his stance to find his balance. If traveling to a new location wasn't enough to make him dizzy, standing hundreds of feet over a rocky surf was. He breathed deeply and smelled the salty spray as he watched the ocean crash into the jagged earth below. His mind finally settled, and he turned to find Marvalaine.

"I still have faith in you," Marvalaine said. "You just need to find the orb, and I'm sure it will all become clear to you."

"Just find the orb? It's not like a missing sock. You haven't giv-en me any clues where to start looking for it. On second thought, maybe it is like a missing sock. Nobody ever knows where they go or where to find them and they remain lost forever!"

"Be patient," Marvalaine said. "Would you like some tea?"

Blake smelled the tea brewing on a table behind him. "Very clever Mr. Wizard, but how am I supposed to be patient with everyone telling me to do go find the orb?"

Marvalaine filled two cups with tea and added sugar to his. He didn't know who else might be pushing Blake to find the orb, and stirred the cup thoughtfully as he said, "You and the orb will come together. It is your destiny."

Blake scowled. Marvalaine was a very charming man, but Blake wasn't going to let some clever witch influence him. He turned his head back to the sea and ignored Marvalaine and his tea.

"Are you sure you wouldn't like a cup?"

"I'm not interested in your parlor tricks," Blake said.

"Too bad," Marvalaine replied. "What about the scones?"

Blake was too hungry to ignore the scones and reached for one.

"The tea too," Marvalaine said. "You must really try the tea."

"Why?" Blake asked. "Is it a magical tea that will reveal the location of the orb to me?"

"No," Marvalaine said, shaking his head. "Although that would be nice. Trust me when I say the orb is as destined to find you as you are to find it, but you must be looking for it or you will pass it by without ever knowing it."

"You speak of it like it was a person."

"Do I?" Marvalaine asked. "Do you believe that only people can have a destiny? Not animals? Not places? Is a mountain not destined to be climbed?"

Blake chewed his scone and sipped his tea.

Marvalaine drained his tea, then closed his eyes and faced the ocean. He took a deep, restorative breath and exhaled. "Trust me young Blake. Seek it out, and the clues will come to you. Then, once you have found it, all will be revealed."

Chapter 9

Richard finished laying out the last of the thick mats on the floor and joined Honey near the bleachers. "Are you ready?"

"I think I am," she said. "Are you?"

"All set here," he replied.

Honey walked out onto the mat. The foam filled cushions squished beneath her feet. "You do know that I'm not going to be demonstrating judo, don't you?"

"I know," Richard said, "but I thought it would make people feel safer. We never really talked about what you planned to do."

Honey frowned and shrugged her shoulders. "Ya know...I don't have a clue where to start."

"We do have schools," Richard said. "They try to teach the children how to light a candle with their minds. I can get some candles, if you want to try that."

"We got schools?" Abilene asked.

"Candles?" Honey asked. "I don't see what good lighting candles is gonna be. We need an army, not a choir."

"A choir?" Richard asked.

"You know," Honey said with a lyrical lilt to her voice, "boys and girls wearing long robes and holding candles while singing Kumbaya."

"Okay," he said, "no candles. How did you learn?"

"I dunno. It's kind of like sex. One day I just up and done it."

Abilene snickered and added, "And she keeps on doing it as often as possible."

"Mama!"

Richard backed away in case Abilene's remark would have instigated any retaliation from Honey, but instead Honey hugged her mother and said, "When you's right, you's right. I s'pose that's something I could really teach them about."

Richard's young assistants returned with the first twenty candidates. "There they are," he announced. "And you'll notice they aren't all a bunch of old farts."

"Not all of them at least," Honey said, "and I see some tits in there, too."

"As you requested," he replied. "Come on in, everybody. Please assemble on the mat. I'm sure that by now, everybody knows why we are here."

The candidates followed quietly behind Richard's assistants.

"And," he continued, "I hope you are all aware of who this is, but it is my honor to introduce her, anyway. Please say hello to Honey."

"Your queen," Abilene added.

An indistinct jumble of mumbled hellos filled the room. Richard frowned at the lackluster response, but Honey took it in stride.

"I wonder," Richard said, "how many of you have been to one of our schools teaching the theory of our ancestral powers?"

A smattering of hands went up.

"Good," Richard said. "You may remember that your instructors taught you the history of how things used to be. They also tried to see if they could inspire any of you to show any hint of the powers that your forefathers wielded, but they were unable to actually demonstrate what they were trying to teach you."

Some heads nodded along with other mumbled acknowledgements.

"Well, this is going to be different," Richard continued. "Today you are going to get a real live demonstration of what our people can do. We hope that with such a practical approach, that you might be able to find the power within yourselves. It is my pleasure now, to turn you over to your instructor," he nodded his head towards Abilene and added, "and your queen, Honey."

"First of all," Honey said, "you're my first students, so I want you to bear with me while I try to figure out how to teach you what I know. Now, I never been to one of them schools that Richard was talkin' about. In fact, I didn't even know that we had schools until just a few moments ago. To be honest, I'm not all that sure how I'm going to teach you, but I sure ain't gonna be teaching you to light no candles with your minds, cause it doesn't come from up here," she pointed to her head, "and it sure don't come from here," she pointed to her heart, "although some of them witches might just get their powers from their hearts. My power comes from down here," she pointed to her crotch. "That's right." She pointed to one of the older men in the group and said, "I don't want to give grandpa there a stroke, so I'm just gonna call it my coochie. I don't tell my coochie when to get turned on or when not to. It does it all on its own. I bet you boys wished it was all in your mind instead of down there. Then maybe you wouldn't have to walk around holdin' a notebook in front of you all the time."

Some of the boys blushed, but nobody laughed.

"Come on," she said. "That was pretty funny and none of y'all laughed at it."

Richard leaned close to Honey and said, "Why don't you try a demonstration?"

"Good idea. Look here everyone." She held her hand out in front of her, palm up, and produced a pulsating globe of fire. Her students gasped and oohed in appreciation, but it was the sound of two small hands clapping in the doorway that drew everyone's attention. Honey turned and saw a very little girl watching her and squealing with delight.

"Well, hey darling. What's your name?"

Richard went to the entrance and took the child by the hand and started walking her out.

"Wait!" Honey yelled. "Where are you taking her?"

"This is no place for a child."

"Well, at least bring her here to meet me for a second."

Richard bowed his head and brought the child forth.

Honey bent over at the waist so she could be closer to the young girl. "What's your name, sweet heart?"

"Tammy."

A teenage girl in the class blurted out, "Tammy! What are you doing here?"

Tammy pointed and said, "That's my sister."

Honey snuffed out the fire in her hand and crouched down to speak face to face with her. "How old are you?"

Tammy held up four fingers.

Her sister came forward and took her by the hand. "I'm sorry. She's always getting into mischief. She drives our parents crazy most of the time. I'll take her home."

"No," Honey said. "It's okay. You need to be here. Let her watch. You can take her home with you when you is done."

Richard took Tammy to the bleacher seats and sat her down.

Honey waved her fingers at Tammy before reproducing the fireball in her right hand, then she created a clone of it in her left hand and turned back to her students. "You like these?" she asked. "Who wants to do this?"

Several hands flew up into the air as Tammy squealed from the bleachers.

Blake floated aimlessly through the endless void and mocked Marvalaine. "The orb will come to you. The orb wants to find you as much as you want to find it."

He eavesdropped on the many memories in the void, waiting for one of them to seek him out, but none came. "Here I am!" he yelled out into the void. "If you want me, come and get me!" He heard numerous random peoples' past lives as they floated past him. He knew it would be an impossible mission before he had even set out, and now it proved to be even harder in actual practice. It was like finding a needle in a haystack when you didn't know that you were looking for a needle.

"Orb," he thought to himself. "Someone say something about the orb. Do you hear me orb? If you want to find me so much, come to me now."

Nothing happened. He hadn't really expected that it would, but he was disappointed anyway and started chanting, "Orb...orb...orb...orb..."

He peeked into a passing memory and heard, "...fifteen seconds to orbital insertion...ten...nine..."

He pushed the memory away. That's not even funny.

He tried again. "...pull the eyeball from the orbital socket..."

"Eeeew," he blanched. "That's just disgusting."

He heard another memory as it floated by. "You saw the Orb of Destiny?"

"The orb of Destiny?" he thought to himself. That can't be a coincidence. He followed the memory backwards to a few moments earlier and reached into the memory. Destiny's image came into view, talking to a dark-skinned girl with wild markings on her skin. He also saw an older woman, a witch doctor, within the dark-skinned girl, as if they were the same person from different times in their lives.

"Why did you give me that last memory?" Destiny asked. "I didn't learn any new powers or anything there."

"That was part introduction," the witch girl said, "and part test. You met him, no?"

"Met who?"

"The Great One. He who is the most powerful of our kind. He wasn't even born yet in my time, but he will be a savior to our people. You descend from his line. He took Nimisen as not only his apprentice, but eventually as his bride. Your blood is powerful."

"I met him, but he didn't teach me anything. He caught Nimisen trying to steal something from him, but it was all a trick. He lured her there, caught her and forced her to be his apprentice."

"He may have tricked her, but she was willing enough. As powerful as he already was, his power only grew when they were together. Hers too. They were each more powerful as a team than either of them had ever been alone. I think their power came from their love for each other. I think they loved each other all along, before they even met. Love is a powerful and mysterious thing, young Destiny. Do not let it be a distraction to you, but do not let it slip through your fingers, either. Love is like a blanket. The blanket not really make you warm, but when you wrap it around you, it doubles the warmth inside you."

"Well, I didn't see any love, but he was kinda cute. Will I meet them again?"

"When dreams not bound by time, you will find that there are those you will run into again."

"I see."

"No, you don't yet, but you will. You saw the Orb of Destiny?"

"Is that what it was called? I have an orb named after me?" Destiny laughed softly.

"Not joke. Not named after you. Maybe it was made for you. Maybe not."

"What? You think that some orb that was made a thousand years ago was made just to wait for me to come along? That's crazy."

"The universe is full of mysteries. That is just one of many possible truths. If the orb is for you, then it will find you."

Destiny's eyes glazed over with the thought that a magical orb waited over a thousand years for her to be born.

Blake returned to the void. He had a name now, but he still didn't know what it looked like. Destiny had seen it. Why didn't she tell him? The witch girl said the orb was for her, but now they all say it is for him to find the orb. He wasn't sure what or who to believe. Maybe if he goes back a little further, he can find the time when Destiny saw it.

He reached backwards into the same memory and found Destiny sneaking down a hallway, but it wasn't really Destiny. She was in another's memory and he was watching both of them.

She kept her hood pulled over her head as she slunk through the servant's hallways. A wizard in the castle had something that she wanted, and she thought that he would surely take the main halls, but still she kept to the shadows. She maintained the pretense of delivering water even as she entered his room, but finding it empty, she closed the door behind her and put the pitcher down on a bench. The apartment was dark, which suited her well. Most of the room was your standard living quarter, a bed, a night table, a desk and some storage. The far end of the room, however, was quite different. There were animal skins and heads on the walls, but not those of a hunter. They were a scholar's display. There was a display of butterflies pinned to a board with their wings beautifully preserved. A table stood away from the wall with odd glass items and jars of various colored powders and liquids. Next to the table, against the wall, she found several trunks and boxes, where she started her search.

Inside the trunks, she mostly found and set aside small bottles of various ingredients, ground herbs and odd animal pieces, until she came to the last trunk. It was a large trunk reinforced with brass straps and had a large lock securing the lid to the trunk. Destiny pulled her hood back and extracted the metal spikes that were holding her hair up. She went to the lock, inserted the spikes, and started to manipulate the tumblers until the lock sprung open.

Inside, she found a much better assortment of items in this trunk. She shoved some items aside, but pulled a few out and slipped them into the secret pockets inside her skirt. Anything with jewels made it to her pocket. She kept digging deeper and deeper, looking for the one prize that brought her here.

"Looking for this?" She heard the voice booming inside her head. She sprang up and spun around to face him. He stood in darkness but held a perfectly round crystal globe that glowed from within, dimly lighting his dark beard and pale face against the gloom behind him.

She stammered a moment, trying to think of an excuse, but he raised his free hand and she was unable to speak.

"It's beautiful, don't you think?" He was young for a wizard of such importance. His eyes were bright blue, even in the dim light from the orb. They pierced her eyes and held her stare locked with his. He stepped towards her and waved the orb back and forth in front of her. She was frozen, completely helpless. She felt like one of those butterflies pinned by his gaze. He stepped closer and brought his face close to hers. She stared at his face. It was young with flawless skin. His beard was dark brown and neatly trimmed. His eyes were light and happy, and when he smiled, his whole face was bright and soothing.

Destiny blushed. "Yes, it is very beautiful."

Blake reached forward in the memory. He'd finally seen the orb and now only needed to learn what the wizard did with it. He saw Destiny leave the room. The wizard held the orb in his hand and let it roll smoothly around his fingers. It seemed to float above his hand as it bounced unnaturally from finger to finger, pulsating from an inner blue light as it tapped each of his digits. He turned his hand palm down, wrapping his fingers around the orb, and squeezed. His hand glowed red for a moment as the orb's light shone through his flesh, then his hand squeezed shut and the orb was gone, but Blake still saw the light of the orb shining from behind the wizard's bright blue eyes. Blake felt as if the wizard were staring right at him, but that couldn't be, as Blake was only a voyeur, watching one of Destiny's memories unfold.

"I told you," the wizard said directly to him, "that you are to find the orb, and I am pleased that you are searching for it, but you will not find it here and you may not keep this memory. You must find it in your own time."

Blake's mouth fell open, and he started to ask, "Marvalaine?" but the memory clouded over and he found himself back in the void, floating amongst the free memories, and unable to recall the orb.

Michelle pulled the hotel curtains closed and looked around the small room, wondering if she was doing the right thing. This hotel was a little fancier than the motel that Zeline had found for them by the airport, but it didn't look all that much more comfortable to her than the waiting room had. It wasn't anything like home and she had the nagging feeling that she should have remained with Destiny, but as soon as she stretched out atop the bed's comforter and felt her back sink into the mattress, she knew that Logan had been right. A good night's sleep was something that she desperately needed. Her skin prickled at the thought that she was accepting life advice from one of them, but she smashed her head into the pillow anyway, creating a comfortable dent in the filling. She was tired, but more than just feeling sleepy, she felt drained from worry over everything that had been going on around her. She closed her eyes, not even bothering to remove her clothes and dive in between the sheets, but her mind was buzzing with too many thoughts to sleep just yet. Focusing on Destiny's current predicament didn't seem to help. She tried imagining the arguments that she might use to convince her granddaughter to return to them, but her thoughts inevitably drifted off to the battle between the two girls. She wasn't even present to see the great Cheyenne conflict in person, but her mind was filled with images from dozens of anonymous witnesses and she had been there at the farm to see the two girls face off the first time. That was the night when Honey had stolen Destiny's amulet and they squared off against each other, with the family standing around them watching.

Having seen them fight in person made it even easier for her to visualize the final battle between the two of them, but she didn't want to dream of the fight. She wanted to picture Destiny stuck in her dream world so she could concentrate on a way to get her out, but it was hard for her to tear her focus away from the battle. She wouldn't have an easy sleep if she kept dwelling on them fighting. She tried shifting her focus to Ashlin instead. She was such a cute little girl, with her bright red hair just like Michelle's mother, but she couldn't picture Ashlin without seeing her mother's face superimposed over hers.

Michelle rolled over onto her side and mashed her head into the pillow some more. She turned the pillow over to feel the cool side against her cheeks. She wasn't in control of her own thoughts and her mind kept drifting back to the fight on the farm when Destiny chased

Honey and her mother off the property. Honey had tried seducing Blake, but when that didn't work, she ran out of his room and into the farm's courtyard with her naked bosom on display to the world. That was only the start of the sparks that led to the fight between the two girls. Honey thought nothing of baring her breasts in public, and most of the men on the farm had already seen them more than once, but Destiny didn't know her that well and only knew that she had tried to start something with Blake.

Michelle hadn't known Honey either, but she knew her mother and could tell that the apple hadn't fallen far from the tree, except in this case, the daughter's ambitions had far outpaced the mother's. Honey was nothing special before she had stolen the amulet from Destiny. She may have been able to produce some sparks that could start fires, but nothing of the magnitude that Destiny could, at least not before she had taken the magical trinket. That was the turning point that changed the spoiled little slut into a super villain capable of destroying buildings and killing people. She thought as little of killing people as she had of seducing them and tarnishing their virtue. She took her stolen powers and tried to claim the world as her prize, and she no doubt still had the same plans.

Michelle sighed into her pillow. She wanted desperately to sleep and dream about Destiny, but she couldn't control the images that kept seeping into her mind. The room darkened as the light against the curtains dimmed to blackness. She wondered how long she had been ruminating about the two girls. It didn't feel like it could have been that long, but it was sure dark outside. It felt like sleep would elude her forever, but she couldn't believe that she had lain there long enough to be night time already. She went to the window and parted the curtains to take a peek.

It wasn't the lateness of the hour that had darkened the world. Thick black clouds had stretched across the heavens while she had tried to sleep. They completely blotted out the sky now, turning everything outside to pitch black, except for a small point of light way down the street by the hospital. The light grew and flashed, but it also spewed out more dark clouds. It was smoke, not clouds. And beneath the smoke was Honey. It was too far for Michelle to actually see her, but she knew instinctively that it was her. Michelle turned towards the door. Destiny was in trouble and she needed her Nana now more than ever before. She slammed her palm against the wall as the anger welled up inside of her. She never should have left the hospital, and she sure wasn't going to stand by idly now while that bitch attacked her little girl, but when she turned to run for the door, she couldn't lift her feet. They had sunk down deep into the shag and were tangled up in the carpet fibers.

Panic gripped her heart as the carpet engulfed her feet, leaving her helpless to save Destiny. She didn't even know what she would do when she got there, but whatever it might be, it would be more than she could do from a hotel bed. Flames arched into the air and surrounded the hospital. She didn't see anyone fighting back. Only Honey and the fire, except Honey wasn't alone. Michelle could tell that there were more people with her. Honey had managed to get some others to join her crusade, and they were making fire, too.

Michelle tugged mightily on her feet, but she couldn't dislodge them from the carpet. Her balance shifted backwards, and she fell back away from the window, landing softly on the bed. She tried sitting back up, but her eyelids were too heavy and fell closed as her breathing softened and she slipped into a peaceful sleep.

* * *

None of Honey's students managed to conjure up any flames, although one of them was able to generate some heat and a tiny wisp of smoke. Despair engulfed her students. Each of them had arrived believing that they would have the gift and go home blasting fire from their hands, especially the older students who thought it was their destiny to be big shots. Some of them even thought that if a country bumpkin like Honey could do it, then surely they could excel beyond her. Such a talent would certainly rocket them to the top of the clan, but one by one, they failed to make anything close to the kind of fire that she could make. Some of the younger students had not been to the sorcerer schools yet, but the older ones recognized the failure and felt even more defeated.

"It's okay," Honey explained to them. "Maybe fire ain't your thing. My mama can't make the fire neither, but she can do something just as impressive." Abilene had been standing off the edge of the mats watching, but Honey went to her and pulled her by the hand. "Come on, Mama. Show them what you kin do."

Abilene resisted at first, out of shyness, but quickly overcame her hesitation and went forward willingly, emboldened by the looks of admiration from the class. "Those were nice words," she said, "but I cain't do nothing anywheres near as impressive as my Honey. If you insists though, I will show you what I can do." She held out her right hand and produced a single ball of electricity. It glowed a soft blue with an undulating swirl of electric tendrils that wrapped around each other in a tangle of threads. The class applauded and Abilene took the ball in both hands and split it into two balls, which she tossed around and received another round of applause. "Well," she said, "I spect I'll have to start learnin' jugglin' so I can put on a proper show." She spread her hands out at arm's length and slapped them together, squashing the two lightning balls into each other, creating a loud clap of thunder. As the thunder reverberated around the hall, she showed her hands to the class, with her palms facing outwards, and small tendrils of electricity forked out of her fingers. She spread her hands out at arm's length again and arced the electric thread over her head.

"Oooh," Tammy said from behind them, "Pretty!"

"Mama!" Honey exclaimed. "I never expected you to put on such a good show!"

Abilene smiled and gushed, "I been practicin' when you wasn't lookin'."

"There you go," Honey said to the class. "Just cause you cain't make fire don't mean you ain't got some other awesome power hiding within you just waiting to come out."

The class roared with approval before being ushered out by Richard's assistants.

"That was good," Richard said. "You were worried for nothing."

"Too bad none of them could make any fire," Honey said.

"I suppose," Richard said, "but one of them did make some smoke. Maybe you just need to give her some more time and the fire will come."

"If you want," Abilene said, "I can try them at lightning."

"Sure, Mama. You kin do that while I work with that one girl. What was her name?"

Richard shrugged and said, "I think she was the one with the funny sounding name."

"Yeah," Abilene agreed. "It was real long and sounded kinda Russian, I think. She was the plain lookin' girl with the dark hair."

Saunders stood nervously outside of Flinch's office before knocking on the door. Even after he had finally rapped his knuckles, he could hear papers rustling around inside before the major eventually responded, "Come in."

He entered Flinch's office and stood at attention, holding his fingers sharply to his temples.

Flinch bit down on his cigar when he saw Saunders salute. They'd worked together long enough to have dispensed with such formalities while in private. Something must be wrong. He must have bad news to report. "At ease. Close the door. Did you find her?"

"Yes Sir, but she didn't make it. I turned the ambulance around when she expired and sent her body to the morgue for research."

That was the best news Flinch had heard since the whole incident had begun. "Well done. I know you were fond of her, but your country is counting on us to figure out what the hell she was. What about the other one? Do we know where she is?"

"Yes sir. The NSA's satellites tracked their vehicle as they left. They stopped to let someone out in Salt Lake, but then continued on to a remote desert also in Utah. Aerial shots of the compound suggest that it might be some kind of a school."

Flinch frowned and chewed the butt of his stogie. "A school? Damn it. There must be more of them. Get some boots on the ground to monitor them."

"Yes, sir."

Richard opened the far doors leading out of the gym to air out the scent of sulphur that still lingered in the room. He would have held the class outdoors if he didn't suspect the government would be spying on them with satellite cameras.

Honey took her mother's arm in hers and headed for the auditorium exit. She could still smell the electricity in Abilene's hair. "You know, Mama, I ain't never been more proud of you. That was a real impressive display. I wonder if I kin do that."

"Do what?" Abilene asked. "Make the fire arch over your head?"

"No silly. That's easy. I mean makin' the lightning like you do."

Abilene stopped before they reached the door and asked, "Why? Is there sumpin' wrong with your fire?"

"No," Honey replied, "of course not. I just want to be more well-rounded. You know, cousin Destiny could do both."

"And look where it got her. It still warn't enough to stop you."

"She did kinda stop me, Mama."

"Well, she didn't kill you. You still come out on top. I don't see how no lightin' is gonna make you any better."

"I know, Mama, but it will make me more special, and a queen should be more special. Don't you think?"

The warmth that Abilene had felt moments ago from Honey's praise evaporated as she realized that her daughter wouldn't need her if she could have both powers. "Maybe it don't work like that. Maybe we all gets only one gift and we should just be happy with what we gots."

Honey frowned. "She could."

"Who could what? You mean your cousin?"

"Yeah. We both seen it."

Abilene scowled. "Your cousin was a freak, and not a freak of nature neithers. I heered talk about how things was before Mr. Frank come and found us, and what she done was pure unnatural. She had both fire and lightnin' alright, but she had the witch powers too, and that just ain't right."

Honey lowered her voice slightly as she admitted, "There was a moment there, when I was fightin' her, that it felt like I was becoming just like her. I felt like I could do anything that she could do."

"And what did it get her?" Abilene asked. "Here you is, training a new army, and she's dead."

Honey stepped out through the door and there, just outside the doorway, was the student that had made some smoke, waiting for them. "You're her," Honey said. "I'm sorry, but I forgot your name."

"You remember me?" the girl asked shyly.

"Of course I do," Honey said. "You're the only one who managed to conjure up any smoke."

The girl blushed and said, "That was pretty pathetic compared to what you can do."

"Maybe it just takes practice," Honey said. "What's your name again?"

"Balletina," she said with a grin. "Balletina Lyoshovna Alkaev."

"Well, Balletina, I have a good feeling about you."

Balletina blushed.

Honey pointed back towards the gym and asked, "Would you like to try again? I have some time."

Balletina nodded her head enthusiastically.

"Thank you for your help, Mama. I think I'm gonna work with this girl some more."

"Sure, sure," Abilene replied. "You go right ahead. We'll talk more later."

CHAPTER 10

Day nine.

People tend to think of a legacy as something that was built in the past, but legacies must start sometime, and that is always in the present. Whether or not this day will be acknowledged by history, it will still be the day in which two legacies were started, but in the end, only one of them will survive the test of time.

Michelle didn't feel right when she woke up. The bed was too soft, or the room was too warm or too cold. The night had started off with her believing that she would never fall asleep, tossing and turning throughout the night, but she had apparently drifted off to sleep at some point, because the clock on the bed stand read seven in the morning by the time that she finally awoke.

She didn't like the uncomfortable feeling that had consumed her and assumed that her sleep must have been rocked with bad dreams, but she couldn't recall any of them. All that she remembered was having trouble sleeping and staring at the ceiling, but she also remembered being utterly exhausted and didn't know why she would have any trouble sleeping. She hated waking up tired and didn't have a good feeling for the coming day, but she was determined to put her best foot forward.

The warmth from the hot shower soaked into her tired muscles and eased the aches in her joints. She remembered when Destiny had first returned from the ancestral memories with the power to heal. Michelle had burned her arm making candles and Destiny healed it, but more than that, she left Michelle feeling young and energetic for the whole day that followed. She wished that she had Destiny's gift for healing right now, so her knees could feel young again, but she accepted what comfort she could get from the warm water spraying down upon her and remained grateful for at least that.

It was nice to be clean again, although, without any fresh clothes, she wondered just how clean she would really be. She found her way to the elevator and down to the ground floor where a breakfast service was setup in the dining area. She was too anxious to see Destiny to dawdle in the dining area and only grabbed a juice and a Danish to go.

The sun had risen just over the horizon, low enough that Michelle needed to shade her eyes to see the hospital. It seemed farther than she remembered, but it wasn't coming to her, so she started walking.

A car pulled up alongside her and rolled down the window. Logan said from the car, "I thought you might try sneaking off like this."

"I warn't sneaking," she said. "I just be walkin'."

"Get in," he said as he pushed the door open.

She had plenty of reasons to question his motives and far more reasons to distrust him than she ever had distrusted Blake, but she wasn't going to turn down a ride.

"I know you're not being sneaky," he admitted. "You're just a very strong and independent woman."

"True dat," she admitted.

"Of course," he continued, "those are just code words for proud and stubborn."

She didn't like his remark, but she couldn't argue with it and chose to pout instead. He pulled the car into the parking lot and jumped out of the car so he could help her out.

"You know how proud and stubborn I be," she said to him, "yet you insist on helping me down from da car?"

"I'm proud and stubborn too," he said, "and I still believe that there are some things that a gentleman should do for a lady."

She accepted his assistance and waited for him to close the door before they started walking towards the entrance. "I sure hopes you didn't steal dis car like you boys done wit' da last one."

Once inside, she didn't even bother with reception and headed directly towards the elevator and up to Destiny's floor. Outside Destiny's room, Ashlin and Zeline were both holding Tempest's hands and talking comfort to her.

"Oh no," Michelle said, "Did Tempest have another one of her anxiety attacks?"

Ashlin left Tempest to grip Michelle around the waist. "Destiny's heart stopped."

Michelle thought for a moment that she would fall faint on the floor. She commanded her voice to speak and barely squeaked out, "Is she…"

Tempest wrapped her arms around Ashlin and Michelle. The corridor wobbled around Michelle as she felt the grave concern pouring out of Tempest.

"Dey is workin' on her now," Zeline said, "but dey keep talkin' like she was already gone and dis be a waste of time."

A doctor came out of the room and said, "She's stabilized, but there's no brain activity."

Michelle heard the doctor think the words, "organ donation" and looked at him with a gaze that might have turned him to stone if Zeline hadn't entered her thoughts and said, "Leave him be. He's just a doctor. He don't know nothin' about us."

Saunders couldn't suppress the feeling that he should have been more helpful to the girl who defeated Honey. She was on their side, and he should have done something to save her. He blamed himself for letting her die and didn't understand why she would be the foremost thought on his mind, but she was all he could think about, if he was actually thinking at all. His thoughts were as blurry as his memory. He found himself walking aimlessly through the base as he brooded over the things that he should have done to protect her. On the outside, he looked like a soldier that was deep in thought, but on the inside, he was beside himself with grief and had no idea why.

Flinch, on the other hand, felt no such ambivalence. He wanted her dissected and her organs analyzed. It made no difference to him if she did turn out to be an alien from Alpha Centauri; he wanted her DNA mapped and preferably weaponized into a serum that could provide her abilities to his soldiers. Saunders shuddered as the image of Flinch's army brushed through his mind. Flinch had only seen the video images, and most of those were from satellite cameras hundreds of miles away. But he wasn't there at ground zero. He wasn't up close to see how their missiles exploded at point blank range without even scratching Honey. It's different when you can see the crater in the ground that was created by the two girls using only their...Saunders thoughts were derailed when he realized that even though it looked like they used their hands; he didn't really know what they used. That's precisely what Flinch wanted to learn. It would be a disaster to give such power to infantrymen. How could you expect such a man to take orders? Saunders didn't know all the things that Flinch was imagining, but he was sure that he wouldn't agree with any of them.

Being there at the battle gave Saunders a different perspective. He smelled the smoke from their fire. It was real old testament stuff; fire and brimstone. A chuckle percolated through his brain when he remembered asking Honey if she was an alien from another planet. He didn't actually ask her, but she guessed what he was thinking. He never would have guessed by looking at her that she could be a demon from hell, but that's exactly what the war between the girls looked like. It looked like hell. It smelled like hell. What did that make the girl who died? Had he witnessed a battle between two demons from hell? Or was the blond girl actually an angel? Had he just witnessed a battle between two celestial beings? He shivered as he thought they might be dissecting an angel from God.

Saunders tried pushing those thoughts from his mind and sighed when he realized how far he had walked. He looked up and found himself at the foot of the steps to the offices of Mortuary Affairs. That's where she would be. Inside that building, lying on a cold steel table, they might actually have the remains of an angelic soldier. He wondered why they would come to Earth as teenaged girls instead of something a little more ominous. Maybe they were so young because angels are ageless, but why girls? Why would they even have a gender? His father might have given him some answers, but then, his father would never have questioned why one of them would have been here to protect them. Saunders wondered if his deep sadness over her passing was because she was a messenger from God. Maybe if he just looked upon her face, he would understand his feelings better.

Tempest and Michelle were beset with grief, and Ashlin was unable to console either of them. The doctors had been telling them all along that Destiny was already dead, but they refused to believe it. How could they? They still heard Destiny's thoughts as if she were still there with them, just waiting to wake up, but when her heart stopped and all the alarms emitted their terrifying tones, fear and doubt crept into their minds.

Ashlin looked past Michelle for Blake, but he hadn't followed her down the hall. Had he already sensed that something was wrong? Or did Michelle finally send him off to find the orb? He should be here. She looked for him in the lobby, but he wasn't there either. She froze for a moment, staring at the door, hoping he would be coming in any second, but he never showed. He should be here. She wiped the tears from her eyes and called out with her mind, "Blake?" She listened for him, but only heard the sobs of Tempest and Michelle.

The hallway wobbled around her as her unsteady legs carried her to the waiting room. She searched for a place to sit and wait out the dizziness. An empty seat in the corner, away from the bustle of the hospital staff, beckoned to her. She took a deep breath as she sat down and closed her eyes. Even with the world throbbing in her ears, she was still able to shut her eyes and slow her breathing so she could draw in deep, purposeful draughts of air, slipping away from the world around her. She felt the void form around her. She had never entered the memories so easily before, but Destiny had told her that she had a gift for witchcraft and it would get easier in time.

Maybe grief was a great motivator, but this felt to her like the void had been searching for her and had pulled her into it.

"Blake?"

"Shhh," he said, "I'm listening for the orb."

"You need to come see Destiny."

"I already saw her."

Even in the void, Ashlin felt the tears streaming from her eyes. "Something has happened to her. I'm afraid she won't come back."

"She's just confused," Blake said. "She's doesn't think that she can come back, but I know she can."

"How can you know that?"

"I know," Blake said, "because he knows, and I trust him. I need to find the orb, and then we can use it to save her."

"Well, you better..."

"Shhh..."

Blake heard a passing memory. "Nobody can ever know that you have it."

Ashlin followed Blake into the memory and found herself staring down into his eyes, but they weren't Blake's eyes, and it wasn't her voice when she asked, "Why, Papa?"

"Because," Blake's host said, "It's been entrusted to us. We are the guardians and it is for us to pass it on through the centuries."

Ashlin flung herself onto the bed where Blake lay and wrapped her arms around his neck. She felt his host's scruffy beard scratch against her cheeks, but she didn't care. "Why can't we use it to save you?"

Blake wrapped his arms around her and said, "I love you, my daughter, and I wish I could be with you longer, but the orb is not for us. It has been passed down since the time of the Great One and must continue its journey until it finds the Chosen One."

Ashlin laid her head on Blake's chest and said, "I wish we were one of the one's it was meant for."

Blake coughed and turned his head to hide the blood from her. "We are," he said. "We are the ones with the honor of passing it down through the ages."

Blake coughed again and entered into a fit of coughs. A matronly woman pulled Ashlin away, and the memory faded for both of them.

"What was that about?" Ashlin asked.

"He told me that I would have to find it in my own time, I guess he was right."

"Still," she said, "a clue would have been nice. All I could tell was that it must be very powerful."

"You could feel its power?"

"Very much," she said. "It's hard to explain, but every part of me felt energized from it."

"But could you feel its shape? How big was it?"

"Sorry," she said. "I could only feel what it was doing to me."

***

Nobody ever returned to the abandoned village, so Destiny adopted it as her new home and settled into the first house on the right. She didn't feel like she had much choice, other than choosing which of the several homes to use. The village had just about anything she could ask for, except for companionship. She tried contacting Marvalaine and Nimisen to invite them to join her and take up residence in one of the other homes, but they refused to even answer her calls. What's the point of an afterlife if you can't share it with other deceased friends? She had managed to get Blake to come for a visit in this world, but he didn't stay long and refused to come see her new home. This could have been the perfect life if only her family would have just accepted the truth and moved on instead of clinging to the hope that she wasn't really dead. She felt as abandoned by them as this village was by whoever had created it. She went to the door and looked out at the small community. There were three different homes and farms that she could see from her porch, but they were all empty. If she wanted to, she could live in a different house every week, but they would all be just as lonely as this one.

She closed her eyes tightly and tried to keep the tears squeezed inside. Blake was the only one she had seen in a very long time. She wished she could see him again, but he had something important to do to save her mother. She missed her mother. How strange life was that she could miss her mother so much when she barely even knew her. Even when she was alive and her mother was locked in the psychiatric hospital, she missed her. The hospital was so far from their home in the bayou that they could not afford to visit her there. Even if they had, her mother was kept in a vegetative state with drugs and she wouldn't have had a real opportunity to know her, at least, not until they had rescued her. She had just started getting to know her mother in these last few days, and now they were separated again. Before she had died, Destiny had big plans to heal her mother's mind. That was the mission that she had given to herself, and she considered it to be her destiny, but her mother was already doing so much better now, maybe it wasn't necessary. Had she tried reaching her mother yet? What about her nana? Maybe she just needs to give them a chance.

She walked up the path to the meadow where Blake had met her. The sun warmed her face and dried her tears. She closed her eyes and thought, "Mama? Mama can you hear me?"

She listened intently, but only heard the wind in her ears. This place was too quiet. There should be insects, and birds! Why weren't there any birds? There was a brook nearby. She liked dangling her feet in the water and just listening to it gurgle. It probably didn't have any fish though, but it was one of the few reliable sounds in this place. There were no birds; no fish, just her. Even the trees didn't rustle. How strange that she could hear the wind, but not the trees.

"Destiny? Is that you?"

"MAMA!" Destiny screamed out loud into her lonely world.

"Are you okay?" Tempest asked. "We thought we had lost you!"

Destiny didn't know how to admit the whole truth to her mother. "I'm okay, but I'm lonely."

"Come back to us. We're all here waiting for you. You don't have to be lonely anymore."

Destiny lay down in the grass and let the sun warm her all over. "I know," she said. "I wish I could be with you, but I can't leave this place."

"I'm afraid for you. I'm afraid that the longer you stay away, the harder it's going to be for you to get back."

"Don't be afraid for me."

"I can't help it," Tempest said. "Remember when you came to visit me in the hospital?"

"Yes Mama. We rescued you that day."

"But you didn't just rescue me from the hospital. Remember how you found me in that dark place?"

"I wouldn't say it was so dark," Destiny said. "I remember bright white walls and the ceiling was made of light."

"It was dark and scary to me," Tempest said, "but you were very brave to come get me out of there. You came into my scary place just to get me and lead me out of it."

"You weren't really trapped, Mama. You were just hiding in that place."

"I thought I was trapped. I believed with all my heart that I was in a place that I could never leave, but you believed differently and came right in there and took me out. Let me come get you."

"This is different. I can't leave here, but I would love to see you again. Could you come for a visit?"

<hr>

Honey grabbed a candle from the box that Richard had set aside in case Balletina wanted it and led her out the back exit. Outside of the gym was a basketball hoop on an asphalt court with some picnic tables surrounded by freshly mowed grass. Honey set the candle on one of the picnic tables and sat down. Balletina sat opposite her.

"When I was little," Honey started, "I used to live on a farm."

"With cows and horses?" Balletina asked.

"Yeah," Honey said, "we had them, but mostly we had witches."

"Witches?"

"Can you believe that? My dingbat grandma up and married a God damned witch, but that was before we even knew what we was. You know how some of our people have been lost and scattered around?"

"Yeah," Balletina said. "I was lost too. I was an orphan."

"Oh," Honey cried, "I'm so sorry. I never knowed my daddy neither and I kinda know what that must have felt like. Anyways, it wasn't till I was in middle school that I learnt that I could make fire. I showed my mama, of course, but she told me not to show no one else. I did like she said and never showed none of them, but whenever we was alone, I would start the wood fires in the fireplace like this." She reached out and touched her finger to the candle wick and it popped to life.

"That's so cool," Balletina gushed.

Honey blew out the flame and said, "Now you try."

Balletina touched the wick, but nothing happened.

"When I first done it, I was getting angry about sumpin', but I don't recollect what it was."

Balletina touched the wick again with no effect.

"What makes you angry?"

Balletina frowned and said, "Not lighting this candle is making me kind of angry."

"You gots to be way more angry than that," Honey said. "Have you ever thought that maybe you weren't really orphaned and your folks just dropped you off at the orphanage because they didn't want you no more?"

Balletina didn't like to think that, but it was one of those involuntary thoughts that had crossed her mind more than once.

"Maybe they thought you was too unfortunate looking and just gave you away rather than have to look at you."

Balletina furrowed her eyebrows and tried ignoring Honey, focusing on lighting the candle instead.

"Did the other orphans tease you for being so ugly?"

Balletina grit her teeth and tried forcing Honey's voice out of her head.

"The other kids probably had loads of fun over your name too," Honey chided.

"Stop it!" Balletina yelled as she slammed her fists on the table. "I don't want to talk about this anymore!"

Honey snickered while Balletina glared at her.

"It's not funny!" Balletina yelled. "They teased me and called me names all the time! And yes, they especially liked making fun of my name! I didn't like it then and I don't like it now!"

The mirth never left Honey's face. She simply smiled and pointed to the candle and the flame that now burned on it.

Logan had offered everyone their own rooms at the motel, but Johnson couldn't adequately protect Blake iff he was in another room, so they agreed to share a room with two beds. Sleep didn't come easily to him that night. Insomnia can haunt anyone, but for some soldiers, their experiences can lead to PTSD, which can make sleep even harder to find. Johnson hadn't seen much action during his tour of duty, and had spent more time being punished than he did actually on the field, but he saw more than enough action after his official duty when he was recruited to track down a mysterious stranger in the bayous of Louisianna. He saw people that could turn themselves into weapons and launch fire from their hands. He had never known fear like that before, and ran for his life, but he couldn't escape them. They were inside of his head, telling him to do things. They knew what he saw and what he thought. They knew what he had done in his past and why he had been incarcerated by the army. They owned him. He couldn't even dream without them knowing about it. He rolled over and tried to ignore the sliver of light from the window.

"Never mind that," the voice boomed in his head. "It's time for you to get up. We have a job for you."

This was just another reason why he had trouble sleeping.

"Don't blame all your problems on us," the librarian said. "You had problems sleeping long before we came along. Now get up."

Johnson swung his legs over the edge of the bed and sat up. He yawned and breathed in heavily, wishing more than anything that he could have smelled some coffee brewing. He needed something to help him sweep the cobwebs and other uninvited guests from his brain.

"We want you to follow Logan."

"You want me to protect him too?" Johnson asked. "I thought he was your enemy."

"He is. He's one of the others, but we are uncertain about his true motives. We want you to spy on him. He's up to something and we want you to tell us what it is."

"What? He's one of them, and you want me to spy on him? I thought you guys were all seeing. Why do you need me for your spy?"

"We mostly see things through the eyes of others. We cannot risk them detecting us if we try to spy through their own eyes."

"But," Johnson complained, "what if he goes back to HER?"

"That's precisely why we want you to spy on him."

"So," Johnson said with an incredulous tone to his voice, "you want me to follow him in case he goes back to her? Are you crazy?"

"No, Johnson, we are not crazy, but we need to know how far we can trust him. He may or may not go back to her. Even if he does, their history has proven to us that they are very capable of betraying each other."

"And you want me to be in the middle of it?"

"No," the librarian said. "We only want to know what he is up to. We would prefer that you do so from a safe distance. Try to be invisible."

"If he's one of them, like you said, then what if he figures out how to make fire with his own hands?"

"You make a good point," the librarian said, "and another good reason for you to spy on him."

Johnson swallowed hard and asked, "What if he catches me and fries me?!?"

"That would be regrettable. We shall make every effort to warn you before that happens."

Silence followed as the librarian waited for Johnson to get moving.

"You need to get started," the librarian prodded him, "as in now. Move out!"

"Alright," Johnson said as he lazily climbed up from the bed, "but it's on you if anything happens to Blake while I'm off playing spy. Especially if I get killed doing it."

Saunders' mind was in a fog as he climbed the steps to the morgue and showed his id to the guard at the entrance. He knew where he was, but he wondered what had brought him here. Was it just random luck or did something mystical draw him to this location? Did the girl draw him here? Maybe angels never really die and she needed him. The guard only needed a brief glance at his credentials before nodding his head to let him in.

He tried to shake off the notion of demons and angels. It sounded too much like his father. His father wanted him to go into the ministry. He would have been the third generation pastor in the family, but he ran from that fate, believing that his feet were too well grounded for a life in the church.

He followed the halls of the Mortuary Affairs building and welcomed the faint antiseptic smell that filled the lobby, expecting it to prepare him for any less pleasant odors that waited inside. The autopsy room was not what he was expecting. There was no large crowd gathered around her body; there was no crowd at all. It was a cold, empty room. He heard the faint sounds of a pen on paper coming from an adjoining office, but his eyes remained glued to the empty autopsy room as he knocked on the glass and asked, "Where's the girl?"

The rustling of paper stopped, and he heard someone moving about in the office, but still hadn't even looked to see who was there when he heard a young woman's voice ask, "What girl?"

"What girl?" he repeated. "What other girl could there be? She's the most significant creature I've ever encountered. I sent her over here yesterday. I expected to see a whole team of doctors working on her."

"You do know that this is the morgue," she said. "Perhaps you wanted the infirmary?"

"Of course I know this is the morgue," he growled. "I wouldn't have sent her here if she weren't dead."

The girl in the office set aside her paperwork and turned to her computer. She looked puzzled as she called up some reports and shook her head.

"What's wrong?" Saunders asked.

The girl shrugged and said, "I don't see any new arrivals for yesterday, or for the whole week for that matter."

"That's impossible," he replied. "I was with her when she expired. I sent her here myself."

The girl shrugged again and said, "Sorry. We don't have anyone new. Perhaps you want the city morgue? We don't actually see much business here most of the time."

"No, I sent her here. She was too important and too classified for the city morgue."

"Classified?" the girl asked. "What made her so special, anyway?"

"She's…" He couldn't tell her that the girl was an angel. He sighed and simply said, "It's classified."

Michelle went to the window and looked out at the hospital parking lot and the street that bordered it. Her heart fluttered as her dream flashed through her mind, but she didn't believe that it was simply a bad dream. It had to have been a vision, and it must have meant something. Two streets bordered the parking lot outside the window. A coffee shop stood across one of them, but across the other street was a small grassy clearing with a couple of pine trees and a jogging path that had callisthenic stations spaced out along the path. It looked innocent enough, but that was where she had seen Honey and her followers gathering. That was where they had launched their fire and attacked the hospital. What was wrong with those monsters? The hospital was full of sick and innocent people. How could they launch their fire on so many poor people? Could they all be as evil and crazy as Honey? She didn't trust Mr. Logan any farther than she could toss him, but at least he didn't seem to be that damned crazy.

Zeline joined her at the window and looked out across the parking lot, but saw nothing out of place. "What's wrong? You been off your game all morning. Didn't you get a good sleep?"

"No," Michelle sighed. "I slept okay, although not at first. It just be dat I seen her in my dreams."

"Who? Honey? I t'ought she left and went back to whatever rock dat she crawled out from. You tink she's comin' back?"

"Uhuh. She's comin' bak alright, and she be comin' here." Michelle pointed to the grassy area and continued, "I seen her right out daer, to be exact. She's comin' here to finish off Destiny and anybody else unfortunate enough to be here."

"I tink mebbe I already knew dat was gonna happen," Zeline said, "but she's gonna have to go through me first."

"She's gonna have to go through all o' us, but she won't be alone. She's somehow found more of her kind dat kin make da fire."

"She probably been teachin' dem."

"Teaching them?" Michelle gasped. "How? I mean, how can a half wit bitch like her teach nobody nothin'?"

"It don't take no genius to make a fist. I tink dat her makin' da fire is sumpin' like if I was to make a fist an' hit you."

"Still," Michelle said, "One o' her be more'n enough. I never thought she would make more of 'em."

"Why not?" Zeline asked. "Didn't you teach your family how to talk without talkin'?"

"Family!" Michelle cried, "Not soldiers! Maybe I should be out there findin' more of our kind."

Zeline sighed and shook her head. "I tink dat's a great idea, but mebbe it be too late for dat already. Asides, we got us a different plan. We just needs to save our one soldier so she can face up agin honey. Ya takes da head off da snake, and da body don't know what ta do. We only needs Destiny to defeat Honey."

"Maybe," Michelle said solemnly, "but I tell you, if I ever gets a chance, I'll kill her my own self with just my bare hands."

"Das another good thought you has daer," Zeline said, "but I tink it might be wiser if you kills her wit' your mind."

Michelle wrapped her arms warmly around Zeline and smiled weakly. "Yeah, you right."

Saunders walked briskly out of the morgue with his cell phone held firmly against his head. He knew that Flinch's secretary would never allow the phone to ring more than twice before he heard her soft, nearly monotone voice, "Major Flinch's office. How may I help you?"

"Millie, it's Captain Saunders. Do we have a dispatch that lists all the civilian respondents to ground zero?"

"Yes, sir. It came in this morning."

He wondered why he walked all the way to the morgue instead of taking the car and started to breathe heavily from his pace. "I need to see a list of all the ambulance services. Can you send a copy to my phone?"

"Sure. Is there a problem? Should I alert Major Flinch about anything?"

Saunders considered whether to tell Flinch yet. Flinch was pretty happy to have her body sent to the base. He wouldn't be pleased to learn that it was missing.

"Captain? Is there anything you want me to pass on to the Major?"

"Not just yet. I need to sort out a few things first."

Logan had a car delivered to the motel and when Johnson saw him get in the car and drive off alone, he thought Logan was bailing on them, but then, before he even had time to panic, Johnson saw him pick up Michelle down the street. He wouldn't do that unless he planned on going to the hospital. Johnson went to the concierge and asked, "Did he order just the one car or two?"

"Just the one, sir."

"He must have forgotten that we'll be needing a second car today. How long would it take to get one here?"

"We'll need your credit card to order a car, but it could be here in forty minutes."

"When Mr. Logan booked these rooms," Johnson said, "did he not tell you to take care of all of our needs and to put it on his tab?"

"He did."

"Well, I need a car. Have them deliver it to the hospital. I'll walk there."

The concierge glanced across the lobby for the hotel manager, but he was busy with a customer.

"What's the problem?" Johnson asked. "You were here when we checked in. I remember you. You heard him clearly tell you personally to take care of the entire group. I know you remember me. I saw how suspicious you were that I was with them."

"I'm sorry, sir. We can't authorize that without checking with him first."

"He's not the kind of man who likes to be disturbed," Johnson said, "but if you think he'll make an exception for you, you'll find him at All Saints hospital visiting his sixteen-year-old niece who is dying. I'm sure he'll appreciate the interruption."

The concierge picked up the phone and dialed the manager, who was still with the same customer. He turned his back towards Johnson and explained the situation, then turned back and said, "We'll take care of it immediately. I apologize for the misunderstanding."

This was not how Johnson wanted to start his day. "Remember," he repeated, "deliver it to the hospital. I'll get it there." He high-tailed it out of the hotel and double time marched the mile to the hospital.

"What now?" Balletina asked. "I've burnt down all these candles."

Honey laughed and said, "Don't forget about the bush you smoked way on the other side of the basketball court."

"I'm hungry."

"Me too!" Honey jumped up from the picnic table and said, "Let's go into town and get us some ice cream."

Honey led Balletina back through the gym and paused in the hallway, pointing to her right. "Is it this way?"

"Follow me," Balletina said as she pushed past Honey and led her down the hall to the main entrance.

Richard was in the parking lot overseeing the office furniture as the movers loaded it onto a variety of trucks.

Honey paused to watch with him and asked, "We're really leaving?"

"I think we have to," Richard said. "They're probably watching us right now."

Honey looked up, but only saw blue sky and a few wisps of clouds. "You really think they can see us with their satellite thingies?"

"I have no doubt that they are watching us right now," Richard replied.

"You mean they can actually see us? They can see my face and everything?"

"Yep," Richard said. "Your face and everything."

"Good," Honey said as she reached up and flipped off the sky. "Take a good look at this, you jerks!" Honey hooked her arm around Balletina's and said, "Come on."

Balletina paused after a couple of steps and asked, "If they can see our faces, don't you think they can see all those trucks?"

Saunders was grateful that the list of ambulances was short. Even better, only two of them had been to the scene of the battle, and of those, only one reported transporting a female. Unfortunately, that was where his luck ended.

"What?" he growled into the phone. "What do you mean, they are on administrative leave?"

"That's all it says in their file," the clerk said.

"Do you know where I can find them?"

"You tell me Captain."

"What's that supposed to mean?" Saunders asked.

"HR would probably have my butt for telling you this, but it was your guys that took them in for questioning. Next thing I know, they're on leave. We're a bit shorthanded and could really use them around here."

Saunders gripped the phone like he wanted to throw it, but stuffed it into his pocket before he gave in to that temptation. Whoever it may have been, it wasn't any of "his" guys, but he knew what that must have meant. Why would they think it was the government? Why would somebody be playing games with his evidence? Does the white house already know what these people are? Why would they still keep it a secret? Could the pentagon know about these people and still withhold what they knew from a soldier like himself that was actually there and had witnessed the whole thing?

Johnson was accustomed to long walks, or rather, long marches. It was just part of being a soldier, even a private soldier for hire, but the time that it took him to cover the distance from the hotel to the hospital gave him plenty of opportunity to worry that Logan might have dropped Michelle off and left already. He wondered if he should have just waited for the rental car and driven there, but covering the mile to the hospital took him far less than the forty minutes they said it would take to deliver a car, and as expected, he didn't see a rental vehicle waiting for him as he approached the main lobby, so he decided that he probably had made the correct decision. That left him wondering about Logan again, but as soon as he entered the lobby, he heard Logan yelling, "I don't care what your medical opinion is. That girl is special and you're not only going to continue caring for her, but you're going to up your game and do better than what I've seen so far!"

"I'm sorry," the hospital administrator said, raising his voice to match Logan's, "but we're not that kind of facility. We can refer you to several more suitable nursing hospitals."

"Where's the other guy? I want to talk to Barry."

"Barry's off today." The doctor stormed out of his office saying, "You're dealing with me now, and I'm transferring the girl."

Logan followed the doctor out to the lobby and said, "I don't think you know who you're dealing with here."

"Are you the president of the United States?" the doctor asked. "That might make a difference."

Logan saw Johnson in the lobby and called out, "Johnson? Come here. Doctor, I'd like you to meet one of my security experts. He is a fascinating character. Did you know that he was a sniper in the war? An assassin, to be more precise."

"Are you threatening me?" the doctor asked. He clicked his stethoscope on the reception desk and said, "Call security...and the police."

Logan jerked his head towards the corridor and told Johnson, "Get the girl."

"Me?" Johnson asked. "Can she travel?"

"Not her," Logan said, "the little redhead."

Johnson nodded and ran down the hall to the elevator.

Several tense moments passed with Logan and the new administrator staring at each other, trying to look more menacing than his opponent, before two uniformed security guards finally arrived in the lobby. The new hospital administrator pointed to Logan and said, "Get him out of here."

As the guards were still approaching Logan, Johnson returned with Ashlin. Logan pointed to the new administrator and asked, "Would you please explain to this man and his friends that your sister needs to stay and they need to take better care of her? Please explain it to him in that special way you did with the other man."

"What's this?" the doctor cried out. "Who is she and why is she in my ICU when she's clearly too young to be visiting? And why is he still here? I told you to throw him out!"

Ashlin liked being needed and said, with the voice, "Her name is Destiny and she's my sister. She's the most important person in the world to me and now she's the most important person in the world to you, too."

The doctor's face paled as the hairs on his neck prickled and his anus puckered.

Ashlin turned to the two guards that the doctor had called and said, "Your duty is to make sure that he takes care of my sister. Don't ever let him move her out of here. You will do anything to prevent him from moving her."

The leader of the guards went to the administrator and poked a meaty finger into his chest, saying, "You heard her. Take care of her sister."

The doctor swallowed hard and said in a raspy voice, "Of course. It's my job. You might even say that it's my life; my passion. Barry must not have done enough to help her, but I'll see to her care at once."

Logan had seen and heard it before, but he still watched with awe and wished he had been born to the other clan.

Johnson had seen it before too, and was glad to have helped, but he really wished that he didn't know about any of this.

Honey climbed behind the wheel of the limo.

"This?" Balletina asked without getting in. "This thing is your car?"

Honey smiled mischievously and said, "In a way, they're all my cars."

"It's kind of lame," Balletina said. "I mean, it's big and expensive, but it's still lame."

"It usually comes with a driver, but I didn't want anyone else to come along and spoil the celebration."

Balletina reached into her purse and pulled out a ring of keys. She dangled the keys in front of her and said, "We could take my car…"

Honey climbed out of the limo and asked, "Which one is your car?"

Balletina clicked the remote on the key ring and a black Audi chirped back at them.

Honey pointed to the racy little car and asked, "That's your car? It looks fast! Your daddy must be rich."

Balletina walked with exaggerated dance like steps to the car. "Almost all of us girls here are rich bitches. Most of the boys too, though some of them just have powerful fathers. Come on. Get in."

"Not me," Honey said as she slid into the leather bucket seats. "Like I told you, I come from a poor farming family."

Balletina pressed the ignition button, and the car roared to life. "That's rough. I don't think I have ever known one of our people that was a farmer before."

"They weren't my real family. I told you how my nutty grandma married us into them, although I have no idea why. I never knew my own pa."

"Why did she do that? Your grandma I mean. Couldn't she do better? I seen what your mama can do. Didn't your grandma have no powers? I would have thought that she would have better options than that."

"If my grandma had powers, we never knew it. Even my mama and me didn't know we had nothin' this special until recently, although mama says she started noticin' strange things when they first moved onto the farm, but it warn't nothin' like we can do now, and she could never find nothin' good to do with her powers. I mean, what's she gonna do? Hire herself out as a mobile battery charger?"

Balletina pulled the car out onto the road and squealed the tires, pressing both of them into the backs of their seats. "You both had powers on the farm?"

"Yeah, pretty much."

"Why didn't you just take your powers and leave?"

Honey pressed her face to the window and watched the world roar by. "Mama says that she tried that, before I was born, but every time she left the farm, she lost her powers, so she went back."

"That's pretty weird, but I guess I'd be willing to live on a farm too, if it meant having powers like yours."

"Not just a farm," Honey said. "Like I told you before, they was all witches on the farm, and we had to hide our powers from them, but mama fixed everything for us. She used her powers to put the old man that was the head of the family out of commission. She took control of the whole damned family after that."

"Aha," Balletina said. "I knew you'd have to embrace your heritage, eventually."

"Our heritage?"

"Yeah. I guess you don't know much about us since you grew up on your own. Our kind have always been the ones with the power; the ones in charge. That's kind of why they have us here in this old abandoned school. We're learning skills that let us infiltrate powerful businesses and the government. That's how we plan to control things without having our powers."

"So me wanting to take over the world is in my blood?"

"Hell yes!" Balletina pulled off the interstate and roared into town. "Here we are."

"This is it?" Honey asked, unable to hide the disappointment in her voice.

Balletina paused the car atop a hill that gave them a clear vantage over the small town, which consisted of about five blocks of enterprises, including a small strip mall. "It ain't much, but our people tend to keep these kinds of facilities in remote locations away from prying eyes. You should see the magic schools. They all look like summer camps and are way more remote than this."

"So, where do we go first?"

"You promised me ice cream," Balletina said, "but don't worry, it's my treat."

Honey didn't like feeling poor. She would have to do something about that.

CHAPTER 11

S aunders sat back on the edge of his desk, feeling more puzzled now than when he had left the morgue. He dialed the number for Flinch.

Millie's familiar voice answered, "Major Flinch's office. How may I help you?"

"Millie. Are we interrogating the emergency medics that collected you-know-who?"

"Not that I've heard of," she replied. "Do you want to talk to the major now?"

"Not yet," he said. "Have you heard any rumors about homeland sniffing around?"

"Why are you asking me? You do know that I'm just his secretary, don't you?"

"Don't be so modest, Millie. Everybody knows that you run the place. Let me know if you hear anything."

"I may be overdue for some leave," she said. "Flinch is going to have a cow if homeland swoops in and steals his thunder."

"Thanks Millie."

"Wait a sec," she said. "I almost forgot. An old army buddy of yours called looking for you. He said his name was Timmons, and that you toured Iraq together and he wants you to call him. He wouldn't tell me what it was about, but he said it was important."

Logan needed to get back to his people if he was ever going to learn anything about this orb that Blake was supposed to find, but first, he would have to say his goodbyes. He found a vending machine in one of the waiting rooms and purchased two coffees. They didn't look great, but they smelled like coffee, so he took them with him to Destiny's room. The women had been allowed back in her room again. "Ms. Boutin," he said quietly, "could I speak with you for a moment?"

Michelle joined him in the corner and asked, "Is something wrong?"

"No," he replied, "not really, but I need to go take care of some business."

He stood awkwardly; fumbling for the right words, then pushed one of the cups for Michelle and said, "Here, this is for you."

She accepted the coffee and took a sip, mostly just to be polite.

Ashlin snuck up behind Logan and asked, "Are you still going to take care of her?"

"Yes," he replied, "absolutely, but I won't be here to ride them."

Ashlin tried looking him in the face, but she had spent the entire night at Destiny's side and her eyes were glued to the remaining coffee that he still held in his hand.

Johnson heard his intention to leave and panicked that his car wouldn't be here in time, but as the shivers ran down his spine, his phone buzzed and a message read that a blue sedan was out front with the keys inside. The text included a five-digit code to unlock the door. He wondered if it was providence, or if the voices in his head had arranged to have the car delivered before Logan left.

"To be honest," Logan said, "I don't think I was all that effective in getting them to keep her here. In the end, it was the two of you commanding them to take care of her."

"The two of us?" Michelle asked while giving Ashlin the curious eye.

"You weren't here," Ashlin said.

"She was fantastic," Logan explained. "After the shift change, the new administrator wanted to move your granddaughter out of here, and he was even more insistent than Barry was. Anyway, the point is that I need to return to my office before someone discovers that I've been helping you."

"We understand," Michelle said. "Will we be seeing you again?"

"I don't know, but don't worry about the hospital bills or the hotel. I have already taken care of them both."

Michelle set the steaming cup down on a nearby table and took his free hand in hers. "Thank you for your generosity."

Logan caught Ashlin's interest in his coffee and handed it to her. "I didn't really want it, anyway. It's okay, I didn't drink any yet."

"I know," Ashlin said.

Logan's spine shivered as he realized how difficult it would be to keep secrets from them. He nodded his head to them and went directly out the door and down to the parking lot.

Johnson was already outside in the rental car, waiting for Logan to leave the Hospital.

Logan had said that he was returning to his office, but Johnson didn't actually believe him until he led Johnson onto the interstate and headed back towards Utah. It was a long drive to Salt Lake, if that was really where they were going, and the last time they made the trip, Logan flew. He didn't seem like the kind of man that would drive himself such a long distance, but here he was, behind the wheel on a highway that went from Cheyenne to Salt Lake, a trip that Johnson figured would be at least six hours. As they settled in to a cruising speed on the highway, Johnson was relieved for the opportunity that he had taken to sleep through the night, or this drive might have been a lot more difficult.

***

Saunders didn't like it. Why would Timmons want to see him now? With all this stuff going on? He hadn't seen or heard from Timmons in years; not since he retired from the army and went into private security. He wondered what in the world his old friend could possibly want, but as he looked up Timmons' number on his cell phone, his curiosity only grew. Timmons was listed under the recent calls that Saunders had made, but he didn't remember talking to him, let alone placing the call himself. He wondered if he should find a more private place for this call, but clicked the call button anyway and waited.

Someone picked up the call on the other end, but when nobody answered, Saunders timidly said, "Timmons?"

Timmons' voice sounded unusually anxious. ""Saunders? Is that you? It's about time that you got back to me."

"Sorry, Millie just told me you called. What's this all about? Why are you calling my superior? You should have called me direct if you needed something."

"Your cell number is listed as restricted, but that's not important. What the hell did you do to my boys?"

"What boys?"

"Don't play games with me. It's one thing if you have them sworn to secrecy about their op, but they sound like they got holes in their memory."

Saunders was getting even more confused. "What op?"

"Really?" Timmons yelled. "After all the shit that we been through, you're going to pull that crap on me?"

"Honestly, I don't know what you are talking about, and I'm not so sure that you should explain it to me on the phone."

Timmons was quiet for a moment, then simply asked, "Lunch?"

"Yeah," Saunders agreed. "Remember the same old spot?"

Timmons grunted and replied, "Yeah. The usual place."

"That was good," Balletina said as she gobbled up the last tip of the sugar cone and licked some of the ice cream from her fingers.

Honey smiled weakly, but she hadn't enjoyed the treat as much as she should have. She was supposed to be better than Balletina, but she needed Balletina to pay for her ice cream, and everybody saw that. It wasn't just that she felt poor; she looked poor too. Several friends had waved at Balletina when they entered the shop, and they all looked like they came from money. Honey looked like one of the locals, or worse even. When Balletina had to pay for them, Honey could feel all of Balletina's friends staring at her and whispering about how dreadful Honey's clothes were.

"What's wrong?" Balletina asked.

"Nothing."

"Awe, come on," Balletina prodded. "Didn't you like your ice cream? I can get you another, if you prefer."

"No!" Honey half whispered. "Don't do that."

"Then tell me. I can't fix it if you don't tell me what's wrong."

"Maybe I don't want you to fix it."

"Okay," Balletina said softly, "I didn't mean to upset you. Let's go shopping. There's a really cute little dress shop in this mall. I bet that would cheer you up!"

"No!" Honey said. "I don't want to go shopping!"

"What then? Is there anything that you do want to do?"

"Take me home."

"Really?" Balletina was crushed. "We came all the way out here just for ice cream?"

"What did you think?" Honey asked.

"Nothing," Balletina said, but her voice sounded like it was something.

"Tell me."

Balletina pouted. "It's just that I thought we would hang out together and I would let all those girls see who I was friends with."

"You what?" Honey sounded mad. "You came here to show off your charity case to your fancy friends?"

"My what?" Balletina cried.

"You heard me. I'm outa here."

Honey jumped up from the table and stormed out into the mall. She wasn't even sure if it should be called a mall; it was so tiny. She wanted to scream, but everywhere she looked, she saw people watching her. She followed the sidewalk down the row of shops and stopped when she saw a fancy dress in the window. "Now that," she said aloud, "is something a queen would wear."

Balletina caught up with her, breathing heavily, and asked, "Isn't it cute? You want it?"

"Of course I want it, but I don't want you to buy it for me."

"I don't know what's going on in your head," Balletina said, "but I never saw you as a charity case. You can't hold it against me just because my daddy has money, and yours doesn't."

"Why not?" Honey cried. "Your daddy has money. All your friends' daddies have money. Y'all are just oozing with money and I ain't got nothin."

"Nothing?" Balletina asked. "You got the one thing our daddies want more than anything. You got power; real power. My daddy would give you all his money just to do what you can do."

"Power ain't gonna buy me that dress!" Honey growled.

"Why not?" Balletina asked. "If you want it so much, why don't you just take it?"

Honey's mouth fell open. She wanted to yell. How dare Balletina talk to her that way? Worse than that...how dare Balletina be right about it? What's wrong with her lately? "You're right," she said softly. "I ain't been myself since Cheyenne. I been nice for some reason and that just ain't like me."

Honey sucked in her breath, then thrust her hands out towards the store window. The window shattered and triggered alarms as shards of glass rained all over the dress in the window, shredding it to tatters. "Oops."

"Maybe we should just go inside," Balletina said, "and find one in your size."

Logan made good time, and luckily for Johnson, he chose a large, busy truck stop to refuel. Johnson was able to keep his distance and fill up at the same time. Logan never bothered to stop at any of the rest stops, which was a huge relief to Johnson, who had worried about what he would do if Logan had decided to stop for a meal or take a nap. Johnson couldn't risk napping himself, or he might miss Logan leaving, but fortunately for him, that never happened. Logan drove straight through, stopping only for gas and once at a drive thru for fast food.

Johnson was surprised to see so many moving trucks when they finally arrived at the facility. If Logan had waited a couple more days, he might have missed them entirely. It worked out nicely for Johnson, however. The trucks made it even easier for him to park in a far corner and watch things from a safe distance, although he had his doubts that any distance could be considered truly safe.

Logan had barely left the hospital before Ashlin had started to worry about what the doctors would try to do without him around. She could always use the voice to control them, but Logan was a doctor and carried a certain amount of authority when he commanded them. It was good to have him around, especially since Captain Saunders wouldn't be returning anymore.

She slipped into an empty corner and closed her eyes. "Mr. Logan?" she thought. "Mr. Logan? Can you hear me?"

She sighed heavily and slumped into a chair when he didn't respond.

"Mr. Logan is not going to hear you like that," Tempest thought to her. "He can't. He's not a witch. It just ain't that simple."

Ashlin frowned. "I thought maybe since we could read their thoughts and Blake can even put ideas into their heads, that maybe it would be possible."

"We should be able to!" Michelle chimed in. "We should be able to talk to anyone! It's not fair!"

"And what about Johnson?" Ashlin asked. "Someone's been talkin' to him in his head and he's not a witch. How do they do that?"

"That's a good point," Tempest said. "There must be other ways, but I don't know any of them and we don't actually know who is talking in Johnson's head or even if they are really our friends."

"I bet the ancestors would know if there's a way," Michelle suggested. "Want me to go search the memories?"

"That's okay," Ashlin replied. "I'll do it. You stay with Destiny."

Blake cracked open one eye and peeked out at the hotel room from his bed. The slender gap in the hotel curtain glowed brightly, casting a warm light into the room. He had apparently slept much later than he had expected, but maybe that was a good thing. He lifted his head for a better look and rubbed the sleep from his eyes. Johnson's bed was made already, with a military style taught cover. "Johnson? Are you up already? What time is it?"

There was no response. Blake groaned as he swung his feet over the edge of the bed and sat up. "Johnson?"

The tile floor was cold as Blake stumbled into the bathroom. Johnson wasn't here. Maybe he had gone for breakfast. Blake knew that Johnson got his orders from a voice in his head. He had always assumed that it was a witch, but he didn't really know who it was, except, of course, that it couldn't have been Michelle. Whoever was in Johnson's head had an agenda for Johnson to help Blake, so it made little sense for Johnson to be gone.

The reflection that Blake saw in the mirror didn't look like someone who had slept enough. Even his barely there beard growth was beginning to show, but he didn't have a razor. He frowned back at the mirror, then threw on the same clothes that he had worn yesterday and headed for the dining area that he had seen just outside the lobby. Johnson was sure to be there. Blake could smell the pancakes and coffee from the elevator. A television high on the wall in the corner was tuned to the news, but the volume was too low for him to hear it. He counted only three patrons having breakfast, and Johnson was not among them.

Michelle wasn't there either, but Blake didn't even have to wonder where she was. Even without his witch senses, he knew that she had gone ahead to the hospital without him.

Johnson, on the other hand, wouldn't have gone to the hospital without him. It didn't make sense for Johnson to have left him behind, unless something had happened to him, or more likely, it was new orders from them. The Johnson that Blake had first met was all about Johnson. Everything he did was for his own benefit, but that was before. What Blake had observed since the incident in the bayou, and especially after Honey had emerged, was a man that only did what he was ordered to do. The fact that Johnson's orders came from a voice in his head might have been alarming if Blake weren't a witch and accustomed to such things. For him to disappear like this could only mean that something had diverted him away from here, and Blake was putting his money on new orders.

He didn't know why he felt so obsessed about Johnson's where-a-bouts, but something inside of him said that he would have to find him. He knew that his most important task was to find the orb, yet he felt compelled to track down Johnson first, and he was learning to trust his instincts.

The smell of the bacon made Blake hungry, but he didn't have enough time to eat, if he was going to track down Johnson. He grabbed a danish and a banana. The cream cheese in the center of the danish only made him hungrier. Johnson would have to wait, but finding him should be easy for Blake. He'd been in Johnson's mind before and had seen some of his deepest fears. Finding him wouldn't even be a challenge. Blake had plenty of time to eat. He returned to the self-serve table of assorted breakfast items and filled a plate with hash browns and scrambled eggs. The sausage and bacon were further down the line of warmed trays and were promptly added to his plate. He topped it off with some juice and found a private table.

As he nibbled on his bacon, Blake closed his eyes and pictured the one thing that Johnson feared the most. A picture of Johnson popped into his head. He was on the road in a car, and far past the hospital. Finding him was as easy as Blake expected it would be, but he would need some wheels. It was a good thing that Michelle was at the hospital already.

Michelle couldn't shake the notion that she wasn't doing enough; Honey was out there building an army while she was just sitting around crying over Destiny. She felt like she had to do something to help, but she couldn't leave the hospital. It might be possible, however, for her to leave the room as long as Destiny wasn't alone. She left Tempest in charge and went to the cafeteria, where she found a quiet spot in the corner. It stood against a large floor to ceiling window that looked out over a small garden where the leaves flickered in a slight breeze. Destiny had so much talent for traversing the memories. She could go when and where she wanted, but Michelle could only drift along until she found one that she could view. The war between the witches and sorcerers had raged on for centuries. There must have been witches in the past that had figured out how to kill a sorcerer and she wanted to learn how. She just had to find an assassin in the ancestral memories and learn their secrets.

She stared at the leaves in the garden as they flowed back and forth in the breeze. A glint of sunlight reflected off the dewdrops and flickered across her eyes. She felt the world shrink away from her until she was looking at it from down a long tunnel, then it was gone.

Killing a sorcerer wouldn't be easy. Witches have always been taught to live in harmony with nature and not to kill, but while that thought was still running through her mind, she realized how that wasn't really true. Wars had been fought between the clans since the beginning of time, with deaths on both sides. She had even killed small animals at times as part of her craft. Honey was nothing more than a filthy beast. She was vermin and if Michelle could sacrifice an innocent bird to help someone, then she could easily find it in her heart to eradicate a monster like Honey for the benefit of all mankind.

"It's not that easy to kill another person..."

Michelle was shocked by the voice in her head.

"These are dark secrets that can end a sorcerer's life, but they come with a cost, and it would be a price that is very dear to anyone who dares to wield them."

Michelle felt the memory tug her into it and found herself looking up into the gentle eyes of an old man. He had kind eyes that were surrounded by a wrinkled face with bushy white eyebrows framing them on the top. A great sadness lived within him as he gazed into her eyes.

"There is a reason that we teach our soldiers how to reflect and redirect the sorcerer's own magic. Dark omens surround the black arts. They cannot be cast without paying a great price."

"But, Grandfather, we are rich enough. We can pay any price." Michelle was shocked by the youthfulness of her voice as her host spoke to the old man.

He smiled sadly and shook his head. "The price I speak of is not a bounty that we can pay with gold. A payment of blood must be made. A life must be sacrificed."

"Fine," Michelle's young host said. "We can sacrifice a servant. They killed my father, so it is worth such a price to put an end to them once and for all. We need only kill their leader and the rest will wither away. Is that not true?"

The old man patted Michelle on the head. "A servant would be no price for you. It must be someone you cherish. You would have to sacrifice me."

Michelle gasped. "Why you? There must be someone else that I can sacrifice."

The old man's face saddened. "I see that just considering this has already cost you some of your humanity. I wish you were not so quick to sacrifice someone's life just because you did not care so much about them, but there is more. Doing such a terrible thing would take a mighty toll upon you, too. You would suffer for the rest of your life and beyond just for doing such a vile deed."

"But that is not fair! Why should they be able to kill us with no penalty to their souls?"

"You think they do not pay a price? I believe they must suffer greatly in the beyond."

"I hate them," Michelle spat. "I hate them all!"

The old man hugged her. "I will grant you that they can be very trying on our patience, but I have come to learn that they are not all alike. Some of them do not cling to their ways so dearly as others, and it is not healthy for us to hate all of them just for the actions of a few."

Michelle felt her host pout.

"Do not feel so bad," the old man said, "we will find a way to stop them. If it weren't for the burden that it would place upon your own soul, I would freely give you this spell and offer myself for your sacrifice, but I could not live with myself, even in the afterlife, if I had damned you to an eternity of suffering."

"Is that it?" Michelle asked, pointing to the parchment on the table.

"Yes," the old man said sadly. "Knowing what I have taught you now, do you still wish to gaze upon it or should you turn your back and forget you ever knew about it?"

"I can read it without paying the price. Can I not? I can know it without ever using it. Is that not true?"

Her grandfather sighed. Just letting her see it and know it already weighed heavily upon his heart.

Michelle read the scroll. A chill ran down her spine. It was both terrifying and empowering. It could be the turning point that saves the world in one single agonizing moment. She read it again, tucking it away into her memory, then slipped back into the void. She now had a terrible secret that could end Honey once and for all. The world would be a better place for it.

She returned to the cafeteria. Nothing had changed while she was gone, but her legs felt heavier and her knees buckled slightly, slowing her pace as she walked back to Destiny's room. What was she thinking? She would do almost anything to stop Honey, but what would be the price the old man had foretold? She would freely sacrifice her own soul to save Destiny, but what of the other sacrifice? She wanted Honey dead, but who else would have to pay a price with her? Who else did she hold so dear?

"You see that?" Balletina yelled over the noise of the alarm as Honey emerged from the dressing room. "They had your size, and it looks great on you."

Honey spread her arms and struck a model pose, showing off her new look.

The shop clerk smiled warmly, ignoring the broken display case in favor of the expensive dress, and even though nobody ever paid cash for such a pricey item, she asked the obligatory question, "Will that be cash or charge?"

"Let me see," Honey said as she held out her palm and produced a perfectly round ball of fire, "do you take fireball express?"

The clerk's face drained to an ashen white as she stepped backwards and bumped into a wall.

Honey shot the fireball into the alarm bell, bringing silence to the room.

Balletina laughed as she turned towards the exit. "Did you see the look on her face when you held up the fireball?"

"Yes!" Honey roared. "I think she peed her panties."

"Totally! I'm sure of it," Balletina said as she continued towards the door.

"Where you going?" Honey asked. "Aren't you gonna get nothin' for yourself?"

"Why?" Balletina asked. "You don't like what I got on?"

"Nah, you look fine. I just figured we were shopping and you might get something."

"I might still, but I'm waiting for the shoe store."

"Good idea," Honey said. "I think I need some new shoes, too. Something to go with this dress." She pushed a wave of force from her palms and blew open the shop's doors.

"Are you gonna teach me that one, too?"

"Sure," Honey replied, "but first you gotta master fire, then we'll see if you can do some other spells."

"Where'd you learn all this?"

"I learnt the fire on my own, but I stole the rest from my cousin."

"Your cousin?"

Honey stepped through the shattered doors and said, "Oh shit."

Balletina joined her on the sidewalk and saw two police cruisers with their red lights flashing. "Are they here for us?"

"Probably so."

One of the police officers pointed his gun directly at Honey and yelled, "Freeze!"

"Are you sure you want me to do that?" Honey asked. "Ain't y'all heard about what happened in Salt Lake and up in Wyoming?"

The police glanced at each other and swallowed hard.

Honey laughed and said, "I'm guessing maybe from the looks on your faces that you has heard of me." She produced a large pulsating ball of fire and said, "It's not too late for you to run, if you want. I'll let you go this time. You know, kinda like a head start."

The two cops looked at each other again. One of them shook his head no, but the other jumped into his cruiser and fired it up.

Balletina shot a fireball into the cruiser and yelled, "She said run, like on your feet!"

The terrified cop bailed out of the burning car and ran down the mall road with his partner close behind.

"Not bad," Honey said.

A tingle ran down Balletina's spine as her skin prickled with excitement. "Wow! What a rush! I never expected something like this to come so fast."

"I guess it's what we was meant to do," Honey said. "This is who we are supposed to be."

"Then why can't the others do it?"

"They will," Honey said, "but some of them might take longer. They don't got the gift same as we do. Now, where's that shoe store?"

CHAPTER 12

Ashlin couldn't shake the feeling that she needed to stay in contact with Logan, but she was unable to articulate why, even to herself, and she'd learned, especially since meeting Michelle and Destiny, to simply trust her instincts. Tempest had suggested that there may be other ways for a witch to contact a sorcerer, and she didn't mean with a telephone. If something like this was possible, then Michelle was probably right when she said that the answer would lie somewhere in the past with the ancestors.

She had barely opened her mouth to ask Tempest if she could be excused when Tempest smiled and said, "Go ahead, and good luck."

"Thanks!" Ashlin skipped out of the room and down the hallway to the waiting room. There were plenty of empty seats from which she could choose, but she didn't want just any seat. She had often wondered what she looked like when she visited the memories, but she didn't want to find out now by making a spectacle of herself in the middle of the room, especially in a hospital where somebody might try to revive her. Fortunately for her, there was a row of four empty seats that were back against the wall.

She settled into one of the empty seats and plunged directly into the void, swooping way back through the voices to where the memories were older and witches had all their powers. She wanted to close her eyes and let her feelings guide her, but this was the void and her eyes had little to do with what she saw there. In fact, there was little to see, but she heard the voices of the ancestors drifting past her. Voices filled her head and surrounded her like an angry mob rushing past her in all directions. There were too many for her to hear just one. She suddenly realized that she didn't even know what to listen for.

"Listen to the sound of my voice," she heard someone say. "What you are about to do is not much different from entering the void, except that you will be staying where you are while your spirit will go forth and walk someplace else in the world."

"What?" she asked, but the voice hadn't been speaking to her. She followed it into a memory and found a gentle old man with a scraggly white beard. He was a teacher, and it seemed like they always had long white beards. He was surrounded by students just a few years older than her age. They were gathered under the shade of a large willow tree that stood between the bank of a stream and a broad green meadow with a quaint little school building. Beneath the large shade tree was neatly manicured grass that reached all the way to the sandy shore that lined the river.

"Lie back," he said with a smooth, hypnotic voice, "and close your eyes. Feel yourselves sink into the grass and lie very still until you don't feel your arms and legs any more. The grass is a soft cushion that floats above the ground. It feels as soothing and calming as floating atop the peaceful waters of the river that flows next to us, slowly meandering along. Feel the river carry you downstream. You are not afraid. You trust the river and you know where it is taking you. Now, instead of entering into the void, which is a place for your mind to go, I want you to think of a real place that you wish you could visit right now. You can make it a very special place full of pleasant memories or you can even make it a place that you've never been, but you have had the fondest dreams about going there. Imagine now that the river is carrying you to that special place. I don't want you to just visualize that place. I want you to feel it, hear it, and smell it. Let that place surround you. In fact, if you put your feet down now, you can get up out of the water and walk around there. You're no longer here under the willow tree with your classmates; you are in that special place now. Go ahead. Explore."

The students' breathing fell into a soft peaceful rhythm. Ashlin watched them lying motionless in the grass as their instructor checked them, one by one, peeking into their minds to see where they had gone. "Jasper, you're just imagining that you are there. You must believe it in your soul or you will never break free of your earthly body." Ashlin heard him mentally check the other students and think, "Very good Raven. That's it Pern."

Ashlin had to see for herself and peeked into Raven's mind. Raven was at the base of a tall mountain, looking up at its towering peaks. Ashlin could feel the young witch gathering her strength and her nerves, then she leapt up off the ground and flew up the base of the mountain, skimming over the trees, climbing ever closer to the mountain's top until there was no more vegetation and only rocks and sand remained in their place. She laughed and giggled as she fluttered like a butterfly, free of the physical world, until she had reached the snow covered top and stood on the highest of the mountain's peaks.

It was the most exhilarating sensation Ashlin had ever known. She felt the freedom to go anywhere and see anything. This was something she definitely wanted to try for herself.

Saunders had already taken a table and ordered a coffee by the time his friend Timmons had arrived. He was the model of calmness as he quietly sipped his coffee, but on the inside, he was a jumble of emotions. He didn't like his friend questioning his integrity, but he was even more concerned that Timmons may have been onto something. Timmons wouldn't have doubted him unless something was truly out of place. The thought that his friend had suspected him of being involved with an op that he couldn't remember was troublesome enough, but the possibility that such holes might actually exist in his own memory was downright frightening, especially since circumstances had already led him to doubt his own recollection of the events. Saunders kept his eyes glued to the entrance, anticipating his friend's arrival, and hoping that he would have more answers for him than questions.

Timmons slipped quietly into the cafe and pointed to Saunders as he whispered something to the hostess, who grabbed a couple place settings and menus to bring to the table.

Saunders sucked in his breath. Timmons hadn't come alone. His palms were sweaty as he stood to shake his friend's hand. He swallowed hard, afraid that his voice would reveal the nerves within him. He put on a thin smile and said, "It's good to see you again, old buddy. Who's this?"

Timmons raised an eyebrow and asked, "What? Have you both been smoking the same hooch?"

Saunders didn't understand or appreciate the reference. "You know I don't do that shit."

Timmons took his seat and motioned for Milton to do the same. "I know, but I also know that the two of you have already met."

Milton shrugged his shoulders and shook his head. "I've never met this man before."

"Yes you have," Timmons said, "you just don't remember."

Now it was Saunders turn to raise his eyebrows and ask, "What are you insinuating?"

Timmons shook his head in disbelief and asked, "Are you seriously suffering from the same amnesia? What kind of super-secret shit have you gotten yourself into?"

"Don't ask," Saunders said. "Even if I understood what it was and tried to explain it to you, you wouldn't believe me."

"Try me."

"Honestly, I have more questions than answers, but have you ever heard the stories about how the Nazis were studying the occult, hoping to find a supernatural weapon?"

Timmons waited for Saunders to continue.

"Or how the Russians were experimenting with psychics to see if they could be weaponized?"

Timmons' eyes glanced over to Milton, then back to Saunders, but he said nothing.

"Well, it's something like that."

Timmons shook his head and said, "You gotta give me something more than that."

"I can't. If what you say is true, that I've met this young man before..."

"Milton," Timmons said. "I guess I should introduce the two of you. Captain Baylor Saunders, meet Andrew Milton."

Saunders gave Timmons a look that his friend understood, but Timmons only grinned back

"I don't know why I can't remember him," Saunders said, "but I guess that would be your explanation."

"That's not an explanation, unless you are trying to tell me that the occult erased your memories."

"I told you," Saunders explained, "that I don't remember anything, but I wouldn't rule that out. Maybe Milton remembers something."

"Andrew," he replied. "Call me Andrew. I wish I could remember something...anything, but what I remember makes no sense."

Timmons snickered and elbowed Milton. "That was a polite gesture of yours, giving your first name, but Saunders here hates it when anyone calls him Baylor."

"Of course I do," Saunders growled. "My father was a Baylor man, and he even named me after his alma mater, but I chose to attend Rice instead."

Milton whistled and said, "Aren't they..."

"Pitched rivals?" Timmons asked. "Yes, they are."

Milton shook his head slowly and said, "That must have made for an interesting household."

"It did..." Saunders said.

"But," Timmons interrupted, "it made it easier when Saunders told his father that he was going into the army instead of the seminary."

"It didn't make that one lick easier," Saunders growled.

"Sure it did. You had already broken your father's heart by going to Rice. Not going into the seminary was just a minor blow to him."

Saunders stared into his coffee and said, "I'm going to need something stronger to drink before we hold that conversation."

Timmons nudged Milton again and said, "Tell him the last thing you remember."

Milton cleared his throat and said, "Well Captain, may I call you Captain? It makes no sense, but I remember waking up in a parking lot. At first, I thought that maybe I was just hungover because of the wedding, but then I remembered that the wedding was a couple months ago. At least I think it was a couple months. I can't remember exactly when."

Saunders looked up from his coffee and asked, "You don't remember anything before waking up like that?"

Milton shook his head. "I remember receiving some orders, but I don't remember what those orders were or where they would take me. Everything is a blank until I woke up in the car."

"Tell him the rest," Timmons said.

"Jimmy, who I was teamed up with, had also fallen asleep. He woke up remembering the same wedding."

"From months ago?" Saunders asked.

Milton nodded his head and shrugged his shoulders.

"Whose wedding was it?"

Milton quickly responded, "Blake's."

"Who's Blake?"

Milton shrugged his shoulders. "No clue. Jimmy remembered that it was Blake and Destiny's wedding too, but neither of us could remember who they were, except that we also dreamed that she was in a hospital bed and Blake was visiting her."

"We?" Saunders asked. "You both had the same dream?"

"I talk in my sleep and he may have heard me."

"If you ask me," Timmons said, "it sounds like a posthypnotic suggestion, so I ask you again; what have you gotten my boys into?"

Saunders slowly shook his head.

Timmons rose from the table, but Saunders said, "Just one more question. Where were you when you woke up? You said you were in a car. Where was it parked?"

Milton stood up and said, "Devlyn Children's hospital. Does that mean anything to you?"

"What about you Timmons? Where did you send them?"

Timmons shrugged. "I gave them your number and told them to call you for their instructions. You wanted it that way. You only told me that it would be a guard detail to protect someone special."

Saunders didn't remember ordering a guard detail to Devlyn Children's hospital, but if he was trying to save the blond girl, it would have been at a hospital. "Thanks guys. I'll look into this and let you know if I learn anything."

Michelle felt unclean, but she knew that it was just in her mind. She settled into a chair in the back of Destiny's room, hiding the shame she felt, though she had no reason to feel so. Her mind held a dirty secret, but it was only that. She learned a spell that could work against Honey, but she couldn't use it. It would be unthinkable, yet she couldn't stop thinking about it. She scanned the faces around her, wondering who it would have to be, and if she actually dared to end Honey. She loved all of them.

The evil bit of knowledge was taking over her thoughts, but she knew that she couldn't keep dwelling on that dark spell, and leapt out of her chair barking, "Come on. Let's go find our Destiny."

"Find her?" Tempest asked.

"Dat boy said she be in her own world now. Iffin' she won't come to us, then we gots to go to her."

"His name is Blake," Ashlin said, "and you should be nicer to him."

"He was s'posed to be with her," Michelle growled. "He went with her to protect her, but where was he when she was fightin' her cousin all by her own self? You stay here and watch over her while we go finds out where her mind has made itself a home."

Ashlin did not want to be left out, but before she could object, Michelle said, "No! I don't want to hear none o' your excuses. You stay here while we go find her."

"You still think I'm just a little girl!"

Michelle sighed and hugged Ashlin, saying, "I don't rightly know if I truly believes dat, but I do know how you wants to be her sister and it's high time you started actin' like one."

"I thought I was," Ashlin pouted.

"Maybe so, but we cain't all go trapsin' off into da unknown. We needs someone to watch over her, and I selected you."

Michelle released Ashlin and led Tempest to the cafeteria. "I ain't got no candles, but I already found us a way to improvise."

"Yes, Mama."

Michelle picked the same table in the corner. A mild breeze blew gently through the lush green plants outside, making the dew on the leaves sparkle in the morning sun. "I'm gonna concentrate on dem leaves. Might be dey works for you, too."

Tempest's voice filled Michelle's head. "Hurry up Mama. I'm waitin' for you."

Michelle glanced over at her daughter, who was already in a trance, then slowly shook her head, wondering what life would have been like if Tempest had ever accepted her training. She turned her head towards the leaves and breathed in shallow drafts as she felt the world fade away, only to be replaced by the void and Tempest.

Tempest called out into the void, "Destiny? It's Mama. I'm coming to visit you."

"I be here too," Michelle said. "Is you gonna come show us da way?"

"Mama?" Destiny called out. "I can't believe you came to visit me!"

"Of course I came to visit you," Tempest replied.

"Especially," Michelle added, "since you ain't been comin' to us."

Michelle and Tempest felt something tug at their bellies as Destiny pulled them through the grey expanse and into her world until the void was replaced with a brilliantly lit meadow.

Michelle landed just ahead of Tempest. She fell to her side and grunted.

Tempest landed on her feet and quickly offered her mother a hand getting up. "Are you okay Mama?"

"I be fine," Michelle panted as she climbed to her feet. "I just has the breath knocked out from me."

"Would you look at this place?" Tempest said. "It's a damned site better than the prison I cooked up for myself."

"Don't you get to likin' it too much," Michelle said as she looked around at the surroundings. "A prison be a prison, no matter how fine it be, and dem storm clouds don't look too friendly to me."

"I was locked away in a mental hospital. It was horrible."

"I knows that," Michelle said. "I ain't gone senile yet."

"That's not what I mean. I'm talkin' about what I cooked up inside my mind. Destiny came in and found me hiding in my own mental hospital. It was a damned prison of my own making."

"It's true," Destiny said from behind them. "Hi Mama."

Tempest turned slowly, afraid she would shatter the magical connection to this place if she moved too abruptly. "Baby."

Destiny had no such fears and leapt to hug her mother. "You look real good Mama. Are you feelin' better now?"

"Much," she said. "It seems that I have adopted another daughter, and she's been a huge help to me."

Destiny looked confused and Michelle said, "She be talkin' about your new little sister Ashlin, but I spect dat Zeline done had a hand in your mama's recuperation too."

Destiny released her mother so she could hug Michelle. "Nana. I'm glad you came too. This way I have both my mama's together. Come see my new home."

"I think that's a good idea," Tempest said as she watched the lightning emanating from the distant thunder clouds. "We should get inside before those storms move in."

Destiny looked right and left, but didn't see any storm clouds.

"Wait a minute," Tempest said as she recognized the bewilderment on Destiny's face. "You don't see them?"

Destiny just shrugged and led them out of the meadow to a narrow gravel path.

Michelle saw the clouds, but preferred changing the subject since Destiny seemed unwilling to discuss them. "Oh!" she said, pointing down the hill. "Would you look at that? I thought you'd be all alone. I didn't expect to see a whole town."

"It's not really a town," Destiny said, "but it could be if I could only get some neighbors to come live here with me. Those homes are all empty for now."

Michelle swallowed a tear. Destiny still thought that all of this was more than just a memory.

"It's not a memory," Destiny said. "It's a dream world. There's a difference. Mala, my teacher from the past, used to make these for my lessons. She was real good at making them."

Michelle smiled politely, but said nothing.

"If you know that it's just a dream world," Tempest offered, "then why do you insist that you can't leave this place?"

"It's not just any dream world," Destiny explained. "It's a very special dream world. This is my final resting place. At least, I think it's final. It could just be a temporary waiting stage, but I don't know why I would have to wait like this, unless I'm being tested or something. Anyway, it seems that I can do whatever I want to make this place feel like home. The only thing I can't seem to do is make more people. I don't think that even Mala could do that." Destiny paused for a moment as her face brightened immensely and she shouted, "I know what I should do! I should invite Mala to come live here!"

Destiny skipped down the path. Below the hill, before they entered the neighborhood, the path widened to a road that was bordered by tall hedges. "My house is right here," Destiny said, pointing to the right. "It's the first one on the right, but I suppose that I could choose any house that I want, at least, that is, until I get some people to move in with me."

At the end of the hedge, a white picket fence bordered a small lawn with a stone walkway that led to a cozy cottage with large picture windows and flower beds on each side. "I could totally live in any of the bigger houses, but this one's about the same size as our home in Cricket Bend."

"It be charming," Michelle said politely.

"Mama!" Tempest elbowed Michelle and whispered, "Don't encourage her."

Destiny sighed. "It's okay, Mama. I expected that you wouldn't accept that I'm gone so easy. Blake couldn't neither."

"Just like you couldn't accept that I was lost," Tempest said.

"You was just hiding," Destiny said. "You weren't blown up like I was."

"But you…"

Michelle interrupted Tempest as she crossed the threshold and said, "I love what you've done with the place."

Tempest glared at her mother, but said nothing.

"You want some tea?" Destiny asked. "I can whip up some cookies too, if you like."

"Tea would be fine," Michelle said as she toured the cottage and admired the pictures on the wall. "I remember this one. Isn't that the party at Mrs. Planchette's?"

"Yup," Destiny confirmed. "You was quite a hit at that party."

"Oh yeah?" Tempest asked. "What did my mama do? Did she have a bit too much to drink?"

"No," Destiny replied. "Nothing like that. Nana read the bones and predicted that strangers were coming to the bayou and someone was going to die."

"Funny," Michelle said, "but I don't remember nobody takin' pictures."

"Don't be silly," Destiny said. "It's a dream world. Do you really think that I can't conjure up a picture from my memory?"

Michelle frowned. Destiny was accepting this fate far too easily, and it wasn't even her true fate.

"You're just in denial," Destiny said. "You just need more time to accept that I'm dead."

"But you're not dead," Tempest said. "Your body lives. It's just waiting for your mind to return to it."

"Come home to us," Michelle pleaded.

"I am home," Destiny said. The humor had left her voice, and she started to cry. "Maybe you should go now."

Something burned inside Michelle's heart. Regardless of whether or not Destiny had crafted this prison in her mind on her own, it all boiled down to something that Honey did and if Destiny wasn't going to return with them to deal with Honey, then she might have to do it herself. "Okay," she sighed, "We's goin', but we ain't givin' up so easy."

Blake felt like he hadn't eaten in forever and wolfed down the sausage links and strips of bacon alongside his Belgian waffle. He felt the distance growing between himself and Johnson and questioned his decision to take time to eat, but weighed that against his ability to track him. Regardless, he couldn't let Johnson get too far ahead, so he forced himself to stop eating before any more time was wasted. He wouldn't even be able to hit the road until he found a car that could catch Johnson without drawing too much attention. The parking lot had a variety of different vehicles, but he was searching for a plain-looking car. He passed a couple of subcompacts, fearing that they wouldn't be fast enough, but found a non-descript older car that looked up to the task. He reached into the tumblers of the door lock and heard Michelle scolding him for his life of crime. She wasn't really in his head, but she had planted the seed of a conscious in his mind and he imagined all the things she would have said to him. He pushed her from his mind and proceeded to turn the tumblers of the lock.

"Hey buddy," a man said as he approached Blake from behind.

Blake should have felt his presence, and might have if he hadn't been obsessing over what Michelle would have said to him. He turned his head to see a short stocky guy in his early thirties.

The stranger pointed to the car and asked, "What're you doing?"

Blake's hand was cupped like he was about to grip a door knob. His palm faced the lock, but he wasn't actually touching the car yet. "Me? Nothing."

"It don't look like nothing."

"Well," Blake explained, "it's nothing that you would believe then."

"How about you go do nothing to someone else's car?"

"Is this your car?" Blake asked as he relaxed his hand and stood up straight. "Sorry. I'll go try someone else's car."

Blake started to walk away when the man said, "Wait. What are you going to try on someone else's car? What were you doing?"

"If you must know," Blake said, "I was asking your car to open its door for me."

The man wasn't sure if he should laugh or hide.

"You don't believe me?"

"Sure," the man said. "I believe you."

"No you don't. I told you that it was something that you wouldn't believe."

The man clearly looked at Blake as if he were crazy. "I believe that you were trying to do that at least, and maybe you even believed it yourself."

"Wanna see?" Blake asked.

"I don't have time for this. Go be crazy somewhere else."

Blake held up his empty hand, but placed the image of five one hundred-dollar bills into the man's head. "I got five hundred dollars that says I can do it."

"No way," the man said. "I'm not falling for that. My daddy taught me that if a stranger comes up to you and bets you that he can pull a mermaid from his ear, not to take the bet cause sure as sure, it was a trick and he was going to do it."

"Oh," Blake said. "I get it. You don't have five hundred dollars."

"Do I look like I would walk around with five hundred bucks on me?"

"Tell you what," Blake said. "If I can't persuade your car to unlock itself for me, then you can have everything that is in my hand, but if it opens up for me, then you have to drive me to Salt Lake City."

The man paused a moment, then pulled out his car remote and made sure the doors were locked. "Okay, then. You got a bet, but no touching the car and no using any tools on it. Do like you said and just ask it to open up for you, but keep your hands where I can see them."

"It's a deal," Blake said. He turned back to the car door and held both of his hands in plain sight while swiftly turning the tumblers to unlock the door. He reached out and with one finger, pulled the door open and put the imaginary money back into his pocket, saying, "I guess I get to keep these."

"How did you?" the man asked while scratching his head. "Never mind. I should have listened to my father."

"So you'll take me to Salt Lake?"

"Sure kid. A bet's a bet. Besides, I got family near there that I can go visit. Hop in."

Zeline felt the anger growing deep within Michelle's heart. She grabbed Michelle by the wrist and said, "Come on. Let's you and me go for a walk."

Michelle looked at Zeline like she was completely crazy. "You know I cain't leave."

"Sure you can," Zeline pleaded. "It don't matter how far we is from her. We be connected in our heads and in our hearts."

"Dat may be, but I cain't…"

Zeline leaned in close so she could whisper. "You gots to. You is emanating an aura of bad feelings all over da hospital. I needs you to go somewhere where you kin clear yo' head or you is gonna affect all da sick folks throughout da whole damned building with your bad juju, and you ain't doin' Destiny no good neithers."

Michelle sighed and rose to follow Zeline. She was right, although Michelle didn't know if a walk would be enough to lift her spirits.

"I heard dat," Zeline said. "Could be we finds ourselves sumpin' to eat."

"Eat?" Michelle asked. "I was thinkin' more of a stiff drink."

"Lord knows I could use a little spirits," Zeline said, "but I tink we needs to keep our wits about us."

Michelle sighed and said, "Yeah. You right again. So what does we do now?"

Zeline shrugged as she led her down the hallway, away from Destiny. "I don't know just yet, but I knows that you ain't doin' no good spreading those bad vibes in her room."

"That's the problem," Michelle said. "I ain't doin' nothin' to help nobody."

"Then lets you and me go do somethin'. What kin we do?"

Michelle thought about it while they were waiting for the elevator. She couldn't share what she learned about the dark spell, but there were other things. "Remember the party when I read da bones and said dem evil men was comin'?"

Zeline grunted as they stepped into the lift. "You sho hit dat nail smack on da head wit' dat one."

"Well, I done some things after that. I set up a bon-fire and burned herbs to keep dose men away."

"Too bad it didn't work none."

"But it did," Michelle said, "for a spell at least. It kept 'em at bay for a bit, and when they did come, dey was just a bit timid at first, but dey overcome da effects in da end. It was da boy dat come first, and he was affected da most. Could be dat's why he turned on dem others."

"Mebbe," Zeline said, "but I 'spect Destiny had a hand in turnin' him."

"Yeah, you right. But he had him some nasty dreams before dat."

The doors opened and Zeline swiftly led Michelle towards the main entrance. "I is all for settin' up some defenses, but I hopes you ain't suggestin' dat we makes a bonfire in Destiny's room."

"No," Michelle said as they stepped out into the fresh air, "but I done other things too."

They reached the parking area, but Zeline didn't stop there and led them across the street to a grassy area. "Is you gonna tell me what dem other tings was or not?"

"I made talismans from ancient bones and other relics."

"What tings did they do for you?"

Michelle sighed and said, "Nothing."

Zeline saw past Michelle's pouting and said, "Is you blind or sumpin'? Even if dem talismans didn't ward off dose evil men forever, dey still did sumpin' powerful good to your heart. I say we makes up a whole mess of 'em to hang around her bed."

Michelle was caught up in her excitement for a moment, then crashed back to reality. "We cain't. All my relics got burnt in da fire. Even if daer was some left, dey would all be back in da bayou."

"What you tinkin'?" Zeline asked. "You tink my granddaddy's voodoo never used no relics to make tings? I jest has to go shoppin' for some supplies."

"Dis ain't Cricket Bend, you know."

"I knows, but I kin find us what we need."

Michelle's spirits lifted. They had something to do. "Where do we start?"

Zeline smiled and said, "I don't tink I could ever explain some old white woman where I's goin'. I tink just knowin' how we's gonna do sumthin' is already makin' you well enough to go back and sit with Destiny. I'll be back soon enough."

Chapter 13

Saunders had questions that he desperately wanted answered, but he couldn't ask them over the phone, especially if the NSA had become involved. He had to go to the hospital and speak with the staff there. He wanted to look directly into their eyes when they saw his face to know if they recognized him. One thing was certain as he approached the campus; he didn't recognize the hospital by either name or by sight. He pulled into Devlyn Childrens' parking lot and sat for a moment, hoping anything about the hospital would register as a familiar memory, but he swore to himself that he had never been there before.

The front entrance had tall glass walls surrounding the double man-trap doors, but that described a lot of modern hospitals. He could see easily into the lobby, but recognized nothing inside. The parking lot around him was equally unfamiliar. He scanned the perimeter, desperate for anything that might trigger a memory, but even the smell of the lot was unfamiliar to him. He paused as he approached the automatic doors when an ambulance pulled out from around the corner and left the premises. A small grunt escaped from his throat as he turned to watch them leave. If he had brought the girl here, it would have been in an ambulance, and not through the main entrance. He followed the sidewalk around the hospital to the emergency room entrance. The main doors were for emergency personnel and gurneys only, but a waiting room stood to the left of those doors.

An admitting nurse sat behind a counter on the far side of the emergency waiting room. Would she recognize him? What would he have to do to get her to reveal whether he had been there before? She smiled at him before he had even reached her and shouted, "Captain! I was wondering when you would get here. You can go on up if you want."

Saunders smiled back at the unfamiliar receptionist and pointed meekly up in the air.

"Yes," she said with a bright smile. "Just follow the hallway and take the elevator to the third floor. You can't miss it."

The hair on Saunders' nape prickled as he walked down the hall, still hoping to recognize something.

Balletina pulled her car back into the compound's parking lot and maneuvered around the moving trucks, unable to find a spot as close as she usually parked. "That was fun."

"Yes it was," Honey replied. "I think that was just what I needed to start feeling like my old self again. Go ahead and pull the car up front in one of the reserved spots."

"Which one?"

"Whichever is closest."

Balletina pulled forward and frowned. "Most of the good spots are blocked by the moving trucks."

Honey twisted her jaw sideways as she thought about the scene outside and said, "I may have to do something about that."

Balletina's eyes lit up. "Are we gonna blow one of them up? Or maybe crush it and brush it aside?"

"No," Honey said laughing. "They got all our stuff in them, but I am gonna talk to Richard about whether we really want to move."

Balletina circled around the trucks and parked the car next to the steps. The alarm chirped as the two of them bounded up the steps and marched victoriously through the main doors. Richard was in the hallway talking to her mother and Logan. Honey recognized Logan from when they lived on the farm and he had recruited them to spy on the Boutin family. She and her mother didn't even know about witches and sorcerers at the time, but he must have already known about them, and he paid the two of them handsomely for anything that they learned.

Honey marched straight up to him and asked, "Where the hell have you been? I thought you was dead."

"Not dead," Logan said. "I've been following the witches around and spying on them."

"By yourself?" Honey asked. "Why didn't you just send someone?"

Logan had never been more relieved that his people didn't have the witches' gift to read minds and recognize lies. "I had to move fast. You had just emerged with your new powers; that was really something by the way, but it didn't leave me much time to organize a team to follow them. I must say, I am really impressed with what you did. I always knew you were special from the first moment I saw you and your mother."

"About that, how come you never told us that they was witches?"

"I wanted to, especially since you were showing some signs of our ancient powers, but I didn't think you would believe me at the time."

Honey nodded her head and said, "I spose it would have sounded kinda crazy."

"Anyway," Logan continued, "after your fight with Destiny, the witches were on the move, and so were you as I recall. I didn't want to risk losing them, so I followed. Who else could I trust with something so important, anyway?"

"Yeah," Honey said. "I been noticin' that not everyone here is up to the tasks that need to be done. Richard? Can I talk to you?"

"Now that Logan's back," Richard said, "I think you should talk to him. He's my boss."

"And I'm your queen," she said flatly.

"It's okay," Logan said. "I can see that you are busy moving the compound. This is no time to interrupt your work just because I'm back."

"That's what I want to talk to you about," Honey said. "Why are we moving again?"

"Because you've announced yourself to the government and they're probably watching us right now with their satellites."

"And you think you can move us to someplace new without their space spies following us?"

"Maybe we should talk in private?"

"No," Honey said. "Like you said, Logan's your boss. He should hear your plan."

"I've hired a lot more trucks than we need just to relocate. My plan was to send them all over the country. They don't have enough satellites to follow all of them. With luck, the real trucks would sneak away."

"It's not a bad plan," Logan said. "It might work."

"With luck?" Honey asked. "What happens if we decide to stay?"

"They'll watch everything we do, meaning, they'll watch you train your army. Even if you train them inside, they'll use infrared cameras to see what you're doing."

"So we won't be a secret," Honey said. "We already aren't a secret."

"Eventually," Richard said, "they'll get up the nerve to bomb this place to shreds."

"They'll need congressional approval for that," Logan said. "That will take time, and I doubt they could keep that a secret from the media."

"How much time?" Honey asked.

"Months at least," Logan said. "Perhaps six to nine months. It would not be an easy sell for the army to bomb an old school on American soil."

"Maybe not so long," Richard said. "You pulled down a high rise, remember?"

Honey smiled wickedly. "Yeah, I remember."

"And," Richard continued, "even if they had to wait for approval to bomb the place, they could mount a police action by combining forces with the national guard and the FBI without waiting so long."

Logan nodded his head. "He's right. They could send in ground troops and hope to keep it secret."

"We'll do whatever you want," Richard said.

"What I want," Honey said, "is to attack them again before they find their balls and try to attack us."

"Alone?" Richard asked. "Without training your army?"

"Not alone," Honey said. "If you bring me the right recruits, it won't take that long. Balletina? Show them a fireball."

Balletina stepped into the group and produced round pulsating globe of fire in her palm.

Logan swallowed hard and felt the sweat gather in his palms.

"What about your cousin?" Richard asked.

"What about my cousin?" Honey parroted Richard. "Master spy? What's up with my cousin? Is she dead?"

"The doctors say that she is gone, but they're keeping her body alive with machines. Her family insists that she can come back. They are trying to locate some ancient artifact that is supposed to save her.

Remember that the witches have the gift of healing, but they don't think they can heal her without finding this thing first."

"Send someone to keep an eye on them," Honey said. "Let me know if they find their thingy."

"Actually," Logan suggested, "I was thinking that maybe I should go and try to find it before they do. For all we know, it might even be in our possession already. We do have a lot of stuff hidden away around the world."

"I like that," Honey said. "No wonder you're the boss, but did you say you wanted to do that yourself?"

Logan patted Richard on the back and said, "Richard seems to be doing a fine job as my lieutenant, and I have gotten to know these witches pretty well. Besides, I think I know what they are looking for, and if we do have it, it may take someone with very high clearance to access it; someone like me."

"Okay then," Honey said, "but let us know how it's going so we don't think you're dead this time."

***

Saunders' mind reeled from his confusion, or maybe it was just the motion of the elevator as it rose up to the third floor and came to a stop. He hated the feeling that someone may have messed with his mind and he wanted to know the truth, but that also meant that he didn't know what he was getting into. His heart raced as he stepped out into the hall and looked right and left for anything familiar, then randomly turned to his right and headed for the nearest nurse's station. He barely took two steps before a nurse called from behind him, "Captain! You're late. We were getting worried that you weren't going to make it."

His heart skipped as he spun around and asked, "You were expecting me?"

"Of course we were expecting you," she said as she took his arm and started leading him the other direction down the hall.

"Then you know me?"

The nurse stopped and looked at him curiously.

"I'm sorry," he said. "I know that it must sound very strange, but I don't remember you."

"That's okay," the nurse said slowly, "because I don't think that we've ever met before."

"But, you were expecting me?"

"Of course we were," she said while forcing a nervous smile. "The children are especially anxious."

"The children?"

She took a step back and asked, "Aren't you here for the army's special youth corps?"

"The army's what?" He shook his head slowly and continued, "No, I'm here looking for a girl who might have been brought in a couple days ago."

The nurse breathed a heavy sigh of relief. "That certainly explains the confusion. I was wondering why you were coming up through the emergency room elevator. The base usually sends over an officer every other week to read to the children, but we haven't seen anyone today. I'm sorry, but when I saw your uniform, I just assumed that it was you."

"Well," Saunders explained, "things have been a little busy at the base these days. They may not be able to spare anyone at the moment."

"That's too bad. The kids will be disappointed. Well, I won't keep you any longer. Good luck finding your girl."

"Thank you." Saunders said as the nurse turned to return to her station. Saunders looked back down the other side of the hall, but he still didn't know where to go, and turned back towards the nurse and asked, "What do they read?"

She paused and replied, "Children's stories. Mostly inspirational hero stories about how they can overcome adversity. Why?"

Saunders smiled and shrugged his shoulders. "I guess I can spare a few minutes."

The nurse smiled brightly, pointed down the hall and said, "This way."

Saunders double timed to catch up with her. "I'm Captain Saunders, but you can call me Baylor."

<hr>

Blake pulled the seatbelt around his waist and fastened the clasp. "My name's Blake."

"Carl."

Carl started the car and pulled it out of the parking lot and headed for the highway. "So, you gonna tell me how you did that?"

"What?" Blake asked. "The lock? You must know that a magician can never reveal his secrets."

Carl laughed with Blake, but he couldn't push it from his mind. It had to be something technological. Maybe Blake had some kind of master unlock transmitter hidden in his pocket, except Carl could see his hands the whole time.

"So," Blake said. "You said you have family in Salt Lake?"

"My older sister and her kids. You?"

"Nothing like that. My girlfriend's cousin is there, but I don't have any real family waiting for me."

"Your girlfriend's cousin?" Carl asked. "You stepping out on your girlfriend? With her cousin?"

"With Honey? No way. We hate her."

"Honey?" Carl asked. "Is that really her name? Sounds like a stripper."

"She dresses like one too. She's in the area, but I'm not going there for her. I'm catching up with a friend there."

Carl waited to see if Blake would volunteer any more details about why he was going to Salt Lake where his girlfriend's cousin lives and dresses like a stripper, but Blake said nothing.

A pot hole in the road jarred the vehicle with a loud thump and the passenger mirror started to flutter. Blake pointed and said, "Your mirror's loose."

"Yeah, it does that. Ignore it."

Blake couldn't ignore it. He thought at first that it might pop free from the mirror cowling and fall to the street, but it only fluttered. As it vibrated in the wind, Blake saw the world outside as a blurry streak. The colors blended together and reminded him of the void. The blur spread outward from the mirror until it consumed the whole world and surrounded Blake with a miasma of colors. It was very much like the void that Destiny had introduced him to, but their void was calm and peaceful while this image was harsh and chaotic. Blake's mind wobbled as he was swept up into the cyclone of colors. His vision narrowed until the world around him turned black with him falling through the inky darkness until he landed on the ground with a thud and rolled to his side.

If it weren't for the ground below him, he wouldn't have known up from down. He climbed to his feet, and the blackness remained around him, except directly in front of him where a faded patch of grey appeared and morphed into the form of a man in a grey hooded robe.

Blake raised his hands towards the hooded figure, preparing to strike him with lightning.

"Fear not young Blake," the figure said to him. "We are not your enemy. I have come here to warn you."

"Warn me about what?"

"You should not follow Logan today."

"I'm not following Logan," Blake said. "I'm following Johnson."

"Johnson is keeping an eye on Logan for us, so you may rest easy now and turn around to return to your destiny."

"You're the voice in Johnson's head?"

Blake saw the grey hood dip as the man inside nodded his head. "I am one of them."

"Well, I'm not like Johnson. I don't like being told what to do."

"Or what not to do," the figure said. "Yes. We know this about you."

"And yet, you still come to me in a dream and tell me what not to do?"

"You play a vital role in what is to come," the figure said. "Surely, he has told you this already."

"Who?" Blake asked. "Johnson?"

"No. We bring you this warning on behalf of our master..."

"Oh," Blake interrupted, "you must mean The Old One."

The librarian cringed and replied, "He is not our master, but he is special to us and I doubt that he would appreciate you calling him that."

Blake laughed and said, "I know. I think Destiny said that they called him The Great One."

The hooded figure laughed with Blake and said, "Actually, he doesn't like that title either. He has told you that you are the one to save her?"

Blake grew suspicious. They knew too much, yet they seemed to be fishing for details. "He said I had to find something."

"Of course," the figure said. "You are to find the orb."

"But you just told me that I should return to Destiny."

The figure shook his head and said, "Not to her, but to your true destiny; the path that lies before you that you are destined to follow."

"Finding the orb?"

"Yes," the figure said with a nod. "Finding the orb."

"I don't suppose you know where it is, do you? Because as far as I know, it may be in this direction where Johnson is following Logan."

"Following them would not be wise."

"You didn't answer my first question. Do you know where this mysterious orb is?"

"We cannot tell you that."

"You cannot?" Blake asked. "Or will not?"

"We only came here to warn you that where you are headed is very dangerous."

"Of course it is," Blake said snidely. "Everyplace is dangerous. Thanks for the warning, but I think I should be going now."

Blake popped out of the vision and returned to the passenger seat. He was tired of other people pushing their agendas onto him like their problems should be his own problems.

"You okay?" Carl asked.

"Yeah, I'm fine."

"You don't look so good. You sure you don't want me to turn around?"

"No," Blake said, more than a little irritated. "I told you I'm good."

"It's just that my daddy always told me that if a thing wasn't meant to be, there was no good in forcing it."

Blake looked out the window and absently mumbled, "Mhm."

"I mean, this whole trip seems kind of weird. It's not giving me a good feeling about what we're doing."

"I'm fine. You're fine. Let's just not worry about it."

Carl sighed and shrugged. "If you say so."

"I just did."

"Yeah," Carl said. "You said the words, but I'm not so sure I believe you. Heck. I doubt that you believe yourself."

Blake shook his head. He hitched a ride with a crazy person.

"I didn't want to tell you this," Carl said, "because some people get spooked, but I'm kind of psychic about these things. My gut is doing flip-flops right now. Something bad is going on and we're heading right for it. I should turn around."

"I didn't want to do this," Blake said. "I'm really trying to be a better person, but you're forcing me." Blake peeked into Carl's mind and told him, "You're not afraid of anything about this trip, and if you ever start to feel afraid, just remember that you're more afraid of me, so keep driving."

Carl didn't bother him anymore after that.

———

Michelle had returned to her usual spot at Destiny's side while Zeline had been out shopping. A rage still boiled within her, but she fought to keep it bottled up while trying to offer some comfort to Destiny. She not only fought the awful anger inside of her, but she also struggled to keep her emotions hidden from her family and was greatly relieved when she finally sensed Zeline's return. She felt her approach the hospital long before she could actually hear her coming down the hall and waited by the door as Zeline approached the room. Tempest watched curiously as Zeline entered the room with a large bag that rattled and clinked as she shifted it from one hand to another. "Come on," she beckoned to Michelle as she went directly to the back of the room where two chairs sat in front of the window. Michelle nodded and followed her.

Zeline waited for Michelle to sit down, then placed the bag in her lap. "I tink I gots everything dat we might be needing."

Tempest just shrugged her shoulders and turned her attention back to Destiny.

Michelle dove into the bag and found bones and feathers along with an assortment of sticks made from different kinds of wood. The bag jingled as she dug through the sticks. She pulled out a bell and asked, "What's this?"

"It's a bell," Zeline said with an evil snicker. "You ain't never seen no bell before?"

"Of course I seen a bell before. You think dat I don't know what it be? I just don't know why you brung it."

"My granddaddy used bells and rattles all da time. If ya stops to ponder it, bells can be used as warnings or as signals to call for someone. I tink dat dey is good for wakin' up da spirits too."

"I guess," Michelle said, wondering what kind of a witch she was dealing with. She grabbed some yarn from the bag and immediately began lashing sticks together the way that she had been taught.

Destiny regretted sending her mother away, but she also didn't like her mother insisting that this was all in her head and that she could still leave this place. She understood that it might have been hard for her mother to give up on her, but she had hoped that her mother would have trusted her enough to believe her when she said that she was gone and just accepted what had happened to her. Destiny had never felt quite as alone as she did right now. She wanted someone to talk to. More than just what she wanted, she *needed* someone to talk to, but nobody wanted to listen to her and she didn't want to be lectured again.

She went to a quiet place near the house where she could sit and listen to the water gurgling in the stream while she leisurely wandered through her memories. There were so few sounds in this world that the small stream was one of her most treasured and tranquil places. She thought it was funny that the quietest place to think would be the one with the most noise, but it was practically the only sound here, and it was comforting. The sun filtered through the trees and glittered off the glistening rocks making it easy for her to visit the void. She liked to just float in the void and listen to other people's memories as they passed her by.

She heard someone mention Blake's name. There were probably millions of Blakes in the void, but she knew that this was about her Blake. She frowned as she remembered him. Their budding love hadn't even had time to blossom. They were soul mates, and had been so throughout time and through several lives, but this one was cut short. Perhaps the next one will fare better.

"I don't care if you are afraid of him, you need to turn the car around and stop Blake from going to Salt Lake."

Destiny peeked into the memory and saw the hooded figure peering into a fire. The sight of the grey hooded robes brought her blood to boiling. She felt the heat rise in her chest and in her cheeks. She didn't know who he was, but she recognized what he was. He was one of the librarians. They tried to kill her once before, and they succeeded at killing her mentor, Mala. She didn't even have to think about it. A fireball formed in her palm. She wrapped her fingers around it and massaged it, but she was only watching this scene unfold. Something was very different about this particular memory, in fact, it wasn't a memory yet. It was happening now, as she watched it, but it didn't include her. When she was alive, she could have traveled to them and done something to stop them, but she was stuck in the quiet little world where her house was.

Her peaceful spot by the brook suddenly felt damp and dreary. The librarians were messing with Blake's life now and she couldn't do anything to stop them.

Ashlin was anxious to try what she had witnessed in the memories, but she didn't want to appear too conspicuous. The students that she had seen in the memory looked almost dead as they lay motionless in the grass. If she looked like that in the middle of a hospital, someone was sure to resuscitate her and break the spell. She needed to find some place even more private than the waiting room. Fortunately, there was a small park across the street from the hospital. It had a few trees, and a manicured lawn with a jogging path. "Tempest? I'm going for a walk."

When Tempest didn't respond, she peeked into her mind and saw the turmoil that was stealing her attention. Tempest was doing as she was taught; focusing on a single voice, but this voice was a young girl crying. Ashlin could feel the overwhelming empathy that boiled up in Tempest's heart.

"Tempest? What's wrong?"

Again, Tempest didn't respond, but the little girl cried out, "I'm scared."

Ashlin felt a deep sorrow for the little girl, but she was too busy to help her now. Tempest should be able to comfort the little girl, and if Tempest needs any help, Michelle and Zeline are both there.

She left the hospital and crossed the street to a spot with soft grass under the shade of a large pine tree. Except for the jogging path that was in the place of the brook that was in the memory, it was a pretty good match for the small classroom that she had seen. The pine needles under the tree were slightly prickly, but they also added some spring to the grass. She lay back and stared up into the tree's branches for a moment before closing her eyes. The instructor had said to sink into the grass until you don't feel your arms and legs. She had to lie very still before she was no longer aware of her limbs. A serene quiet surrounded her like a blanket. This may not have worked if the nearby street had been crowded with motorists, but the silence filled her ears and was not unlike the moment when she crossed into the void, right before hearing the voices of the past. She imagined that she was floating in the water and focused on Logan's voice. She felt the world change around her, but when she opened her eyes, she didn't see Logan.

"You came!" the little girl exclaimed.

Ashlin sucked in her breath when she saw the swollen bruises that covered the girl's face. She was a very small girl in a very large hospital bed. A woman stood on the opposite side of the bed, crying softly into a man's chest. He held his arms firmly around her shoulders. Ashlin wondered if the woman would have remained upright without his support.

"What's your name?" the little girl asked.

"I'm Ashlin. What's yours?"

"I'm Patty, but my mommy always calls me Pumpkin. Have you seen my mommy? I'm afraid she might be lost."

Ashlin looked up to the crying woman and only then realized that she was only seeing her spirit. "Your mommy is here with you. She's very sad that you can't see her right now, but you should know that she is with you."

"Why can't I see her? Mommy?"

The woman left her husband's arms and tried to brush Patty's cheek.

Patty's father looked at Ashlin wondering how their daughter could see her and not them, but he wasn't angry.

"Can you feel that?" Ashlin asked. "Your mommy is caressing your cheek. Even though you can't see her, she is with you. Your daddy is here too."

"I love you Mommy."

Ashlin backed away from the bed so Patty's father could come around to this side.

"Wait!" Patty cried out. "Where are you going?"

"Your parents are both with you. I'm so sorry that you can't see them, but you don't need to be afraid anymore and I have other people to visit."

Patty sucked in her breath as her father kissed her forehead.

Ashlin felt like she was intruding and faded out of the room. She found herself staring up into the tree branches again.

Tempest's thoughts whispered in her head, "Thank you."

Michelle knew hundreds of patterns and started with some of the more common figurines. Her hands were a blur as she bound the sticks and bones together.

Zeline paused what she was doing to watch Michelle. "I knows that you done this recently, so you is practiced, but you looks like you kin do that in yo' sleep."

Michelle half-smiled and said, "I made me a whole mess o' dese when dem men was a-comin'."

Zeline pointed to Michelle's work and asked, "What is zat? It looks like a man."

"It is," Michelle explained.

"When my granddaddy made dolls, he used scraps of clothes and bits o' hair."

"If I ties a feather to da head," Michelle said, "it affects da mind. A chicken feather makes a man hungry, but a goose feather makes a man sleepy."

"Only men?"

"No," Michelle said, "women too, but I never had me many men comin' for my help agin no woman."

"Das a good ting," Zeline said, "dat dey works on women too, acause we ain't fightin' no men dis time." Zeline changed from tying figures like her grandfather had taught her and started copying Michelle's figures. She undid and redid her figures several times before she felt she had them right, then held it up to show Michelle, but Michelle didn't see her.

Michelle's eyes had glassed over, but her hands worked steadily, building a new figure on their own. It wasn't anything like the other figures that Michelle had made. Four long sticks were lashed together into a tall pyramid with bones providing cross beams for support. She hung a bell inside the structure and was apparently finished with it.

Zeline cocked her head to the side and asked, "Does dat mean sumpin' special?"

Michelle blinked as she returned from her altered state. "What was that?"

"I was askin' about da tower you built."

Michelle looked at the icon in her hands and shrugged her shoulders. She didn't know why she created a tower. "I tain't never seen nothin' like this afore."

"Best put dat one someplace safe," Zeline said. "If dat come to you in a trance, den it must have some powerful magic behind it."

<hr>

The sound of the tires against the road droned in Blake's ears. He leaned his head against the window and heard the road sound directly through his skull. Carl found a stretch of freshly paved black top that produced the soft kind of white noise that made sleep more attractive. Blake yawned and asked, "Hey, Carl? You mind if I close my eyes for a few?"

"Nah. Go for it. I'll let you know when we make a pit stop."

Blake let his lids fall shut and lazily searched for Johnson. Johnson wasn't moving anymore. He must have already arrived where he was going. Blake thought about peeking into Johnson's mind so he could see where he was at, but the soothing vibrations from the new road lulled him into a deeper sleep.

His slumber presented him with a dream in which he found himself on a long empty highway surrounded by the desert. Down the road, a stand of evergreen trees stood off to the side, in stark contrast to the flat desert around them. Blake stood in the middle of the deserted road that stretched off to the horizon in both directions. The other side of the road, across from the evergreens, was sand, tumbleweed and Joshua trees framed by purple mountains that stood far off in the distance. The strange stand of trees formed a perfectly square barrier that was large enough to hide a city block and could not have looked more out of place.

He stayed on the main road and walked until he was even with the unnaturally placed trees. A small asphalt lane left the main road and led directly to the center of the trees. From where he now stood, Blake could see an open gate at the end of the road with more asphalt and some buildings beyond the gate. He shook his head and wondered where Johnson had led him. The road may have been deserted, but the building was not. Dozens of tractor trailers lined the parking lot in front of the building, but it did not look like a warehouse to him. As he neared the gate, he saw Johnson slunk down in his car in a far corner of the parking lot. Blake hiked across the lot to Johnson's passenger door and knocked on the window.

Johnson jumped in his seat and yelled, "Oh hell, man! Don't do that! What in the hell are you doing here?"

Blake climbed in and said, "I was looking for you."

"Why?" Johnson asked. "Aren't you supposed to be looking for some crystal ball or something?"

"It's an orb," Blake said. "And I thought you were supposed to help me."

"I got new orders, and I doubt that you'll find your orb here."

"Why not?" Blake joked. "I have no clue where to start looking, so this place is no worse than any other."

"Well, I don't think you'd be too welcome here."

Blake had already felt the knot in his stomach ever since he had crossed the gate. It was a familiar feeling that he had lived with for almost as long as he could remember. The sorcerers were here for sure. "Is she here?"

"I sure hope not. She's one scary crazy bitch."

Blake stretched his feelings out towards the buildings and felt something call for him. It didn't call him by name, but he felt something tug at his soul. The old man said the orb would try to find him. "It's here."

"Yeah," Johnson laughed. "Very funny."

"I'm not joking."

"What makes you think it's here? Have you seen it?"

"No. I can feel it."

"Well," Johnson said, "if it's here, you got a big problem trying to get it."

Blake grimaced. "I know."

He left the car and snuck around the lot to the side of the building. He felt like he had a homing device built into his chest that was pulling him towards the orb. A window had been left ajar at the end of the building that looked like easy access to the inside. The tug on his chest grew and told him that the orb was close. He lifted the window, climbed over the sill and hid behind a desk. The pull on his chest left him breathless and led to the other end of the room, but the feeling seemed to end at the far wall, where a painting on the wall smiled at him. He crossed the room and nodded to the painting. It nodded back. It was too surreal for him to be afraid, so he reached out and pulled on the picture frame. The painting swung out of the way to reveal a hidden wall safe.

Blake looked at the simple combination lock dial and smiled. This was going to be easier than he had anticipated. He turned the tumblers with his mind and pulled the handle, swinging the heavy door open. But instead of an orb, there were only documents and folders inside the safe. A faint glow from a file folder caught his attention, but as he reached to grab it, the drapes in the window blew into the room and the force of the wind slammed the desk chair into the desk. Blake spun around to see what the commotion was and saw an apparition floating in the middle of the room. The misty creature was vaguely human, but not human enough. It pointed an astral, but bony, finger at Blake and asked, "Who the hell are you?"

"Excuse me?" Blake asked. He reached out to touch the specter, but his hand passed through the floating mist. "I'll tell you who I am if you first tell me what in the hell you are."

The ghost smiled broadly and said, "I am the owner of what you seek."

"You?" Blake asked. "You don't look like someone who could own anything, at least not anymore."

"But it was mine in my time, and in my time, I was very important amongst our people, and I swore an oath to never let that secret out of our family. Now, I have told you what I am, so tell me, please, who you are."

"My name is Blake, but I'm still curious. Who were your people? Were you a witch?"

The specter spat a disgusting glob of ectoplasmic snot onto the floor. "Do I look like a witch to you?"

"Frankly," Blake said, "you look like the steam that rises from a stale pond, and forgive me for saying this, but you smell kind of like a stagnant pond, too."

The specter's face clouded over and grew red with anger. Its chest heaved as its breath turned deeper and smoke snorted out from its nostrils, then it calmed down and shrugged its shoulders. "You may be correct about the odor, but my current circumstances notwithstanding, I was a king in my time and unless you are one of my descendants, you simply don't belong here. You should leave."

"Gladly," Blake said, "but first I need to have a peek inside of that folder."

The specter shook its head and said, "That is for family only, and since you are not family, I don't think that I will allow you to have what you seek."

Blake produced a perfectly round ball of fire in his palm and asked, "What makes you think I'm not family?"

The specter's belly bounced as it laughed from deep inside and said, "Just because you have the gifts does not mean that you sprung from my loins."

"You've been away for a long time," Blake said. "Too long, maybe. These are desperate times that I live in, and we must unite the clan as one family to survive. Have you not noticed how long it has been since someone came to you with the gifts?"

The specter grew quiet for a moment. What Blake said was true. Until recently, he had not seen a bona fide sorcerer or witch in centuries.

"And you may not see another one for a while," Blake said. "The witches ruined magic for all of us, but that's all about to change."

The specter's face turned a dark crimson. "Can you hear my thoughts? By God, you are not one of mine. You wear the foul taint of a witch about you and I suspect that you may be one of that bastard Marvalaine's whelps. You shall never see these files."

Blake lunged for the safe and grasped the folder. He barely had opened it to the first page when the apparition enveloped him in fire.

Blake was overcome with the stench of his own burning flesh as the apparition filled his ears with a hollow laughter.

Blake sucked in his breath and tried to scream, but his voice was paralyzed.

Carl poked him in the arm and asked, "You okay dude? That must have been one hell of a dream."

Blake tried retaining the picture of the folder in his mind, but all he saw in it was the picture of a girl with dark hair and a single word: Britain.

One of Destiny's doctors entered the room and saw the strange artifacts scattered around Michelle and Zeline. He didn't think much of it at first glance, and assumed it was just some strange kind of hobby. It wasn't uncommon for women to knit or crochet while their loved ones slept. His reaction changed, however, when he saw Zeline tying a feather onto a stick figure. "Is that a feather? You do know that the ICU is a clean zone, don't you?"

"Don't you worry," Zeline replied. "It be a very clean feather."

The doctor took a closer look and asked, "Are those bones? You can't possibly think that this is an appropriate place for bones."

"It's okay," Michelle said, "whatever they died from ain't catchy."

"Not no more, anyways," Zeline added with a snicker.

"This is no matter for jokes," the doctor objected. "This ward is where we care for our most serious cases. We cannot risk infection under any circumstances."

"You listen to me," Michelle said, "my little girl here be more important than you can possibly understand. Not just to me cause I loves her, but to da whole damned world. Dis hospital dat you wants to keep so clean is gonna be reduced to a pile-o-ash iffin my girl don't wake up to save us all, and I ain't seen you doin' much to help bring her around, so it falls to us to do what we can."

"I'm not listening to any more of your delusions," the doctor said, "I'm calling security."

"No, you ain't," Michelle said with the voice, "you is gonna help me to protect her cause you knows what I knows. We must protect her and we must save her. We be protecting her with these talismans just like you is trying to save her with your medicines and all dose machines. This just be us doin' our part and you be okay wit' da whole thing cause you knows dat our part is just as important as yours is."

The doctor paused awkwardly for a moment. His mouth still hung open from the arguments he had been making, but he cocked his head as if that gave him a better view of their things and said, "Why are you hoarding them all? Shouldn't you be placing those things around the room already?" He reached for one and said, "Here, let me help you place them."

Zeline took his hand in hers and said soothingly, "Dat be okay. We be fixin' to put dem up presently, but dere be a small ceremony dat goes wit' puttin' dem up."

The doctor stood up straight and tugged on his white frock. "Of course. Carry on."

Flinch's door was open, but he was on the phone, so Saunders waited in the doorway for him to finish his call. Flinch saw him waiting and held up a finger to signal him that it would only be a moment. "Yes sir," he said into the phone. "Right away sir. I'm on it." He replaced the handset and beckoned Saunders to join him.

Saunders came in and closed the door behind him.

"Go ahead and take a seat," Flinch said, a little rattled that Saunders felt the need to close the door. "That was the pentagon. Congress is demanding an explanation. They don't seem very interested in waiting for an investigation."

Saunders frowned as he asked, "Do you think that they may have launched their own investigation already?"

"I'm sure they have," Flinch replied.

"They didn't say anything though? You're just guessing?"

Flinch shook his head. "Why? Did you want to conduct a joint investigation with them?"

"No. I was just wondering if they had already engaged the NSA to look into the matter."

"No doubt. I'm sure they have a lot more satellite imagery than the few paltry photos that they have offered to us."

"I was thinking of something a bit more personal, like assets on the ground."

Flinch detected something curious in Saunders' tone. "Why? Have you seen something? Are their agents already here?"

Saunders shook his head slowly. "I can't confirm that."

"But you suspect it."

"Sir, I may need to step down from this investigation. I think I've been compromised."

Flinch thought it was a joke and started to laugh, but Saunders wasn't smiling. "You think you've been compromised? You're not sure?"

"I don't remember. That's the problem. There are holes in my memory. Something happened when I took the girl from the field, but I can't remember."

"And you think the NSA did something to make you forget?"

Saunders shrugged. He didn't know what had happened to him, but he wasn't about to suggest that an angel from heaven had altered his memory. It was easier for him to believe that the NSA had drugged him and done something to his memory. "I don't know, but I can't rule that out."

Flinch scratched his chin. "If what you suspect is true, then they must be taking this threat pretty seriously for them to do something like that to one of our own." His face grew dark before he continued, "I don't like it one bit if they have launched a black op against one of MY own people. That's an attack against me, but it must mean you are pretty close to something. I can't afford to bring anyone else in on this. The less people that know about this, the better. You keep on it, but don't let them know what you suspect. Perhaps you'll come across something that will jar your memory."

Chapter 14

Day ten.

Explanations of the destruction in Salt Lake and Cheyenne blanketed the networks, but it was mostly misinformation propagated by the government. The internet was abuzz with counter theories. Opinions varied, and there were too many witnesses for the government's cover-up to stick. Never before had the conspiracy theorists had this much fuel to kindle their fires. Firsthand accounts and videos of the destruction found their way to social media, where they were promptly removed, but the government couldn't control the dark web where videos were rapidly shared with new ones appearing every hour. Popular social media was flooded with more and more first-hand accounts. The government couldn't keep pace and ultimately couldn't prevent the world from seeing one deranged girl crushing tanks and burning soldiers with only her hands.

News of two burned police cruisers was lost in the noise.

Balletina had been roaming the hallway outside of Honey's apartment, waiting for her to get up. Honey hadn't even finished closing her door when Balletina approached her.

Honey flashed a bright smile and greeted Balletina. "Good morning sugar. Are you alright?"

"Let's go do something," Balletina said breathlessly.

"We just did something last night," Honey replied. "Has you been waiting out here for me to get up?"

"Maybe. Let's go do something."

"Are you stalking me now?"

"Come on!" Balletina cried. "Aren't you listening to me? I want to go do something!"

"We just did something last night," Honey repeated herself.

"I know, but I want to do more!"

Honey laughed. "It's like a drug. Ain't it?"

Balletina's eyes quivered in their sockets as she recalled their exploits at the mall. She loved the juice it gave her and craved more.

"Wow," Honey said. "You're really tweaking. Are you on something?"

"I'm on a power trip," she replied. "I just need to burn off some steam."

"Well, alright then," Honey said, "but I ain't even had breakfast yet. Why don't we go outside and burn something?"

Balletina raced down the hall to a back entrance and burst through the doors. Honey was curious to see what she was going to do and ran behind her. Balletina sprinted through the basketball court to the field outback and sailed rapid fire balls of flames into an oak tree.

The tree burst into flames, sending a large black bird into the sky to escape the searing heat.

"Oh no you don't," Balletina yelled. She pointed to the bird and fired a long stream of fire at the bird, but her flames trailed behind it. She shot multiple fireballs all around the bird, but never hit it. "Arrrghhhh! What must I do to hit you? Stupid bird!"

Honey snickered and said, "Nice shooting, Tex."

"I ain't done yet." She took careful aim ahead of the bird and fired a ball of flame that expanded as it flew, but the bird simply turned away to avoid the slow-moving flame.

"You done, now?" Honey asked. "I'm hungry."

"No!" she growled. "It's just that the fire is too slow."

"Then try something else."

"How?"

"I dunno," Honey said. "Ain't you been to magic school?"

"Yeah, but they didn't know anything. They told stories of how it used to be, but they couldn't do any of this shit."

Honey laughed. She liked Balletina, but she especially enjoyed watching the girl's failure. "Just cause they couldn't do it don't mean they didn't know about it. Don't they always say that those that can't do it teach?"

Balletina bit her lip as she recalled her training. The bird landed on a fence post near the burning tree. She tried to recall her lessons about lightning, then pointed her finger and arced a slender bolt of lightning across the field and into the unsuspecting bird.

A chill ran down Honey's spine as the mirth evaporated from her face. "Where'd you learn that? Did my mama teach you that behind my back?"

"No, it wasn't your mother. In fact, it was your idea, just now," Balletina explained. "You told me to try recalling my training. I guess they did know a thing or two, even if they didn't know how to actually do it."

"Let's go inside," Honey said. "I'm hungry."

Blake had been staring absentmindedly out the window when he heard Carl say, "Salt Lake: one hundred miles."

Blake closed his eyes and felt for Johnson's presence. "What the...? Slow down."

"You want to help this guy out?" Carl asked. "I dunno if that's such a good idea. He looks like trouble to me."

Blake looked down the road and saw someone standing next to a vehicle while vigorously waving his arm to flag them down. They were too far away for Blake to actually see his face, but Blake didn't need to see him to know who it was. "I don't think he's trouble. Let's just see what his story is."

Carl pulled the car over to the shoulder, raising a cloud of dust and dirt, stopping just behind the other vehicle.

Blake climbed out and fanned the dust away from his face. "What in the hell are you doing out here, Johnson?"

"They told me that you wouldn't listen to them," Johnson said.

"I'm not you," Blake replied. "I don't have to listen to them."

"Why are you here? Don't you know how dangerous it is?"

Blake shrugged and said, "I was following you. You know that I need to find that orb. I don't see how I'm going to do it without you. I thought you were supposed to be helping me."

"They gave me a new job. I'm following Logan now."

Blake walked to Carl's window and knocked on the glass. Carl rolled down the window and Blake told him, "Thanks for the ride. You can go now. I got it from here."

"Really?" Carl asked. "You're going to ditch me to get off in the middle of nowhere and hitch a ride with a complete stranger?"

"You and me are strangers, Carl. Besides, believe it or not, this is the guy I was coming out here to meet."

"No. No. No," Johnson protested while waving his hands and shaking his head. "You can't send him away. You need him to take you back."

"I'm not going back," Blake said.

"Well, you ain't goin' with me!" Johnson practically screamed.

Carl looked around and saw nothing but sand and tumbleweed. "You sure you want me to leave you here? He doesn't seem too happy to see you and it's a pretty strange place to meet someone..." Carl's mind was flooded with all the not so good reasons to meet in a place like this. "You know what? Just never mind. It's none of my business and I don't need to know nothing. You take care."

"You too, Carl. Thanks for the ride. Mind your father's advice in the future."

Johnson was still arguing as Carl pulled out and raised another cloud of dust and dirt behind him.

"He's right," Blake said. "You picked a terrible place to meet."

"I wasn't here to meet you. I was only supposed to stop you and convince you to turn around. Who was he anyway?"

"Just some dude that caught me trying to break into his car."

"You were breaking into his car and he gave you a ride all the way out here?"

Blake smirked as he explained, "He was very understanding."

"Uhuh. You did your Jedi mind trick on him."

Blake just shrugged and climbed into the car.

Johnson slid behind the wheel, shaking his head and said, "I'll drop you off at a bus station, 'cause you can't go where I been."

"I must go where you are going. The orb is there, or something. I can't explain it yet."

"Logan went to their compound. That dark-haired bitch is there and now she has a friend. They both are no good if you ask me."

"Fine," Blake said. "Let's just not get caught then."

Johnson's stomach felt queasy as he reluctantly started the car and headed back towards the sorcerer's compound.

Saunders flipped through the many files that he had collected regarding the two incidents in Cheyenne and Salt Lake. He paid particular attention to the eyewitness testimony, the most credible of which had been collected from soldiers and police officers.

He personally had witnessed the Cheyenne event where Honey and the blond girl had withstood direct hits from missiles. The missiles' payloads had detonated in the air over their heads and erupted all around them, but had no effect upon either of them, as if they were protected by an invisible bullet and bomb proof dome. The tank shells and sniper bullets were equally ineffective. All of the army's great might had done nothing to stop her. They couldn't even slow her down. It was the other girl that stopped her, and he had her, but he lost her. At least, he thinks he had her.

On the road from Salt Lake, the one that called herself Honey had tossed tanks around like they were paper toys, but it was the downtown building in Salt Lake that disturbed him the most. She brought a high-rise down onto the street. She just thought it, and the building turned into a pile of rubble.

He didn't know what she was...what they were, but whatever she was, she was dangerous. She said they weren't aliens, but what else could they be? He searched for a logical explanation, but kept coming back to the notion that she was an angel...well, the new girl was, anyway. Honey could only have been from the other place.

Why Cheyenne? For that matter, why Salt Lake? Did she just pop in from the gates of Hell and decide to attack Salt Lake? Is that where the plane of Hell intersects with Earth? Or were there other incidents that had come before Salt Lake?

Saunders opened a new window on the computer and started a search for other outlandish police reports. Honey said she was from the Gulf. He didn't know if she was telling the truth, but they must have come from somewhere. Maybe they didn't start with Salt Lake. He just had to follow the trail back to where they started.

He stared at the computer monitor and wondered how you searched for something that defied explanation.

"Blake?" the deep voice rumbled in Blake's head. "You don't need to do this."

"Seriously?" Blake asked. "You don't think it's kind of rude, not to mention an invasion of privacy, for you to interrupt my thoughts like that?"

"Apologies," the voice said, "but matters are too grave and I can no longer spare the time to be polite."

"No?" Blake asked. "You must know who I am. Have you ever asked yourself if you can spare the time to be dead?"

"Are you really threatening us?" another male voice asked.

"We thought you were turning over a new leaf," a third voice said.

"Now there are three of you?" Blake yelled from his mind.

"Please forgive the intrusion," the second voice said, "but my brother was correct. You should not continue in this direction."

"So, you're brothers?"

"A figure of speech," the third one said. "You already have your clue. There is no need to go there anymore. Would you like some help?"

"No."

"No?" the first voice asked. "The orb is an elusive thing. I doubt that you can find it alone."

"I didn't ask you."

"Perhaps you should," the second voice said. "We could lead you to the right clue without you walking blindly into a hostile environment and getting yourself killed."

"Again," the third said.

"Nobody killed me," Blake said. "It was only a dream."

"But," the first said, "we all know how well that went for you. The danger ahead of you is real. The dream was just a foreshadowing."

"The orb is real, too," Blake said. "I could feel it calling for me."

"And what did you see?" the third asked. "Did you find the orb, or did you merely find a document with only your gut feeling telling you that it is somehow connected to the orb?"

"Why are you asking me if you already know everything?" Blake asked. "I found a file folder. Why? What do you know about it?"

"Only that it was a clue," the first said.

"And if you hadn't been killed so fast," the second said, "you would have found a picture within the folder and a document telling you that the face came from a family in Europe."

"England," the third said. "All you felt were the documents that had been brought here from England. They may be connected to the orb in some way, but they are only clues."

"I think I saw a picture," Blake said, "but just for a split second."

"Very good," the third said. "Now that you've already seen the clue, there is no need for you to go in there and actually get yourself killed for real."

"I don't know," Blake said. "How do I know if I can trust you?"

"Ask Johnson," the first said.

"Ha. Ha. He works for you."

"You are more important to us than you can possibly realize," the first said, "and in time, you will learn to trust us."

***

Saunders didn't know where his investigation was going to lead him and he would never be ready to reveal any of his occult suspicions, but he needed to continue his research and he needed to do it without letting Flinch know what he was looking into, so he left the base and went to the public library hoping to backtrack Honey's trail by finding another newsworthy incident that happened before Salt Lake. He knew that the library now offered internet terminals, but he was still surprised by how many people were there. It hadn't occurred to him didn't think anybody read anymore, especially young people. He hadn't been to a public library since his schooldays and had arrived expecting the place to smell like musty books, but the air was pleasantly fresh. What he was looking for wouldn't be found in a book, or even in the periodicals. He walked briskly past the tall bookshelves to the far corner where the internet terminals were organized in compact little rows. He had hoped that he could have found a relatively private station in the corner where he could do his research unobserved, but the library was far busier than he could have anticipated. Short walls divided the stations, but didn't provide the kind of intimacy that he would have preferred. The best he could do was a terminal against the wall, but the wall behind him was a large glass window to the outside world. A hedge outside shielded him from the sidewalk and should keep him away from prying eyes, but it still left him feeling edgy.

The real news about Salt Lake and Cheyenne wouldn't be found in the traditional news channels, and if it had ever made its way there, it would have been quickly swept away by the government, but personal accounts continued to pop up in social media. The government tried to control the spread of that information too, but it was an impossible task. He quickly found personal posts with headlines about what happened in Cheyenne, but most of them were dead links pointing to deleted pages. After sifting through them, he found some links to the events in Salt Lake. People were already starting to connect the two of them. More links led to other places, but most of them seemed to stray off topic to people's personal agendas and wacko conspiracy theories. He chuckled at the thought that any conspiracy could be crazier than the reality he suspected. A pattern emerged where the most outlandish topics had no deleted pages. The number of dead links seemed to be a good indicator of which events were being controlled by the government. Those were the ones that were the most credible and required the bulk of his attention.

One link that he found led him to a much smaller event at a restaurant near the border between Utah and Wyoming. According to the report, several police cruisers were burned and human ashes were found inside the restaurant, but the most interesting point in the report was that they had shot someone whose description matched Honey's and she had been declared dead. She didn't remain dead, however, and several reports had been devoted to the inept medical staff that had failed to find a heartbeat. Saunders didn't doubt that she may in fact have been dead and came back. That's just what he would expect from a supernatural being.

He closed his eyes and tried concentrating on something other than her being a demon from Hell, but he couldn't shake the thought that he might have to consult with a priest, or worse, his father.

The sorcerer's archives contained a variety of ancient scrolls and documents that had been collected over the centuries, but they also held a number of bona fide artifacts that dated back several millennia. The bulk of the material in the archives had been replicated digitally and was available worldwide to any clan member interested in viewing them, but the actual relics themselves were randomly scattered around the world in various locations in the clan's more elite archives with the rarer items privy only to a few select members with sufficient rank to grant them access. There had been too many wars between the sorcerers and the witches to risk keeping such powerful items together in one place. Instead, after they were all photographed and copied, they were scattered around the world. Before the days of photography, sketches were made and copied for distribution. Every fifty or so years, they held an Umstellung in which the artifacts and documents were randomly transferred around the world, but all the libraries had access to the sketches and photographic copies that were made, which had been transferred into digital archives towards the end of the twentieth century.

Logan was very ambitious, and though he had not yet achieved any truly noteworthy rank, he had risen to the lower cusp of upper management and had access to all but the most secure items. Students and workers at the facilities were encouraged to take advantage of the recorded documents, but young people these days weren't particularly interested in pursuing a hobby that felt like homework. The archives weren't used very often, but they were used.

It wasn't that many weeks ago when Destiny had been the first from either clan to develop real powers in over a thousand years. Her feat registered around the world in an inadvertent wave of power that was felt by the sorcerers as it passed through them. Her energy wave was declared a prophecy level event, and the archives saw a spike in activity by those with ambitions to make names for themselves. Logan had already known about Honey and Abilene, who had shown glimpses of the old abilities, but he hadn't crossed Destiny's path until one of his protégés had located her and tried taking her on himself. He paid the ultimate price for his ambitions, but he had also started the chain of events that led to Honey's rising. Logan was initially interested in only cleaning up the unfortunate events enough to segregate himself from his subordinate's failure. It wasn't until later, when Honey had developed her powers and declared herself queen of the world, that he became genuinely interested in the lore buried within the archives.

The library was empty when he had arrived, which wasn't surprising. While usage of the archives was up worldwide, it was still quite common to find any given library empty. Logan logged into a terminal and searched for the word orb. He was rewarded with over six thousand references. Browsing through a few of them, he found nothing that stood out for him. He poured himself a cup of coffee from the thermos that he had brought with him and settled down for what promised to be a long night.

Ashlin still felt abandoned by Logan. She knew that he was doing his part to help locate the orb, but she still liked his confident way of ordering the hospital around. She was especially impressed by the way he could control them without using the voice like she had to do. He wasn't anything like Honey. He was proof that the clans could work together. The memories had not shown her a way to communicate telepathically with him like she could with the other witches, but they had taught her how to astral project.

The waiting room was more hectic than usual and she didn't know if she could achieve a full trance with all the noise. She was still afraid that she would look too conspicuous in the full trance required to astral project, but she didn't want to venture too far from Destiny. Most of the seats in the waiting room had thin vinyl covered cushions and were not overly comfortable, but an overstuffed chair sat in the corner and seemed more inviting to her than the rest did, and it was unoccupied. She sank down into the luxurious cushions and closed her eyes. It was still too noisy. She concentrated on the steady rhythm of her breathing, looking for that one focus point to replace the candle and take her into her trance, but even as the sounds of the nurses and the carts melted behind the sound of the air rushing through her nose, she found it difficult to focus because her breathing had grown shallower and she could barely hear her tiny sips of air.

Her head throbbed. It was the steady beat of her heart that pulsed in her temples. Her breathing deepened as the throb appeared now in her wrists. Her whole body had become a gentle throb, and she felt like she would finally slip into the trance she sought, until she was startled by the unsteady tapping of fingers on a keyboard. She was never going to achieve a satisfactory calm state with interruptions like this, but when she opened her eyes so she could leave the hospital to find a new place to crash, she was surprised to see Logan typing into a computer.

She crept up behind him to see what was on the screen. She didn't recognize anything on the display. The screen had a black background with bright green letters and none of the familiar images that she was accustomed to seeing on the internet. He turned to the side and referred to some notes that lay alongside the keyboard. She thought that she had come here to talk to him, but now she found herself fascinated with what he was doing and held her breath, hoping that he wouldn't notice her. After running his finger down the page of scribbled notes, he returned to the keyboard and typed a word, then pressed enter. It looked like he was searching for something, but it definitely wasn't Google. The interface on the screen was totally unfamiliar to her. Why wasn't he just using one of the regular search engines like she was taught in school?

A list appeared on the screen and Logan used the arrows on the keyboard to move the cursor down the list and typed a number on one of the rows. The screen was promptly replaced with a picture and some text. The Orb of Lancey was a gift from the king of France. It is rumored to have had the power to break a witch's concentration. No reliable data exists on how to activate or deploy it.

Logan hit the escape key, blanking out the screen and replacing it with the green list again. He frowned and mumbled, "That's not going to help me." He pressed the page down key on the keyboard and the list was replaced with a new green list full of different items. His mood grew foul as he growled at the screen, "I'll never be able to wrest control from that stupid little bitch if I can't overpower her. That damned orb must be in here somewhere!"

Ashlin gasped and stepped backwards, afraid that he must have heard her. She spun around and scrambled for the door, but as she flailed her arms around in front of her, she could see through them like they were mere wisps of smoke. She wasn't really there and when she looked back at him, she realized that she was apparently in no danger of being discovered. Still, she had learned his secret and had to return.

The hospital had apparently not noticed the young red head's limp body, but the woozy spinning in her head left her wondering if this had been the best place to try her astral projections. Her knees buckled slightly as she pushed herself out of the chair and she wobbled a bit as she made her way back to Destiny's side. She needed to rest and lay her chin on the edge of the bed, then let her eyelids droop shut, wishing that she could curl up beside Destiny.

Saunders widened the scope of his search for extra-normal events to include the entire nation. He remembered a time when such a request would have taken days, even on their best computers. Worse yet, the odds of those old computers having enough events for him to scan through would have been extremely low, but these days, data was collected from everywhere in the world and stored on massive central repositories. The computer systems that drove the searches were tremendously powerful and could return results in seconds. Unfortunately for him, they returned a lot more data than he could possibly digest.

He scoured through the search results, unsure of exactly what he should be looking for. He tried a variety of different search criteria. He looked for explosions, fire bombs, collapsed buildings, and burned corpses. There was no shortage of information for him to browse, but none of it smelled supernatural to him.

He knew it would just be a matter of finding the right combination of keywords for his search, but the various combinations of search terms were limitless. He searched for angels and demons, and when that came up empty, he looked for devils and black magic. The internet was full of stuff about every conceivable subject, but nothing led him to the origin of those two girls. He was on the verge of giving up when he tried unusual weather patterns. The world is an interesting place, full of strange weather, but not much of interest to him, until he found an article claiming that thunder, lightning and earthquakes took place in a very tight area. In fact, they all occurred on a single evening and all within the borders of a solitary small farm, and it was only a few weeks ago.

Not long ago, he would have cruised past such an article and simply assumed that it was a pot farm and everything had been hallucinated, but his thinking had expanded in the past few days and he wasn't so quick to dismiss a report like this anymore.

He searched for other incidents that might have happened on or near that farm and learned about a small military incursion. This was even more outlandish than believing angels had come to Earth to hold a battle. He could understand burglars and home invasions, but for a military force to surround and attack a tiny little farm was beyond belief, except for one simple fact: it happened on the same day as the strange weather.

The story became even more incredulous when he searched the dark net and learned that there were no casualties. Apparently, a well-armed band of mercenaries infiltrated some no-name family farm, but were later found bound at the wrists in the back of their vehicle. Saunders found as many denials to the event as he found accusations. Knowing soldiers as he did, he had no doubt that a competitor leaked the information onto the net. What wasn't clear was the connection between the mercenaries and the unusual weather. He might have to go see for himself.

***

Destiny rumbled around her new house, banging cupboard doors and tossing things on the floor. She wanted to scream, but there was nobody there who could hear her.

"What's wrong?" Ashlin asked behind her.

Destiny spun around, startled to hear someone's voice, but nobody was there. "Ashlin! Where are you?"

"I'm in the hospital by your bed. I've wanted to come visit you before, but Michelle and your mother always make me stay with you. It's as if your nana is afraid that if one of us isn't in the hospital with you at all times, they'll take you away like they keep saying they're going to do. But even after your mama and nana returned from vising you, they still wouldn't really tell me where you were, so I called to see for myself."

"I hope you're not going to try convincing me that I'm crazy like they did."

"Crazy?" Ashlin asked. "Really? I don't remember anyone ever talking about you being crazy. Confused, maybe, but that's understandable after everything you've been through."

Destiny sighed. "So you think I'm crazy too?"

"I don't think you're crazy. I think you're comfortable. What you went through was hell. You kicked Honey's butt, but from the looks of things, it must have been a brutal battle. It was hell out there. You'd have to be crazy to want to return to that."

"I'm not crazy."

Ashlin sighed. "I know. So, are you gonna tell me how to get there?"

"Another time, perhaps. I would really love to see you, but right now, I need you to do a favor for me."

"Sure," Ashlin said brightly. "That's what sisters are for."

"I need you to deliver a message to Blake for me."

Ashlin twisted her lips as she wondered what was wrong with her sister. "Why me? Why don't you do it yourself?"

"I've been trying, but I'm not sure if I can."

"Why?"

"It's complicated. I can't leave this place and lately, I'm not so sure if my thoughts can leave either."

"Oh," Ashlin said grimly. "You should at least try."

"Sure," Destiny said. "I'll keep trying, but will you be my backup in case I can't do it? It's too important to take chances."

"Okay. What's the message?"

"Warn Blake that he should watch out for Johnson."

"Why?" she asked. "What's Johnson ever done to us?"

"Nothing yet, but he works for the librarians and they are bad people. They're the ones that killed Mala and they are going to try to stop Blake from doing something and I just don't think that he should completely trust Johnson."

"Okay, I can do that for you. Now, can you show me how to get there?"

"No!" Destiny squealed. "You need to go warn Blake. Go! Now!"

"Is the food here really that good?" Honey asked as she followed Balletina into the cafeteria and measured the length of the line.

"Not really," Balletina said, "but they never have enough of the daily specials and you gotta be here early if you want any of the better stuff."

"You mean we might not get anything good?"

"Us?" Balletina asked. "No way." She shoved the people at the end of the line aside and growled, "Out of the way."

The first few people gave her dirty looks, but the fifth one in, a dark-haired girl in a designer dress, shoved her back and said, "Piss off. I got as much right to be here as you do."

"You think so?" Balletina asked. "Do you really think so?"

"Yes, I do," the girl snarled directly in Balletina's face. "You should know who I am and who my father is."

"I know who you are," Balletina replied, "and more importantly, I know who you think you are, but it just doesn't matter so much anymore."

"Oh yeah?" the girl asked. "Who the hell made you queen? My father sure didn't, and he's got about a billion reasons why I'm more important than you, not to mention he's on the elder council, so get the hell out of my face."

Honey laughed. She slinked her way down the line to the girl in the designer dress and said, "I don't believe I have ever heard anyone in such fancy duds brag about how much money her daddy had while she was waiting in line at a soup kitchen before." She winked at the cook who had been so kind to her before and mouthed the words, "Sorry."

"I want to know something," Balletina said. "Can your daddy, with all his money, buy you one of these?" She held up her palm and produced a fireball that she spun around for everyone to see.

The fancy girl's eyes widened as she quietly backed away.

"I didn't think so," Balletina said. "You're going to have to reassess your net worth around here, and this goes for everyone. You may have thought that you were big shits around here because your fathers had money. I know I did, but I also know that some of you thought you were more important than me just because your fathers had more money than mine did. Well, I think you're going to find out that we have a new currency around here. Your value isn't going to be measured by your daddies' wealth anymore. It's going to be measured by this." Balletina produced fireballs in each of her hands and waved them around as she walked in a small circle for everybody to see. "And if you're thinking that maybe you're more important because your family goes back to the Stone Age or your father is a high-ranking official, guess again." She glanced over at Honey and said, "Here, catch." She lobbed one of her fireballs over to Honey, who easily caught it in her palm. "You were right," Balletina continued, "when you said that your father did not make me queen. I'm not your queen, but she is, and she didn't need your daddy to make her queen; her power makes her your queen. Your high ranking fathers are only minions to her. They will bow before her, and so will you." Balletina turned to face the girl in the designer dress. She walked slowly up to her until they were face to face and said, "I better not hear any more about who your father is ever again. Is that clear?"

The fancy girl's eyes never left the fireball that still glowed and danced in Balletina's palm. She bowed her head and dipped her knees. Balletina thought she was going to curtsey for a moment. "I want to hear you say it."

The poor girl trembled. She wasn't sure how to address Balletina without offending her. She dipped her knees again and said, "Yes, ma'am."

Honey smiled broadly as she popped the fireball and clapped her hands. "That was great. Really good, but I'd like to add something." She paused a moment and slowly panned the room so everyone would know she was addressing all of them. "I'm sure that all of you have become accustomed to your little power clicks over the years. And I can see how you like to hang out in little groups together. I also seen how you whispered about me when I arrived, but that's okay. Water under the bridge. Today is a new day. Like Balletina just said, I am your queen, but Balletina here is the 'A' crowd and the rest of you ain't, except maybe for you." She pointed to the cook and said, "You are definitely on my 'A' list, but the rest of you are all on my 'Z' list. You get it? You have zero value until you prove yourselves. You'll have to work your way onto my 'A' list. And you might have to kiss Balletina's ass on the way, because I'm putting her in charge of the 'A' crowd, so pucker up everybody. One more thing. In case y'all didn't get the memo, I'm not just going to be your queen, I'm gonna be queen of the whole God damned world. That means that we are going to rule the world, especially my 'A' team. So, if you play your cards right, y'all have a chance to help me rule the world. Now, if you don't mind, I'm hungry."

Everybody ahead of them in line moved voluntarily out of the way so Honey could go to the front of the line. Balletina grabbed two trays and plates and started sliding them down the buffet tables. She started to scoop out some baked ziti, when the chef said, "No. No! That is not for you. I have some freshly prepared plates for the two of you. You go find your table and Pablo will bring your food in a jiffy."

Ashlin's head was still a little woozy as she returned from her conversation with Destiny. She lazily opened her eyes and Michelle snapped, "Where in da blazes have you been?"

"I was just..."

"I thought you was supposed to be her new little sister! Why wasn't you here?"

Fear set in as Ashlin felt the anger seething from Michelle and asked, "Why? Did something happen?"

"No!" Michelle barked. "But what if somthin' did happen, and you was of traipsin' around who knows where? You don't see none of us goin' nowhere!"

"You visited Destiny," Ashlin said flatly.

"Don't you give me none of your sass..."

"Or what?" Ashlin growled. "Are you going to throw a tantrum? What's next? Are you going to hold your breath and turn blue until someone notices you?"

Michelle's cheeks reddened as her mouth fell open. Ashlin used to be such a sweet loving little girl and now she had turned against Michelle and it was all Honey's fault. Heat gathered in her ears as her embarrassment grew and flamed her fury. She turned away from Ashlin and tried to ignore her. Now she hated Honey even more.

Saunders pulled his jeep off the main road and onto the long driveway that led to the small family farm that he had spotted in the news. Trees lined the road on the left-hand side, with a white fence standing between the road and a green pasture on the right. A small crowd had collected at the end of the road to greet him.

He pulled the jeep to a stop, and climbed out, saying, "Good morning. I'm Captain Saunders and I was hoping to ask you a few questions."

They knew who he was, just as they had known that he was coming, but they didn't say so. A stern-looking woman, barely in her thirties, stepped forward and looked into his mind long enough to hear Honey's name. She thought to the rest of the family, "He knows that bitch, Honey, but I didn't see if he was friend or foe."

He cleared his throat and continued, "I was hoping that maybe I could have a word with you about something that might have happened here a couple of weeks ago."

Brie Boutin took another step forward and without introducing herself, said in an accusing voice, "Was dey your men?" She knew they weren't, but she wanted to put him on the defensive and establish her dominance in the conversation.

"No ma'am," he replied. "I don't know who they were, but I sure am curious about what happened that night."

She believed him and said, "Let's go inside then and have us a talk. The rest of y'all kin go back to work now."

Brie set her jaw and flipped her dark locks over her shoulder as she spun around and walked briskly across the lot to the front porch. She waited impatiently at the foot of the steps for him to catch up.

The family dynamics had changed since Michelle had visited them. She had opened their minds to the gifts of their ancestors. Where before they could only see the past, and a select few may have had some glimpses into the future, now they could all peer into people's minds and talk to each other over great distances. With the absence of Abilene, the family needed to find their own leadership and with Zeb still incapacitated, they had fallen back into a matriarchy. Abilene was never the family matriarch. She was just the villain that had stolen Grandpa Zeb's place of leadership. With her gone, Brie had assumed the role of family head. She wasn't one of the elders, but her gifts were strong and with them, she had the best insight of any of the family members. Nobody objected to her role at the head of the family, and she had never done anything to dissuade the trust that they had placed in her.

Brie climbed the steps when Saunders had almost reached her and held the screen door open for him, where she waited for him to cross the threshold. The screen door slammed shut with a thwang from the long spring as she pushed past him and led him into the kitchen. She pointed to an old kitchen chair with tubular chrome legs and vinyl padded cushions, saying, "You can have a seat there while I fetch us some lemonade."

Saunders pulled the fragile looking old chair from the table and tested his weight on it before relaxing.

Brie was still in the fridge when she said, "I don't know what it is that you was expecting to learn here. Tain't much we kin tell you about them soldier boys."

"So," Saunders said, "you knew they were here. I was led to believe that they were discovered some distance away from the farm. Did your boys do that?"

The ice cubes clinked against the glass as Brie put the pitcher on the table. "Oh heavens no. We didn't do that. We would have filled them with shot if we had caught them."

"But you knew."

Brie put a couple of tall tumblers on the table and filled them. "Of course we knew, afterwards at least. Word travels fast in these parts."

"I see," Saunders said as he sipped his lemonade. "Mmmm. This is real good. Do you grow your own lemons?"

Brie sat down and replied, "No sir, but I don't think you come here to talk about lemons."

"No," Saunders said as he put his glass down so he could look more serious. "I wanted to ask you about the storm."

"The storm?" Brie asked coyly. "You'll have to be a little more specific. We get lots of storms around here. They're good for the crops, you know."

"That night," Saunders said, "when the soldiers came to the farm, there was a storm directly over this farm, but it wasn't like a regular storm. It had thunder and lightning, and I understand there was also some seismic activity, but no reports of rain."

Brie pretended to look confused. "Size-ma-what?"

"The ground shook."

"Oh that," she said. "What's the army want to know about our funny little earthquake for?"

"Did it seem natural to you?"

"Hell no!" Brie shouted. "We never gets them earthquakes around here. It was kinda excitin' though. Why? Is you suggestin' that them soldier boys made the ground shake? Was they testin' some new experimental weapon on us? Why on earth would they want to do that? Did they steal it from you?" She was toying with him and pretending to lower her IQ by at least a dozen points.

Saunders frowned. The interrogation was getting away from him. "Besides the soldiers, did you notice any strangers around here that day?"

Brie tried to hide the reaction from her face, but Saunders caught it anyway. "Strangers?" she asked. "Like who?"

"I don't know," Saunders replied, feeling a modicum of control in the conversation. "Was there anyone who didn't belong here? Maybe someone who had only just arrived?"

Brie shrugged and said, "There was only family here."

"Do you know anyone named Honey?"

That definitely got a reaction from Brie. She looked into his mind and saw the battle between Honey and Destiny, but she couldn't see how it ended. More importantly, she didn't see why he was here or what his connection with Honey was.

Saunders leaned back and narrowed his eyes. "You don't have to answer. I can see that you knew her."

"She was family too, sort of."

Someone outside screamed her thoughts into Brie's head, "No she warn't! Don't be telling him that!"

"Family?" Saunders asked. "You were related?"

"Not really," Brie explained. "Her mama had come to us when Cousin Pete up and married the whore's mother, Honey's grandmama. It was a real scandal to most of us, but Grandpa Zeb took it all in stride. Cousin Pete actually had the nerve to raise that little tramp right alongside his own little girl, but when the little tramp turned up pregnant with Honey, his ex-wife took their thirteen-year-old daughter away and I cain't say that I blames her none. We don't know nothin' about Honey's daddy, only that he warn't one o' our men."

Someone outside thought, "Why is you tellin' him so much?"

Brie couldn't answer. She could only continue her story. "Most of us thought Grandpa Zeb would step in and tell Pete and his whore to leave, but that never happened."

"Yeah," another family member thought. "Grandpa Zeb must have knowed what she was and wanted to keep his eye on them two. Too bad he let her hurt him until he lost his mind like that."

"So," Saunders said as he gathered his thoughts, "She wasn't really from here. Do you know where she came from?"

Brie wanted to end the interview, but a strange feeling inside of her compelled her to continue. "I think her mama mighta come from Baton Rouge. It was somewhere south. That's for sure."

"Did you ever notice anything unusual about Honey?"

Brie didn't sense any concern for Honey's well-being in his tone. "'Course I did. She was a good for nothin' whore like her mama and we is glad to be rid of her."

"But did she ever do anything that you couldn't explain?"

"She slept with Cousin Daniel. He ain't exactly handsome, and he never been right in the head. I cain't rightly explain that."

Someone outside thought, "She slept with all the men."

Someone else outside added, "And the boys."

Another family member thought, "It warn't just the men and the boys. She slept with anyone she could connive into bed. Boy or girl, it didn't matter none to her."

Saunders sighed. She was hiding something, and he didn't think he was going to get her to talk. "Did you know a girl about this tall with blond hair?"

Brie panicked. He used the word "did" as in past tense. Something must have happened to Destiny.

"Why does that frighten you?" Saunders asked. "Was there something unusual about the blond girl?"

Brie didn't answer. She looked into his mind for answers, but she saw only smoke.

"Did Honey have anything against the blond girl?"

Brie reached out to her family and thought, "I need help. Something happened to cousin Destiny, but I cain't see what it was."

Chapter 15

Johnson had seen the expression on Blake's face throughout the trip and pulled the car into the furthest, most remote corner of the parking lot that he could find.

Blake cracked open an eye as his mind returned to the real world. He looked around at the eerily familiar scene and asked, "Is this it?"

"Yeah," Johnson replied in a hoarse whisper. "You okay? You kind of zoned out there during the trip. Were you doing one of your Jedi things again or what?"

"Something like that," Blake said. "I had a vision. In it, I thought the orb was here. I even thought I could feel it here, but when I went inside, all I found was a document from England. Your bosses told me that the document was all that I was going to find here. They said that I should skip going inside here to find the orb and just go to Britain to look for it."

"That's good advice," Johnson said. "It's dangerous here."

"Tell me about it," Blake said. "In my vision, I found the document in a safe, but I was discovered and killed."

"Did Destiny's cousin kill you?"

"No," Blake said. "Don't ask. You really don't want to know."

Johnson really didn't want to know. He wished he didn't know anything, but it creeped him out that there was something worse that Blake didn't think he would want to know. "I think you should go to England like they said."

"I don't know how much I really trust them, but I have a feeling that this time they are telling it to me straight."

"I have no choice whether to trust them or not," Johnson said. "I can only listen and do what they say, or they'll drive me absolutely mad."

"Yeah," Blake snickered. "I can see how they could do that."

"Listen, man, I wish I could go with you, but I'm still keeping an eye on Logan. I suppose, though, that I could give you that ride to the bus station, or the airport maybe."

"Nah. You're busy. I see my ride coming now."

Johnson looked out the car window and saw one of the tractor trailers leaving the compound.

Blake jumped out of the car and flagged down the truck. He pushed the driver to offer him a ride.

"Where you heading?"

Blake chuckled and said, "England."

The driver also laughed and said, "I don't think I'm going that far."

"How about the airport?"

"Hop in."

Michelle felt bad for speaking so harshly to Ashlin, but the time had come for the young girl to recognize the evil influences of Honey and hopefully avoid them. She needed to start thinking more of the family and less of herself.

The matronly woman didn't know why she should be the only one with her sights set on the true prize, but everyone else seemed more focused on their own personal agendas. She looked around the room and recounted to herself how each of her friends had strayed off the true path.

Tempest was certainly determined to see her daughter well again, but not for the right reasons. Her motives were more personal and selfish. She had missed out on seeing Destiny grow and mature and saw this as an opportunity to rekindle the bond between a mother and a daughter instead of a necessity to stop Honey and her kind. Bonding with her daughter was a fine reason to want to save Destiny, but it blinded her to the kind of evil that Honey represented.

Zeline was just along for the ride. She had been shunned for so long as a crazy old coot that she was thrilled to finally be accepted into the clan as a real witch. Michelle couldn't really fault her, though. Zeline had never known Honey except for what they had told her. Still, this whole incident with Honey represented more of a metamorphosis for Zeline than a crusade to save the world.

Ashlin's motives were clear. She wanted Destiny for a big sister. But, as Michelle thought about it, maybe her motives weren't really so transparent. Maybe Honey's influence had already infected her so deeply that Ashlin wanted something more than just a family from Destiny. Maybe she wanted to be Destiny; to have Destiny's powers for herself.

Michelle's parade of growing paranoia was abruptly interrupted when a nurse came into the room and checked the machines that were keeping Destiny alive. She took Destiny's chart from a hook at the end of the bed and copied some numbers from the machines onto the clipboard. Michelle knew nothing of the nature of these high-tech devices that were monitoring Destiny's vital signs, but she was pretty sure that they should be able to read those numbers from some central computer somewhere. Everything was done by computers these days and the computers all talked to each other. She couldn't fathom why they would have someone come in here and interrupt everybody to write down some stupid numbers that a computer could have done so much easier. "Why are you doing that?" Michelle asked as the nurse returned the clipboard to its hook. "Why does you waste your time and our time to come in here and write down those numbers? Why don't you do something more useful, like helping my granddaughter to wake up instead of coming in here and gawking at all of us? Not just you neither. I mean the whole damned hospital. This girl needs your help, and you know something else? Y'all need her help too. That's right. Without her, this world is going to be nothin' but a pile of ash. You should be doing more to help her instead of just interruptin' us and writin' down your silly numbers."

Tempest tugged on Michelle's arm and whispered, "It's not her fault. Besides, I don't think you should be telling her so much."

"I'll tell her whatever I god damned want to tell her. She ain't doin' nothin' to help."

"Stop it!" Ashlin snapped. "I don't know what is going on in that head of yours, but you got to settle your emotions!"

Michelle ratcheted her voice up a notch as she yelled back, "You cain't talk to me like that! You're not my moth..."

Zeline jumped into Michelle's head and shouted, "What are you doing? This ain't like you!"

The nurse had seen this kind of reaction before, where family members were overwrought with emotions and lashed out at the staff, but still, the tears welled up in her eyes.

Tempest led her out of the room as Michelle turned to Zeline and barked, "You too? Is you gonna turn against me now? Ain't you got no appreciation for what I done for you? I let you in with us and now you gonna turn on me? Is all of you plannin' to go join Honey's army against me?"

Honey was still waiting for Pablo to deliver her lunch when Richard seated himself across from her. "That was a good speech. You sounded like someone that our people might follow."

Balletina leaned back and crossed her arms. She still saw Richard as part of the old guard. He didn't fit in with the new regime that she had just described to everyone.

"Stop givin' him the evil eye," Honey said to her. "He's done okay by me, and I trust him."

Richard privately harbored some doubts and was glad that Honey couldn't read his mind like the witches could. "One thing though. Before you set out to gain world domination, you're going to have to deal with the witches, and sooner would be better than later."

"I already dealt with my dear sweet cousin," Honey said. "Did you think she would be coming back from the dead?"

"She wasn't the only witch in the world. She wasn't even the only witch that had some of our powers. Her boyfriend was like her and I bet he's pissed as hell with you."

"So?" she asked. "I showed him a taste of what I got and he nearly dumped her for it. Besides, what's he going to do when I have a whole army trained up?"

"You don't think the witches are making an army of their own?" Richard asked.

"Oh yeah? You think they're all gonna be like my cousin with some of our powers?"

"I don't think it's going to matter whether they have our powers or not. We've had our armies before and we've had wars with them. They have their own powers and they have their ways to defeat us. If we allow them to build an army and prepare for war against us, you're going to find that we have our hands full."

"So," Balletina said, "we hit them first. We hit them fast, and we hit them hard." She paused and laughed. "Sorry, I didn't mean to sound like a football coach from an old movie, but maybe we don't need a whole army. Maybe just the two of us going out now, before they are prepared, will be enough."

"Don't underestimate them," Richard said. "They have their ways, and they can…"

Richard stopped abruptly and Honey asked, "What's wrong?"

Richard nodded his head to Honey's right and said, "I think you have an admirer."

Honey turned her head and saw little Tammy holding a cupcake with a lit candle in it. "Well, hello darling! What's this for?"

Tammy squealed, "Happy Birthday!"

Misty came running after the little girl and shouted, "Tammy!"

Honey chuckled and accepted the cupcake, saying, "But it's not my birthday, sweetheart."

Tammy didn't care and just clapped her hands while Honey blew out the candle.

Misty took Tammy's hand and said, "I thought I told you not to play with fire. Who lit the candle for you?"

Tammy just shrugged her shoulders and waved goodbye to Honey as Misty led her away.

Honey waved back to Tammy. "She's such a sweet little girl."

Balletina winked at Tammy as she left.

"About the witches," Honey said. "Is there any way for us to know how prepared they are?"

"We have our spies," Richard replied, "and our technology, but there's no way to guarantee that we'll know when they're ready for us. What really matters is that you know who our enemy is and all the many ways they can counter us."

Michelle didn't want to leave Destiny surrounded with traitors, but she needed to get away from them so she could regroup and clear her thoughts. Honey had to be stopped and unless Destiny returned, she might be the only one that knew how to do it. The parchment with the spell written on it was etched in her memory. It would be so easy for her to end it all, and it seemed like she didn't have as many loved ones as she had thought, so the consequences might not be so dire after all.

She was so lost in her thoughts that she had paid no attention to where she had wandered off to until she noticed that she had found her way back to the cafeteria by the garden. She sat down next to the window, but turned her face away from the garden. This wasn't a time when she wanted to enter the void to visit Destiny. She had to figure this out for herself, but her mind had called out for Destiny, anyway. This must be some kind of madness if she couldn't control her own thoughts anymore. First, her mind kept reciting the words to the dark spell, and now it called out for Destiny when all she wanted was some peace and quiet. It was probably some curse one of the others had put on her.

"Nana?" Destiny replied. "Is that you? Are you comin' for a visit?"

"No, Cherie. I ain't comin' to you this time. I gots to work this out on my own."

"Why?" Destiny asked. "And what are those words you keep repeating?"

"Don't you pay no mind to them words. Your nana is losing her mind and dem words just keep rambling through mah head."

"What language is that?"

"Tain't nothin'," Michelle replied. "It be gibberish. Nothin' more, but I cain't stop 'em from repeating. They is probably meant to drive me mad."

"It don't sound like nothin' to me. Those words sound ancient, like maybe the ancestors are trying to tell you something. Why don't you come visit me and we can figure them out together?"

"No!" Michelle barked. "We don't need to know what they mean!"

"Why?" Destiny asked. "If the ancestors think you need to know it, then maybe it's something important to help stop Honey."

"And maybe it be something that could unleash hell on all of us!"

"That's why we should figure it out. It might be something important. Maybe it's a warning, or maybe it's a key to stopping Honey. Maybe you and me are the only ones that kin figure it out! Together!"

Michelle did love Destiny. In fact, at this very moment, Destiny might be the only one that she really loved, which was even more reason for her to forget that she had ever seen the spell. With everyone else turned against her, Destiny was the only one left to pay the price.

"What price?" Destiny asked.

"Are you listening to my private thoughts?"

"How am I supposed to tell you were only thinking them? It sounded the same to me like when you are telling me something. It also sounded like you already know what those words are."

"Yeah, you right. I know what dey is alright, but they is a terrible curse that I wished I could forget."

"Why?

"Because," Michelle explained, "I learnt how to kill a sorcerer. I knows how to kill Honey, but it comes with a terrible cost. Someone near me; someone that I loves, would also have to die."

"Is that why you said everyone had turned against you?"

"No, I ain't told dem about it. I think dey is just losin' sight of the future. Honey is probably building an army of others dat can do what she does and I don't think we can stop her."

"Except for you," Destiny said plainly. "You can stop her with that spell."

"Ain't you listenin' to me? It comes with a terrible curse! The worst curse I ever heard of!"

"But sometimes we have to do what we have to do."

"I don't think I can bear it. Someone I love has to die."

"Are you sure?" Destiny asked. "I heard you say that I was the only one left that you loved, and I'm already dead."

"Don't say that," Michelle cried. "You ain't really dead and I cain't be da one that kills you for real."

"Not even to save the whole family? Not even to save the whole world?"

Michelle put her face in her hands and cried softly. It was too much for her to bear.

Between Logan and the mysterious librarians, Blake wasn't sure who he could trust and couldn't help feeling like he was being sent on a wild goose chase just to get him out of the way, but the notion of the orb wasn't new to them. Destiny had seen it and he had seen the visions of Destiny in the hospital and her mother urging him to get the orb. These guys in the grey robes didn't just dream that up, but did that really mean that the orb was actually in England? He didn't know, and leaving Destiny behind strained his heart, but he wasn't going to lose her just because he stayed at her side and did nothing.

The trucker pulled off the highway, but didn't take the exit to the airport. "Sorry, kid, but the departure zone wasn't really designed for big rigs."

"That's okay," Blake said. "I'll manage. Thanks for the ride."

Blake waved as the truck pulled away, then turned to face the airport. A slight breeze blew through his hair as he examined the tangle of roads that lead towards and around the terminal. None of them had sidewalks and all of them seemed more like frontage roads to different sections of the airport, but none of them screamed main terminal to him. His feelings weren't providing the insight he thought he needed, but he chose a road anyway and started walking. He stayed on the gravel covered shoulder and wondered if he had chosen the wrong road until he saw the welcome sight of a jet coming in for a landing, then another, and another at evenly spaced intervals. The streets may have left him feeling lost initially, but once he saw the lights of the terminal far off down the road, he quickened his pace.

He was surprised by how far away it was and quickened his pace when an airport police cruiser pulled alongside him and asked, "Where are you heading?"

"I'm trying to get to the airport," Blake replied.

"Well, you can't walk along this road."

"Honestly," Blake said, "I'm not so keen about walking on this road either, but I got a ride here on a trailer truck, and he didn't want to take his big rig through departures."

The cop looked at Blake suspiciously and asked, "What's your business here?"

"I'm going to England."

"With no bags?"

Blake shrugged and said, "I like to travel light, but this is a bit lighter than usual. I'll just have to resupply when I get there."

"Can I see your tickets?"

"I don't have them yet. I was going to buy them at the counter."

"You?" the officer asked, giving him a good look from head to toe. "You don't look like someone who can afford last minute tickets overseas."

"No," Blake said, "I guess I don't, but looks can be deceiving."

The cop reached for his radio and Blake could hear his thoughts to call for backup.

"You don't need to do that," Blake said directly into his head. "You probably have seen me in the movies and you know how eccentric they say I am in the tabloids."

The cop squinted at him and said, "You look kind of familiar to me. Do I know you?"

"I get that a lot," Blake replied.

"It's not safe to walk from here. Let me give you a ride."

Blake flashed him a big movie star smile and said, "Thanks. That's much appreciated."

Ashlin was still angry at Michelle, but she was also relieved when Michelle had rejoined them in Destiny's room. She couldn't explain the older woman's earlier behavior, but she could tell that something was deeply troubling her. With Blake, Johnson and Logan all gone, the once crowded hospital room had seemed lonely to the young red head and Michelle was a welcome presence in the room. Tempest had remained with her through the night, but sometimes Tempest was more of a challenge than she was company.

Michelle approached Ashlin with her head hung low. "I want to apologize for snapping at you before."

"It's okay," Ashlin said. "I can tell that something's been bothering you, but I don't know what it is. Would you like to talk about it?"

"No," Michelle replied, "I don't believe that I would, but thank you for offering. You look dreadfully tired and I be here to keep Destiny company now. Why don't you go get yourself some rest?"

Ashlin sighed softly as she contemplated what some rest might feel like. "Have you seen Blake?"

"No Cher, did you need something?"

"No," Ashlin replied. "I was just wondering if he'd left to find the orb yet."

Michelle frowned as she watched Ashlin's face. "What else be botherin' you?"

The young girl curled her lips and blew a few stray bangs off of her face, then sighed, "Nothin' really."

"Well, all right then," Michelle said, unconvinced. "If it tain't nothin', then I won't worry about it."

"It's just that I got this bad feeling about Johnson. Sometimes I can't tell if he's here to help us or to stop us."

Michelle hugged Ashlin and said, "I gots me that very same feelin'. Mebbe not so much about Johnson hisself, but about dem voices in his head. You go get you some rest now."

Ashlin went out to the lounge and found a soft chair to crash in, but it wasn't as inviting as a bed would have been. The hotel that Logan had arranged for them was only a mile or so away and she knew how to drive, sort of. Grandpa Zeb used to let her drive the tractor on the farm. She could probably keep a car on the road long enough to reach the hotel, and a real bed would be so much better than this.

"You'll do no such thing," Michelle said in her head. "I already gots me one granddaughter in the hospital because o' dat bitch Honey, I don't needs you addin' another child in here for me to worry about!"

"Yes'm"

Ashlin fell into the chair and closed her eyes, thinking to Blake, "Are you coming to see Destiny?"

She waited for an answer, but heard nothing back. She leaned her head back into the chair and closed her eyes, peeking through her lashes at the nurses and doctors walking back and forth just beyond the waiting room. The sounds of the hospital were routine. She heard clipboards snapping and the soft whir of the trolley cart wheels. Occasionally, the intercom would ding, followed by an announcement. The sounds merged together in her head as she drifted off into a deep slumber.

Work slowed on the farm as the Boutin family gathered outside the kitchen and peered into Saunders' memory for a glimpse of Destiny and what may have become of her. Visions of fire and explosions flashed through their minds. They saw tanks lined up outside a government building, but the tanks were turned in odd random directions and some were even crushed. Smoke billowed out of a crater in the ground.

"What we seek is in there," someone thought, "in that crater."

The family tried to see into the crater, but the smoke was as black as midnight.

"Woah," someone thought.

"What's up?" Brie asked. "Marge? Was that you?"

"Yeah," Marge replied. "I'm standing at the rim of the crater."

Marge's son chuckled and thought, "We're all looking into the crater, Mom."

"You might be looking," Marge replied, "but I'm actually there, but I feel like I'm there. I can even smell the gunpowder. I'm going in."

Brie was still looking at Saunders when she thought, "Does anybody else feel like they are actually there?"

Nobody answered and Brie added, "Be careful, Marge."

It wasn't a particularly steep crater, but the walls were littered with debris that Marge had to climb over to get to the bottom. She coughed from the thick smoke that assaulted her lungs.

"You okay Marge?"

"I'm fine, but it's hard to see anything, and the footing is ter-rible." The hard debris from the tanks stood in sharp contrast to the soft and crumbly ground that easily gave way to her footfall. Each step, as she descended, sunk a little deeper into the soft turf. The smoke thinned as she delved down into the hole and turned into a layer of smoke that remained mostly over her head. "Oh my god," she gasped. "I see her. I see cousin Destiny, but she don't look good."

"What's wrong with her?"

Marge cried softly, "I think she's dead. That soldier fella is with her. I think he's trying to help her. He's yelling at the ambulance driver, but I cain't hear him. They're taking her on a stretcher."

"Then she must not be dead," Brie thought, to everyone's relief. "Where are they taking her?"

"I don't know," Marge replied. "My feet are stuck in the ground and I can't follow them no more."

"So," Brie said to Saunders, "you were saying something about a blond girl. What happened to her?"

"I don't know. How did you know her?"

"What makes you think I know her?"

"I can tell that you know her. What are you hiding?" Saunders asked. "Why can't you just be truthful with me?"

"Me?" Brie asked. "You're the one that brung her up, but now you act like you don't know who she is."

Saunders grimaced as he grit his teeth and thought to himself, "It's more like I don't know what she is," but he didn't want to ask her that. "I don't know who she is. In fact, I don't know anything about her. I was hoping you could tell me."

"Tell you what? That I used to know someone named Honey, and I also knew a blond girl about yay high?"

Saunders sighed. She wasn't going to volunteer any information. He rose from the table and said, "I'm sorry to have bothered you."

Brie may not have seen what had happened to Destiny, but she felt the anguish in Saunders' heart. Something was really bothering him, but more than that, he was deeply concerned for the blond girl that he didn't know, even if he didn't know why. "No," she blurted out, "Don't go. Her name was Destiny...is Destiny. Oh, please tell me she is okay."

"Destiny?" Something clicked in Saunders' memory. Milton had dreamt of Destiny's wedding. "Honey and Destiny? Did Destiny come here with Honey?"

Someone outside thought, "Don't tell him too much," but Brie was being guided by some inner instinct to reveal more than she wanted.

"No," she said, "Destiny came to us much later, after Honey and her mother had already taken over the farm."

"They took over the farm? By force?"

"You might say that," Brie admitted cautiously.

"But things changed, didn't they? After Destiny came?"

"You might say that too."

Saunders sucked downed his lemonade and asked, "Did Destiny already know Honey when she came here?"

Brie shook her head.

"No?"

Brie shook her head again.

"What about Blake? Did Destiny know someone called Blake?"

Brie's eyes widened a bit as she nodded her head.

"Did he come here with Destiny?"

Brie nodded her head.

"Were they married? Destiny and Blake, I mean."

"Noooo," Brie hung on to the syllable to emphasize the point. "They was only sixteen years old."

Saunders raised his eyebrows and cocked his head.

"We ain't like that here," Brie volunteered. "They were good kids."

"What about Honey? Did Blake already know Honey?"

"No, but it warn't like that tramp didn't try gettin' to know him, if you know what I mean."

The picture in Saunders' mind wasn't getting any clearer. "So they both came here, out of the blue, and neither of them had ever known Honey before?"

"Nope, but her nana sure did, or, at least, she knew Honey's mother."

"Destiny's grandmother was here?"

"Yup. They come here with Michelle. Michelle was family. I already told you about Cousin Pete, may he rest in peace. Well, Michelle was Cousin Pete's little girl. The one that ran away with her mama after that bitch Abilene come here. I don't think none of us ever knowed Destiny before they come here."

"So what happened between Destiny and Honey?"

Brie's hands quaked as she refilled Saunders' tumbler. "It started with Michelle and Abilene. Michelle used to live here on the farm, but her mother naturally didn't take too kindly to old Pete bringing Abilene's tramp mother to live with us, and not just 'cause she was shacked up with Pete, neither."

"They were still married?" Saunders asked, unable to suppress the shock in his voice.

"Oh, hell no. After Pete brung his Jezibel here to the farm, they was divorced faster than you kin say armadillo. Faith hated Abilene's mama and Michelle hated Abilene just as much, but it warn't just because they stole her daddy away. There was somethin' else that she despised about Abilene, so they just up and left. That was long before Honey was born and to tell you the truth, I don't rightly know who her daddy was. Abilene slept around a bit, just like her bitch of a daughter. I even seen her sniffin' around Grandp Zeb a time or two, but I think he was a couple decades past knockin' that tramp up. Most likely, she laid some poor soul what come here to deliver somepin', but maybe I'm just hopin' dat Honey don't got no genes from our family tree."

Saunders counted on his fingers. "Destiny's grandmother and her great-grandmother lived here, but left. Did you ever know Destiny's mother?"

Brie shook her head. "She wasn't born yet when they left. In fact, Michelle was a good girl and a smidge too young to be with child at the time when they left. We never seen Tempest until they came here, but even then, none of us ever got to know her."

"Are you sure that they were family?"

"Michelle was. Plenty of us remembered Michelle."

"You can't possibly be old enough to remember Michelle before Destiny's mother was born."

Brie blushed. "Not me personally," she lied, "but plenty of the family remembered her. Abilene sure did."

"But you can't be sure about Destiny."

"Sure I can. Her family resemblance was unmistakable."

Saunders was confused. She couldn't have been family if she was sent here from heaven.

"Do you know where Destiny came from?"

Someone outside thought to her, "Don't tell him," but Brie nodded her head slowly and said, "They was livin' in the swamps in Louisiana."

"In the swamps?" Saunders asked.

"Out in a bayou called Cricket Bend. We never seen the place, but judgin' by how Destiny turned out, I'd say they done alright there."

Saunders was more confused now than when he had arrived. How could those girls have family here if they were supernatural beings? For that matter, how could they even have mothers and grandmothers? If they weren't angels or demons, then what were they? If Flinch was right, and they were aliens, then it wasn't some kind of an invasion, but how long have they been here? And what does that make these people? If they were an alien sleeper cell, then they probably wouldn't be telling him so much.

Ashlin's dream took her back to the place where she had seen Logan searching for the orb on the computer, but the room was dark and empty. A cold shiver swept across her skin as she sensed a dark force looming outside of the room. She closed her eyes to see what was going on, but all she saw was the door that led out of the library. The hairs on her head prickled as she left the dark room and followed the hallway to the end, where a staircase took her down to the main level. The hall was cold and dim, but the stairwell was even darker. Her senses told her that the danger she felt was down those stairs, and the hackles on the back of her neck told her to leave it alone. She clung to the banister as she slowly delved down the stairwell, though her ghost like fingers could not actually grip the rail. Her skin shivered as she descended onto the lower floor, but she didn't know if it was actually cold or if she was just scared. At the base of the stairs, children huddled together just inside the door that led back out into the lower hallway. They held their hands over their ears and cried out in pain. Ashlin couldn't hear what they heard, but she saw the agony in each of their faces.

The hallway itself was quiet, but was filled with people pushing away from the front of the building and away from the outside windows. All of them showed pain on their faces and held their hands covering their ears. A few brave souls separated from the younger students and pushed forward to see what was outside in spite of the pain that was evident on their faces. Bright lights flooded the front of the building as vehicles filled the parking lot and trained their search lights onto the building. Ashlin didn't have to push through the crowd, her wispy body passed right through the throng of onlookers and straight to the front door.

She tried opening the door, but her hands passed right through the door handle. She sensed the terror in the people around her, but didn't feel it in her own heart, yet the hairs on the back of her neck remained at full attention. The danger outside and the fear inside simultaneously pushed and pulled at her body. Whatever was happening was coming from out front. Ashlin pressed her face through the thick wooden door and saw the army collecting outside. Tanks and armored vehicles flooded the parking lot. Men in silver suits lined up in front of the vehicles and were preparing to come into the building. This was an army of men, and there was no wonder why they were here. The skies were blotted out with black smoke that carried the taint of Honey's magic.

In an instant, Ashlin saw what the army had seen. Whole neighborhoods had been flattened by Honey's reign of terror. It wasn't hard for her to look forward to see the whole world in flames if someone didn't stop her, but could it be that the army would be their savior? Was Destiny not the one that they had waited for, after all?

Chapter 16

Blake tried keeping his mind clear and his thoughts to himself. If Michelle ever learned how he pushed his way to get a ticket for England, she would throw a fit. He couldn't stay completely off of the psychic grid, however. He would have to tell Destiny where he was going. Finding some privacy in the airport was impossible, but he found a gate that had just emptied into an airplane, leaving only a few scattered seats that were still unoccupied. He chose a row facing a window and settled into a seat with a clear view of the tarmac. The luggage carts snaked around the jets outside as he propped his head up to one side, with his elbow not so comfortably set on the chair's armrest. The ground crew scurried around, throwing luggage onto the conveyer belts that carried them up into the bellies of the planes. Boredom set in and Blake found himself listening in on their thoughts. He heard them complain about their lives, both at home and at work. They griped to each other about their wives, their girlfriends, and their boyfriends.

It all sounded the same to Blake. People may think that their lives are complicated, but in truth, they have very simple existences without magic complicating things. Their ignorance is their saving grace. They can live their lives without ever knowing how close they could be to annihilation. That thought reminded him of the safe little dream world where Destiny was hiding. He didn't know if he was ready yet, but that memory and his desire to tell her what he was about to do transported him into her dream without his even trying.

"If you came back to tell me that I'm delusional again," Destiny said crossly, "then you can just leave." As soon as the words left her mouth, she regretted them. She was torn between her loneliness in this place and the unending defense of her death.

"No," Blake said. "I can honestly say that I did not come here with the intention of drawing you out of your delusion."

Destiny furrowed her brows and bit her lip. "I don't think I like that answer so much."

"I guess you wouldn't," Blake said, "but I did want to tell you something."

"I don't want to hear no more talk about what's wrong with me."

"It may come as a surprise to you," Blake said with just a hint of irritation in his voice, "but the world does not revolve around you. War with the sorcerers is coming whether you choose to hide in here or not."

Destiny definitely did not like that answer and turned her back to him.

Blake raised his right hand and said, "I swear that I did not come here to discuss your situation, not exactly, anyway."

"What's that supposed to mean?"

"I'm going to England."

"You're what?" Destiny snapped back at him. "You just told me that war was coming and you're leaving? Don't you know that my mama and nana are going to need your support?"

"Don't worry," Blake said. "They support what I'm doing."

"Why in the world would you go to England?"

"Because I found a note that said it is there, or at least it was there. I'm looking for clues."

"Clues for what?"

"Clues to find the orb. You saw it once before. He called it the Orb of Destiny."

"Oh, that thing," she said, almost laughing. "I thought it was pretty funny that we shared the same name. I guess that with me gone, you'll be needing the extra power from the orb to fight off Honey."

"Yeah," Blake said. "Something like that."

"You want to stay for some tea?"

"Tea? Since when do you drink tea?"

"I always liked tea," she said. "Now-a-days, it's almost all we drink around here."

"We?" Blake asked. "Did you finally get someone else to join you?"

Destiny frowned and faced him again. "No, but I still have hope. I don't know why I said that. Maybe I'm going crazy in this place."

Blake wanted to suggest that she leave if this place was driving her crazy, but he said he wouldn't and kept quiet about it. "I should be going," he said as he wrapped his arms around her. "Getting the orb may be dangerous. It feels like someone out there has been trying to keep me from it."

Michelle saw the discomfort on Tempest's face and walked around the bed to be at her daughter's side. She had seen this look before. When Tempest was young, she was easily overcome by the voices in her head, but they weren't crazy voices, they were normal ordinary thoughts of people around her. Her gifts were powerful, but she didn't like other people's thoughts mixing with her own and had refused training as a child and consequently struggled to deal with them on her own now. Michelle wrapped her arm around Tempest's shoulders and asked, "You want me to go get Ashlin for you? I seen what a comfort she be for you."

"No mama, that ain't what's bothering me right now, and besides, Zeline's been helpin' me with that, but if the two of you don't mind, I think I'll go sit with Ashlin for a spell anyway."

"Of course. That be fine too," Michelle said. "Zeline and me kin watch Destiny."

Tempest hadn't been completely honest with her mother. The voices were crowding in on her, but she also saw that something had been troubling her mother and she had seen what a comfort Zeline had been for her, so she didn't want to split them up. She left the small room to find Ashlin, but the hallway seemed to lean to the left and as she looked down the length of it, she felt like it had stretched farther away from her than it actually was. She had seen all this before. Her brain tried shutting out the voices, but it left her feeling dizzy. Ashlin told her not to block out all the voices, but to focus on a single voice. That voice had always been Ashlin's, but she was silent now. Tempest leaned on the wall as she worked her way out to the lounge.

A nurse came to her and gently held her arm to steady her. "Are you okay?"

"I'm just dizzy. I think I'll be fine if I just go sit down with my niece."

The nurse stayed with her all the way to the lounge. "Which one's your niece?"

"The redhead in the corner."

"Ah, yes. She's been there all morning."

"We were up all night with my daughter. She's in a coma."

"That's right," the nurse said. "I remember them trying to ship your daughter out of here. I know they have rules about how we use the ICU, but I still liked the way your family insisted on keeping her here. She's a lucky girl to have a family like yours."

"She's too important to give up on. We just gotta convince her to come back."

The nurse felt a tug on her heart. She'd heard so many families express similar feelings when their loved ones were locked in a coma. "Here you go," she said as she settled Tempest into the chair next to Ashlin.

"I know what you're thinking," Tempest said. "You think that she's gone; that she's brain dead, but she's not. She's different. We'll bring her back."

Ashlin opened her eyes and asked, "What's up?"

"Oh you know," Tempest said. "I been having that thing again. You know, that thing that you help me with."

"Your aunt got dizzy," the nurse said, "and no wonder. She's been up all night. You really should think about getting some sleep, like your niece here."

"That sounds good," Tempest admitted, "but we shouldn't be sleeping in your waiting room."

"Now you sound like our administrator," the nurse said. "I tell you, he'd rent out these chairs if he thought he could get away with it."

Tempest laughed. "He wasn't very nice, and I don't think he wanted to help us very much."

"I really didn't like him," Ashlin said. "And he wouldn't have helped us at all if I hadn't made him…I mean, if I hadn't made him feel guilty."

"Well, whatever you did," the nurse said, "it seemed to have worked. Would you like something to drink? I'm going to go get your aunt a juice. Would you like some chocolate milk?"

Ashlin nodded her head enthusiastically.

"Whew," she said when the nurse left, "I almost let it slip that I used the voice to force the doctor to let Destiny stay."

Tempest hugged Ashlin and said, "I doubt she would have believed that anyway, but even if she had, I get the feeling that she wouldn't have cared."

"What's with the long face?" Balletina asked. "Did you think it was going to be easy?"

Honey smirked and said, "I kinda did. I never thought them witches could ever do nothing to hurt us."

"Maybe you should get back to training us some more. I can't be the only student able to pick up your powers."

"That's a good idea," Richard said. "Would you like me to bring some of our teachers here to help organize the classes?"

"Why?" Honey asked. "What can they do?"

"You saw me pick up lightning," Balletina said. "They taught me that, except they couldn't actually do it and neither could I until I was with you, but still, I got a lot of the concepts from them."

"They could organize the students into different classes," Richard said, "and they could even help evaluate the students for you. You would only have to go around and show them how the theory is put to use."

"It's possible," Balletina said, "that they know some spells that you could learn too. You'd be more powerful, and you'd have an army behind you."

"That sounds good," Honey said. "You really think I could learn some more spells?"

"According to the ancient texts," Richard said, "Our people used to know some really wicked spells. How would you like to throw blades from your hands like you do with the fire?"

Honey's face filled with anticipation. "Blades? That sounds pretty cool."

"More than cool," Balletina said. "You don't think them army boys aren't going to show up here one day in those silver fire proof suits?"

Honey laughed as she pictured it. "You're right. I bet they wouldn't be blade proof."

"Let's go," Balletina said as she tugged on Honey's arm. "I can try to remember what else they told me. We can see if you can pick it up, too."

As they neared the hallway, they heard a girl outside say, "She wants to be queen of the world? I mean, I know she's bad ass and can make fire and all that, but this chick wants to rule the whole planet?"

"Whose gonna stop her?" another asked. "You?"

"Did you hear that?" Honey asked.

"Never mind them," Balletina said as she led Honey down the hall away from them. "They're nobodies."

Honey glanced back at them. They wore expensive clothing like so many of the girls in this place that thought they were special. "They talk like they think they're better than me."

Balletina stopped walking and said, "I know them. You want me to talk to them?"

Honey thought about it. They heard what she had said to everyone, but they didn't believe it. Something had to be done to show them in a way that they couldn't deny. "Yeah. Go talk to them. Invite them to my next class and make sure they understand that it's not optional."

Honey walked further down the hall and turned to watch from a distance while Balletina walked straight up to the girls.

"Do you mind?" one of the girls asked. "We're having a private conversation."

"Not private enough," Balletina said. "We heard you."

Two of the three girls shrunk away from Balletina, but the third stood her ground and said, "Don't you know it's rude to eavesdrop on other people's conversations?"

"Rude?" Balletina asked. "You're worried about me being rude? You should really be more concerned about the stupid things that come out of your mouth."

"Who in the hell do you think you are?" the girl asked. "You're nobody and you can't talk to me like that. It's a free world, and I'll say whatever I want."

"There you go again, saying something stupid."

"If you're not going to go away, then you might as well say what's on your mind and run along back to your new friend."

The girl was really getting under Balletina's skin. She wanted to slap her right there, or better yet, fry her, but she restrained herself and calmly said, "I came to invite you to a training session."

"Not interested."

"It wasn't really a question," Balletina explained. "Your presence is required at the next class. If you want to talk like you're so special, then it's time you come and prove it."

"I don't have to prove anything!"

"Yes you do," Balletina said as the other two girls tried sneaking away. "You too. Both of you. Class starts in ninety minutes."

"And what if I don't?"

Balletina balled up a fist, not sure if she was going to punch her or form a fireball, but one of the two other girls grabbed their friend by her arm and said, "Stop it, Angie. She's serious. We'll go to her class."

"Yeah," the other said. "It might be fun."

***

Finding the right Cricket Bend wasn't easy, but Saunders had a couple clues to separate it from the myriad of other Cricket Bends in the country. It was in Louisiana and it was somewhere in the bayous. The problem was that it wasn't on the map. He found vague references to it, but nothing that led him directly there. He did find one tidbit of information that helped. There had been a mysterious fire and an even more mysterious trial held there.

He took a commercial flight to Lafayette and rented a vehicle. The trial records included an address that was on an interstate of sorts. He thought that he was already in the swamps as the road divided a jungle and was lined on both sides by indigenous trees, but it wasn't until he reached the gas station and the local store that highlighted Cricket Bend, that he actually saw the true swamp.

He pulled up to the diner, thinking that it would be the best place for him to get some information. Even if he had to sift through a lot of gossip and rumors, he wouldn't mind a bite to eat.

Marie didn't think much of him when she saw his rental car drive up, but when he exited the car and she saw his uniform, she went to the door to greet him. "Bonjour. Bonjour."

Saunders smiled broadly. "Good day."

"Zis way," she sang sweetly as she guided him to an empty table. She had grown accustomed to police and federal investigators coming in to learn about the strange fire. Most of them were too cheap to purchase a meal. "You must be here for ze information, but first we eat. Would you like to start with some coffee?"

Saunders nodded. "Coffee would be fine. Black, please."

Marie smiled as she put a menu on the table and left to get him some coffee. Too many of the men who came here wanted to find something disturbing about Michelle and Destiny, so she had learned her own ways to deal with them. She poured a cup of bitter coffee with chicory and brought it to his table. Saunders was still looking over the menu when she asked, "'ave you decided yet?"

Saunders turned the single-page menu over, but found the back side blank and returned to the front. "I'll have a tuna sandwich and a side salad."

Marie smiled politely, but grimaced on the inside. The further these big city folks lived from the Bend, the more they ate like they were afraid of their food. "Oui, monsieur. Will zat be all?"

Saunders sipped his coffee and puckered his lips over the sour mixture. "Do you have any sugar substitute?"

"No, monsieur. We usually dip ze beignets in ze coffee to tame ze flavors."

Saunders put the cup down and nodded his head. "I'll have some of that then."

"Right away." Marie skipped into the kitchen and delivered his order to the cook, then grabbed the tray of sugar-coated beignets that she had already set aside and brought them to his table. She was wickedly delighted when he frowned at them. Most outsiders thought of them as little more than doughnuts that looked like fritters.

Saunders picked one up and shook off some of the powdered sugar.

"No!" she said. "Don't do zat. It is ze sugar dat helps ze coffee."

Saunders sighed and stared at the sugar laden confection before dipping the nugget into his coffee and eating the coffee drenched end. It had been a while since he had allowed himself to indulge in anything this sweet. He silently apologized to the spare tire that had started to accumulate around his waist and went for another dip.

Marie returned to the kitchen to wait for his food.

<hr>

"Tempest?" Ashlin thought directly into Tempest's mind. "Tempest? Can you hear me?"

"I hear you," Tempest said, "but I hear everyone else, too."

"I told you before that you can't force all the voices out of your head. You can only pick one and focus on it until the others fade into the background.

"I know," Tempest said, "but you were sleeping and I couldn't hear you. That's why I came out here to be closer to you."

"You need to learn to focus on other voices, too. I won't always be around when you need me."

Tempest sifted through the myriad of voices and picked out a little girl, who was crying. "Okay," she said, "I found someone, but she's crying and it's making me sad."

"You don't want to listen too closely," Ashlin said. "If you get too close, you'll not only hear her voice, but you'll feel her emotions too."

"I can't help it," Tempest said. "I want to help her."

"Then pick a different voice."

"I have to help her first." Tempest reached further into the little girl's mind and thought, "You are not alone. I may not be in your room with you, but I am here and I feel your pain."

"Who are you?" the girl asked.

"I'm a friend. I'm here to see my daughter, but I heard you crying."

The girl's mood improved. "My mommy's not here. I'm all alone."

"Maybe you were all alone," Tempest said, "but I'm with you now."

Ashlin tapped Tempest on the shoulder and asked, "How many voices do you hear now?"

Tempest was surprised by the question, but even more surprised by the answer. "Just the one."

"See how it works?"

Richard had a frown on his face when Honey and Balletina arrived in the Gymnasium.

Honey put on a fake frown and played with his collar. "What's the matter Ricky?"

"It's just not safe," he replied. "They're sure to be watching this place and you're just giving them more to see."

"We're indoors," she said as she pointed to the roof overhead. "How are they going to see us? Do they have..." she paused dramatically, then giggled as she wiggled her fingers and accentuated the last word, "...magic?"

Richard ignored her theatrics and said, "Something like that. They have infrared cameras that can read our heat signatures. They can watch us walking around, roof or no roof. You can damn sure bet that they'll have a real good view of your pyrotechnics."

"My pyro what? Oh, never mind. I'm givin' these classes and trainin' my army. If you don't want them to watch, then why don't you come up with some way to hide us?"

"Yeah," he said, unconvinced, "sure."

"If you ain't up to it, maybe Frank can do it. He spends most of his time in the libary and it could be that he runs across a spell that can help put your mind to ease."

Richard left the room before his grumbling became too vocal. He bumped into Angie and her friends and saw the looks on their faces. He didn't need to be a witch to have a bad feeling about this session and was glad to be leaving the room.

"Oh look," Balletina said. "They showed up."

"I'll be damned," Honey said. "I guess I owe you a dollar. Come on in girls. Shyness don't get you nothin'."

Angie's friends stood on each side of her and pushed her ahead of them.

"I'm glad you could join us," Honey said.

"Did we have a choice?" Angie asked with her voice laced heavily with attitude.

Her friends nudged her and said, "Shhh."

"You should listen to your friends," Balletina said.

Angie twisted her shoulders right and left, yanking her arms from the other girl's grips. "You call these my friends? They're just my entourage. That's French. It means 'little people who like to hang out with more important people'. Lately, it seems like they aren't even very good at that."

Her friends took a step away from her. Their faces registered both their feelings about her statement and their fear of the consequences.

"And," Honey said, "you must think you're pretty important. Is that right?"

"That's right," Angie said. "I heard what you said in the cafeteria. It's always the poor people who are trying to make it sound like money isn't the true power, but it doesn't matter what all you poor people say. Anything you have to say doesn't really count in the end."

"I see," Honey said, turning to her friends. "And what about you two? You don't look like you agree with her."

"No, ma'am," they said in unison.

"Ma'am? Did you just call me ma'am? Do I look like a ma'am to you?"

The two girls did not mean to insult Honey, but they didn't know what to call her and began shaking out of fear for their lives.

"It's okay," Honey said, "I'm just messin' with you. Since Angie don't seem to respect you none, maybe you'd like to be in my antoorahjee."

Angie snickered at Honey's pronunciation.

"Did I say something funny?"

Angie sneered. "Just about everything you say is funny."

Angie's friends left her side and walked over to stand with Honey.

Honey cocked her head to the side and said, "I guess you don't respect me none."

Angie didn't reply, but she didn't have to. The expression on her face said it all.

"Okay then," Honey said. "Let's start our class now. Angie, I want you to stand over there on the mat with the red dot, while your friends stay here with us."

Angie crossed her arms and refused to move.

Honey reached out and gripped a force field around Angie, and moved her to the mat she had indicated. Angie was unable to resist and registered true fear on her face as she lost her footing and stumbled onto the dot on the floor. Honey smiled wickedly and asked, "Do you still think that money is power?"

Angie just glared back at Honey.

"Stand up!" Honey commanded.

Angie did not want to do anything that Honey said, but she also refused to be on her knees before a penniless country bumpkin. She not only climbed back onto her feet, but she held her head up high. "My father will hear about this, and it won't go well for you."

Honey ignored her and turned to the other two. "Hold your hands up like this."

They did as they were told.

"Now picture that you are holding a piece of paper in your palm. Imagine that you have a magnifying glass aiming the sun onto the paper until it starts to smoke and catches fire."

The girls did as she asked, but nothing happened.

"Twist your hands around. Feel the heat in your palms. Visualize the paper as it starts to turn brown then catches fire."

One of the two girls got excited when smoke emerged from her palm.

"Yes!" Honey exclaimed. "That's it! Now flick it to Angie."

The excited girl flicked the smoke and a brief bright cinder shot out towards Angie. Squealing and laughter erupted from the doorway.

Honey looked over her shoulder and saw the little girl, Tammy, watching them. "Again!" she shouted to her new students.

The two girls concentrated on their palms. Having seen what her friend could do, the other felt a surge of confidence and created a cinder of her own that struck Angie in the leg.

Angie cried out, "Owww. Why are you doing this? Stop listening to her, you ungrateful little bitches!"

"Good!" Honey shouted. "Good! It takes time to master."

Angie tried leaving the spot, but Honey held her in place. "Who the hell do you think you are? You can't do this to me! My father will hear about this and you will pay! You…"

Honey added a small force to hold her mouth shut and said, "Balletina? Show them what happens when they get real good."

Balletina joined the two girls and asked, "Singe her eyebrows?"

Honey released the force on Angie's jaw and asked, "You think you've learned your lesson yet?"

Angie set her jaw and looked down her nose at them.

"No," Honey said as she shook her head. "I guess not. Full force. Hit her with everything."

"What are you doing?" Angie screamed. "Don't you dare!"

Balletina looked sadly at Angie and said, "You brought this on yourself, Angie." She produced a softball sized flame and held it for a moment.

Angie's eyes grew large. She tried running, but Honey held her in place. "You motherless little skank! You stupid little..."

Balletina had heard enough and launched the ball onto Angie. She screamed as the fireball struck her and rapidly spread around her body, travelling up and over her head, squelching her screams as the flames engulfed her. Honey watched her shrivel within the flames and waited until she was fully charred before she released her and let the ashes fall to the ground.

"I expect you girls to be at all my classes," Honey said. "I think y'all look like 'A' list material to me."

Tammy came running in from the doorway and flung her arms around her sister, Misty.

Abilene clapped from the doorway and sang out, "That's my baby! The queen is back to her old self. Long live the queen!"

"Hey Mama," Honey said. "I guess I have been a little off my game lately."

"No worries," Abilene said. "You went through somethin' that was more than any of us can ever understand. How about you and your mama go get us some ice cream?"

Tammy jumped up and down shouting, "Ice cream! Ice cream!"

Honey laughed and asked Misty, "Is she going to come with you all the time?"

A tear gathered in Misty's eye as she hugged her little sister and Ramona explained, "Tammy has to come with Misty now. Their parents died last night."

"Oh no," Honey said. "Just last night? Wow. You've been through so much in such a short time!"

Ramona nodded blankly, still staring at Angie's ashes.

Honey felt genuinely sad and asked, "You mean this precious little thing ain't got no parents now? What happened?"

"It's still under investigation," Ramona replied, "but they lived in the employee wing with their father, and so far, they said that it looks like their father was smoking in bed and the apartment caught fire. Only Misty and Tammy survived. I'm letting them stay with me in my dorm room until we figure out something better. I hope that's okay."

Honey knelt down and hugged Tammy. "That's terrible. Of course you can come for ice cream with us."

Honey took Tammy by the hand and waltzed up to her mother, offering her other arm to Abilene and said, "That sounds pretty good, only they're coming with us."

"Go ahead," Ramona said, with her eyes locked on Angie's remains. "I don't feel like ice cream right now."

"You go," Misty said to Tammy. "I'm going to stay here with Ramona."

Honey looked down at Tammy and scrunched up her face. "Is this something that the old me would have done?"

Abilene shrugged and said, "Maybe we just takes the best of the old you and the new you and puts them together."

Michelle was completely unaware that it was her own recent behavior that was more out of character than everyone else in the room. In her mind, she was the only one that had remained unchanged and it was all of them that had been acting strangely, but she was acutely aware that their eyes were all on her, although she saw that as just one more sign that they were all behaving a bit different.

She didn't care. Well, she did care, but she wasn't going to let them prevent her from doing her duty. If Destiny wasn't going to return to save the world, then she would have to step up and do it for her. Maybe they'll all thank her in the end, or maybe they're too far gone already. If they had truly turned against her, then she couldn't risk revealing her plan, or the dark spell that she had learned.

Her private reverie was interrupted when she heard the ringing of a small bell. Her eyes darted around the room to see who had rung it, but not only did none of them have a bell, they showed no signs of even having heard it. If they believed that they could distract her by using their magic to make sounds that only she could hear, they were mistaken. It rang again, and she traced the sound to the small bell tower that she had made. The bell glinted as a single ray of sun pierced through the closed blinds to highlight the small metallic object.

She tried looking as nonchalant as possible while she quietly stepped over to the tower and picked it up. This talisman was important and the ringing she heard was proof of its importance. Somehow, she knew, deep inside of her, that the bell was a key to the spell that she had learned. The parchment said that it required something to pierce the target's defenses. She thought, at first, that it had meant a weapon of some kind, but now it was all clear to her. The high-pitched tone of the bell pierced into her mind and it was as if she had known it all along.

The bell tinkled as she sat down with the tower in her lap. She couldn't feel any power emanating from it, but she had faith that it wouldn't have been revealed to her if it had not meant something special. She brushed the polished metal with the tip of her finger. It was cool to her touch, but still gave off no cosmic sense of power. No matter.

She held it to her bosom and closed her eyes, thinking, just call upon me when the time is right. I won't let you down.

***

Marie waited for Saunders to finish his lunch, then slid into the other side of the booth facing him. He'd tried several times to start a dialog with her, but she had neatly fended him off each time with food and drink. He was still trying to figure out how to engage her in a conversation when she smiled at him and said, "Zis is ze part where you ask me ze questions and I decide if I should give you ze answers."

"Oh," he said with a sly smile, "you're a cynic."

"No Monsieur, but I have seen your kind before. You come in here demanding answers and flashing your badges, like it was our civic duty to help you."

"Isn't it?"

"No. My first duty is to my family and my friends. Where is your duty?"

Saunders sighed and slouched his shoulders. "I'm not so sure anymore. I mean, I have a duty to my country, and I take that very seriously, but lately, I've been too busy trying to find someone."

"You are trying to catch someone? You are not ze police."

"Not to catch someone. I think I'm trying to protect her, but I can't remember her."

"How can you do zis if you can't remember her?"

Saunders folded his napkin and said, "Honestly, I don't know, but I keep hoping that I might finally remember her when I find her. I found her family. They told me that she used to live here, but I'm not so sure that she really came from here."

"You sink ze family lied to you?"

"No," he said, shaking his head, "but I wonder if she told them the truth."

"Do you know ze girl's name?"

"Yes. Her name is Destiny. She's about this tall with blond hair." Saunders' mood perked up when he saw Marie's reaction. "You knew her? She really was from here?"

"Oui. I knew her. She lived here as long as I can remember."

Saunders frowned, but he should have been happy. Living here a long time didn't fit with being an angel or any other supernatural being. He was no closer to knowing what she was. "The family said that her home burned down. Do you remember a dark-haired girl coming to visit her that day?"

Marie thought about it for a moment, but shook her head. "No. Only ze four men and ze boy came, but ze boy was her friend. I don't sink ze other men were friends."

If Destiny had lived here a long time and Honey was not the one that came and burned down the house, what else could have happened here? Saunders wanted to go back to their first assumption that these were aliens with supernatural powers. He could probably fight aliens better than demons. "Can you tell me where I can find the home?"

"No. Zat is, even if I knew, I don't sink you'd ever find it." Marie pointed to the swamp and continued, "She lived out zare in ze bayou."

He looked out through the dirty window, at the untamed swamp where she was pointing, and replied, "Oh," unable to suppress the disappointment in his voice. He pulled out his wallet and put some bills on the table. "Thank you for your time."

"I'm sorry Monsieur. If I knew where ze home was, I would show you personally, but I was never at ze house."

"I understand. Can you tell me where I can get a boat?"

Marie pointed next door and said, "In ze general store, but you better tell 'enry zat Marie sent you. He don't like strangers so much since dose men come and make Michelle go away."

Ashlin couldn't shake the nagging concern that Johnson was up to something. She went to the window to look out into the parking lot, as if she thought he would suddenly return. An ambulance sat out in front of the emergency room, with its red and yellow lights blinking on top of the driver's cab and more lights tracing the outline of the box shaped back. She rested her tired head against the window, staring absently at the ambulance, and sighed deeply from exhaustion. The ground reflected the red and yellow glow as the flashing lights spread wider in her vision and flew across the sky, landing on the ground all around her, bursting into flames that blasted her with heat. She refocused her eyes and saw more lights streaking across the sky towards her. A barrage of lights streaked across the sky towards her, one after the other, bursting on the ground around her. It wasn't safe in the middle of the field where she stood. A nearby blast forced her to duck behind a boulder, but she still felt the heat through the large rock. Tears pushed to escape from her closed eyes. The last one landed too close for her to feel safe. She brushed her hands through her hair, afraid that the heat from the blast might have singed her hair and left it smoldering.

Someone behind her yelled, "Run!" She took off sideways towards the attackers instead of running away. Something inside of her wouldn't let her leave yet. She needed to get a better look at them. She felt the flames burst behind her, but they landed farther away now. The attackers didn't see her get away. She ran to a tree and shimmied up for a better look. It was a large pine tree that jutted straight up into the air. She climbed as far up the trunk as she could and almost wished she hadn't. Hundreds of sorcerers filled the field, casting fire balls that arced through the air and landed on the witches behind her.

"This can't be," she thought to Tempest. "There are too many of them."

"Too many of who?" Tempest asked as she stroked the youth's fine red hair.

"What are you doing up here?" Ashlin asked when she heard Tempest's voice.

"Up where?" Tempest asked. "Are you feeling okay?"

Ashlin's head swirled as the waiting room bobbed up and down in her vision. "I think I should sit up for a minute."

"Sure," Tempest said. "Let me help you."

"It was her," Ashlin said. "It was cousin Honey, but she had hundreds of others with her and they all learned to launch fire."

"What? You saw Honey? She's coming back?"

"And she won't be alone next time."

"Neither will we," Tempest said. "We can't be. We had better do something to prepare."

***

Three librarians huddled around the fire in their special meditation room. The hoods on their grey robes were all pulled forward, trapping the warmth from the glowing coals and blocking out any distracting views of each other from their vision. They stared not into the fire, but through it into the interior of a small office at the Salt Lake Airport. It was the same airport where Blake waited patiently for his plane. A solitary man sat in the security room scanning the monitors that continually rotated from camera to camera throughout the complex.

"Let us hope this works," the first librarian said.

"And let us hope," the second librarian said, "that he doesn't eventually catch on to us. We don't want him getting mixed signals since we were the ones that sent him there."

"Fear not," the third said confidently. "He is unaware of the alternate time lines where his mission failed because he arrived too soon."

"That may be true," the first said, "but the girl is already aware of us and she won't hesitate to warn him if she senses our involvement."

"And," the second added, "she knows that we meddled in her past already."

"That wasn't our fault," the first said.

"Wasn't it?" the second asked. "It was one of our own that killed her mentor."

"Yes, yes, yes," the first conceded, "but it wasn't our plan. Nor was it his plan. Our operative went off script…"

"And nearly killed the girl," the second interjected.

"He shouldn't have done that," the first admitted. "He was in there too long. It does things to the mind. He was only supposed to block her training, not harm the girl."

"Agreed," the third said. "The girl is necessary and so is the boy."

"Especially the boy," the first said. "Let us continue."

The librarians pushed their wills onto the TSA computers, and Blake's picture popped up in a window on one of the monitors. A mild alarm sounded on the computer, alerting the man in the room that the computers had a possible identification based on facial recognition. The monitors simultaneously showed Blake's location in the terminal.

The TSA officer picked up a radio and clicked it twice. "Harry? What's your twenty? The computers just popped up an I.D. for someone of interest in G35. I'm sending a photo to your phone."

"Roger that," Harry said. "I'll be there in five."

"The suspect is seated by the windows looking out."

Balletina stood alone, staring at Angie's ashes. Angie was a bitch. She had always been a self-centered, condescending bitch and Balletina couldn't imagine anyone who deserved to be punished more than her, but did she deserve to die for being such a smart mouth? She did ask for it. In fact, she seemed to be daring someone to do it, but maybe just giving her a good burn would have sufficed. "Probably not," she sighed in a barely audible whisper. She would have just run crying to her daddy, who was just as bad as her, and eventually they would have both been reduced to piles of ash. Of course, when he finds out, he may come looking for blood and could still end up burned to a crisp.

Angie's ashes stirred as a breeze came in through the open door. Despite the rush of adrenaline when she had released the fireball, Balletina wished that maybe it hadn't been her who had delivered the fatal blow. It wasn't remorse that she felt, it was the consequences that she may face. She will have to be more careful in the future. Just because Angie's father didn't have powers didn't mean that he wasn't dangerous. He has enough money and clout to hire an assassin to come for her, and then his hireling would end up as a charred corpse too, unless he sneaks up on her.

"Are you okay?" Ramona asked as she tentatively approached Balletina. They had heard the rumors that Honey had been giving her extra training, but they had no idea that she could unleash that much power, and Ramona did not want to be on the receiving end of her rage.

"I don't know," Balletina said. "I killed her. I didn't even think about it. It was almost like she was begging for it."

"She was asking for it. You don't need to feel guilty about anything."

"Why would I feel guilty?" Balletina asked, incensed by the notion.

"You shouldn't," the frightened girl replied. "That's what I was saying."

"She was a bitch," Misty added. "I'm not going to miss her."

"Yeah," Balletina agreed. "I doubt that any of us will actually miss her, but her father will."

"I doubt that he liked her all that much," Ramona added, "but he'll probably be pissed, anyway. I wouldn't worry about him, though. He doesn't have your kind of power. He just has money, and like Queen Honey said, money isn't power anymore."

"It's still a little power," Balletina said. "He can afford to hire a ninja to come kill me."

"So? What's a ninja going to do against your kind of power?"

"Sure," Balletina said, "if I see him, I can fry him, but what if he sneaks up behind me and kills me by surprise? What if he comes while I'm asleep?"

"We'll just have to all stick together then, so you're never alone."

Balletina looked surprised. Misty and Ramona were only a year or two behind her, but they had always looked down on her.

"Why would you do that for me? We've never been friends. You've never even liked me."

Misty dropped her face to stare at the ground and admitted, "Angie was right about us. We were just sheep following her around because we're nobodies. She told us who to like and who not to like."

Balletina was surprised by her frankness. She shook her head and said, "You each made smoke and cinders on your first tries. I don't think you'll be nobodies around here anymore."

"Then we got your back. We're all A-listers now, aren't we?"

Balletina nodded her head. "Yeah. We are the A list."

CHAPTER 17

Michelle felt like she had cracked an ancient secret when she realized that the bell was supposed to work together with the spell to kill Honey. It was as if the cosmos had known in advance that her granddaughter was not going to fulfil her destiny, so they turned around and reassigned it to Michelle. It couldn't be a coincidence that Zeline had gone out alone to shop for supplies and had returned with a bell. Michelle had never used a bell before, but she fashioned the bell tower as if making it was her most important role in life. As Zeline had said, the bell tower must be a powerful totem for Michelle to have created it while in a trance, but if it held a special power within it, she couldn't feel it now. She held it to her face and touched the cold metal to her lips, but she felt nothing but the coolness of the silver from which it was fashioned.

"Michelle?" Zeline's voice was like a splash of cold water on Michelle's face. "What is you doin'? Did you just kiss dat bell?"

Michelle snapped her eyes open and saw everyone staring at her. "No! I didn't kiss it. That's ridiculous."

"Den what exactly was you doin'?"

"Dis bell is special. You knows how special it is."

Zeline sat down in the chair next to Michelle and asked, "So you kissed it?"

"I told you no."

"Den you was just whisperin' sweet nothin's to it?"

Michelle looked harshly at Zeline. "Is you mad? I mean, has you completely lost hold of your senses?"

"Has you?"

"No. It's just that I learnt why I made da bell."

Zeline waited for Michelle to continue, but when nothing followed, she prodded her, "And?"

"And nothin'. Its purpose has been revealed to me and what dat purpose be is between me and da bell."

Zeline whistled and slowly shook her head. "You has really lost it."

"Not at all. In fact, instead of losin' sumpin', I actually found sumpin'. We all been waitin' and prayin' for Destiny to come back to us, but maybe she ain't never gonna return. I wants her back more'n just about anybody, but maybe da cosmos has revealed something to me. Mebbe da powers dat be has moved on and selected another way to save us all."

Ashlin gasped.

"It be okay," Zeline said to Ashlin. "She said she still wants Destiny back. I don't tink da rest of her story makes much sense."

"Actually," Ashlin said, "it kinda does makes sense. I had a vision that the army was attacking Honey."

"The army?" Tempest asked. "You mean da soldier boys? Didn't dey already try that? Twice even?"

"This time will be different," Ashlin explained. "They are going to do something to those kids. I can't explain it. I couldn't hear what they were doing, but I saw what it did. They figured something out and all of them were covering their ears to block something out, and it was hurting them."

"Hmmmph," Michelle said. "Tain't gonna be no army dat takes down Honey."

"Whatch you mean?" Zeline asked.

"Nothin'," Michelle said. "I said too much already."

"You ain't said nothin'!" Zeline growled. "But it's high time you start tellin' us what in da hell is goin' on in dat head of yourn!"

Michelle barked back at her, "I ain't tellin you nothin'! To be true, I ain't even sure where your loyalty lies no more and I sure ain't gonna tell no spy for Honey what I knows."

Before Zeline could yell back, Tempest held up her hand to stop her and said, "Mama, I loves you dearly, but you is talkin' crazy. Maybe I should get you a doctor."

"You'll do no such thing!" Michelle snapped back. "There ain't nothin' wrong wit' me! I must say, though, dat after ever' thing you been through, I never imagined dat you would turn on me too!"

"Nobody is turnin' on you Mama! We are all your family and we love you! It's just that you are worrying us with your strange talk and the way you been acting lately."

Michelle frowned and thought how much better off they would be if they didn't love her.

"What's that supposed to mean?" Ashlin asked.

Michelle pointed her finger at Ashlin and screeched, "Didn't we teach you no better than dat? Is you crawlin' around in my head?"

"We all heard you," Tempest said. "You kinda thought it out loud."

"Well, you just never mind my private thoughts and go on about your business."

"Okay," Tempest said soothingly. "We aren't trying to pry, but I am still worried about you."

"You don't got nothin' to worry about!"

Tempest pointed to the tower and said, "Except maybe for the way you is hugging and kissing that tower."

"Don't you worry none about my bell neither! Ya hear?"

"I'm not worried about the bell, mama. I'm worried about you. I'd feel a whole lot better if you just put the bell over on that shelf for a while."

Michelle felt all the heads nodding around the room. She reluctantly placed the bell tower on the shelf and said, "There! Is you happy now? You best not be messing with my bell, though. I'm gonna be needin' it when da time comes. Da powers dat be has revealed its purpose to me and I is not gonna fail them. Your mama is gonna take care of everything. Just you wait and see."

Zeline and Tempest shared a look and shrugged their shoulders.

Henry, as Marie had suggested, was happy to rent Saunders a boat, especially after he told him that Marie had sent him, but he wasn't able to tell Saunders how to find the site of the Boutin home. Saunders wasn't quite sure if Henry was unwilling or if he really didn't know.

He already knew the general direction, however, and he had copies of maps that were included in the arson investigation, but they looked like child drawings done with crayons. He pushed the boat away from the dock and guided it out into the bright green water. There was something vaguely romantic about shoving away from the dock, like an adventurer heading out into the unknown, just trusting his guts and going 'that-a-way'. The swamp immediately divided in three different directions. To the right and left, the water followed a wide curve like the bend in a river. He'd read the history of how Cricket Bend had derived its name from Crooked Bend and immediately understood that the shape of the water must have been how it got its name, but the maps that he had didn't go right or left. They pointed directly into a thick stand of trees that were across the water ahead of him. The trees grew straight up out of the water. He pointed the boat towards them and goosed the throttle.

The bayou changed dramatically as he plunged into the thick trees. Gone was the bright sunshine and equally bright carpet of duck weeds that floated on the surface of the water, giving it the bright green coloration. Sunlight filtered through the trees, casting god rays through the mist that rose from the warm water. The canopy of the trees glowed overhead, providing a soft ambient light that hid most of the shadows, but it was still dark and shadowy below. An ungodly stench rose from the murky water. It was just the kind of place where he would expect to find a foul creature from the under-world, but not where he would expect to find an angelic creature of the light.

The small motor chugged away as Saunders lightly twisted the throttle. A thin grey trail of smoke followed the boat, adding its own foul odor to the bayou that already smelled like death. Saunders guided the small boat, not only between the large trees that jutted out of the water, but also around the long looping vines that hung down into the swamp. He wondered how many of those vines were actually snakes waiting for him to make just one mistake. He snickered as he heard his father's voice advising him not to accept an apple from them.

Small islands and sand bars rose here and there from the water. The wake behind his boat lapped up against the sandbars, leaving a rippled pattern across their lengths. The unpleasant odor intensified as he plunged deeper into the dark interior. It smelled like old dead leaves that had been raked into a pile and left there to grow moldy after a heavy rain. He steered the craft to the left to avoid a log floating in the water, but the log had eyes and swam a safe distance away on its own.

Occasionally, the canopy broke to show the blue color of the sky. It was in one of these openings where he saw an island and could still smell the faint hint of smoke. As he neared the island, he found a small pontoon dock and pulled his boat alongside it. A short path led him up from the water-level, where he found the burned carcass of a home. This had to be the place, but he was amazed that he had actually found it. The maps weren't really good enough to find this spot. Was he guided here by heavenly forces, or was it just luck?

He stared at the ashes and charred wood. The remains of an old refrigerator stood next to some fallen pipes and a kitchen sink. A solitary power wire led off in the general direction of the mainland, but he had never seen any evidence of it from Henry's dock or he could have followed it. The sink only had drain pipes with no faucet or running water. This was rougher living than most of his camping trips. On the other side of the home, he saw the burnt springs of a mattress surrounded by broken shards from a mirror. Ashes covered the floor, but had been blown smooth from the weather, yet he still found a few small telltale signs of tiny trowels that had been drawn across the floor, probably by the arson investigators collecting evidence.

He shook his head slowly. He wasn't sure what he had hoped to find here, but this wasn't it. The ashes weren't going to reveal who the girl was or who the men were that came for her.

Saunders felt like he was caught in some bizarre movie where four mercenaries were sent by the church to rid the world of demons hiding in the swamp. He wished he'd been here sooner, much sooner. Any trails that may have been left by the men that had come here had already been washed away by rain and wind. If they were military men, then maybe he could deduce their movements by planning how he would have assaulted the island. They would have needed a spotter with a good view of the home. The arrangement of the trees surrounding the home didn't leave very many directions for someone to recon the structure, but there was a gap in the trees that might reveal where their camp would have been. He returned to the boat and left to search some of the neighboring islands for any signs that they may have left behind.

Blake's heart beat uneasily as he watched the planes roll in and out of the terminal. He arrived at the airport way too early for his flight and he felt increasingly uneasy about this trip. He couldn't help feeling that the world, or at least part of it, was against him finding the orb. On the one hand, he had people pushing him to go, and even giving him hints that it would be somewhere in England, while on the other hand, he had other people that were constantly warning him to give it up. What if this trip was just a ruse to get him out of the country and away from the orb? What if the clue he saw in the safe was false and the orb really was in the sorcerers' compound? Most of all, he wondered if he was just paranoid and this nervousness was just his body's way of telling him that he was hungry, because he was famished.

There were plenty of places to get food in the terminal, and his flight was still several hours away. He left the gate and headed back towards the center where the different terminals connected, stopping at the first hamburger stall he found. He grabbed a paper napkin on his way to the counter. They had a short menu. Burgers; burgers with bacon and chicken burgers, all served with fries.

A tall lanky boy with a pimply face greeted Blake, "Welcome to Damn Big Burgers. What can I get you?"

"I'll have a bacon burger and fries with a chocolate shake."

Blake watched the kid on the other side of the counter punch in his order. He was probably Blake's age, but he seemed younger.

"That will be eight seventy five."

Blake wasn't surprised. Nine bucks for what was essentially a fastfood burger. He didn't hold much hope for it being as big as either its name or the picture on the menu. He handed the clerk one of the folded napkins and pushed the image of a ten-dollar bill into the kid's mind. The clerk put the napkin in the register drawer and counted out Blake's change. "Nine and ten. Your order number is two seventy three."

Before Blake could even thank the kid, a large TSA officer put his hand on Blake's shoulder and said, "Okay, kid. Let's you and me go have a private conversation about the severity of passing phony money."

Blake turned to face the man and calmly said, "Do we have to do this now? I'm really hungry." As he spoke, he placed the idea in the man's head to let him go.

"Yeah," the man said, ignoring Blake's planted suggestion, "We have to do it now." He clasped Blake's arms behind his back and slapped handcuffs on his wrists. As he started leading Blake away, the clerk called out, "Don't you want your meal?"

Blake turned back to the clerk and asked the officer, "Can't we take my food so I can eat and talk?"

"You'd have to pay for it first," the officer said.

Blake entered the man's mind and placed the thought, "You saw me give him a ten-dollar bill."

Blake took another step towards his food when the cop turned him around and said, "Didn't you hear me? You can't have your food unless you pay for it first."

"Wait," Blake said. "Look at the kid behind the counter. He wants me to have that burger. It's just going to go to waste if you don't get it for me. Please?"

"If I let you have your food, will you stop giving me so much trouble and come with me?"

"Sure," Blake said. He didn't know how this man was able to resist his influence, but he was sure that he would find some more opportunities to straighten it all out. At least he would get his food.

———

Michelle stood next to Destiny's sleeping body, wishing she had her granddaughter's gift of healing. "You remember when you first come outa your trance and healed your nana's burnt arm? Dat be da proudest day of your nana's life, and I had me plenty of proud days dat it beat out. Da regular people has a saying about physician, heal thyself. I does wish dat you could fix what's ailing you. I miss you something terrible! We all be here, most of us, anyways. Why is it you cain't come out and be here with us? I knows that you feel like you is lost and you is in a better place, but it be a false place. We don't just miss you, we needs you real bad. I got da feeling in mah bones dat your cousin ain't done wit' her messin' around and we needs you to lead us agin her. You should be here to see your mama. She be doin' real good, but she still hears da voices. Cousin Ashlin does what she can to help, but I gots me da feeling dat you could be da best cure for your mama, if you only comes back to us."

Tempest wrapped her arms around her mother.

Michelle pressed her cheek against Tempest's arm. "I knows dat some part of her can hear us."

"Maybe," Tempest said, "but I don't think it is getting through to where she is hiding. I've been there. I didn't know about nothing while I hid inside my own little prison, but when she pulled me out, it all come to me in a rush of memories."

Michelle sighed. "I wish I could reach her better. Could be we just has to get her to come part way for her to hear dem memories."

"Could be," Tempest said. "It's getting late Mama. You should get back to the hotel and get you some sleep."

"What about you?" Michelle asked. "You ain't been to the hotel at all yet. You should take Ashlin there to get a good night's sleep."

"We're still young," Tempest replied, "and I feel like I been asleep for all my life. Besides, Ashlin and I both got a good sleep in the waiting room. They got surprisingly soft chairs there."

"I am a bit tired," Michelle admitted. "Maybe I'll just go see how soft those chairs be."

"Oh, mama. You know that your back ain't as young as ours. You go on back to the hotel that the nice Mr. Logan got for us."

"That be twice now dat you called me old."

Tempest pressed her forehead to Michelle's. "Mama. You know I love you, but go look at yourself in the mirror. You is old. It might be my fault. I was a handful, I know, and I probably added more than a few grey hairs to your head."

Michelle sighed again. "Mr. Logan been gone all day. So has dat boy and da soldier. You and Ashlin be here. Dat hotel gonna be a lonely place with dat boy and his friend gone too."

Tempest squeezed her mother in a hug. "He's growin' on you. Destiny will be glad."

"He ain't doin' no such thing."

"Come on now," Tempest said as she pushed her mother towards the door. "You git now. And take Zeline with you so you won't be so alone. I spect she could use a good night's sleep too. While you're at it, get yourself something to eat. I can feel how hungry you are and you won't be no good to my baby girl if you starve yourself to death."

"All right," Michelle surrendered herself. "I'm goin', but you make sure to feed that child out there."

"I will," Tempest replied, "but I'm not so sure I'd call her a child. Sometimes, when she gets into my head to help me, I feel like she's the oldest of us all."

Saunders pointed the boat in a direct line away from the island. There were a handful of small plots poking up from the swamp that he would have to navigate around, but they were far too small to support a four-man camp. Large trees grew from some of these plots and Saunders wondered which was here first? Did the trees spring up from the small islands, or did they grow out of the water until silt and sand were deposited against their sides and the island was born?

Beyond these small sand bars, he finally found an island that was large enough to have served as a base, but when he shimmied up a tree to spot the burned home, his view was still blocked by the trees on the smaller pieces of land. He boarded the boat again and circled around to his right, looking for the right sort of island. He couldn't even be sure that they had made a base camp, but it's what he would have done if he had been leading an armed incursion.

On the third such island, he found a discarded cardboard box and a couple empty tin cans, but no signs of a campfire. Were they already aware of what she was? Did they eat cold rations to avoid detection?

He scoured the ground looking for anything out of place and spotted something shiny in the grass. A small bolt on the ground caught the sun as the light filtered through the trees. It wasn't part of a gun, but it might have fallen off of a pair of field glasses. It might even have even been a spare part that fell out of someone's pack.

He picked up the bolt and started searching again when he heard a faint metallic clink coming from above his head. Craning his neck upwards, he spotted a rope dangling down alongside the trunk, swinging freely in the breeze. He couldn't see where the rope led and had to climb the tree to follow it, but near the top of the tree, he found a parabolic dish antenna pointing directly at the burned out home. This was definitely the place and whoever the soldiers were, they weren't demons from the netherworld. This was technological and that meant humans; probably mercenaries. They camped here, and either left in a hurry without retrieving the dish, or what seemed more likely to him, it may have been the last day of their lives.

Saunders pulled out his penknife and cut the straps so he could lower the dish to the ground and take it back with him. Even if they were only human, they knew something. They knew enough to find this place before anything extraordinary had happened, at least, before anything he had learned about. Could they have worked for Honey? She didn't seem either smart enough or organized enough to order something like this, but then, he didn't know much about how demons' minds worked.

The TSA office was a spartan room with no expense wasted on decoration. A couple desks lined one wall with monitors whose screens rotated through the various views of the airports wings. Blake was led through the office to an even sparser interrogation room where they sat him down at the lone table in the middle of the small bleak room. He placed Blake's handcuffs in a lock, effectively chaining him to the table, then left the meal on the end of the table out of his reach and started to leave.

"Excuse me?" Blake prompted him.

"What?" the officer asked.

"Can you remove my handcuffs so I can eat?"

The officer curled his lips maliciously and said, "Sorry, kid, but that wasn't part of our bargain."

As soon as he had left the room, Blake manipulated the locks with his mind and freed his hands. Opening locks was one of the first powers that he had discovered, and it always got easier for him each time he used the skill. In the beginning, it was little more than a means to commit mischief and play pranks on the school mates who mostly hated him, but this time, he made far better use of his talent. He tore into the burger and wasn't sure if it was as good as he thought it was or if he had just gotten that hungry anticipating it, but it definitely wasn't as damned big as its name. Only the burger and fries made it into the bag. He missed out on his shake. The clerk also neglected to include any napkins in the bag. Blake could have wiped the grease on his shirt, but he still had a long trip to England ahead of him, so he chose to lick the abundant layers of grease from his fingers. He was still sucking the bacon flavored grease off his little finger when the officer returned and asked, "What the?"

"Where's my shake?" Blake asked. "I thought maybe you were going back for my milkshake."

"How'd you get out of those?"

Blake shrugged and said, "I dunno. I guess you didn't do them very good."

The cop stood there with a blank expression on his face until Blake burst out laughing. "I'm just messing with you, man. Some other dude came in and let me out so I could eat. What did you think?"

The TSA officer looked over at the mirror, which Blake had no doubt was a two-way mirror. Then he turned back and shut the door.

Blake finished the last French fry and rolled up the bag, then deftly tossed it into a trash can in the corner. "So, what's this about?"

"You don't seem to be taking this very seriously."

"Taking what very seriously?" Blake asked.

"We don't like people coming in here and passing fake bills around."

"You mean fake money?" Blake asked. "I don't blame you for not liking that, but what does that have to do with me?"

"You didn't use real money to pay for your meal."

"What?" Blake asked. "Are you accusing me of using counterfeit money to buy my burger?"

The TSA officer tossed a plastic evidence bag on the table with a plain brown napkin inside. "It was a paper napkin."

"It was?" Blake asked. "Why did you just tell me it was counterfeit money, if it was just a napkin?"

"Because you used it to pay for your meal."

"Even if I did do what you say, how are you going to convince anyone that a paper napkin is counterfeit currency? It's just a piece of paper. It doesn't even look like money."

The officer stopped for a moment. Blake was right. He saw Blake hand the kid a paper napkin, not a phony bill. He didn't know how Blake had done it; maybe some kind of hypnotism, but it didn't matter. He was wanted for questioning, anyway. The computer had already picked him out.

Blake still didn't know how this guy could resist his suggestions. Maybe he was a witch and didn't know it, but he had never met a witch who was immune to his powers before. Whatever this guy was, Blake was not going to trick him into letting him go. He would need to get someone else in here to let him go; preferably one of this guy's superiors.

"It seems to me," Blake said, "that you are in a bit of a quandary. Maybe you should get someone else in here to help you sort this out."

Honey was already seated at a table in the cafeteria with her mother when Balletina arrived. Word of Angie's death had already spread throughout the facility and the line parted for Balletina as she approached it.

"Oooh," Ramona said as she and Misty followed Balletina up to the front of the line. "This is nice. Looks like you're famous now. My name is Ramona, by the way."

"And I'm Misty."

"I know who you are," Balletina replied coolly, failing to hide the irritation in her voice.

"I wasn't sure," Ramona said. "I know that everybody knew Angie, but I thought you might have just thought of me as one of the nameless girls that hung out with her."

"You were, weren't you?"

Ramona sighed and hung her head. "Yeah, I guess I was. That's why I thought you might not know who I really was."

"We've known each other for years," Balletina said, "but in all that time, you never took the time to talk to me."

Ramona frowned and said, "I regret that, but Angie always said you were some kind of a foreigner."

"So what if I was a foreigner?" Balletina asked.

"You're right," Ramona said. "It doesn't matter to me if you're Russian or something."

"Oh my God," Balletina said as she held her hand up between them, hoping that Ramona would stop talking. She pointed to the meatloaf and said, "I'll have some of that."

Misty nudged Ramona in the side and whispered, "Why did you have to upset her?"

"I'll take care of her," Pablo said as he shoved his assistant aside. He nodded towards Honey and asked, "You're with her, aren't you?"

Balletina saw where he was looking and nodded her head.

"You go ahead and take your seat. Pablo will bring you your food."

Balletina turned without thanking Pablo and took three steps towards Honey, then paused and looked over her shoulder to say, "They're with me."

Pablo saw which meals they were pointing to and said, "I take care of you, too. You ladies go find your seats."

Misty motioned for Tammy, who had been hanging back, to come join her.

Pablo waved his fingers at Tammy and said, "Pepe already knows what the little one likes."

Blake stretched his senses beyond the mirror in the room and located a woman that he thought might be in charge. "This is going to get you in deep trouble," Blake thought to her. "If you don't put a stop to this and let this boy go, you could lose your job."

Having planted the suggestion, Blake leaned back in his chair and watched the TSA officer, who stood there and studied Blake's face for any reaction.

"What's going on in your head?" his interrogator asked him. "You look like you know something that I don't know."

"I'm sure that wouldn't be too hard," Blake said. He may not have been able to plant ideas into this guy's mind, but he sure could push his buttons and read the anger coming from him. Even if he weren't able to read the frustration directly from the man's thoughts, anyone could see the scowl on his face.

The interrogator sucked in his breath as he leaned over the table to yell at Blake, but stopped abruptly when his commander burst into the room.

"I've heard enough," she barked. "Son, I apologize for the inconvenience. You're free to go."

Blake stood and gave the surprised interrogator a mock salute as he left the room.

"Tell me again why we did that?" one of the librarians asked. "We didn't make him miss his flight, we just distracted him a bit. So, he didn't get his milkshake. So what? Did that change anything?"

A second librarian shrugged his shoulders. "The big guy told us to do it. If all we ended up doing was to feed into his paranoia, well, maybe that's all we had to accomplish. He'll be more alert now."

"Hmmph," the first librarian scowled. Maybe it was just that simple, but it required a lot of effort for something with such little tangible gain.

It was still bright outside of the hotel room, so Michelle pulled the curtains shut and turned out the lights. She climbed into the bed and sighed as her weary bones sunk into the mattress. It wasn't the softest bed she'd ever slept in, but her muscles didn't seem to care as they luxuriated into whatever comfort that it provided. "Tain't no wonder," she said out loud. "I done slept in a mess of strange places these past few days."

"What was that?" Zeline thought from the next room.

"Oh, nothin'," Michelle thought back, "I was just ruminating on some o' the odd places I done slept this week. Good night Zeline."

"Good night. Sweet dreams. See you in the morning."

Michelle closed her eyes and shut away the outside world. The sound from beyond the room's door faded to a mild murmur, and she felt herself drifting off towards sleep. She was afraid that even asleep, she might go visit Destiny and wake up without getting any rest, and as much as she would love to see her granddaughter again, she was too tired to let that happen, so she cleared her mind and tried to dream of nothing.

The world must have become a sick and twisted place for her to not want to visit her own granddaughter, but it was supposed to be Destiny's duty to change things, and she wasn't doing that. It was her destiny to save the world and that boy's destiny to save her. If she doesn't come around and return to them, then Michelle would have to...she abruptly ended that train of thought. She did not want to resort to that. She needed Destiny. They had to rescue Destiny from herself.

They had to rescue Destiny from herself.

They had to rescue...

Michelle slipped into the dreamless sleep that she had hoped to find.

The chagrined TSA officer continued to watch Blake on the monitors, but he didn't approach him again. He didn't know why he should have been chewed out so severely. It was the computers that initially pointed suspicion to Blake. It was their highly prized facial recognition programs that picked him out as a person of interest. They should spend more time blaming the computer and less time humiliating the soldiers on the ground.

He didn't know who Blake was, but he saw him mesmerize the food clerk and pay for a hamburger with a paper napkin. That shouldn't be allowed, but his supervisor gave him a direct order to back off. As aggravated as he was to see Blake in his airport, he was actually relieved to see Blake finally board his plane and officially get out of their hair. He would be someone else's problem now. Now he was free to deal with the headache that had been building behind his eyes ever since this whole thing had started.

CHAPTER 18

Day eleven.

The world still didn't know the truth about the evil that it had just faced, or how close it might have come to annihilation, and the way things were going, it might never know before it is too late to prepare. Government efforts to squash firsthand accounts were almost unnecessary, as the video accounts were met with more skepticism than fear. The world had come to believe that each new account to surface on the internet was just one more videographer wanting his fifteen minutes of fame in just another "me too" event. Worse yet, while the world had an opportunity to recover from what had just transpired and prepare for what was coming next, the small handful of men that knew the truth kept the truth of those events a secret from the world, believing that they alone could safeguard humanity from these creatures that can spew fire from their hands. The government's hubris could get everyone killed, and without the truth being shared with the world, everybody went about their daily business, paying little heed to the ridiculous rumors that circulated the internet.

Blake had thought that he had known all about flying first class. Their jet to Cheyenne was a private plane and about as luxurious as he could have ever have imagined. It put his flight to New York to shame, but the overseas leg surpassed his wildest expectations. He didn't just get more leg room and a roomier seat; he got a small cocoon that served as a private cabin for him. It made sense when he stopped to consider the length of the flight, but he hadn't expected the seat would fold all the way back into a bed with a private television and a choice of movies to watch.

He hadn't paid any attention to the cost of the flight. He simply pushed the ticketing agent to approve it, but now, as he stretched out in comfort, he wondered what the price tag actually was that he wasn't paying. This level of comfort must come at an enormous cost. Michelle would be furious if she ever found out, but he was too tired now to worry about her sensibilities.

He settled into his seat and reclined it into the bed position. It was a shame that he was too tired to take full advantage of all the comforts that the suite provided; it seemed to have a lot to offer, but he would probably sleep through most of the trip.

Destiny's voice wafted into Michelle's dreamless sleep. "Nana… You can't not dream, Nana. It just ain't healthy."

"Shush," Michelle said. "I don't need someone who has locked herself into a dream world telling me how I can or cannot dream."

"I'm just saying that if you want to sleep, your mind is gonna do what it wants to do."

Michelle didn't want this. She knew that if she let go and allowed her mind to have its own way, it would go back to the spell and she wanted a few moments of rest without worrying about that damned parchment that she had read, but here she was standing in a broad green meadow, right where she didn't want to be thinking the words she didn't want to repeat.

"You mean that dusty old spell you was repeating?" Destiny asked. "Are you gonna tell me what it meant?"

"No," Michelle replied, "I don't believe I will. I don't even want to think about it right now."

"Why?" Destiny giggled. "Is it something embarrassing?"

"No, tain't that. It just be something that I might have to do iffin you don't come back to save us. You see, I has been given a duty, only it comes with dire consequences."

"I certainly understand havin' a duty," Destiny said. "It can be a heavy burden to carry."

"Do you?" Michelle asked. "I mean, do you really understand duty?"

"Why do you ask?"

Michelle spun around, scanning the green meadow for Destiny, but she still stood alone. "It just seems to me that you has a duty, but you ain't doin' it."

Destiny sniffled. "I tried, but I died. I just didn't know that you held it against me like that until now."

"No, you didn't die, but you just keep tellin' yourself that so you don't have to go out there and face your real duty. It be a callin', ya know? And you be shirking your duty and hiding away from the world, pretending that you is dead. Now I gots to step up and do what you has refused to do, an' it might get me killt, or worse."

"So that's it," Destiny replied. "The ancestors have given you something to do. It must be awfully important to have you so riled up about it."

"It is, but it could damn me to hell for all eternity if I goes through with it."

Destiny sucked in her breath, but remained silent.

"What?" Michelle asked. "You got nothin' to say to that?"

"I'm sorry Nana. I didn't know."

"Of course you didn't know. You is hiding in your own little world like a ostrich with its head in the..." Michelle stopped speaking and snapped her head around. "What was that?"

"What was what?"

"You didn't hear that?"

"No," Destiny replied, "I didn't hear nothin'."

It wasn't until that moment that Michelle had realized that she hadn't wandered into Destiny's dream world. She was standing in a meadow very much like the one outside of Destiny's little cottage, but something was different. "It sounded like a bell. There it goes again."

"Nope. Are you hearing things? Maybe that spell is making you crazy."

"No doubt that," Michelle replied as she spun around again to see the world around her with a new perspective, "but I definitely heard a bell." She turned slowly around, examining this new world in more detail. It had a broad meadow, but it wasn't exactly like Destiny's world. She felt like she was in a painting where all the colors were pastel and the broad brush strokes hid all the sharp details. The bell rang again, and she said, "I don't think I'm just hearin' things. I kin feel it too. It's like it be tuggin' at my very soul. There be something very powerful in dat bell. Like it has da power of life and death."

"Wow," Destiny said. "You can feel all that from a bell in the distance?"

"I be a witch too," Michelle snapped. "You was once da Chosen One, but maybe dat ain't you no more. Mebbe someone like me has to take up da reins and do what you refuses to do. Could be that dat bell is daer to help me find mah way."

"Wow, you really have changed, Nana."

Michelle started walking towards the bell. "We all has to do our part. I just has a new part to do and you ain't doin' nothin'."

Logan was disappointed when he heard about Honey's escapades in town. He had hoped that she would have kept a low profile and remained dormant a little while longer, but he had always figured that her uncontrollable nature would surface, eventually. He spent most of his time in the library where his research into the orb bore little fruit, but he did find a blurb from one of their most ancient texts that referred to an inheritance of power. It was a series of letters between two scholars that indicated how the war with the witches was not going well, but that they had taken the orb of power from the witches and now it was their duty to secure the orb so the witches would not capture it back. Attached to the file was an image of one of the author's headstones with a caption that he carried the orb of destiny, and it was his descendants' duty to preserve it forever from the vile witches. Logan reread the letters in his mind. If it was truly a magical inheritance, and they had taken it from the witches, then they must have done the unthinkable; a witch and a sorcerer must have co-mingled, or worse yet, married.

A little more research located the same author's headstone in an old graveyard in England. If this was the same orb that the boy was told to find, then this was the first clue as to its location. It made sense as he thought about it; the orb predated the Americas and if it was truly an inheritance tied to a family bloodline, then it should be found in either Europe or Asia. If he was to secure the orb for himself, before Blake, then that is where he would have to start. He might actually try to find the mysterious headstone, but first, he would try one of the archives in England. He could get lucky and find the relic already in the archive, but at the very least, he hoped to find another clue.

England was just as dark and overcast as Blake had always heard it would be. He walked down the steps from the plane to the tarmac and was immediately cloaked in a cold fog that swirled around his head. It was an obscenely thick fog that must have made landing the plane a challenge. He brushed his hands past his face, but that only stirred the mist before him, replacing one fog with more fog. A string of street lamps in the distance created small globes of light in the mist that marked a stretch of road running roughly right to left. It was quiet, with only the sound of Blake's heals scraping on the hard ground as he approached the barely lit street. Darkness and shadow surrounded him. The fog thoroughly blanketed the sky, blotting out the stars entirely. The brilliance of the full moon could barely penetrate enough to form a soft glow in the fog over his head. The fog ended abruptly, bordered by the street while behind him, the brightly lit airport had faded entirely into the fog, but even as dark as the fog had been, nothing around him was as dark as what he saw on the other side of the road. He peered across the street and thought he saw something shift in the inky blackness, but he hoped, as he clenched his fists, that it was only his imagination getting away from him.

The sound of his footsteps ended as he reached the edge of the road and came to a stop before crossing. The fog was little more than a thin mist around him, but a heavy blanket of clouds still blacked out the sky. The vague scent of jet fuel had gradually faded and was replaced with the dank musk of old decaying vegetation. Blake recognized the fetid odor of a rotting swamp. He had met Destiny in just such a putrid wetland. A chorus of crickets rose to serenade the night across the street. That, too, reminded him of the bayou. The roar of the jets was a forgotten memory. Blake turned around to see the silent airport, but all he saw was the dark fog reflecting the dim light of the street lamps.

He stepped out onto the road and wondered why there weren't more vehicles traveling down it to get to or from the airport. Even as the thought still echoed in his mind, headlamps appeared at the far end of the road, but they were still far enough away for him to cross safely. The damp ground reflected the headlamps in a long streak of light that would have made a bleak and terrifying painting. Blake shivered as the hackles on the back of his neck stiffened. He stepped out onto the road, wondering why he felt so apprehensive, but it was an instinctive feeling that he couldn't shake. He told himself that this was just a road, and that was just a car that was nowhere near him in a country that did not know who he was, yet his bones quaked and his skin turned cold.

A cat screeched from deep within the darkness across the street. He might have stopped and waited for the car to pass, but the crickets beckoned him onward. He answered their call by stepping forward, but his shoes stuck to the road. The wet asphalt should have been slick, but instead, he felt the soles of his shoes stick to the shiny black surface. He pulled hard to separate his shoe from the road top. It felt like he had stepped on gum, except that it felt like the whole road was made of gum. He pulled harder, but that only served to fasten his forward shoe to the sticky asphalt. Each step took more strength than the step before it, and the headlamps were bearing down upon him.

Something was wrong. He'd seen enough magic to know when something wasn't the way it should be, and this wasn't natural. He lit a small ball of fire to see the road better. The road reflected his fire and blinded his eyes, but he had seen enough to see that he was walking across a layer of tar. His front foot sunk into the black muck as his rear foot pulled out with a resounding pop. The headlamps were nearly on top of him.

The thick tar gripped his shoes and the approaching vehicle wasn't slowing. He sprayed fire onto the tar to soften it, but that only made it stickier. His shoe sunk even further into the softer tar until it was so deep that he pulled out a bare foot with his shoe and sock remaining stuck in the black goo.

The headlamps were on him. Blake fell to the ground and felt the rush of the air as the lights flew over him, but there was no vehicle attached to the lights. He was stuck in the tar and could barely raise his head to see what had passed over him. The tar's fragrance filled his nose and mouth and felt like it would stick to his taste buds as it had stuck to his shoes. The lights stopped a short way down the road and Blake clearly saw two specters glaring at him. He wished now that he knew more about spiritual creatures, because he was sure that they were some kinds of ghosts. Something inside of him, like an instinctual memory, told him they might be wraiths. He had never believed in ghosts before, but that was before he met the one guarding the safe.

The wraiths returned and floated over him. A woman's voice, with a sweet Scottish brogue, said, "You're a gey stubborn young laddie. Ye shouldn'a come this far."

Blake got a better look at the two apparitions as they floated over the tar. They were much more human looking than the specter guarding the safe. The one who had spoken to him had a pretty face framed in flowing red and black hair, but her body was merely wisps of smoke with a light burning where her heart should be.

A deep man's voice rumbled next to her, "Ach. He's nothin' but trouble, 'n' I canna say that he looks so young to me. Let me murdurr 'im 'n' be done with it."

"No," the woman said, "Deep doon in 'is heart, he's still one o' us, but he's not our kin 'n' he canna stay here."

The man poked Blake with a wispy finger. "Did ye hear that, laddie? I dinnae ken if ye truly be one of us, bit only our kin be allowed here. You hasta go. Go now 'n' don't ye ne'er come back or mibbie I'll take me own advice next time."

Blake couldn't move. His legs, arms, and face were stuck in the tar.

"Did ye nah hear me?" the wraith bellowed. "I said to git out o' here!"

The harder Blake pushed, the deeper he stuck into the tar.

"Get up! Get up! Get up!"

The wispy apparitions popped out of Blake's vision and instead of being stuck in the tar, he found himself collapsed on the ground just inside the doorway leading out of the airport. A man in a leather bomber jacket growled at him, "Get up, you wanker!"

A small girl pointed at Blake and asked her mother, "Is he okay?" Her mother took her by the hand and pulled her away.

Blake climbed unsteadily to his feet, unsure how he had gotten himself to this point.

Sweat dripped from Saunders' face as he tied the small boat to the dock where he had gotten it. He grabbed the rope that hung from the surveillance dish and slung it over his shoulder. It clinked and rattled as he crossed the street and returned the boat keys to Henry.

Henry eyed Saunders suspiciously when he saw the equipment that Saunders carried. "You find da place okay? Dat don't look like nuttin' Miss Michelle would be owning."

"It's not," Saunders said. "Those men that came here looking for trouble used this to spy on them."

Henry spat, "I hope dey burns in hell."

Saunders smiled. "Most likely, they burned right here. I suspect that they may have perished in the fire. Do you have a backpack or maybe a duffle bag I can put this in?"

Henry nodded his head and stepped towards the back room. "I'll be bag in a jiffy."

Saunders put the dish on the counter and checked out the gear as he waited. The dish was a stock parabolic reflector, but it didn't have a microphone. He wasn't an expert, but if he had to guess, he thought it looked more like a microwave receiver. The electronics could have been anything and judging from the antenna that hung from it, he was pretty sure that it had some kind of a radio transmitter, but he also spotted a computer jack that seemed completely out of place for a listening device. It made sense to have a transmitter, but he didn't know why it would have a plug for a computer, unless it was digital.

"Here you is," Henry said as he emerged from the back room and plopped a duffle bag on top of the counter next to the dish. "That will be twelve seven'y five."

Saunders gave him a twenty and started putting the dish into the bag while Henry was counting out his change. He hung the bag over his shoulder and accepted the money Henry held out to him. "Thank you. You have a nice day."

Henry nodded his head as he stared out of his window and wondered what had become of Michelle.

Johnson was sleeping with his head leaning against the car window when the morning sun lit upon his eyelids. He growled softly as he squinted his eyes and turned his head aside.

"Good," one of the librarians said in his head. "You're awake."

"Finally," another librarian added.

"Finally?" Johnson asked. "It's still early. The sun just came up."

"The sun rose a while ago," the second librarian said. "It only just rose high enough over the building to wake you for us."

"You needed the sun to wake me?" Johnson asked. "Good to know."

"No," the first librarian said. "We could have woken you up any time, but you were tired, so we let you sleep."

"Wow," Johnson said. "Thanks guys. Why were you waiting for me?"

"It's time for you to go. We need you to watch over Blake again."

"You could have told me that yesterday," Johnson said. "I could have gone with him."

"Yesterday," the third librarian said, "we needed you to keep an eye on Logan. Today, we need you to watch Blake."

"Why?" Johnson asked. "Did you grow tired of Logan?"

The second librarian snickered and said, "You can watch Logan, too. He just scheduled a flight to England."

"Speaking of which," Johnson asked, "how did you expect me to get to England?"

"We're working on that," the first one said.

"Blake could have done his Jedi thing and taken me with him."

"We'll figure something out by the time you reach the airport."

Johnson started the car, but before he put it in gear, he said, "I thought you guys were supposed to be from the future. How is it you didn't see any of this coming?"

"Time has become a bit chaotic," the third one explained. "We see multiple outcomes. It is difficult to predict which one is most likely to come true and which one will lead to our time."

"But you're in the future," Johnson said. "Why must you predict anything?"

"You need to get going," the first one said. "We found a flight for you, but it's leaving in a couple of hours."

Blake crossed the threshold leading out of the airport. He was surprised by how familiar everything looked once he was outside. He merged onto the crowded sidewalk, but the further he walked into London, the more familiar things appeared to him. It wasn't just the cityscape; the people were familiar to him too, and he didn't feel like they were all friendly to him. He recognized a particularly evil wizard, so he turned the corner into a crowded alleyway to avoid him. The crowd thickened, and he brushed shoulders with people going both directions as he tried to stay ahead of the wizard that he had spotted, but he saw more bad sorcerers ahead of him. He turned around another corner, and the crowd grew even denser. People coming the other direction bumped directly into him, except he wasn't so sure that all of them were even people anymore. He weaved his way past a variety of non-human looking pedestrians, and they were all looking directly at him. Uncomfortable from their stares, he ducked into a shop's doorway and felt someone tap him on the shoulder. He turned to see who it was, but nobody was there. Another more forceful shove to his shoulder shook his whole torso, and he caught a glimpse of a round glowing orb right before the world went dark.

The world spun around him, even with his eyes closed. Blake cracked open his eyes and saw the cabin attendant standing over him. "Please raise your seat in preparation for landing."

He was grateful to be free of the nightmares, but he had arrived in England already and still hadn't given any thought to how he was going to find the orb. It was a big country. In fact, the U.K. was several countries and the orb could be in any of them. Outside his window, he saw the approaching land as the plane descended and touched down. With no plan to guide him, he could only trust his instincts. He smiled warmly as the attendants thanked him for riding British Airways and walked down the Jetway along with all the other passengers.

Blake was the only passenger without any carry-on items, and he could already feel the security agents eyeing him suspiciously. Wait till they learn that he did not bring any checked luggage with him.

The passengers were ushered into a line that passed by the luggage carousels. Blake walked nonchalantly past the other passengers and into the queue for customs. The line took him to a window where a stern matronly woman asked him, "Do you have anything to declare?"

"Declare?" Blake asked.

"Your luggage," the woman said. "Do you have anything to declare in your luggage?"

"Oh," Blake said with a shy smile. "I don't have any luggage."

The woman frowned and deftly pressed a small button to get a supervisor. "You came here from America with no luggage?" Her voice was laced with a practiced coldness that alarmed him to the core.

"No ma'am," he stuttered. "I mean yes ma'am. That is, I don't have any luggage. I came on a whim."

"A whim?" she asked. "You just decided to hop onto a plane and fly to the British Isle?"

"I've always wanted to come here," he said, "but whenever I tried making plans, something got in the way. So, I came without a plan."

The woman's supervisor arrived and gave Blake an equally stern eye. "What do we have here?"

"This boy comes here all the way from America and he has no luggage."

Blake suggested, in the supervisor's mind, that there was nothing going on here, and he should explain it to her.

Her supervisor gave her a vexed look and asked, "How long does it take to declare nothing?"

"But Felix," she said, "Don't you find it rather odd that he should arrive here empty-handed?"

"What I find odd," Felix said, "is that you somehow expect the poor lad to declare nothing."

The woman was dumbfounded.

"I'm sorry to have bothered you," Felix said to Blake. "You obviously just came here on holiday. I hope you enjoy your stay."

The poor customs inspector couldn't look Blake in the eye as she said, "Very well, then. Carry on."

Tempest didn't want to sleep. She told herself that she had already slept through her entire life and needed to stay awake, but the soft whir of the lung machine and the rhythmic beat of the heart monitor were more than she could bear. She sat at Destiny's side, holding her hand, and even though her head remained upright, her eyelids drooped and her breathing deepened.

Outside Destiny's room, the sky grew black with smoke. Explosions in the distance flashed against the blackness like camera flashes, followed by a loud boom that reverberated against the hospital windows, rattling the glass. Tempest went to the window and looked down onto the streets. Bands of sorcerers and witches roamed the rubble filled streets and erupted in sparks and flames when they met. It was easier for the sorcerers. Fire and lightning were their most basic skills. Their ancestors would have scoffed at them for using such rudimentary weapons, but they were easy to use and much easier to learn than the witches' counter spells.

She saw a few witches down below that had learned some of the old spells and cast their glowing nets across the skies to descend upon the sorcerers and contain their destructive magic, but far too few of the witches could master these spells. The sorcerers continued their march and grew ever closer to Destiny. Tempest wished desperately for Blake to arrive with the orb. They needed Destiny to defend them against the sorcerers' attacks. Destiny could learn the old spells. That was her gift. She merely had to experience any kind of magic, and she instantly knew how to cast it back. They needed her, but she still lay dormant in her hospital bed. The doctors called it a coma, but Tempest knew that it was much more than that.

She exhaled onto the window glass and wiped it with her sleeve, but the oily black smudges were on the outside. The image of gloom and destruction still shone through the dirty glass. She saw a band of sorcerers approaching from down the street. They were here already, but they took their time as they held an orb high in the air so all could see. She felt her breath drain out of her, taking her hope with it. They already had the orb. All was lost, unless she could find another way to wake her daughter.

Tempest's head nodded forward and woke her from her dream, but she knew that it was more than just an idle dream. It was a foreboding premonition. She squeezed Destiny's hand, knowing that she needed to wake her and prepare for the possibility that Blake would fail to recover the orb, and worse, the sorcerers may already have it.

Chapter 19

Michelle woke from her dream with a renewed sense of duty. The bell still reverberated in her memory, and even though she never located it in her dream, she felt confident that she now understood its significance and dressed rapidly to return to the hospital. The bell, her bell, was there, and it was waiting for her. Nothing else in her life mattered as much as what she now had to do. She couldn't worry about the consequences any more. Her duty was clear, and her objective was too important for her to concern herself with her personal fears. She had to end Honey to save the world, even if it required her personal sacrifice, and she needed her bell to fulfill her duty.

Honey stood with Balletina in the center of the auditorium, waiting for her next batch of students to arrive. The scent of sulphur already filled the gymnasium from Ramona and Misty, who were off to the side practicing their fire spells. Ramona had learned to create a spray of sparks which looked more like a fireworks display, but Misty had actually produced a tennis ball sized ball of flame and had held it in her palm. Honey glanced over at them and said, "They're doing good."

"Uh huh," Balletina agreed, but there was a sad hollowness to her answer.

"What's wrong?" Honey asked. "You don't sound very happy."

Balletina shrugged and said, "Nothing," but as she spoke, she traced a somber semi-circle on the floor with her toe.

"Come on," Honey urged her. "Tell me what's wrong. I can't have my number one girl moping around when we have so much work to do."

"Am I?" Balletina asked.

Honey waited for more, but Balletina just stared back at her, waiting for an answer. Honey shrugged her shoulders and asked, "Are you what?"

"Am I your number one girl?"

"Of course you are!" Honey exclaimed. "Just look how fast you learned to make fire."

Balletina slumped her shoulders and said, "Look how fast they're picking it up."

"So?" Honey asked. "You were still first."

"If they can pick it up," Balletina said, "then anyone can. What if I'm nothing special at all?"

"So what if everyone else can pick it up?" Honey asked. "You'll still be my friend, even if you do turn out to be a big disappointment in the magic department."

Balletina felt a hollowness in her chest as her mouth fall open and she slowly backed away from Honey.

"I'm just kidding," Honey said.

"It's not very funny."

"Look," Honey said, "The other students are arriving now. I need you to help me teach them. It will make the training go faster, and it will make you look better to them too."

───────────

Ashlin had overheard Michelle talking with Tempest about Destiny being stuck in her own make believe world, but she had never been included her in any of those conversations. She felt like an outsider who was only called upon when they needed something from her, and now she could see the look on Tempest's face and knew that something was going on inside of her. She felt the fear and anxiety that Tempest was feeling from her vision, but it wasn't the same kind of turmoil that Tempest usually went through when she heard too many people's thoughts all at once. With Tempest zoned out like that, Ashlin was essentially alone with her adopted sister, and she might never have a better chance to sneak away and go visit her than right now.

Tempest was on one side of the bed, holding Destiny's hand, so Ashlin pulled a chair up to the other side and sat down with her chin resting on the edge of the mattress. She closed her eyes and effortlessly slid into the void. "Destiny? It's me, Ashlin. Can I come visit you for a bit?"

Destiny had been hoping someone would come back for a visit. Time seemed to pass faster in this world, or maybe she was just uncommonly lonely. She regretted sending her mother and nana away so abruptly. It was rude, and it ended up leaving everybody unhappy. She needed them to give her a second chance.

"Destiny? Can you hear me?"

"Yes," Destiny replied. "I hear you, and of course you can come visit me! You don't have to ask."

"Actually, I kinda do have to ask," Ashlin said. "I haven't been there before and I don't know how to find you."

"Ooops," Destiny giggled and guided her in, but when she heard Ashlin land, she snapped her hands into a threatening posture and demanded, "Who are you? Is this some sort of trick?"

"What do you mean?" Ashlin asked.

"You know what I mean. Who are you?" She cocked her fist behind her and warned, "Don't think I won't hurt you if I think you're lying to me."

"Destiny! It's me! Ashlin!"

She sounded like Ashlin, but Destiny saw an old woman standing in Ashlin's place. "You don't look anything like Ashlin. How long have I been dead?"

"Dead?" Ashlin asked. "You're not dead. Who do I look like if not myself?" Ashlin looked down at herself and saw the same dress she was wearing an hour ago, but when she reached down to pull the skirt back so she could see her feet better, she saw old-lady hands covered in wrinkles and liver spots. She held the frail old hands up in front of her face and turned them back and forth so she could examine both sides. "Ooops. What is this? Did I do something wrong?"

Destiny saw the honest confusion on Ashlin's face and burst out laughing.

"It's not funny," Ashlin cried.

"Yeah, it is."

"I don't know how this happened. I guess I'm just not very good at this stuff. You should come back and teach me."

"You too?" Destiny cried. "Why does everybody refuse to understand that I can't leave this place?"

"You can't? Why not? They don't tell me anything. Have you tried leaving?"

"Come on," Destiny said. "Let me show you my place. That is, if you think you can make it. Did you bring a walker with you? Or a cane maybe? Should I go fetch you a walkin' stick?"

"Ha ha," Ashlin replied dryly. "Lead on."

"You look pretty good for your age," Destiny chided her, "that is, if you were like a hundred years old."

Ashlin rolled her eyes. Destiny wasn't going to let this go.

"I know I have some tea, but I should probably look for a shawl first, so you don't catch cold."

Ashlin ignored her and tried changing the subject. "Blake would probably come visit you, but he's out there looking for the orb. He's going to England."

"I heard."

"He hasn't reported in yet," Ashlin continued, "so I don't know how his flight was."

"I already heard about your plans to get the orb and rescue me from here, but I tell you: I don't need rescuin' and I sure don't need to hear another of you tellin' me how much I do."

"Maybe so," Ashlin said, "but you haven't heard it from a wise old woman like me yet."

"I heard it from Nana."

"Oh."

Destiny walked slowly so Ashlin could keep up with her. "I wonder why you look like a old woman? If it's so easy for us to change our age, then why didn't nana look like a young woman? At least that would make some sense."

Ashlin had no answer.

"I'm kind of surprised that you're not out there with Blake lookin' for the orb."

Ashlin giggled. It was an infectious giggle that grew into a snicker until she finally burst out laughing.

Destiny held open the front door and said, "This is my place, but you're gonna have to tell my why you're laughin' so hard."

Ashlin took deep breaths to contain her laughter until she could finally say, "Your nana would never let me go with Blake to look for the orb..." she paused and struck a pose with her arms spread wide, "...because I'm too young."

Destiny caught the contagious laughter and the two of them bent over at the waist. "That ain't right."

"I know," Ashlin said. "Just look at me and tell me I'm too young."

"I wish I could," Destiny said, "but like I said, you must be a hundred years old and it ain't right for you to be laughing so hard. You could croak up a lung or something."

***

Richard entered the training room mid-class and saw several students conjuring various degrees of smoke and fire. He joined Honey in the center and said, "It's really working. You're actually creating an army, but doesn't it bother you that they're all so young?"

"I can't help it if they're all so young," she replied. "You brought me some old dudes at first, but they just stopped coming."

"Were they unable to summon any powers?"

"Maybe, but I think the old farts just didn't want to learn from someone as young as me."

Richard whistled and shook his head. "Who wouldn't want to learn this?"

"You? Are you saying you'd like to join my class?"

"I'd love to," Richard replied, "but I don't really have time right now. Perhaps after we fill in a few more ranks, things will start to run themselves and I can. Speaking of which, how are you ever going to find time to be our queen if you're so busy being our teacher?"

"Look at Balletina. She's a natural, and a good teacher too."

"You have another teacher already? I guess I shouldn't worry about you so much."

Honey caressed his check and asked, "You were worried about me? That's so sweet."

Richard pointed over to Ramona and Misty. "Those other two look like they're advancing pretty nicely."

"Yup. Makes you wonder how good their friend Angie might have been if she hadn't had such a big mouth on her."

"Yeah," Richard said. "About that. Her father heard stories about what happened. I don't know how much of them he believes, but the word I hear is that he's gathering support to shut us down."

"What can he do?" Honey asked. "He doesn't have power like ours. He's just rich. If he comes here and makes waves, then he can have a rich man's funeral."

Balletina heard them talking and left her students practicing to join them.

"He has a lot of friends," Richard said.

"Then they can choose new friends," Honey snarled, "or they can all have rich man funerals too."

Balletina said, "It won't be long before our army is a force to be reckoned with. Ramona and Misty already have my back. There's nothing that Angie's family can buy that we can't fry in a blink."

Richard smiled grimly and nodded his head. "Have you ever wondered why you can suddenly train our people to make fire again?"

"No," Honey said, "but I wondered how our people managed to lose it in the first place."

"That's in the archives," Richard replied. "The witches did something to us. They claimed that it wasn't them, but they issued a threat to us that we would lose our powers right before it happened, so we know it was them. They even tried claiming that it was a prophecy, not a threat, but that's just what we would expect them to say. Their prophecy said that eventually, one person would bring magic back, so we've been holding training sessions for almost a thousand years looking for that one phenom who could make the old magic, but we never found anyone that could even make a spark."

"Maybe you just needed someone who could actually do it to teach them."

"Maybe," Richard said. "But you weren't born with it. You had to..."

"Steal it?" Honey asked. "Is that what you were going to say? You forget that Frank found me before she ever came along and I could already do things, only they weren't very powerful then. Besides, so what if I did steal the big fire from her? My bitch ass little cousin wasn't doing anything with it. At least I'm making it work."

"Are you?" He asked. "She did stop you."

"It's like Mr. Peters used to say in history class. She won the battle, but not the war."

"The way I hear it," Balletina said, "it was more like a draw."

"Even so," Richard said. "She was the first. She found the magic that had been lost for centuries."

"And I stole it," Honey said. "Now I'm sharing it, and she's dead."

"Is she?" Richard asked.

***

Blake stood in front of the airport, feeling like he had been there before, but fully aware that it had only been a dream; a really strange dream. His mind spun from the overwhelming tasks that he had to do, which left him standing dumbly as he watched the cars wiz by. He had always known that drivers drove on the other side of the road in England, but in his state of mind, actually seeing the traffic in person made the image look like some bizarre kind of mirror world.

A man in a heavy overcoat brushed by Blake hauling his luggage to the cabbie stand where he was met by a short squat driver who helped load his luggage into the trunk. Blake followed him to the queue, and as the cab drove off, another took its place. Blake barely raised his hand to signal the driver when the gaunt young man rolled down the window and said, "I see ya. Nothing for the boot?"

"What?" Blake asked.

"The boot," the driver repeated. "You've got no luggage?"

"Oh," Blake replied sheepishly, "yeah, no luggage."

Blake climbed into the back of the cab, looking a bit dazed.

"Where to?"

"Good question," Blake said. "I'm looking for a really old college with a large library."

"Ah," the man said. "We have plenty of those. You'll be wanting Oxford, or maybe even Cambridge. Are you a student? Is that why you have no bags?"

"Something like that," Blake said. "I'm searching for an old book, and I figured a university would be as good a place as any to start."

"You're from America then?"

"Yeah..."

"I have a mate in California. Maybe you know him. Are you from California?"

"No," Blake replied. "I'm from a lot of places, but not from California. This is my first time here. I wasn't expecting such nice weather."

"Why not?" the driver asked. "Did you think that California was the only place with sunshine?"

"I'm not from California."

"Oh, that's right," the cabbie said. "You probably..."

The man stopped mid-sentence and was quiet for several blocks, then he turned the corner and pulled into the campus drop-off zone and announced, "Here we are. Out you go."

"This is it?" Blake asked. "I thought it would look...older."

"Out you go," the cabbie repeated. "I have more customers waiting for me."

Blake climbed out and before he could push the man to believe that some random brochures he collected at the airport were money, the cab pulled away and squealed down the street. This was not the library. The street was lined with trees on one side and lots of construction on the other. A white sign stood on the far corner. Blake couldn't read it from that distance, but he clearly saw arrows pointing right and left. He walked to the corner and followed the sign towards the library, but before arriving there, he came across a prominent looking building with a plaque out front, "Surrey University, founded 1966."

"What the...?"

He turned back to where the cabbie had dropped him off, but his ride was long gone.

Logan didn't find Richard in his office, and was about to give up and leave for the airport when he passed the auditorium and saw Richard inside. Sulphur laced smoke filled the room and leaked out into the corridor. He swallowed hard when he saw how many students were creating fire already. If he didn't find that orb soon, or if the orb wasn't as powerful as he had hoped, then wresting control from Honey might become impossible.

Richard saw Logan enter the room and said, "Hey Frank. What do you think? Pretty impressive, huh?"

Logan whistled. "More than I expected so soon. What about the thermal imagery from the satellites? Aren't you afraid that they'll see what's going on?"

Richard stepped aside to talk more privately with Logan. "I've already ordered some supplies, but if I had known that the training was going to progress this rapidly, I would have rushed the orders."

"So, you have a plan to hide this?"

"I think so. I'm going to cover the roof with a sandwich made of two thermal reflective blankets and a thermal absorptive layer in between. Just for good measure, I'll put a non-conductive layer between each of the thermal blankets. That should mask what's inside and make the whole God dammed roof match the surrounding desert all the time."

Logan nodded his head approvingly. "I'm heading for the airport. Take good care of my girl while I'm gone."

"Did you find a location for the witches' artifact? Is it in one of our archives?"

"I haven't found it yet, but I found a clue. It's someplace for me to start looking at least."

"Excellent," Richard slapped Logan on the back. "You sure you don't want to stick around for a few minutes? Watching them is quite fascinating."

Logan checked his watch, but it wasn't really necessary. He was taking a private jet and wasn't bound by the same kind of schedules as commercial flights. "Sure, I can watch a bit."

Balletina took a young girl aside and said, "You're still stuck on the smoke."

The little girl shied away from Balletina and stared at the ground.

"What's the matter?" Balletina asked. "You almost have it."

The girl shrugged her shoulders and twisted back and forth at the waist.

Logan whispered to Richard, "How old is she?"

"Ten, I think. Maybe nine."

Logan whistled. "That's young. You know, I've been spending a lot of time in the archives. In the old days, it was mostly boys that had the power. I don't remember any young girls, at least, not that young. In fact, the archives made it sound like the girls couldn't get their powers until puberty."

Richard shrugged. "That may still be true, but I've seen articles that girls are reaching puberty at younger and younger ages these days. It's probably something in all the junk food we eat."

"Hmmm," Logan replied. "You'd think the boys would too."

"Maybe they do, but we may have some issues getting our boys to take instructions from a girl. We do have a couple boys that show some promise. The rest of them will come around, eventually. They'll have to if they don't want to be left behind."

"I think it's bigger than just a few boys falling behind in these skills," Logan said. "If we don't have some boys learn their powers, and only girls have the magic, then our whole clan could change into a matriarchy and we'd be slaves to the women."

Balletina knelt down next to the young girl and hugged her. "It's okay. You can tell me. Are you afraid?"

The girl nodded her head. "I got burnt from fire once."

"Normal fire burns," Balletina said, "but this is a special kind of fire that we can learn to hold. Our hands are made for handling our special kind of fire, and you are going to see that it doesn't burn us at all." Balletina knew that she was over simplifying her explanation for the little girl. She could easily produce a fire that did burn, but for this lesson, she flipped out her hand and produced a small ball of fire that pulsated as it rested on her palm. The little girl tentatively pointed her finger to touch it. After a few gentle pokes, Balletina whipped the ball away from her and said, "Turn your palm up and straighten out your fingers." The girl did as she was told and Balletina placed the ball in her hand. "You see? Does that burn?"

The little girl shook her head no.

Balletina snapped her fingers, and the fireball popped into a puff of smoke. "Now you try. Imagine that your hand is hot, and it itches.

The itch is driving you crazy, but it's deep inside of your hand where you can't scratch it, so you want to push it out of your hand and into the air."

The little girl grunted as she tried to imagine how she might push an itch until a small flame appeared in her hand. "I did it! I did it! And it doesn't burn at all!"

Logan was surprised by the simplicity of it. Balletina's description certainly wasn't what he remembered them teaching him when he was young, but they couldn't actually make the fire and nobody had done so for centuries. He turned his palm up and imagined a burning itch. Richard saw what he was doing and watched intently as Logan pushed a small flame out of his palm.

"I'll be damned," Richard said.

"Frank!" Honey exclaimed. "Look at you!"

Logan couldn't help the giddy smile that stretched across his face. "You were right when you said this is real power. I was appointed to my position, and I may have even earned that to some degree, but not like this. This is real power, and I really earned it."

"That's a good thing," Honey said. "I need some real men with real power in my 'ministration. And you know how to run things too."

"Speaking of which," he said, "I have to run. I'll be out of town for a few days at least. What you're doing here is amazing. I thought it would have taken months."

"If you ask me," Honey said, "this is what we were born to do. We was always supposed to be makin' fire like this. It's in our nature. We're just learning to lift whatever them witches put on us to make us forget how it's done."

"Yeah," Logan said softly. That was the most intelligent thing he had ever heard her say. Not bad for such a crazy bitch.

***

Johnson's trip across the Atlantic wasn't nearly as pleasant as Blake's. He had room for his legs and the seat reclined, but it didn't leave much room for him to move around. He wished that he would have picked up a book on the way to the plane. There was precious little for him to do, and sleep was as hard for him to find as comfort was. He kept his eyes closed with his head turned against the backrest and managed to drift in and out of something resembling sleep, but it was a dreamless, restless time leaving him with a stiff neck and a headache by the time he arrived in England.

Customs was a long slow-moving line, during which Blake just got further ahead of him. He tried guessing what all the other travelers were doing there. He hoped it would help him pass the time, but he didn't have Blake's insight and quickly bored of the game. A funk hung in the air that reminded him that he hadn't showered recently, but a quick glance around him allayed his concerns, because he was clearly not the only one. He shuffled his feet as the line inched forward, and when he arrived at the front of the line, the stern-looking agent sighed heavily when she saw that he had no luggage, but waived him through, preferring not to receive another lecture from her supervisor.

Outside the terminal, Johnson looked up and down the road, hoping vainly to spot Blake, but he knew that he was too far behind to find him that easily. One of the librarians snickered in his head. "Of course you don't know where he is. You're not psychic. Proceed to Oxford University and wait for him outside the library there."

Johnson hated them being in his head, but he appreciated the help and proceeded to find a taxi.

Destiny brought a pitcher of ice cold tea to the table and handed a tumbler to Ashlin. "Do you know the real reason why Blake needs to find the orb?"

"To save you," Ashlin replied without any hesitation or question in her voice.

"No, that's not it at all. It's a mystical object and you probably won't find it unless you know why you really need it."

"We need it to save you," Ashlin insisted.

"Not me," Destiny objected, "my mother. My mother is a lot stronger than anyone realizes. You need to find the orb to save my mother."

"Your mother needs to be healed," Ashlin said, "and you're the only one with the power of healing."

"The orb will heal her," Destiny said.

"That's not what I heard," Ashlin said. "The orb will add power, like a battery, but it can't do anything on its own."

"It has to," Destiny said. "I always knew that I had to find the orb to save my mother, but now that I'm gone, you all need to use it to save her for me. Someone who is still living needs to use it to heal my mother."

Ashlin frowned. Destiny wouldn't listen to her. "I should be going, but I really wish you'd try to understand. Only you and the orb together can save your mother. That's why it has your name. The power of the orb is meant for you."

"What are we talking about? My mother is almost saved already."

"She's doing much better," Ashlin agreed, "but I wouldn't call her saved."

"Not yet, maybe, but you'll save her."

Ashlin sighed heavily and said, "We'll talk later. I really should be going now. Being this old is kinda exhausting."

Chapter 20

For thousands of years, the sorcerer clan raised their children to believe that they were the master race, and for the most part, it wasn't merely idle boasting. They easily lorded over the non-magical humans, and there were many times in history when they ruled the land. Their advantages over the humans made them impossible to oppose and their practice of marrying within the clan led many nations to the believe that their bloodlines were descended from the Gods. Rising above the humans was easy, but they were cruel and greedy masters and found themselves always at odds with the witch clan who repeatedly found ways to topple their regimes. Even after both clans had lost their powers, the sorcerers and their descendants continued to feel that they were superior, and those who were aware of the history of their clan blamed the witches for their misfortune.

They not only fostered the idea among their children that their clan was superior to both the humans and the witch clan, they also raised their offspring to believe that boys were superior to girls, but this was an increasingly unpopular notion that pit them not only against the witch clan, but also against enlightened men and women of the human race. Honey had already conveyed to Richard that she didn't want to see a boys only class of students, and Richard had dutifully provided an even mix of boys and girls, but the boys arrived believing that this would be easier for them to learn than it would be for girls. They had a tendency to push to the front and expected the girls to relinquish their spots to them.

Honey had seen this, but had moderated her temper. She could have fried any one of them on the spot and ended any superiority they felt over the girls, but the way the class was progressing, she didn't think she would have to. The boys showed no increased aptitude towards making fire than the girls had. In fact, their belief that it should be easier for them left them putting out less effort than the girls. Being as competitive as the boys were, those that were unwilling to try harder left for other pursuits rather than admit defeat and naturally blamed it on the unfair system that put a girl in charge of training. Honey didn't mind their leaving and appreciated the boys that were open-minded enough to see past their prejudices and put in some extra effort to learn. Some boys, however, were too stubborn to give up their self-anointed superiority and continued to bully their way through the classes.

It was common for new students, be they boy or girl, to be stuck on making sparks and embers; unable to launch a full-blown fireball. Balletina was working patiently with one such girl, who was nearly in tears, when a boy joined them and took aim at her target. The girl gripped his arm before he could take a shot and yelled, "Hey! That's my target!"

The boy had seen that she had not managed to launch anything at it and replied, "Well, you weren't using it!"

The girl glanced over at his target and defiantly answered back, "Yours doesn't look like it's been used any more than mine!"

"Something's wrong with mine," he said flatly, as if sounding factual would make it so.

"Like what?" She asked. "What is wrong with your target?"

"Nothing is wrong with his target," Balletina said, and as she said it, she fired two rounds of fireballs at it. "See? It works fine."

The girl shoved the boy and said, "Go away!"

The boy growled and reared back to hit her with a fist, but when she threw her hands up to block her face, a lightning bolt sprung from her hands and struck him in the chest, knocking the surprised young man backwards onto his butt.

"Wow!" Balletina said. "Where did that come from? What's your name?"

"Caroline," the girl said meekly. "Carol. My name is Carol, and I don't know how I did that."

"It doesn't matter how. It only matters that you can do it again. I liked it. Keep practicing."

Michelle stared blankly ahead of her as she entered the hospital. Nurses and attendants swarmed right and left around her as she passed through the lobby, but she saw none of them as her feet automatically followed the corridor to the elevators. If any of them would have looked, they would have seen two detached and unfocussed eyes, but she was as invisible to them as they were to her. Even the cab ride from the hotel was less than a blur in her memory. If she ever did remember the cab, she would never remember how she had found it or how she had managed to pay for it. Her mind and body occupied two different spaces. In her mind, she saw only the bell tower that awaited her in Destiny's room. When she had finally arrived, she walked directly past everyone without uttering even a syllable of greeting and took the tower into her arms and hugged it to her bosom, oblivious to the strange looks on the faces of her family and friends.

Blake balled up a fist and punched a sign that pointed to one of the Surrey dormitories, then immediately regretted his action as he flexed his now hurting knuckles. He still needed to get to Oxford. It didn't make sense that a university founded in the 60s would hold any worthwhile clues for his quest. He spun around, looking for another taxi. The Surrey campus wasn't exactly deserted, but there were no cabs that he could see. He saw two guys huddled around a girl in front of a fountain and walked up to them, asking, "Excuse me, but a crazy cab driver dropped me off at the wrong university. Is there someplace around here where I can catch another taxi?"

The girl pushed one of the guys away and asked, "Where did you want to be?"

"Oxford," Blake said.

"You?" one of the guys asked with an incredulous tone to his voice. "A raggedy bloke like you goes to Oxford?"

"Not as a student," Blake said.

"Don't tell me that you're a teacher," the other guy said laughingly. "You don't look nothin' like a teacher."

The first guy laughed. "Of course he's not a teacher, you prat. They got standards over there. Just look at 'is baby face. 'e looks like a bit o' a uphill gardener if you is askin' me."

The girl pushed past them and said, "Nobody's askin' you. Maybe he's one of those American geniuses."

Blake blushed and said, "I'm just trying to find their library. I'm looking for an old book."

"Ah," the second guy said. "You're a librarian then. You do look more like a librarian."

Blake pictured the mysterious strangers in the grey robes. He didn't like being called a librarian.

"If it's a rare book you be looking for," the first guy said, "then you'd be wanting the long library in Dublin."

"It's the long room," the second guy said, "not the long library, and it's in Trinity College."

"Dublin?" Blake asked. "Isn't that in Scotland?"

"No," the girl said, "it's in Ireland."

"Close enough," the second guy said with a hearty laugh.

Blake eyed them suspiciously and asked, "Are you sure you're not just trying to get rid of me?"

"Are you a rare book collector?" the girl asked.

"A rare book collector?" the first guy asked. "Are you daft? Look at him. Those rare books can really cost a bomb. I doubt he has it in him."

"Cost a bomb?" Blake asked.

The girl took Blake by the arm and said, "Don't listen to them. I never judge a book by the cover."

"By the cover?" the second guy roared. "Good one."

"About that cab," Blake said as he tried to pull his arm free from hers. "Can you tell me where to find one or not?"

The girl hung onto his arm and said, "Come with me. I'll show you to the taxi queue."

"Why?" the first guy asked. "You don't even know him."

She ignored her rude friend and said, "In fact, I've always wanted to see Oxford."

"You?" the first guy asked. "What's Oxford got for the likes of you?"

The second guy said, "You don't need a cab. I'll take you."

"Blimey," the first guy said, "do you realize that trip's at least an hour each way? Probably more!"

"So?" the second guy replied. "I expect that this might be interesting. I'm dying to see how he gets into the library there."

"An hour?" Blake thought. That would be one very long cab ride.

Ashlin returned from her visit to Destiny and was immediately struck by the tension that filled the room, and it all seemed to be centered around Michelle, who sat in the corner hugging one of the talismans that she had whipped up with Zeline. "Hey Michelle," she said sweetly, hoping to break the ice, "what's up?"

Michelle didn't even hear the young girl's question.

"Guess what?" Ashlin continued. "I just got back from visiting Destiny. You won't believe what happened…"

Again Michelle didn't react.

"Are you okay?"

"No," Zeline said flatly, "she ain't okay. I tink dat maybe she be possessed. I seen her leave da hotel. She looked like a zombie."

Ashlin walked directly in front of Michelle and softly asked, "Is that true?"

Michelle didn't even look at her.

Ashlin frowned and cocked her head as she studied Michelle's face. "What is going on inside your head? If you don't come out and tell us, then I'll just have to go in and see for myself."

Michelle continued to stare off into space.

"She's gone," Zeline said, pointing to the tower in Michelle's arms. "At first I was tinkin' dat maybe dat bell tower was a good omen when she made it, but now I don't be so sure."

Ashlin snatched the bell tower from Michelle's hands and yelled, "Michelle!"

Michelle blinked and finally saw Ashlin.

Ashlin waved the bell tower around in the air and yelled, "What the hell have you gotten yourself into? You've been taught better than that! What is this thing? Have you been meddling around in dark magic? You know that you can't go around messin' with powers that you don't understand!"

Tears clouded Michelle's eyes. "I'm sorry Mama. It just be dat I gots sumpin' dat I gots to do. It be a terrible deed, but I gots to do it 'cause I'm da only one dat can do it and I need dat bell when I do."

Ashlin looked around the room, hoping that someone would know what she was talking about, but Zeline and Tempest only shrugged. Ashlin looked back into Michelle's eyes and asked in her sweetest little voice, "What is this terrible thing that you have to do?"

"I cain't tell you, but iffin Destiny don't come back to us, then it falls to me. I knows a way to make things right ag'in, but that's all I kin tell you."

"I don't know what you think you're going to do," Ashlin said softly, "but I can tell you that it don't all fall to you. I have some plans of my own, so maybe you don't have to go all crazy on us. I'm gonna give this thing to Zeline, since she helped you make all this fine stuff."

Michelle reached for it and said, "But I need it with me."

"Let's see how things go. If they don't go so well for us, then maybe you can have it back, but I don't believe that I want you doing a terrible thing, as you called it, at least not just yet. I have a plan and I think I should check in on it."

"But..."

"Don't you but me!" Ashlin scolded her.

Michelle bowed her head and said, "Yes'm."

Ashlin handed the tower to Zeline.

Zeline looked awkwardly at Ashlin and asked, "Did she jest call you mama a moment ago? Never mind. You don't has to answer. I been tinking all along dat you seemed a might old for your age."

Ashlin recalled her visit to Destiny and could only muster a half smile.

Logan didn't need to maneuver through the same congested TSA lines like Blake had. He had a jet ready and waiting for him at a terminal reserved for private traffic. He breezed through the nearly deserted terminal with no crowds to slow him down. The lighting in this part of the airport was more subdued than it was on the commercial side. The softened illumination wasn't purposefully designed to provide the private patrons with additional privacy over their commercial counterparts, although they undoubtedly appreciated the relaxed ambiance, but the lack of gaudy shops and restaurants vying for customers kept this part of the airport more intimate.

Logan had always appreciated the dusky atmosphere in the past, but not on this trip. Every chance he had, he was holding up his palm to produce a small flame, but the low lights made it very difficult for him to keep it hidden. Fortunately, he'd be on the jet shortly and away from prying eyes, but he couldn't wait for that and stretched out his fingers again, producing a small flame. Making the flame wasn't enough. He tried controlling it to make it dance for him and succeeded at moving it around and across his palm. Squashing it formed a fat base to the flame, then releasing it, let it spring upwards.

He wondered if Honey could do that.

Blake watched England roll by through the car window. If he read the signs correctly, they were circling along the outskirts of London. He tried keeping track of their route, but his attention was at least partially on his new companions. Something didn't quite make sense about their eagerness to drive him to Oxford. The tension from the two guys was unmistakable, but that was all from their interest in the girl. It seemed strange that the two of them would sound jealous over the attention that she paid to him, but harbored no jealousy towards each other. He wondered if she was fawning over him purely to push their buttons, since both of them seemed to desire her for themselves, or did they want her for both of them together?

He did his best to remain aloof, but she sat with him in the back of the car and clung tightly to his arm. He couldn't shake the feeling that something was wrong with them. There was no doubt in his mind that he could handle the guys if things got physical, but he wasn't so sure what he could do about the girl.

"You never answered my question," she said as she leaned her head against his shoulder and looked up into his eyes. "Are you a rare book collector?"

Blake shook his head. He was intensely aware that her signs of affection were disturbing the other two. "No. I'm just doing some archeological research."

The second guy, behind the wheel, smiled slightly into the rear-view mirror, but the first guy looked at Blake sideways and said, "You don't look like an archeologist either."

"I'm not," Blake admitted. "It's more of a personal interest."

"Wha'?" the first guy asked. "You flew all the way 'ere on a hobby? Are you stupid?"

"Daft as a bush," the second guy added, "if you is askin' me."

"Never mind them," the girl said. "Did you really fly all the way here just to research a book? On a personal interest?"

Blake shrugged and said, "Yeah. Something like that."

The second guy glanced at the first and said, "It all sounds a bit dodgy to me."

"I s'pose everything would sound a bit dodgy," the girl said, "to a right diddler like yourself."

Blake didn't know what was going on with his new companions, and he didn't really care. What did matter to him was that they weren't all in agreement, which probably meant that they weren't some kind of conspiracy cooked up to stop him from finding the orb. He looked out the window again and sighed. He didn't like feeling so paranoid all the time.

Ashlin didn't know what Michelle had planned, but she was serious about finding another way to deal with Honey, although she had no plans in mind just yet. She cried softly as she rested her head on the edge of Destiny's bed. Everything was such a mess, and the doctors weren't doing anything to help Destiny, so she could come back to them to fix it. The whole hospital just seemed to be waiting for Destiny to die, and her family could only plead for Destiny to return. Destiny herself was doing nothing to come back and help them. Things outside were rapidly becoming a disaster, and they didn't have Michelle to hold them together. The army had apparently figured something out, or maybe they were going to figure something out, but she had little faith that they could execute such a plan and see it through to the end. She had even less faith that they could fairly and justly wield such power if Honey ever was defeated and the disaster was averted.

That left only Logan. He wasn't really on their side, but he was at least against Honey, and he knew about them and what they could do. It was hard for her to trust him, but they might still need to use him. He wasn't completely crazy like Honey was, but he still wanted the power of the orb for himself, and if he ever got it, who knows how bad he might become?

She closed her eyes and searched for him. She had already seen what he was planning and easily found him in the airport. This wasn't good. He must have already learned where the orb was and was going to retrieve it for himself. She had to do something before he beat all of them to it.

Logan stepped quietly through the airport, trying not to attract any undue attention, but he couldn't stop himself from playing with his fire. He produced small flames in his palms and turned them around, running them across his fingers and around the back of his hand. The more he played with them, the easier it got for him to produce them.

"Wait!" Ashlin called from behind him. "Mr. Logan!"

Logan squashed the flame in his palm and turned around to see Ashlin's familiar red hair bouncing down the hallway behind him. "How did you..." he stopped abruptly when he saw her image shimmer slightly. "Oh, this is one of your witch tricks?"

"I need to talk to you."

He turned his back to her and resumed walking. "I don't have time for this. I have a flight to catch."

"No, you don't," she said, "I mean, yes you do. That is, you do have a flight to catch, but you have plenty of time because it's a private plane and you don't really have to rush like this."

"I'm still in a hurry."

"You don't want to do this," she said. "If you get the orb for yourself, she'll end up with it and that will be a disaster."

"I suppose you've seen all this."

"I have. You need to stop."

"What makes you think she can take the orb from me? If I have the orb, I'll be stronger than her."

Ashlin ran up ahead of him and turned around to stop him. "I can see things that you can't."

"I don't care what you can see, and I don't care how many friends she has with her."

"She has friends?"

"I thought you said you could see things. Yes, she has friends."

"That's kind of hard to believe," Ashlin said. "I've known her all of my life and she's never had any friends before."

Logan stopped before he ran right through her. "That's easy enough to believe. Maybe friends is the wrong word, but they follow her and she's teaching them to make fire."

Without a thought, Ashlin found herself rummaging around in Logan's memory. She saw Honey in an auditorium with groups of girls and boys that were all staring at their hands. Some had managed to issue small flames from their palms, while others, with more constipated faces, could only conjure up bare wisps of smoke. Off to the side of the room, more advanced students were throwing bona fide fireballs at smoldering targets. "So, she's teaching others to make fire now? That explains the vision I had where she had a whole army that could conjure up flames. It's still hard to understand what kind of person would follow her."

Logan stared at her image. She didn't shimmer any more like she had at first. He reached out and tentatively touched her.

"Did you think you were dreaming?"

"It had occurred to me." He tousled her hair and said, "This is a pretty good trick. How did someone so young become so powerful?"

"Maybe I'm not as young as you think."

"Perhaps, but it emphasizes even more why I need to go find the orb."

The last image that Ashlin pulled from his mind was a round glowing orb floating beside Honey. Why would Logan be searching for the orb if she had already obtained it? He certainly wouldn't try to go against her if he thought she already had it, and it wasn't a premonition if it had come from his head.

"Excuse me," Logan said as he stepped around the young redhead to continue towards his plane.

"I don't get it," she said. "Why do you say that it is even more important for you to find the orb?"

"Because I don't want to live in a world dominated by witches any more than I want to live under her regime."

Ashlin frowned and let go of her astral projection.

"Let's go to town," Honey said.

"Now?" Balletina asked. "Don't you have another class to teach?"

"I ain't teaching them nothing no more. I just oversees their exercises."

Balletina peeked into the auditorium and saw the students assembling. She called out to them, "Can I have your attention, please? I want you all to keep practicing what you've learned so far while we go into town. You're doing real well. I want you to know that."

Honey stepped through the door and added, "That's right. In fact, I think you are doing so well that pretty soon, I'm going to pick some new instructors out of your group."

The assembled students roared their approval and doubled their efforts to master the creation of fire.

Honey and Balletina headed for the exit when Richard called out, "Where are you two going?"

"To town," Honey said. "Wanna come with?"

"No," he replied. "I think I need to start getting more students transferred here."

"You mean more soldiers," Honey said. "Are there other places like this one? We may need to send some instructors out instead of bringing students in."

"What's going on?" Richard asked. "I thought you were stoked about teaching them fire."

Honey exhaled and slumped her shoulders. "To tell you the truth, I was really stoked about having an army at first, but I'm tired of teaching them the same thing over and over."

"Ahh," Richard said. "You might want to visit the library."

Honey laughed, then stopped short and said, "Oh, you're serious?"

"Our people used to do a lot more than just make fire."

"And lightning," Balletina added.

"A lot more," Richard said.

Honey rolled her eyes. "First you want me to be the teacher, and now you want me to be the student? I got to get out of here."

"Okay," Richard said, "but at least think about it."

Blake was grateful when the car had finally grown quiet. The girl kept her head nestled on his shoulder with her arms wrapped around his. He tried watching the city fly by, but his suspicions grew too great and he couldn't let his guard down while he still didn't know what they were up to. He considered peeking into their minds to learn what they were thinking, but what if they were witches and not necessarily his friends? It was more important that he didn't alert them as to who or what he was, but he just couldn't shake the feeling that there was something wrong about them, so he watched and listened.

"What's wrong?" the girl asked.

"Nothing," Blake said.

"Not you," she replied, pointing to the driver, "him."

The guy behind the wheel pulled the car off the highway until they reached a small round-about, then pulled over to the curb on the other side of the circle and said, "Out you go."

Blake sighed heavily as he looked around and said, "This doesn't look very much like a university."

"I'm done with you," the second guy said. "Get out."

"What're you doing?" the girl asked. "He's our friend."

"Bollocks," the second guy said as he slammed his fist into the wheel. "There's something wrong about him and he's got to go."

Blake looked into his mind and suggested, "There's no need for this. Just calm down and drive to Oxford like you said you would."

The other guy looked back and forth between his friend and Blake, but said nothing as the driver turned to look at Blake. His eyes were blank. He parted his lips as if to say something, but didn't.

Blake pushed a little harder. "You've changed your mind. You want to take him all the way to the Oxford library."

The driver still didn't respond, and instead twitched his head to the left while he stared through Blake.

Blake wasn't sure why it didn't work, but the car was still at the curb. It was like the security officer at the airport. Was he losing his powers? He looked at the girl for help, but she was focused on her friend, whose face was now twitching in half a dozen muscle spasms. Blake let himself out and said, "I better go. Is he going to be okay? Can you get back alright?"

The girl was too busy checking on her friend to have even heard Blake. The first guy walked around the car and pulled his friend out

of the car, then helped him around to the passenger side. It was as if
Blake weren't even there.

Ashlin stroked Destiny's hand, afraid of what she had seen in Logan's
mind and wishing more than ever that her new big sister would
return, but she had to face the fact that she might have to handle this
herself. She had not only seen the interior of the gym where Honey's
classes were held, but she had come away with its location in the
desert and knew how to find it.

She closed her eyes and projected herself above their headquarters. Just as with entering the void, projecting her astral self was
getting easier with practice. She tried forming an invisible image,
but the best she could do was closer to clear soap bubbles floating in
the air. She hovered around the complex, counting how many people
roamed around outside and noting where the entrances and exits
were. It looked like an old boarding school. How could that dimwit
Honey have found a school where she could teach them fire? She
must have had a lot of help.

A breeze brushed across Ashlin's face as she floated around the
perimeter of the building to the front steps and waited until the
coast was clear, then descended behind a bush near the steps where
she materialized into her true form, but to be sure, she checked her
hands to make sure she didn't show up as a wrinkled old woman.
Satisfied that her hands were their youthful selves, she took a step
towards the sidewalk, but before she could emerge from the bushes,
a school bus pulled up and dropped off a dozen girls and boys. She
crouched down behind the shrubbery and watched the kids file out
of the bus and congregate in front of the steps. They were mostly
around her own age and, from the looks of wonder on their faces,

she surmised that this may have been their first trip here. The bus belched out a cloud of diesel smoke as it pulled away, and the new kids formed a line and began to climb the steps. Her heart pounded in her ears as she waited for all of them to pass by, then she impulsively stepped out from the bush and climbed the steps as if she were the last of the new arrivals. She was grateful that her projection did not experience or apparently cause any of the alarming cramps they get when witches and sorcerers were near each other.

They were led directly into the auditorium, where a man met them. "Hello. My name is Richard. I'm sorry, but our instructors are out on an errand today. However, you are welcome to take a seat on the bleachers and watch the other students practice their lessons. After class, you'll all be assigned rooms and given a tour of the school."

Ashlin followed them to the seating area and sat down to watch. They were more advanced than what she had seen in Logan's memory. A couple of them launched lightning bolts to their targets, but most of them created fire balls that engulfed their targets in flames. Murmurs circulated amongst the new arrivals as they watched the astounding display and anticipated joining their ranks.

Balletina drove while Honey sat quietly in the passenger seat, mulling over what Richard had said to her.

"Where to first?" Balletina asked as they approached the small town.

"I dunno," Honey replied. "Do you suppose that maybe he was right?"

"Who? Richard?"

"Yeah. Should I really be spending more time in the libary learning what other things our people used to do?"

"Maybe," Balletina replied, "but what if you can only make fire? What good would the archives do you if fire is your only power?"

"I can do more," Honey said defensively. "I pushed a car right off the road once."

"Really? I wish I could have seen that."

"And I crushed a bunch of army tanks like they was paper bags. Maybe I can do even more than that, but just don't know it yet."

Balletina pulled the car into the mall and parked in the middle of the lot, away from the ice cream parlor.

"You gonna make me walk there?"

A sinister smile crossed Balletina's face. "I wonder if we can make it hot in there without catching it on fire."

"We?"

Balletina ignored her question and said, "Maybe we can make it so hot that all the ice cream melts."

"What's with this we?" Honey asked.

"Why? You don't think I can learn something new?"

"I didn't say that, but..."

"Haven't you seen how easy everyone is picking it all up?"

"Yeah," Honey said, "but..."

"Don't you want to be at least one step ahead of everyone else?"

"Well sure, but..."

"So do I," Balletina said. "I can't stand all those late comers learning everything we can do."

"We again?"

"You know what I mean. You've always been special. Because you were the first. I want to be special too."

Honey understood. "So? The ice cream? You want to spoil the ice cream? Should we go get a cone first?"

"Why wait? Let's do it from here."

"From here?" Honey asked.

"Sure. Why not?"

Honey climbed out of the car and started to focus her energy on the ice cream parlor.

"Wait!" Balletina yelled as she jumped out of the car and pointed to the left of the ice cream parlor. "Look over there!"

An armored car pulled up in front of the bank branch.

"Knock it over!"

Honey laughed and asked, "You want me to knock over a bank?"

"No!" Balletina squealed. "The truck! Knock over the truck!"

"You do it!" Honey said. "You wanted to learn something new."

Balletina stared blankly at Honey, then turned towards the truck. Two guards pulled a bag from the back of the truck and entered the bank. Balletina focused on the truck and swung her arms around. "Nothing's happening. How'd you do it before?"

"As I recall, I was pissed off. Imagine it just cut you off on the road. Then imagine that it's just a toy car that you can reach out and pick up."

Balletina scowled at the truck and reached out to grab hold of it, but it just sat there. She imagined it was laughing at her, but that was Honey. She closed one eye and reached out again, envisioning the truck between her thumb and finger. Honey only laughed louder and Balletina growled back at her, "Stop laughing!"

"I can't help it," Honey said. "You should see yourself."

Balletina tried again, but failed and yelled while shaking her fist at the truck. The truck squashed down and popped off one of the front hubcaps. Balletina froze and asked, "Did I do that?"

Honey stopped laughing and said, "I think so."

She punched her fist at the truck again and the rear door popped open, sending a bag of cash out onto the street. Balletina pointed her finger like a gun and blew the imaginary smoke from her fingertip.

"Now, can we have some ice cream?" Honey asked. "Or did you want to scoop up that bag of money?"

Balletina batted her hands around and the flat canvas bag of cash flopped and slid until it settled under a nearby pickup truck, then another swipe of her arm slammed the armored door shut. The guards came out of the bank carrying three new bags of cash. One of the guards opened the back of the truck while the other tossed the new bags into the back.

Balletina waited for them to drive off, then drove up in front of the pickup. "It would be a sin to leave it there."

"I thought you was rich."

"My daddy's rich, but there ain't nothing like being self-sufficient."

Balletina tossed the bag in the trunk and Honey asked again, "Now can I have my ice cream?"

"Yes," Balletina said with a curtsey, "Her royal majesty can now have her ice cream." Balletina pulled a couple of bills from the bag and added, "I'm buying."

For the first time, it didn't bother Honey to let Balletina pay.

Saunders had barely breached a toe into Flinch's office when Flinch, who had been looking down at a report on his desk, asked, "Well? Did you find the girl?"

Saunders sighed and slowly shook his head. "No, sir. Not yet."

Flinch growled as he chewed on his cigar. "Damned shame, but it's time to stop wasting your time on a wild goose chase."

"I wouldn't call it a complete waste," Saunders said. "I've learned a few things about her. Her name is Destiny Boutin. She's from Louisiana and she grew up in the swamps with her grandmother."

Flinch turned to look out the window while he waited for Saunders to say something useful.

"Don't you get it?" Saunders asked. "If she grew up in the swamps and wasn't first generation here, I think we can rule out an invasion from Mars."

Flinch grunted and replied, "Nobody ever said anything about Mars, per se. Besides, wherever they are from originally, they could still be sleeper cells waiting until the time was right." He watched a dozen men march by outside. That's what soldiers were supposed to look like; marching together with stern expressions frozen on their faces. He longed for the simpler days when men fought other men and needed weapons to do it. "None of that was much use to us. What about the other girl? Did you learn anything about her?"

"I'll get to that. Ask me why our girl left the bayou."

Flinch turned and raised an eyebrow. "Games? Do you really think this is a good time to play games?"

"Ask me."

Flinch continued to look out the window as he removed the cigar from his mouth and said, "Okay. I'll bite. Why did the little blond girl leave the bayou?"

"Because their home was burned down to the ground."

Flinch's jaw fell slack as he turned back around to face Saunders. "She burned down her own home?" Flinch chuckled and added, "I thought you said she was the good one."

"I still think she is," Saunders said, "and she didn't just burn the place down. She was probably defending it."

"Defending it?"

"Yes. From soldiers. Mercenaries most likely. They assaulted the home, and I think they ended up paying for their poor judgement."

"Poor luck, most likely." Flinch chewed his cigar some more and continued, "They just didn't know what they were getting into."

"I'm not so sure," Saunders said. "I found some surveillance equipment. It wasn't your garden variety listening device either. I think these guys knew exactly what they were getting into, and I'm guessing that they had some pretty sophisticated gear to monitor the girl's power."

"Really?"

"I'm just waiting for our labs to examine the equipment I brought back to know for sure, but that's what I think."

Flinch sat down and unfocussed his eyes as he gazed up past Saunders. "Now, that is interesting. You should have led with that instead of playing games about her burning down her home. Let me know what they learn. If you're right about that stuff, and if we can learn to use it..."

"My thoughts exactly."

Saunders turned to leave, but Flinch said, "Wait a sec. What about the other girl?"

"They're family..."

"That makes sense," Flinch interrupted, "but where do they come from?"

"Not so fast. They're only related by marriage. Honey's grand-mother married into the family and it didn't make the family too happy."

"So the two girls had bad blood from the start, but where did they come from? Originally, I mean."

Saunders simply shrugged. He couldn't give him a straight answer to that question and he wasn't going to suggest that one of them fell from heaven and the other rose from the other place.

Blake stood numbly in the cool breeze as he watched the three college students drive off. They circled the round-about twice, with the girl waving at him, but the first driver still stared blankly off into space from the passenger seat as they left. When they were gone, Blake looked at the area around him and felt like he had been dumped on the border between two different farms. There were no homes directly around him, but he saw what looked like a neighborhood further down the street, but that was going away from the highway and he was nowhere near Oxford. He was going to have to walk, and he doubted that he could walk on the highway, but the highway was the only way he knew to get him back to Oxford. He circled around the round-about hoping that he might at least find a service road that ran parallel, so he could continue on his way.

He left the round-about behind him and just as the students' taillights disappeared from his view, another pair of headlights passed them, heading in his directions. A chill ran down his spine as he recalled the two Scottish wraiths. He had a long walk yet and quickened his gait. There was no other traffic on the road, and the whole area was blanketed in a deathly silence, except for the sound of the solitary car's wheels as it passed him on the road and circled the round-about. It was a lonely road, until he heard car wheels crunching debris in the street behind him, but no car drove past him. He held his arms close to his chest to keep warm and stepped a little livelier. The car kept pace with him. The sun had disappeared behind the buildings on the west side of the street, but the car had yet to turn on its headlamps. Blake had nothing to fear. He could take care of himself, but he had a bad feeling about this and his heart quickened, anyway.

He stopped at the next intersection and looked each direction, wondering how far they had taken him after leaving the highway, and which would be the way to Oxford. The car pulled in front of him and rolled down the window. "Are you lost?"

"You could say that."

"American, eh? Where you heading?"

Blake didn't feel like explaining it again, but saw no use in avoiding the truth. "Oxford."

"You?"

"I know," Blake said. "I don't look like a student and I don't look like a teacher. I heard it all before."

"Why would a young lad like yourself, who admittedly does not look like a student, claim to be heading to Oxford?"

"Because it's the truth, but I'm having a bit of a problem getting there."

"And you're walking? You have a long way to go. Must be at least 75 kilometers."

"I had a ride," Blake explained, "but the guys got jealous because their girl was paying too much attention to me. They just dumped me on the curb a little way back from here."

"How about you let me give you a ride?"

A shiver ran down Blake's spine, and he shook his head and said, "Thanks, but I don't think..."

The man climbed out of the car and opened the back door. "I insist. I'm Inspector Brighton of Scotland Yard."

"Really?" Blake asked. "This doesn't look like a very high crime neighborhood. What's Scotland Yard doing out here?"

"I should hope there's not much crime here. My home is just down the street. Now, won't you get in?"

Blake sighed and climbed into the vehicle.

"Do you have business at Oxford?"

"I'm looking for a book."

"Ahh," the inspector said while nodding his head. "They have a pretty good library."

"But not as big as the one in Dublin, I hear."

"You mean Trinity? Aye. They have a really big library. A big musty dust trap, if you ask me."

Blake laughed. "Are you sure you know the way to Oxford?"

"I can assure you that I know the way."

"It seems to me that we have turned in a different direction."

"You have a good eye," the inspector said. "I'll grant you that. I have to drop something off at headquarters."

The hackles on the back of Blake's neck prickled. "By something, you mean me."

The inspector just grinned and kept driving.

Blake suggested to the inspector's mind, "You really don't need the extra paperwork. Wouldn't it be easier just to drop the kid off at the library?"

The inspector ignored Blake's suggestion and continued driving.

This was getting irritating. Was it something about England that was interrupting his ability to persuade people? No. The security guard in New York also resisted his suggestions. If he was losing his ability, what about his other powers, like fire and opening locks? His spine shivered as he refocused on his current situation. "How long will this take?"

"Not too long, but I'm afraid the library will be closed long before you can get there."

Blake grimaced, but it was getting dark, and at least he wouldn't have to find a place to stay.

Ashlin watched in awe, mesmerized by the hand movements employed by the students to produce fire. They all started with an open palm and proceeded to undulate their hands and fingers with barely perceptible little movements that produced a variety of different looking fires, but how they moved their hands after that produced a remarkable number of effects on the flames. She had never known the witch clan to have ever used any similar gestures, but then, the witch skills were all mental rather than physical. Moving the hand to manipulate a ball of fire in the palm made sense.

She wanted a closer look and left the bleachers to walk out onto the mat so she could get up real close.

Misty saw the look in her eye and flashed a big smile. "Hi. I'm Misty. You're one of the new girls, right?"

Ashlin slowly nodded her head, unable to speak, with her eyes locked onto the fireball that Misty rolled across her fingers.

"Do you want to try?" Misty was hoping to earn a spot as an instructor like Balletina had done.

Ashlin held her palm up and mimicked some of the subtle motions she had seen, but nothing happened. Of course, nothing happened, she admonished herself. Fire is a sorcerer skill.

"You got the motions right," Misty said, "but there are still two things that you have to master. Number one, you must believe with absolute certainty that you can do this. You have to know deep inside of you that you were born to do this."

Ashlin nodded her head enthusiastically, but inside, she knew that it would be impossible because she most definitely was not born to do this.

"Number two," Misty continued, "you have to imagine the fire. Imagine it is already inside your hand, and it itches, but instead of scratching it, you want to push it out of your palm. Think of it like squeezing water out of a sponge."

Ashlin tried, hoping vainly that she could be like Destiny, but it was futile.

"That's okay. None of us got it on our very first try. Watch Paige here and work with her. She's struggling with it too. Maybe you can work on it together."

Ashlin nodded and the girl that Misty had been working with waved meekly and said, "Hi, I'm Paige."

Ashlin smiled back and said, "I'm Ashlin." Ashlin's eyes were glued to Paige's hands, but her mind was wandering. Misty and Paige weren't the monsters she had come to expect. Even without the magic, Honey was a horrible person, but these girls seemed really nice. If it weren't for them wanting to push fire out of their palms and their willingness to follow Honey, they could have been two of her friends.

Destiny liked having visitors, especially when they weren't trying to convince her to come back with them. She appreciated them even more after not having any visitors for a while. She tried breaking the monotony by wandering around her little world, but she was alone and there was nothing new left for her to discover. Every day became like the day before it. She knew her little town and each of the homes in it by heart. She wished there were cats and dogs wandering the streets, or at least wild birds in the sky. Any kind of movement to catch her eye once in a while would be welcome, or maybe a little sound to break the silence.

She went to her favorite place by the brook. The sound of the water soothed her like nothing else in this place, mostly because there was nothing else, but even it had become boring. It never changed. It sounded the same and looked the same, and even though she hadn't really been here very long, she knew that it wouldn't change with the seasons, if there even were any seasons.

She lay back on a soft mound of grass along the bank of the stream and let her feet dangle in the water while she looked up into the cloudless sky. It was too perfect. Everything here was too perfect. When she first had arrived here, she had thought that this place might be heaven, but the boring routine of it made her wonder if it would turn into hell for her.

She closed her eyes and longed for her nana. "Nana? Can you hear me? Did you know that Ashlin came for a visit? She's a funny girl. She was even older looking than you! I hope you'll watch over her for me. Can you hear me?"

Only the gurgling of the water broke the silence, and it was just about the only sound that there was in this world, although if she listened to it long enough, it seemed to repeat like an endless loop.

"Ashlin? Can you hear me?" She heard her words in her mind as if she were actually speaking them. Even the voice in her mind conveyed a desperate, lonely soul. "Ashlin? Blake? Can't anyone hear me?"

She slipped into the void between worlds and drifted. The voices of her ancestors were quiet, but a cacophony of noise erupted from behind her. "No!" she shouted as she turned to face the racket. "I don't want another memory! Surely someone must be thinking about me!"

The void swirled before her and morphed into a parking lot.

"Now, can we have some ice cream?"

Destiny tensed up in her core. She knew that voice. It was a voice that she hated more than any other.

A dark-haired girl pulled some money from a bag in the trunk of a car and said, "I'm buying."

Destiny formed her hands to throw a fireball at her cousin, but she couldn't bring forth the flames. She hadn't traveled here; it was just a memory, and not something that she could change.

Honey and Balletina entered the ice cream shop and cut to the front of the line. Others in line objected, but when one brave boy with a letterman jacket walked up to face them, Balletina waved her hands and shoved some tables and chairs between them. The boy glared at her, but backed off.

"I don't need to see this," Destiny said. "I already know she's an evil bitch, and I don't want to know about how many other bitches have come along to follow her."

She closed her eyes to conjure up the void again, but was interrupted by the sound of sirens. The street around her quickly filled with police vehicles. Officers poured out of their vehicles and trained their weapons on the ice cream shop just as Balletina and Honey were about to leave with their favorite cones.

"Seriously?" Honey yelled. "Don't you guys ever talk to each other? Haven't you ever heard of me before?"

The cops glanced at each other and shrugged.

"Here," Honey said. "Hold this." She handed Balletina her cone and rapid fire streams of flames into the three nearest cars. The police scattered away from the burning vehicles, but kept their guns pointed at the pair of girls.

"Don't you want to run?" Honey asked. "It's probably the safest thing for you to do."

Honey had seen all this before. First, one cop discharged his weapon, then another. The heat surrounding the two girls rose tremendously. Honey raised a fire shield around them and the bullets stuck in the fire, then fell to the ground in soft blobs.

"You done?" Honey asked. "I guess it's my turn again."

"Let me," Balletina said. She dropped the cones and reached out, grabbing one of the burning cars, then lifted it off the ground and dropped it onto another car, which burst into flames and exploded. More bullets flew into their fire shield.

"You want more?" Balletina yelled. She swung her arm in an arc and sprayed fire out in a wide circle that struck the men in their body armor. The burning men shrieked. She balled up her hand in a fist and the flames grew around the men until the screaming stopped and only pillars of ash were left.

Destiny closed her eyes and turned her back. She didn't need to see that either.

Blake's skin prickled as he sat alone in the cold interrogation room. He breathed into his hands and rubbed them together to warm them up, but his feet and hands felt like ice. A simple fire ball could have warmed up the whole room, but he was certain that someone was watching him, either through the large half-silvered mirror on one wall or from the camera in the corner of the room.

The solitary door opened, and a youngish woman entered the room. She paused a moment in the doorway to straighten out her pencil skirt and give him a good looking over. At least she wasn't wearing a uniform. She was pretty enough, but she didn't act like she thought she was, or maybe she thought she couldn't command men if she was too pretty. "So," she said before even sitting down, "you're visiting our fair city from America. Is that right?"

"Yeah," Blake said. "I just flew in, and boy, are my arms tired."

His interrogator's face was colder than the room. "Perhaps you don't realize how serious this is."

"How serious what is?" Blake asked. "Am I being charged with anything? What is it? Suspicion of suspicion? Is walking a crime? Is being dumped in a random neighborhood by some college pranksters a crime in England? Or is this just how you like to treat all Americans?"

"When did you enter the U.K.?"

"You don't already know? You emptied my pockets. I'm sure you've seen my ticket stub. You've probably already spoken with customs. They questioned me too, you know. I mean, of course you know."

"And why do you suppose they questioned you?"

"They question everybody that enters the country. It's their job."

"But you?" she asked. "What do you suppose made you so interesting to them?"

"To be honest," Blake said, "I think it's some kind of conspiracy to keep me from what I came here for."

She jotted some notes onto her notepad. "And why did you come here?"

"I'm on a quest."

"What?" she asked. "Are you another nut bird looking for the holy grail?"

"Yeah," Blake said, seeing the parallel for the first time. "Something very much like that."

"Well, I guess we had you all wrong then," the inspector said with a laugh. "We thought you was suspicious, but you're really just a bit daff."

"You don't believe in the grail?"

"The cup of Christ?" she asked. "I'm sure there was one like a thousand years ago."

"More like two thousand," Blake corrected her.

"Yeah, whatever, but I sure don't go for all this nonsense about Arthur and the round table."

"What about Merlin?" Blake asked.

She burst out laughing. "You mean the magician?"

Blake smiled and said, "It does sound pretty ridiculous, doesn't it?"

"Totally."

"And yet," Blake postulated, "people believed in magic as much as they believed in religion at one time."

"Sure they did, but they also believed the world was flat."

"True," Blake said. "But what if the legends were based on real people?"

"You mean to say that you believe there really was a great sorcerer that they called Merlin?"

"Perhaps there was a man named Merlin and he could do things that people didn't understand."

"Like what?"

"Maybe he was a brilliant engineer and invented match sticks. That would probably look like magic to them."

"I suppose," she said. "Is that what you think?"

"I think there was a man," Blake explained, "who was very smart and did some very clever things. I don't know if he was really called Merlin, but I think that they considered him to be a wizard."

"Did you research all this?"

"Yes," Blake said.

"So you're just a college boy, after all? You seem okay to me. I don't know why those wankers thought we should 'ave a look at you."

"That's me," Blake said. "I was just trying to get to the Oxford library to do some more research."

She turned to the mirror behind her and said, "Did you 'ear that? He's just doing 'is 'omework. Let 'im go."

"Now?" Blake said. "In the middle of the night? The library is closed already."

"Yeah? So?"

"Where am I supposed to stay? It's getting cold out there."

"That's not our problem," she replied. "You're the one that come here with no luggage and no transportation."

"Did I mention that I'm actually descended from Merlin? I think there's a book at Oxford that will teach me how to inherit his powers."

The inspector laughed. "Now you want me to believe that you are a nut bird? You want that I should call you a cab to take you to the nearest looney bin?"

"No," Blake said. "That won't be necessary. I have a busy day scheduled. After I inherit my powers, I'm supposed to break into the Tower of London to reclaim my staff."

The door burst open and a stocky man with long sideburns stepped in. "I've heard enough. We'll be locking him up for the night until we can see a magistrate in the morning."

Blake just smiled up at the girl. He held his wrists up to her. At least he'll have a place to sleep through the night. He'll worry about getting out in the morning.

Chapter 21

"That was great," Honey said as she entered the auditorium with Balletina, "and I think you were absolutely right."

"That was fun," Balletina agreed, with a malicious grin spread across her face, "but what was I right about?"

"We need more divestiture."

Balletina looked confused.

"You know," Honey explained. "Like you said before. We need to learn more different spells. If some of them ain't good at fire, then they need to learn what they are good at."

"Oh," Balletina swallowed a snicker as she replied, "you mean diversity."

"Whatever," Honey said. "Just look how many of them are using lightning like my mama. We need to teach them that if fire ain't their thing, then it's important to discover what is."

Balletina pointed over to the bleachers and said, "Well, it looks like we have a whole new batch of students to try that on."

***

Michelle had long ago given up any notion of keeping her head upright, or her eyes open. She rested her head on Destiny's mattress while Tempest stood on the other side of the bed, holding Destiny's hand. The soothing and monotonous tempo of the heart monitors echoed through the room as Michelle slept until a sound caught her attention and woke her. She opened her eyes and looked around the room expectantly.

"Did you hear that?" Michelle asked Tempest.

"Hear what?" Tempest asked.

Michelle got up and walked around to the other side of the bed, next to Tempest, and placed her hand over both Tempest's and Destiny's. "You didn't hear nothing? I thought I heard her calling for us."

"Oh that," Tempest said. "I hear that all the time. I can't seem to stop imagining that she's waiting for us to come find her."

"If only dat were so," Michelle said with a heavy sigh, "but I don't think she be ready to be saved yet."

"If you think she was calling for you, then I'm not the right one to ask." Tempest nodded her head towards Destiny. "Go on. Ask her yourself."

Michelle returned to her original chair opposite of Tempest and wrapped her fingers around Destiny's hand. She felt destiny's pulse in her fingers as she stared into the blinking lights of the heart monitor. The screen traced a line that flickered like a candle and Michelle quietly slipped into the void. "Destiny? Where you be?"

"I ain't gone nowhere," Destiny replied. "Cain't you git back here without me guiding you every time?"

Michelle followed her voice. "I just needs to hear your voice to find you."

"Hurry. I seen something about cousin Honey that you should know."

Michelle sneered at the sound of her name.

"I know Nana. I hates her too."

"She be da one dat put you in here. If I had your gifts, it would be a might easier for me ta do something about dat girl."

"You can say it, Nana. She's a bitch."

"Dat she is."

"But if you had my powers, you might just end up in here with me. Lord knows I can use the company, but I don't want to wish that on you or nobody."

Michelle landed softly in the field outside Destiny's home and followed the path to the front door. "So. What's your cousin been doin now?"

"She robbed a bank, but that's not the worst part. She been burning the police up again." Destiny let Michelle into the house. "Want some tea?"

Michelle had worked up a bit of a sweat walking the road from the field and fanned her face with her hands. "Thank you. Some ice cold tea would surely be nice."

Destiny pulled a pitcher of iced tea from the cooler and poured two glasses. The ice swirled around in the glass and twinkled in the light from the window. The room faded away and was replaced with an image of Honey holding a glowing trinket.

"That's it!" Destiny blurted out.

"What?" Michelle exclaimed. "You nearly scared the life out of me."

"Sorry Nana, but I saw what you just saw, and that's the orb! I seen it in one of my first memories."

"You mean that be the orb that your boyfriend be lookin' for? She already has it?"

Destiny sighed at the mention of Blake, but couldn't let his memory distract her. The image of Honey blurred at the edges like an old-fashioned photo that was vignetted at the corners. "I can't tell," Destiny replied. "It might be now or it might be in the future."

"We cain't let her get it," Michelle said. "If dat bitch gets da orb, we'll never save you, and I might have ta resort to..."

Destiny smiled because her grandmother finally called Honey a bitch out loud, but she couldn't let her finish that thought. "Don't say it, Nana. You don't want to resort to that spell, but you still want to find the orb so you can save my mama, although I suspect that Ashlin is takin' pretty good care of her."

"True dat, but I means it when I says we still intends to save you."

"Fine," Destiny said. "You believe that if you want. Just don't let Honey get the orb. Do what you can to help Blake."

"Sure thing, Cher, but dat boy be gone wit' da wind. We ain't seen hide nor hair from him in quite a spell."

"Find him. I'd know if he were in trouble, at least, I think I would."

Michelle smiled warmly. "I'm sure you would."

Honey walked directly up to a couple girls that were striking their targets with lightning bolts and said, "I think it's really good that y'all have embraced electricity like that. You don't need to be ashamed that you cain't do fire. Not everone kin do fire like me. Even my mama does the ligihtnin' like that."

Balletina cringed a bit as she heard Honey's somewhat less than inspiring words.

"I think that as we grow, we're gonna learn that there are new ways to embrace our powers, even if it ain't fire. Our power is passed on to us from our forefathers, scratch that, I think that from now on, we'll call them our fore mothers. Not that we have four mothers, because that would be impossible, but because we can be pretty sure who our mamas are. We is only guessin' about who our daddies might be. Fire and lightning are good beginnings, but I think we're going to expand to find new powers that were lost a long time ago. It's called divinity, no that's not it. What's the word I'm lookin' for?"

Balletina cleared her throat and said, "Diversity."

"Yeah," Honey said, "what she said. I want all of you to feel for that special inner power that might be unique to just you. Maybe your grandmamma had the power to control animals or something..."

Balletina leaned over and whispered, "That's the witches."

"Okay," Honey said, "No controlling animals, but I want each one of you to recognize if you ever does something special and unique. We'll just work with that and find ways to make it more useful."

Ashlin shrunk down when she heard Honey enter the room. She had always disliked Honey. All the women on the farm had, and even though Ashlin was too young to have had a boyfriend for Honey to steal, she saw what Honey did and how it affected the other women. Honey was an enemy to all womankind, and it was only a matter of time before Ashlin would have been old enough to join their ranks.

She may have disliked Honey from the start, but her feelings had graduated to full-on hatred when Honey had put Destiny in the hospital. Destiny had quickly become Ashlin's new older sister, and now Destiny was lost in a dream world, believing that she was actually dead, and it was all Honey's fault. If Ashlin could generate a flame now, it wasn't going to be aimed at a target dummy.

She tried again to squeeze a flame from her hand, but it wasn't easy. She wasn't like Destiny who wasn't restricted to only witch powers. Destiny was like a tape recorder that could repeat any magic that was used against her. Ashlin wished she could be more like Destiny as she tried pushing fire out of her palms. She was so focused on her own hands that she hadn't even noticed the great light that Paige had produced right next to her.

Several other students, however, had noticed and had gathered around them. Paige's hands were surrounded by a brilliant white aura.

"What is it?" Misty asked.

Paige slowly shook her head and meekly replied, "I don't know. I just did like she said and tried to feel what was naturally coming out of me, and this is what came to me."

The commotion could not be ignored, and by the time Honey had paid any attention, too many students were gathered around them for her to see what was going on. All she could see was a bright light projecting out of the center of the crowd, but it couldn't be fire, because there was no smoke with it. The students parted for her as she came to see what all the excitement was.

Blake had barely managed to slip into a light sleep when they escorted three unsavory characters into the cell with him. He cracked open an eye and saw three stocky men with well-worn sports jerseys on. They sang loudly and repeatedly shouted something unintelligible about Manchester. Blake rolled over to face the wall, but he doubted that he would be able to sleep through their ruckus.

The clang of the door slamming shut marked the official end of Blake's sleep.

"Oi," one of them said while nudging Blake in the shoulder. "Who d'you like?"

Blake yawned and was immediately overcome with the mixed scents of booze and piss that wafted from their clothing.

"I seen that," the drunkard said, while leaning over and tickling Blake's earlobe. "You can't fool me. You're awake enough."

Blake tried pushing the man away, but only succeeded in twisting him around.

"You like Manchester?" the drunk asked. "We just come from the game. We're all for Manchester."

"No kidding," Blake said sarcastically. "I never would have guessed."

"So," the drunk slurred, "you're American? I seen your American football, but it's nothing like real foo'ball." He turned to his fellow drunks and shouted, "Wouldn't you say so, lads?"

One of his compatriots was too close to passing out to respond, and the other barely perked up enough just to notice if someone might have spoken to him.

"What brings you here?" the man asked with a loud, but mysteriously clear and sober sounding voice.

"I don't think your cops liked the fact that I have no luggage."

"Not here," the drunk laughed, "I meant why did you come to London?"

"Why do you care?" Blake asked. "It has nothing to do with either football or getting shit faced drunk."

"No foo'ball? No booze? What else is there?" He held a serious face for a moment, then burst out laughing, "Just curious, mate."

"I'm here looking for something."

"I thought you yanks had everything you could ever need. What could we possibly have that you need to find here?"

"Something very special," Blake said, "and old."

"Tha' explains it," the man slurred. "We have plenty of old stuff. Did you really come here with no baggage?" the man asked. "You come all the way here without even a change of underwear? No wonder they locked you up."

"Is that why they locked you up, too?" Blake asked. "Because you need to change your underwear?"

"What was that?" the man sounded incensed.

Blake waved his hand in front of his nose. "You smell like you had an accident."

"Did you hear that?" the man asked his friends. "The boy here says we smell like piss."

The larger of the other two laughed and said, "We do."

"Sure," the first man said, "but that don't mean that I need to hear some little snot tell me I smell like piss!"

"To be honest," Blake said, "you smell a bit like vomit too, but mostly piss and booze."

"You must have some kind of a death wish," the first man said.

"Maybe I'm just not afraid of you." Blake was growing tired of the whole incident and didn't like the drunkard infringing on his space. "Maybe I can totally take care of myself. Maybe you should back off. In fact, why don't you back off all the way over there so I don't have to smell you anymore? You really reek."

That caught the attention of the other two, who now came to stand in front of Blake. "Perhaps you hadn't noticed that there are three of us."

"I can count," Blake said. "I just don't think any of you are worth counting."

"That's it," the larger man said. "I'm going to pound you now."

Blake pushed his palm forward and hit the large man with an invisible force that knocked him back to the opposite wall.

The third man, who had been quiet up until now, said, "So, it's like that, is it?" His face morphed into the gaunt features of a corpse. Maggots fell from the raw flesh on his face as he sneered and grabbed Blake by the wrist.

Blake wagged a finger on his free hand and said, "I wouldn't do that if I were you."

"Oh, no?" the corpse asked as his flesh started to droop off of his face.

"No," Blake said. The bony, rotting fingers that wrapped around Blake's wrist grew hot and started to smoke.

The first man laughed and said, "You must think you're pretty special." He held up his palm and showed Blake a flickering flame.

Blake increased the heat on his wrist, and the corpse's hand burst into flames.

"You never should have come here," the first man said. "You don't belong here and you'll never find what you're looking for."

"If you say so," Blake said, "but you're sure not going to stop me." Blake produced another invisible force and slammed the first man and the corpse into their friend, then he shot lightning from his hands into the first man. The electric bolts bounced from the first man to the corpse and then into the third man.

The big man stepped forward and yelled, "Go Home!" He held his hands to his chest and pushed them towards Blake, sending a stream of sharp blades flying into Blake. The corpse sucked in a lung full of air, then blew a green, noxious cloud onto Blake's bleeding body.

"Not so cocky now," the first man said, "are ya?" He then held his hands straight out from his sides at arm's length. He wiggled his fingers and laughed to his friends, then brought his hands forward like he was crashing two cymbals together. Blake's eyes rolled back in his head when he felt the impact on both of his ears and the world faded away.

Honey reached the center of the crowd and said, "Well, well. Look who we have here."

Misty beamed with excitement. "This is Paige. We're not sure what it is yet, but it's definitely something new."

Honey ignored both Misty and Paige and walked straight up to Ashlin. "Hello cousin. What in the hell are you doing here?"

Ashlin panicked. Trying to create fire was a futile exercise, and now she had been caught by the one person she hated the most. She remembered how it felt when Logan touched her astral projection and wasn't too keen on feeling anything new that Honey might throw at her, but she wasn't ready to leave without saying something. She bucked up her courage, stuck her chin out, and said, "Destiny asked me to come check up on you."

"Destiny?" Honey laughed. "You're lying. She's dead."

"Nope," Ashlin replied with a quick shake of her head. "Not dead."

Honey laughed again. "I still don't buy it. The only part of your story that makes any sense is that she would send you because she's too afraid to face me in person."

Ashlin felt her temper growing inside of her, but she took a deep breath to remain calm. "How do you think I got here? Who do you think taught me this?"

"Taught you what?"

Now it was Ashlin's turn to laugh. "Oh, you can't tell? You didn't really think that I would come here in person, did you?"

Honey looked around. Everyone had been glancing back and forth between the two of them. "Are you tryin' to say this is some witchy trick? You cain't just be in my mind, 'cause everyone else here can see you too." She turned to the crowd and asked, "Ain't that right? Y'all kin see her too, right?"

The spectators didn't quite understand the question, or why it would even be a question, but they nodded their heads and a few mumbled something in the affirmative.

"Of course they can see me," Ashlin said smugly. "Destiny taught me how to astral project myself and make it look real. They can even touch me, too."

"Oh yeah? Well, if they can touch you, then I figure I can touch you too, and if I can touch you, then I can fry your scrawny little ass." Honey whipped out a fireball and slammed it into Ashlin. Ashlin didn't even have time to regret what she had said as she whipped up her hands to cover her face. The fireball hit against her hands and wrapped around her head, then spread down her body until she was thoroughly engulfed in flames. The students backed away, leaving only Honey and a burning Ashlin in the center of a large circle. They watched in amazement as Ashlin was engulfed in flames, but she didn't turn into ashes and crumple over like Angie had.

Ashlin felt the flames surround her, but it was like a warm breeze blowing around her rather than a raging fire ravaging her skin. Her silhouette could be seen inside of the massive column of fire, guarding her face with her hands until the fire burned itself out. When the flames died away and Ashlin dropped her hands from her face, her skin glowed blue, but she was unharmed.

Michelle wished Destiny would worry a little more about herself and less about everyone else, but then she might not have received the gift of healing if it hadn't been for her empathy. On top of that, they were all putting the fate of the world onto Destiny's shoulders, and if she had really seen Honey with the orb, then they were all in trouble.

She retreated to the chair in the corner of the room and plopped down into it. It wasn't like the cushioned chairs in the lobby, and she squirmed this way and that, trying to find the most comfortable position. She wasn't like these young ones. They seemed to have learned how to pop in and out of the void at will, but she grew up using candles and a comfortable, relaxed position to reach out into the memories. Even if she had learned to substitute other lights for the candle, it was getting harder and harder to find a comfortable spot. She couldn't see the heart monitor clearly from this distance, and she wanted desperately to reach out into the void to find Blake. Candles were what she knew best, but there was no way they were going to let her light a candle in here. She could have used the voice to force the doctors and nurses to allow a candle, or even to be blind to it, but she didn't even have one with her, so it was a pointless thought.

Zeline's eyes followed Michelle from across the room. She still held the bell tower firmly in her crossed arms, out of Michelle's reach. A thin shaft of light streamed through the blinds and glittered against the silver rim of the bell.

Michelle wished that she could have known what had possessed her to make such a talisman. She never had before, and the shape had no previous significance to her, but there was something about it that had consumed her until Ashlin had stripped it away from her. The bell rocked gently with Zeline's breathing. Its polished surface twinkled and flickered in the light until Michelle's eyelids fell shut and she was in the void. "Blake? Is you there?"

No response came to her, but she felt a tug in her belly, pulling her to a memory.

"No," she said to the void, "I don't have time for this. I need to speak with Blake."

A woman's voice said, "You'll sure as hell make time for me."

"Mama? Is that you? How kin you be here if you is…"

"Are you sure you want to finish that thought?"

Michelle was sucked into a small room with blue walls and no furniture.

"Things are changing," her mother said. "You've all seen the evil that awaits if you don't do something."

"Yes mama. We needs to find da orb, but that's da thing. Destiny says that dey might already have it."

Michelle's eyes darted around the room. She couldn't see her mother and wanted to locate her voice, but the walls were alive. Dark blue swirls spun and undulated against a light blue background. Michelle was alone in the room, but she wasn't afraid. Her mother wouldn't have brought her anyplace dangerous, but the eerie movement of the colors on the walls was unnerving. "Where is dis place?"

"It's no place Cher. It just be somewhere dat we kin talk."

"Okay. If you say so, but I still needs to find da boy."

"You needs to find yourself. You ain't been you lately, or maybe you is da old you from when you was young, dat only I remembers so much."

"I don't understand mama."

Michelle felt her mother's hands slip onto her shoulders from behind as she whispered into her ear, "I know you don't understand. The young ones are going to fight this fight and you gots to be a rock of strength for them. They need to look up to you. You cain't be one of them. Not now."

Michelle turned around and gasped, "Mama, your hair!"

Her mother smiled warmly. The shocking red hair of her youth that had long ago turned white was bright blue. "I know, but it's nothing for you to worry about. You go back there and be the sage old woman that they needs so they kin get through what's coming."

"I cain't just sit by when I knows a way to end this!"

"Don't you dare speak to me about dat damned spell. You was never supposed to know that!"

"How can you say that?" Michelle cried. "The ancestors give me that spell for a reason."

"The ancestors didn't give you nothin'! You practically stole it from daer rememberin's. You don't want to bring that kind of curse down upon our family."

"I don't want to," Michelle sobbed, "but I might have to. Anything would be better than the future dat we seen."

"It be a bleak future. I'll grant you that. And almost anything would be better, but not that. You don't even know what kind of future you seen. You go now and do as I told you. Be there for them and help them through what's coming."

"But what is coming?"

Her mother and the room faded away with only the echoing words of her mother: "You'll see. Trust in your family."

Ashlin was as surprised as anyone that she so easily withstood Honey's attack. She smiled slyly as she turned her hands over to admire the blue glow of her skin. At least they weren't old hands with liver spots.

"Oh my God," Honey exclaimed. "She's a God damned Smurf!"

"Tell me," Ashlin said. "Did you really think that you could just walk all over everybody to rule the world? Did you actually believe that after thousands of years of struggles between our clans, that an uneducated country bumpkin like you would be the one to dominate where so many others have failed?"

All heads in the class turned to Honey. They expected an answer from her, but all she could do was scream.

"What was that?" Ashlin taunted her. "I didn't quite get it."

Honey pumped her fists up and down as she growled and blasted Ashlin with a continuous stream of fire, but Ashlin just struck a series of model poses from within the flames, and just like before, the flames burned away leaving a glowing blue Ashlin in their place.

"Again?" Ashlin struck another pose and asked, "What do you think? Is blue a good color on me? I think it is."

Honey jumped up and down as her temper seethed through her pores and ignited her whole body into a human torch. "I'm going to destroy you!"

"I get it," Ashlin said calmly. "You can't burn me, so you are going to burn yourself instead. That's kind of pathetic, if you ask me."

"You don't get it," Honey said. "I'm going to destroy all of you."

"Check your archives," Ashlin replied. "You'll learn that it's not so easy. You do know about the archives, don't you? We know you have archives. Your people have been writing stuff down for thousands of years, probably ever since someone invented writing. We don't have to, you know, write stuff down, I mean. We can visit the past any time we want and see things for ourselves. More than just the past, we can see the future too. That's why your kind never wins. You do know that, don't you? Your kind has tried before. It never ends well for you."

"Oh, yeah?"

Ashlin laughed when Honey had nothing more to add. "Snappy comeback."

Honey spread her flaming arms wide to the sides and said, "Look around. I won't be coming alone."

"Seriously?" Ashlin asked. "Did you think that we would be alone? We can talk to each other across continents. We are NEVER alone!"

"I don't care how many of you there are. You can't hurt us! We got the power to destroy you. What do you have? Are you all gonna hold your breath and turn blue?" Honey smiled and laughed, believing that her comeback was particularly witty.

Ashlin struck another series of poses and said, "You really should get down to the archives. You might learn a thing or two. Maybe you can take one of these girls with you to explain the big words. You might learn that we have our ways and we are preparing for you."

"Well, maybe I'm not going to wait for you to get prepared. Maybe I'm going to bring my army to you right now!"

Ashlin sucked in her breath. They weren't ready.

"Aha!" Honey laughed. "Where's your sassy little remark now?"

"I just came to show you that we will be waiting for you. If you are in such a hurry to get yourself and all these nice young kids killed, then be my guest. Just be fair to them and let them know that you are marching them into a trap and they are all going to die. You might want to watch your back, though. It might be that after you teach them fire, they don't want to follow you to their deaths. Your people haven't exactly built a strong reputation of loyalty or trustworthiness."

Honey started to reply, but Ashlin shimmered away and was gone.

Tempest watched Ashlin from the other side of Destiny's bed. Ashlin's head lay quietly on the bed, but she wasn't sleeping. Tempest sensed the turmoil from within Ashlin and thought that she might be in the memories, but the anxiety she felt from the young girl grew until she had to walk around the bed and rouse her.

"Ashlin?" Tempest gently shook her shoulder. "Ashlin sweetie?"

Ashlin moaned before she rolled her head and saw Tempest. "What's wrong?"

Tempest looked directly into Ashlin's eyes and thought she saw a blue glow deep within them, but it was only there for an instant before it faded away.

"What's wrong?" Ashlin repeated.

"You tell me. Where did you go? What happened?"

Ashlin sat up and rubbed her eyes. She swallowed hard before admitting, "I think I did a bad thing."

"It was just a dream then. You were sleeping."

"I wasn't sleeping, and I wasn't dreaming. I astral projected to find Logan and saw where Honey was training more sorcerers. She's teaching a bunch of them to make fire, and they're all just kids. My age even!"

"Okay," Tempest said. "That sounds like a good thing, actually. We need to know what they are up to."

"I'm not done. I astral projected to one of their classes and joined in. They're not so bad, you know. The kids I mean. They're just like us, except for the fire thing. I fit right in! Nobody could even tell that I was a witch. I guess my astral projection doesn't cause the cramps like we usually get."

Tempest chuckled. "So, you saw these kids learning to make fire, and you joined right into their class? That's a bold move."

Ashlin nodded her head. "I thought that if Destiny and Blake can do it, then maybe I could, too."

"What? You thought you would try to make fire?"

"Mhm."

"And you thought you would try to do it while you were astral projecting into their class?"

Ashlin nodded her head.

Tempest chuckled again and said, "I think it's sweet that you would want to help enough to try that, but it's still not such a bad thing and it would have been pretty cool if it had worked."

"Honey saw me."

"She saw your astral projection? Where'd you learn to do that, anyway?"

Ashlin shrugged.

"Did she recognize you?"

"Oh yeah. She even attacked me and tried to burn me."

Tempest chuckled yet again. "She tried to burn your astral projection?"

Ashlin became acutely aware that Michelle was also in the room and was listening to them. "I was kind of solid at the time."

"Wait. You can astral project in solid form? Are you sure? How is that even possible? I don't think I've ever heard of that before."

"I have," Michelle said from the corner. "I seen it in the memories. It be a very rare gift and very advanced. Where'd you learn to do that?"

"I told Honey that Destiny taught me, but that was a lie and she didn't believe me, anyway. She was convinced that Destiny was dead."

"But," Michelle insisted, "where did you learn it?"

"Honestly," Ashlin said with a shrug, "I don't know. I learned the astral projection part in a memory, but the solid part just sort of happened. When I visited Mr. Logan in the airport, he mussed up my hair and that's when I knew."

"You could feel him?" Tempest asked. "How about when Honey burnt you? Did you feel it?"

"I kinda felt it, but I did something to block it."

"You could block da fire?" Michelle asked.

"What did you do?" Tempest asked.

Ashlin shrugged. "I don't know exactly. I just put my hands up to block my face and the fire surrounded me. It was still there. I could feel it, but it didn't burn me any. Then, after the fire burned out, my skin was all blue."

Michelle gasped, "Blue you say?"

Zeline had only heard the tail end of the conversation from the doorway. "Is that something we kin all learn so we kin protect ourselves?"

Michelle shrugged. "I never come across nothing like that before, not in the memories at least."

"It still sounds like a good thing to me," Tempest said with a reassuring smile. "We should search the memories. Maybe we can find someone that knows how it's done and then we can figure out how to protect ourselves."

Michelle sighed heavily. "Dat was Destiny's best gift. She could learn new stuff just by bein' there."

"We better hurry then," Ashlin said.

"Why, exactly?" Tempest asked.

"Yeah," Zeline said. "Why exactly does we have to hurry?"

"Honey is teaching a whole bunch of them how to make fire and stuff."

"You told us that," Tempest said.

"But she's preparing them to attack us!"

Michelle nodded. "She's right. We needs to be ready for dem."

Zeline raised an eyebrow and asked, "Why does I get the feeling dat there's more dat you ain't tellin' us?"

Ashlin lowered her head and softly admitted, "I may have told her that we were preparing an army too."

"Oh Lordy," Michelle said.

"And," Ashlin continued, "she may have said that she wasn't going to wait for us to get ready. She was going to come for us and destroy us right away, before we can make an army."

"That was pretty brave," Destiny said.

Ashlin snapped her head around to see Destiny, but she was still asleep. "Destiny?" she thought.

"Yeah it's me."

"You could hear me?"

"I heard. I'm so proud of you, but I think you're going to have to help protect everyone, since I can't be there."

"But you heard me! I'm standing right next to your hospital bed. Don't you see what that means? It's like we've been saying all along. You're not dead yet. You could hear me, and if you can hear me, then you can wake up! You just have to want to enough."

"You aren't listening to me," Destiny said. "You need to take my place protecting everyone. You need to take Nana's place leading the family."

"But I'm just a kid and I'm not even part of your family. We only adopted each other as sisters."

"You can drop the act. We all know who you really are. Just like I share the same soul as Nimisen, you share the soul of Nana's mother, and I'm so glad that I got a chance to meet you. I was just a baby when you passed."

"But…"

"No," Destiny said. "It's time to stop denying the truth."

"I could say the same thing to you," Ashlin said, "and if you believe what you're saying, then that would make me your great-grandmother and you have to listen to me."

"If I could leave this place, I would."

"Then you just keep trying," Ashlin said. "That's all I ask. Don't give up on leaving that place. Don't let yourself become so complacent there. You just keep trying to come back to us and you will figure it out."

A ripple ran up Ashlin's spine as she sensed everybody looking at her.

Tears streaked down Michelle's eyes as she saw both Ashlin and her mother in the same space. "Mama?"

Ashlin sighed heavily. "It would seem so, at least, that's what Destiny believes, but I'm still myself, too. I guess I'm both, somehow."

"I knew it all along," Zeline said triumphantly. "I always said you was da old child."

To be continued...

Jonni Jordyn was born in Oakland, California in 1957. She started writing at an early age, writing music, poetry, short stories, radio, film, and stage scripts. She didn't start writing novels until later in life, after she retired from playing music, and found herself travelling away from home for extended periods.

She currently lives in Denver, Colorado.

www.ingramcontent.com/pod-product-compliance
Lightning Source LLC
Chambersburg PA
CBHW021331310726
48971CB00001B/84